Becoming Gabriel

By

Amber

Anthony

Paperback and eBooks by Amber Anthony

Appetite for Blood. Prequel to The Blood Trilogy

Blood Rising, The Blood Trilogy, Book 1

Blood Emerald, The Blood Trilogy Book 2

Blood Dragon, The Blood Trilogy Book 3

Arise, My Darling

Becoming Gabriel

Roman's Revenge. Roman's Adventures Book 1

Roman's Rules, Roman's Adventures Book 2

Roman's Return, Roman's Adventures Book 3

Blood Fugue, Tales from the Gaoler Book 1

Are you a Tea Drinker?

These teas are blended with the different characters in mind. Your purchase supports book related charities with a 5% donation.

https://www.adagio.com/ Blends, tagged Amber Anthony
https://www.adagio.com/signature_blend/my_blends.html

Gabriel's Love, Grace is Rooibos with the flavors of Almond and Caramel, as refreshing as Grace. Naturally caffeine free.

From Gabe to Gabriel is Decaf Ceylon Tea, Decaf Ceylon, Natural Vanilla Flavor, Natural Spice Flavor, Orange, Cinnamon, Ginger, Cloves and Cardamom.

Becoming Gabriel is Pu Erh Chorange, Black Tea, Honeybush Tea, Orange, Cocoa Nibs, Natural Chocolate Flavor & Natural Orange Flavor.

You Can Follow Amber Anthony:

https://www.amberanthonywrites.com/

https://www.facebook.com/WriteAmber/

https://www.bookbub.com/

https://www.goodreads.com/

https://allauthor.com/author/amberanthony/

Twitter: @writeambera

Praise for Becoming Gabriel

"This story is a rollercoaster of emotion and love so strong that it cannot be broken."

– Anon, Kobo

"All the familiar corners of Fell's Point and Harborplace are the settings for this intricate tale. The Russian mob and a lascivious billionaire get between them. Which way do they go? What inflicts the greatest pain? I was swept away within their drama. A love story for the city."

– LR, Kobo

"The romantic buildup between Grace and Gabrielle was priceless. Multi-dimensional facets of the protagonists' personalities made the plot come alive for me…The book has an old-world charm."

-AMD, Amazon

"Five stars, an intense story that captivates. Will these two ever catch a break and have a second chance for happiness?"

– MJE, Amazon

Credits

Thank you to the members of the Virtual Season Writing group for listening and giving salient feedback.

Thank-you to Connie Wiegert, Janet Pineau Rivenbark and Randi Bricker for their time, patience and feedback.

Thank you to the third character of this book, the City of Baltimore. *Although its façade is not always 'Charm City'*, it's where I was born and the roots from where the tendrils of my family spread out across these United States.

Moving from Paranormal to Contemporary Romance we made an effort to embrace the largest city in Maryland and represent it as the diverse background for our characters to cross paths.

We have fictionally portrayed some places as well as created sites for our adventures to unfold. When the Reader finishes our book, I hope that it is appreciated as a romance as colorful as the complicated Maryland flag.

P.S., *When in Baltimore, don't forget to try the crab cakes.*

Dedicated to

Those who seek to change their lives. Those who have supported us as we have changed our lives through writing. And those who need a kick-start to change.

We believe it's not who you are, it's who you become.

This is a work of romantic fiction. Yes, the people are working class... *it doesn't take a billionaire to fall in love.*

1

Gabe Lee waited behind the heavily tinted glass of the physical rehab facility, avoiding Baltimore's sweltering June humidity. He was finally going home after emergency surgery followed by six weeks of rehab. Yeah, he'd lost some weight, but ironically, that was beer and pizza bloat. Physical therapy cut him a new physique. He was buff, and the tattoo on his chest now rose and fell over a defined six-pack. His handsome face appeared leaner and sculpted enough to make an artist weep. Gabe's expressive blue-green eyes shone clear and focused.

Traffic snarled when an SUV broke to make an illegal left turn and the truck behind it slammed into the back end. Chrome kissed metal violently, replicating the sound of gunfire. Gabe flinched and turned away. His mind propelled to lying in the emergency room, hearing the evening news' reference, 'a gunfight at Middle Branch Park'.

The gravel pressed into his flesh until he felt only cool dampness. The bullet wound in his upper thigh was his focus. It was an anxious pain. *My woman shot me. Yeah, she was aiming at the drug dealer, but she shot* me.

The second shot thundered louder and more ominously. Gabe heard Carla squeal. Lifting his face from the clammy gravel, he extended his hand toward her, and then the world went black. Gabe lacked the strength to even open his eyes, he was bleeding hard and fast. Carla's moans silenced, and his world changed forever.

During his recovery, Gabe had many discussions with the treatment team about destructive relationships and the undesirable events in his life. High school tedium introduced him to sex, beer, and pot. He wasn't a delinquent, he was bored. Finally, the shooting with Carla showed him alcohol and drugs were going to kill him by inches. He hated that her death was the instrument that woke him. Growing up in Baltimore city may have dealt him a crappy hand, but he was only making it worse with a dead-end job, beer, and pot. He was never tempted to buy meth or heroin like Carla. Hell, all he wanted was honest work and a decent life.

Gabe wasn't absolutely sure how to make that happen in his present circumstances, but he was determined to find a way. He'd been clean for six weeks, without so much as a cigarette. Was it physical therapy? The decent food? The regular bedtime schedule? He wondered if he could stay clean? The last time he lost his sobriety it was out of boredom and frustration. If he worked as hard at staying clean, as he had entertaining a directionless woman, maybe he wouldn't be looking at more bullet holes. *I definitely need to meet a better class of people.*

He ran a tense hand through his hair, shaking off the memories. The rehab doctor said the PTSD might stick with him a while, and that probably included loud noises that sounded like gunshots. He turned to his favorite nurse. Middle-aged and comfortable, he thought maybe she was what a mother *should* be like. "As good as you all were to me, you'll understand if I don't want to mess up like this again."

The nurse grinned. "You're only twenty-three, Gabe, that's a great age to start fresh. You know you don't have to white-knuckle it." She handed him a couple of pamphlets for A.A. and N.A. "These folks can help you."

"I know. Thanks." He gave a shy glance from under his lashes. "Listen, if you or anybody here, ever have trouble with your cars, give me a call. No charge."

A horn honked outside, and Gabe checked through the glass door. "Uh, looks like my cab is here. Thanks for everything." He gave her a standard patient-hug and was out the door and back into the real world.

****

"I always thought this was your best side, just like your Momma." Grace Margaret Lerner, eighteen years old, and a newly graduated prep-schooler shut her eyes in dismay. It was her step-father, Arthur Darby's despised voice. He caught her bent over, removing bed linens from the dryer. She felt an adrenaline surge as she processed this new reality. Arthur returned home earlier than expected from a 'second honeymoon' with her mother. Just two more days and she would have been out of his reach forever.

She gauged his stance in the doorway with her peripheral vision. *Stay down until he moves closer.* Grace's hopes to evade him evaporated when Arthur lunged, throwing two strong arms around her waist.

"Where's Mother?" She demanded, shock momentarily freezing her movement.

Her stepfather yanked her to a standing position, his hot whiskey breath peppering her neck. His hips thrust into her backside. "Turns out, I detest Bali. I told your mom to stay and enjoy." He nuzzled behind her ear. "I need some playtime at home."

Her attacker was a muscular, fit, forty-year-old man, but he was still shorter by a few inches. She had the advantage of surprise and height. "Get off me, Arthur." Maybe the months of planning to escape empowered her to fight him in the daylight. "You touch me again, and I will kill you!"

"Oh, Cici, I love a hell-cat. Your mother used to be a hell-cat."

Bile rose in her throat. He insinuated his knee between hers and momentarily loosened his arms around her waist to paw her breasts. Grace's arms sprang up to dislodge his grasp. With a fierce stomp, she pounded her sneakered heel on his instep. He howled at her assault on his sandaled foot and teetered, unbalanced. Grace grasped the handle of a gallon bottle of fabric softener and swung. She caught his jaw with a hard-plastic punch. His shining blonde pompadour shook free of its slick perfection. Great spurts of viscous, blue fluid doused his handsome face. Arthur's furious wail intensified with Grace's knee to his groin. His well-defined ass hit the slippery floor, and fabric softener rained down on him.

Grace bolted down the long hallway and headed for her keys and purse in the mudroom, next to the garage. Her cell phone was in her back pocket. She prayed she could beat Arthur to the door. Punching the garage door opener, she flung herself into her car and keyed the ignition.

Arthur's furious threats trailed after her. "You really do want to die!"

Time stood still as the door lifted. His fist smacked the button to re-close it. She countered with her opener, and as the door rose above her trunk line, she gritted her teeth and floored the car in reverse. He kept smacking the wall control impotently. Yes, she ripped the bottom of the door in her escape, but wouldn't it be a fine story for him to explain to the neighbors?

Grace's mind whirled. Where could she find safety? *I should ditch the car as soon as possible. He'll have the police after me. Where can I be lost in plain sight?* She sped directly toward the country club exit where she'd be lost in the crowd.

As she drove, Grace racked her brain for a plan. Her mother was always frustrated with the workings of her smartphone and continually asked Grace to get her into her realtor's website. She knew all her mother's log-in info. There had to be a vacant house somewhere in Baltimore that would offer temporary safety. As soon as she could stop, she'd log in.

****

Gabe limped into his Fell's Point garage apartment, throwing wide the door to let the diesel and oil fumes loose into the neighborhood. He shuffled through heaps of gamer magazines, a tangle of audio wires, CD cases, and fast food wrappers. His muddled senses were shocked into working when he went cold turkey in the hospital. Now, his sober body caught the olfactory assault of stale smoke and rotted food. It sickened him enough to grab three or four garbage bags and scourge through the apartment like Christ in the temple.

By nightfall, he didn't recognize the place, the lemon pine cleaner almost transformed the studio. He threw his three ratty towels, two remaining pairs of blue jeans and three tee-shirts in a pile near the door to take to the laundromat. He saw how little he actually owned and wanted to toss it all in a pillowcase and hit the bricks.

Why don't I? Because I have $8.80 in my wallet, a pit-bull of a parole officer, and my only legal means of income is the garage on the other side of the wall.

****

Grace bit her lower lip as she drove, keeping a sharp eye on the rear-view mirror. *Damn it!* She'd had the car packed and ready to go. She was just doing a final load of wash before she took off. *Damn it! Damn it!* She pulled all the money out of her bank account and credit card yesterday, figuring she'd need cash to slip away without a trace. That cash now sat inside her bedside table where she'd put it for safe-keeping, and she had pathetically little in her wallet.

In the middle of the afternoon, the best place to plot her next move was a nearby mall. *How many blue Toyota Corollas like mine are there?* Actually, the car next to an open parking space was similar. With a bit of prowling, she switched license plates and then drove the hell out of North Baltimore.

In a fast food parking lot, she logged into the realtor's listing service and found a vacant home in a city neighborhood where everything was within walking distance. There was ample on-street parking for blocks around. The car would hide in plain sight, without finding her.

On her way to the empty house, she stopped for temporary spray-on brunette hair color. She entered the drugstore's bathroom and cut her hair in a shoulder-length shag according to YouTube directions. She twisted her head side-to-side in the mirror. *Not bad for my first try.*

The neighborhood was quiet as she strolled down the treed avenue, several blocks from where she'd parked her car. The chicken dinner she carried smelled good, even though it was fast food. Confidently, the brunette toted her backpack up the porch steps, and gaining entry, she was 'safe.'

She plugged in her phone. *Bingo! There's power, but couldn't they trace me?* Grace turned off the phone. Night fell, and despite having power, Grace sat in the dark and ate her dinner. This place was a Band-Aid on a mortal wound. She needed a stable place to live and a job. *Any woman who gives birth to a daughter and allows that daughter to be sexually abused loses the right to be called 'Mom'*. It was a wound Grace could never forgive but losing her adored father to suicide was an unforgettable trauma. She feared her mother would follow the same path if Grace made a rape accusation against Arthur. Leaving was a clean break.

****

It wasn't Gabe's habit to spend his last dime at a grocery store, yet it seemed like the thing that would keep him on the straight and narrow. He walked, fighting the desire to smoke a cigarette he didn't have and returned with a bag of rice, a bag of beans and a near expired, reduced-price ham hock. While the ham hock simmered, he dug around in the cupboard to find teabags and some sugar. He over-brewed black tea and sugared it heavily.

Day one of his public sobriety ended with Gabe standing alone in the shower stall, hot emotion flushing over him when he grabbed the peach shower gel Carla lifted from the dollar store. How screwed up would it be if he used the sweet, viscous liquid to beat off? If all the emotionally charged cleaning hadn't worn him out, the blunt force trauma of a six-week-overdue orgasm drove him up the stairs to his sour bed.

The linens were pungent. The wrinkled sheets moved over him, crackling recollections of gymnastic sex. Gabe threw back the shroud of his dead relationship and grabbed his pillow. He headed back down the stairs, leaning heavily against the supporting wall, hiking up the blanket to avoid tripping. *It would be just my luck to trip on the stairs on my first night home and break my other leg.*

He spied the white hospital bag he'd avoided on the coffee table. Carla's stuff sent over by the Coroner's Office. His relationship with Carla had been complicated. By the time of the shooting Gabe wasn't exactly sure he even liked her, forget about love. But… He opened the coin pouch, and there on a gold chain was a blood-spattered profile the size of a quarter. His hand crushed around the gold charm. She was the mother of his unborn son, and this celebrated their decision to name him Gabriel Carlos when he arrived this summer. Dazed at the loss of his son, Gabe's vision blurred with tears. He moved to the sink to clean off Carla's blood.

It dried into the engraving, and he used dish soap and his thumb to gently erase her from the charm.

Back on the sofa, Gabe unhooked his own gold chain and threaded it through the bail. He stared at the gold trinket sparkling in his palm. "You never got a chance, son. I need you in Heaven to keep your eyes open for me. I need to live right so I can see you one day. Your life has always counted to me." He fastened the clasp around his neck and raised the charm to his lips. "You'll always be with me." The weight of the simple charm danced over his heart, as he drew in several calming breaths.

He threw the pillow against the armrest of the sofa, and flopped down, exhausted. The hollows of his brain reverberated with a horse race of anxieties. As Gabe fell into a troubled slumber, it was a win, place and show finish for sobriety, honesty and his son.

****

Grace sat in the corner of the empty bedroom, the full moon casting a broad swath of cold light on the pages of her new journal. It was a left-over composition book she'd found in her backpack tonight. She'd heard a psychologist talking about nightmares on NPR the other night. He'd suggested journaling to stop them. The words flowed through the cheap Bic pen as if a phantom held her hand and formed the letters. When her eyes drooped, she placed the pen in the seam of the book and closed it. Would writing it down really make the dream stop?

****

Gabe struggled toward reality. The alarm didn't ring, it was the miserable radio from upstairs waking him, shocking him into the morning. *Friggin' six A.M., Monday.* Yesterday, he'd come back to the apartment Wally rented him for one hundred dollars a week. He was Wally's junk-yard dog.

This morning, he trudged up the stairs and smacked off the radio. Gabe dragged himself to the kitchen to brew a pot of coffee, black, strong coffee. He walked around naked in the damp-aired studio apartment. The light glared through the wire-reinforced glass while he dug out the Dickies coverall and slid it on commando. Maybe he could talk Wally out of a few bucks for a trip to the laundromat? Fishing around the back of the

7

workbench doubling as a kitchen counter, he found a hard pack of gum, it was six weeks since his last cigarette. *I can do this*. He would chew brass tacks rather than smoke. *If I could just munch on something...* In the kitchen drawer, a lonely cellophane wrapped mint toothpick rolled into view. *Perfect.*

It was a hell of a Monday, a series of females whining about a noise in the front, a noise in the wheel... By 5:45 that night, Gabe was ready to call it a day. He won a ten spot playing cards at lunch with the cocky bastard from the towel service. Gabe was counting on a five-dollar foot long and some clean clothes.

He picked up the pillowcase of dirty laundry and headed to the sub shop in the strip mall on Fleet Street. June nights in Fell's Point sweltered. The brick row homes held humid heat like brick ovens. For every fashionably renovated address, there was a clean, but out of date series of Formstone rowhomes with window air conditioning units dripping excess moisture. Working class taverns stood catty-corner from trendy microbreweries.

He favored the leg with the healing bullet wound and mourned the loss of his car. *I loved that SS, it was cherry.* The police towed it from where he haphazardly parked it the day of the shooting. He'd called the impound lot, to learn the Chevy SS was sold when no one claimed it in thirty days.

Yeah, right, one of those sharp-eyed motorheads counted the minutes until they could take it home themselves. Talk about a steal! I am starting over, again.

Gabe watched the girl on the sandwich line load the foot-long with every free topping she could cram on the bread. Hungry and wanting a cigarette so damn bad, hell, he realized, he wanted a joint. He just wanted to wrap his lips around any burning tobacco stick... It was a few hundred feet to the laundromat, and it was 'Smoke-Free' so there was some sweet relief.

I don't have money for smokes, anyway. Good God, it's all about the damn money. It's all about what I don't have.

2

He put the rest of the cash into the change machine, and it chunked back quarters. All the way over, he thought about sorting the stuff into proper loads. Between the price and his cash on hand, he threw it all in one load. He needed that ninety-nine cents for a Slurpee on the walk home. He watched the grainy TV while he opened the foot long and picked at it. *I need to make this last.*

Then, *she* started banging on a machine, wailing on it like it was attacking her. Watching her was better than Entertainment Tonight. She couldn't be more than eighteen, in her Our Lady of the Mount sweatshirt. *That's a chi-chi girl's school in North Baltimore. What's she doing here?* Her chocolate hair was wild and loose around an angelic face that quickly approached demonic.

"Crap, crap, crap!" She smacked the machine with a wallop, and he realized no one else paid her any attention. He could see how lost and frustrated she was.

"Did it eat your money?" Gabe got up and moved toward her. Not like he could help her out with money…

She looked at him, wide-eyed, caught and cornered. "Huh? Money… yeah, it won't start. I've got the soap in there," She pointed to the front load washer. "My money is in there," She pointed up to the coin slot. "And, it's not working! I am so damn mad!" Her voice could have been whiny, but it was creamy and sweet like a milkshake even when it advertised her pain. She glared at him like she glared at the washer. When she realized he meant to help her, she stepped back, fearful.

Was he too close? He stepped back, put a hand up to let her know he wasn't after her. "I come here all the time, check this out." Gabe reopened the washer door and looked at her before he stuck his hand into her clothes. He nodded, and she nodded, and his bare hands dug into her silky garments and shuffled the uneven load. He slammed the door and wiggled the lever. Gabe never knew a woman who owned clothes like this. *Oh, the sensation of that silk and soft lace.* Gabe's face flushed in reaction to the fabric as he watched her from under his lashes. The water flowed, and he saved her day. She was folded-up like a lawn chair, arms crossed over her sweatshirt, head down, chewing on her thumbnail.

"Hey, it's okay, now, it's running." Even that didn't get her attention. Gabe stood there a beat, deciding how to help, and then gave up. He turned to walk away from her when her hand flew up to reach for him. She stepped up to him, and he jumped at the unexpected touch. Sudden movement still spooked him. He flinched and tried not to show she scared the hell out of him.

"I'm sorry." She apologized and sought peace on the other side of the room.

Gabe went back to his sandwich, open on the wax paper wrapper. He felt her invasive scrutiny. She didn't have anything – it was all in the washer, and he knew it. Gabe held up his hand and caught her attention, drawing her from a blank stare. He waved and pointed to the sandwich. "Hungry?" He offered half of what he had and wished he'd bought the chips and the soda, too. She looked around the room like he was talking to someone else. She nodded and rose warily to drag a chair close to him.

"What's on it?" She asked, not reaching for it yet. *This princess can't be that hungry if she's worried about what's on it.*

He pushed the sub halfway between them. "Cold cuts, with everything, I mean everything." Gabe laughed softly as she picked the short end, and he was glad. He just realized the extent of his hunger. Neither spoke. He chewed every bite, thirty or forty times. Gabe wanted to know he was eating something with his bare hands after all those soft meals on a tray. She lifted the bread and began to squeamishly pick off peppers, onions, and tomatoes, wiping her fingers on the wax wrapper.

"You're not going to eat that?" He pointed a long finger. She shook her head while she took her first bite. She wolfed it down while he gratefully shoved the extras back between his bread. She was done with her half before he'd half-eaten his. He watched her swish her tongue around her teeth like she wanted to brush them. *This Princess is out of her comfort zone*. He let her watch him eat, well, she watched him.

"My name's Gabe. I've never seen you around here, did'ja just move?" She took his napkin, so he wiped his mouth on the back of his wrist. Her eyes widened, and he realized even his 'barely there' mother would have agreed with her.

Her body language closed again as she scoped out the room and then answered. "I'm Grace. Yeah, I'm kinda new. I just moved down here."

Grace. Princess Grace. He nodded at her; his mouth still full of the last bite of sandwich. He saw her perfectly straight, brilliantly white teeth. The kind of teeth you see on T.V. She rested her hands on the table, and he caught this year on her distinctive girl's school class ring. *She's just graduated, makes sense, she looks like a college freshman.* He saw a lot of the school's alumni, they brought their Benzs and Jags into Wally's shop. Their thirty-something, pinched expressions screamed long hours and big paychecks. Juan, their Honduran detail specialist, professionally detailed their cars, and the insides never needed real cleaning, no Cheerios, and no spilled baby bottles.

This girl was light years away from her neighborhood. "Have you moved down here for college?" Hell, he didn't know what to talk about. Her attention was on the street. *Is somebody after her?* Everyone else walked out for a smoke and hell, he didn't have any, so he waited, wishing he was blessed with the gift of small talk.

A beat too late, she shook her head. "I'm taking a semester off."

Ah, that gap year stuff I've heard about. He wanted to press for more, but she took so long to answer, he thought she was avoiding conversation. It was clear she had no intention of getting chatty. Their washers stopped, and he shook out the load before he stuffed it into the dryer. He watched her count her change. Clearly, she didn't have enough to run a dryer. "You wanna share a dryer?" *You would think I asked her to blow me right here in the doorway... Is she going to cry?*

She pulled herself together and nodded. He shoved the rolling basket over to her with his foot, and she shook out her damp clothes preparing to throw them in with his linens and jeans. She rolled the basket back, and he stepped out of her way while she filled the dryer. He knew her all of fifty-five minutes, and he'd shared half his food and money. *What the hell is she doing here? What the hell am I doing with her?*

****

They sat across from each other while their laundry danced in the heat. He wished he'd charged his phone; they could have played a game to break up the dryer's drone. Gabe couldn't think of a thing to talk about, and the T.V. didn't cooperate.

I can deal with a pain in my ass if she doesn't shoot me and leave me for dead. I can deal with a drunk if they sleep most of the time like my Mom. Evidently, I can't deal with a silent debutante.

He was intrigued by Grace's vulnerability. She stuck out in this laundromat like stained glass in a beer bar's window. She was all softness and freckles, pale skin with hazel eyes. He tried to see through those eyes, into her heart. Each time he searched, she ducked away like he was a thief. When she tucked her head, it reminded him he'd *been* a thief, and she wasn't giving up the keys to her kingdom because he shared a sandwich and a dryer. *Was she as stuck up as the garage clients?*

He thought about the women in his life, none of them was anything like Grace. She might have been from Baltimore, where neighborhoods changed from one street to the next, but she wasn't from his working-class neighborhood.

Carla once lived around the corner in Perkins Homes, the squatty public housing building with her broken family. He hadn't gone there except to pick her up. Her old man, Carlos, hadn't given him the time of day. Gabe thought he might have stuck a buck into Gina's thong before she was Carla's stepmom, which was kind of freaky.

Grace made his gut churn. She was way out of his league, but she was on his turf. She needed someone who could keep her three feet from the Fells Point bogeymen. *Being a reformed bogeyman, myself, makes me the right guy for the job. I did say I wanted to meet a better class of people.*

12

He stalked through the minefield in his head, wondering what would spark a conversation and was saved by the bell. The dryer dinged, and she jerked at the sound of it. He remembered the same reaction from guys behind bars, guys who were buggered and beat and slept with one eye open.

She joined him, pulling the dry laundry into the basket. He smiled at the warm sheets and towels. He'd finally get to be in his place with clean stuff. He made a point of not looking at her underwear, two, maybe three designer sets of bras and panties, but he remembered their silkiness. She nervously scooped them into her backpack, and then neatly folded the two pair of jeans and a couple of blouses, sliding them into place with a bit more care. Once he stuffed his things into the pillowcase, he checked the room for his detergent and grabbed his stuff to go. He was headed for the door when he realized her backpack looked cumbersome. "Need help to your car?" He figured the white Prius with the college sticker was hers.

Grace froze, "I walked, that's okay."

He was glad he hadn't picked it up without asking, there was an odd look on her face. "Can I walk you home?" He tilted his head toward the door.

"*May* I walk you home?" She corrected, and then covered her lips with her hand as if flies left her mouth.

Why is she asking me if she can walk me home? Before he gave it much thought, she stepped toward him. "I have a horrible habit of correcting grammar. My Mother always did it, and I hate it, but now I do it." She shook her head and lowered it in dismay. "Please forgive me, I'm so sorry I did that."

Her shoulders fell until he responded with a, "No sweat." *Yeah, she's correcting my grammar, and I'm too thick to know it! Damn, I feel stupid. I don't even know what I don't know.*

"Thank you, Gabe, you've done enough, I don't have any cash to pay you for the sandwich or the laundry. May I take your number? I can call you when I cash my check." She crossed the threshold and walked away, pointedly.

And that, ladies and gentlemen, is what it means to be blown off. That's a half a sandwich I'll never see again.

"It's not safe for a girl to walk alone after dark." He called after her, but she turned, continuing to walk backward, that hand up again.

"I'll be okay." She turned and took off like a scalded dog. He let her run, even though he knew she was heading away from the downtown condos to an old neighborhood with narrow streets and harsh realities. In this area, a wrong turn could take you from a working-class district to a no-man's land of boarded up rowhomes. He hung back and watched her bob and weave down the broken sidewalk. She jerked into a side street, and he headed for the convenience store on the corner.

3

"**A**ngel! My man! You back on the street? I got ya Natty Boh in the twenty-ounce cans -- ice cold." Lamar beamed at him; his café au lait skin sported a saddle of dark brown freckles that danced when he smiled.

Gabe held up his hand and wandered to the Slurpee machine for a frozen root beer, and then wandered back to catch up with Lamar. "You have to save the Natty Boh for those college kids. I'm six weeks sober."

Lamar raised his paw-like hand. "High five, sir. You givin' up beer too?"

Gabe nodded. "Got to, anything starts me up."

Lamar hunkered over the counter and whispered. "Did you really shoot Carla?"

Gabe shelled out the coins for the Slurpee and leaned toward Lamar. "What's the word out there?" He nodded toward the street.

Lamar took the coins and stepped back from the counter. "They out there sayin' she shook a gun at you… and you popped her." The wiry man crossed his arms over his chest and leaned back. "Of course, I don't listen to that talk. I know you wouldn't shoot your woman."

"A drug dealer shot my woman."

"No shit?"

****

Grace turned up South Washington Street, to check on her car and it was a good thing she did. There were two black and whites, red lights flashing to warn away the traffic and they were all over the Toyota. *Well, dammit, there goes my T.V., laptop and most of my clothes.* She swallowed her fear and fought pure panic when she saw the cops starting to question pedestrians, she'd better get out of there. She strained to stroll casually back the way she'd come, but the more she thought about her current situation, the longer and faster her strides became. *I can't go back to the rowhouse, too risky; I have no transportation, but practically nothing to carry. The second house on the MLS is around the corner. I've got to think. I've got to make better decisions.* By the time her mind settled on a plan, she was trotting.

****

"…Working at Wally's… trying to get my life back…"

Gabe was halfway through his drink when Lamar pointed. "Go ahead, get yourself a refill. You deserve it."

He walked toward the dispenser when he saw a blur he could have sworn was Grace, run past the store window. He sat the forgotten drink on the counter and raised a hand in farewell to Lamar. "Gotta go." He saw her turn into an alley. Three of the Point Boys were right behind her, stalking their prey. Gabe's leg burned like hell, but he jogged as best he could to catch up to the boys. She was deep into the alley now, and Gabe wanted to stop this thing while the gang was still on the corner.

He called out; hoping his recent street cred over the shooting would keep them from a fight. "Pauly! Aren't you late for dinner?" The three miscreants eyed Gabe warily and stood down, with a minimum of posturing.

"Hey! G! Hey, hey! I did not know the lady is yours!" Pauly and Gabe began their handshake ritual.

Gabe put a friendly hand on the ginger-headed man's shoulder. "Your Momma know you chase preppies on the street?" Gabe kept one eye on Grace as he watched the gang retreat. "Let Joe know I'm home now, okay?" Gabe leaned hard on his good leg as he watched Grace from a decent distance. *Why isn't she going to the front door?* He wondered. She put her weight into jerking the lockbox on the garage. The evening's inky darkness dropped as he slipped down the dark alley. Gabe heard rattling

and cuss words, and then he saw her lean back to put her shoulder into the door, several times, progressively harder with each lunge.

Was her cry from frustration? Pain? He watched her slide down into the long shadows, her back to him, bent over the backpack she clutched, whimpering. She beat a fist against her thigh. "No, no, no! This can't happen! No!"

Gabe's heart broke. Did Grace snap her key in the lock? *Hell, I know how to get into a building…* He wasn't used to the hot knot tied in his chest. *Was this what the rehab shrink called empathy? Curiosity? I can't remember the last time a woman's tears affected me.* The women he knew never cried. Crouched in the sharp cone of the door light, she drew into herself until she looked like an empty heap of clothes.

She shrieked at his approaching shoes defiantly, without looking up. *Does she even know who she's talking to? Of course, not.* "What do you want? I don't have any money. You can rape me, but you don't scare me!"

He walked out of the dark, into her space, got closer and crouched next to her. "Grace, it's Gabe. What's wrong, do you need help getting into your place?" He waited for her to look up. She was shaking, and he wanted to reach out and hold this aching beauty. "Did you snap the key in the lock?"

"No." Her defiant tone faded. "I said I was okay, Gabe, I don't want to bother you." She bawled, breaking out in fat tears, communicating more than words. Gabe could still smell the fabric softener radiating out of her backpack, and the whole mixture of tears and powdery flowers just about broke him.

Grace sniffed, obviously trying mightily to turn off her torrent, which slowed but wouldn't stop. "You've done too much already. I'm not your problem."

Sitting down next to her, he leaned against the wall but kept his trap shut. He wasn't going to screw up this part. They sat in silence while the city's din played with their senses. After a few moments of police sirens, he chided. "So, this crying in the alley is working for you?"

She stifled a laugh and hiccupped a sob. "I lost the place where I was living."

"What? Show me where they are. I'll make 'em let you in."

Grace ignored Gabe's offer and folded in on herself, again. *Did I cross a line? She doesn't want* my *help.* An ambulance's shriek faded as it drove north, and Gabe grew exasperated by her obstinate silence. He leaned forward to get up, and she caught the back of his calf. It was a jolt like a baseball bat at the back of his knees. He stayed down, pivoted to her and barked. "What? What do you want from me, Grace?" There was an ugly nickname for girls from her Hunt Valley neighborhood. It rhymed with Hunt and began with 'c', was she one of those *Hunt Valley Princesses?*

She clutched her backpack and stared at him, frozen in fear. Grace wasn't the princess he thought she was, or, if she was, she'd fallen far from her kingdom. "I was hiding over on South Anne. The police found my car on Bank, most of my stuff was in the trunk. I don't dare go back to where I was hiding. It's an empty house for sale, but they'd almost certainly find me…"

"What do they want you for?"

"I'm not sure." She hiccupped, wiping tears on her sleeve, trying to quiet herself. "Could be anything from assault to grand theft auto." She tilted her head back toward the building and sat with the vacant stare of the shell-shocked.

Gabe held new street-cred respect for her and more than a little curiosity. He knew there was a hell of a story here. *Am I ready to do this?* He leaned over her and asked gently, "Do you trust me?"

"Why?" Her voice was sullen.

"I have a place, not too far, you can take the bed upstairs, and I'll sleep downstairs."

"I can take the sofa…"

Closer to the door… Gabe felt Grace's cautious gaze.

"No." Her hands flew up to wipe her face. "I can't take your bed, really."

"Honestly, you'll be safe upstairs. You'll thank me later the sofa isn't great."

"Oh..." She rose to walk beside him, giving the old concrete building a final look before they plodded through the alley to the sidewalk. They were preoccupied with their own thoughts during the walk, and Gabe's mind raced. He was glad the garage was situated in a better area than her last hideout. God knew what she was thinking. *She must be genuinely desperate to trust a guy she met at the laundromat.*

Gabe unlocked the door and pushed it open for her to enter first. He expected a groan. Even with the cleaning job, the place was rough. Grace stood inside the door, scanning the two-story room while he studied her. Girls didn't usually venture into the apartment. It was attached to Wally's Garage and was never improved from the raw, concrete walls. The second floor was half of the room, an elevated deck built to hold the box spring and double mattress. Clothes hung on a pipe suspended from the wall. Functionally basic, not lady-approved.

He pulled out the clean towels and put them on the shelf over the toilet. Grace stood still, watching him move around the room. The 'kitchen' was along the back wall, and the bathroom was old and small. It was worse than old and small; it smelled like motor oil and diesel fuel. It was amazing no one suffocated there. Along the length of the kitchen, he poked around for snacks, he was still hungry. He found microwave popcorn and the last four tea bags from Asian takeout.

"Could you eat some popcorn or maybe a cup of tea?" He offered, as she circled the room, still clutching the backpack, eyes wide, reading the story of his life in the room's contents. Her eyebrows rose, and she nodded.

"Do you ever put parmesan cheese on it?" Unshouldering the backpack and sliding out of her sweatshirt, she voiced her preference with smiling eyes.

"On the popcorn, right?" He checked her sense of humor. Could they find a middle ground? Would she feel welcome, could he make her laugh?

"Yeah. We put garlic powder on it too." She followed him to the microwave and watched him unwrap the cellophane. He dug into the drawer, remembering the pizza guy left packets of cheese two months ago, and they rested in the junk drawer. There was one packet of honey from a take-out chicken meal, and he set it aside for her tea.

"Honey?" He held up the packet, and her eyes widened at the endearment. Seeing the packet, she smirked. Her eyes were clear, her nose was dry. He grabbed two mugs the muffler supply salesman left and ran water into them. She stepped up to him and out came that hand of hers…

"May I make the tea?" She proposed. Gabe nodded, and she eyed the containers on the shelf of the kitchen.

"Do you have a pot or a teakettle to boil water?" He thought for a minute and pulled out the three-quart saucepan from under the counter. She wiped it out under the stream of water and then filled half the pan and set it on the gas burner. *Do we need that much water to make two mugs of tea?* She rinsed out the mugs and opened the teabags. Each step was measured and precise.

Gabe shook the popcorn and found the takeout baskets, splitting the bag between them. He sprinkled the cheese over the steaming snack and dug for any other spices while they waited for the water to boil.

He was mesmerized by her process. As the water rolled steam, Grace took the potholder and poured hot water into the cups, swished the mugs and then poured off the boiling water to heat the cups. She poured that water out and poured fresh, still boiling water over the tea bags.

"Now, we let it steep!" Her comment was like a magician's announcement to wait for the surprise. *I'm confused, all this time I've been doing it wrong.*

When the tea was ready, they sat on opposite ends of the sofa with the baseball game low in the background. "This is way better than when I stick the bag in the cup, pour water and nuke the whole shootin' match." It was his awkward way of saying she did a great job. "I like the popcorn, too." The cheese stuck to the butter coating, and he decided he'd never eat bare popcorn again.

Their conversation was sparse. There were strained smiles and silent nods between bites and sips of tea. Gabe worked out the kinks in his long-forgotten manners, carrying her empties to the sink, offering her another tea bag; all the while she shook her head and raised that cautioning hand.

"Do you want to get a shower? There's a lock on the door. I won't bother you." Grace's body language was on guard, he figured the last thing she wanted was a guy pawing her. She nodded but didn't move toward the bathroom

"I can boil my toothbrush if you want. I have some clean tee-shirts if you'd rather sleep in a tee-shirt."

She rose, her gaze sweeping the room and then she walked toward him, unmistakably close. She raised her hand to his forearm, and her fingers glanced his skin for a split second.

"Thank you." She exhaled. "Thank you, Gabe." She walked into the bathroom; he heard the lock click and the water start.

He was stunned by her thanks. He fought to understand why a girl of substance and apparent wealth would squat in a rowhouse. What would it take to understand her? He wanted to arouse her smile and look into her hazel eyes, straight into her heart. When she smiled at him, he felt human again.

While she showered, he moved upstairs and made the bed. After it aired out and was covered in clean sheets, it wasn't the hell-hole he remembered. He looked around his place and felt pretty good.

Hearing the shower turn off, he hurried down the stairs. Gabe was stunned by her appearance. Her brunette hair was unexpectedly strawberry blonde. Her jeans were skinny legged, the polo shirt, fitted. Her complexion blushed in the steam of the tiny bathroom, and she looked like a classy sketch dropped off a deluxe car calendar.

It was hovering around bedtime and as much as Gabe wanted to stay up to talk or watch baseball, tomorrow was an early day, and she looked exhausted. He gestured toward the loft. "Let me show you upstairs."

She followed him but stayed across the room until he left for downstairs. When he heard her pull back the covers, he imagined her legs falling onto the bed with the sheets rustling over her.

She'd left the bathroom cleaner than she found it. The damp towel held her scent, hanging over the shower door. In her short time in the room, she'd branded it. Gabe slid out of his clothes and prayed for enough hot water to wash him clean. He needed to overcome the lump in his heart. Standing where she'd stood only cultivated that lump. Leaning under the shower, he rinsed himself. The shower gel was hers now. When he touched it, it was as if he touched her. He felt she was still within arm's reach, a prize he ached to caress and cherish.

Gabe knew he was coarse, where Grace was refined. He knew he was painfully ignorant, where she was educated and polished by wealth and travel. It haunted him. She must have been badly hurt to run the way she did. She talked about rape like it was inevitable. As if it wouldn't hurt her. How can that be? *Only a psychopath would rape a woman, and I am many things, but I am not a psychopath.* Gabe knew about his scars, what were her permanent scars?

The hot water staunched the aches he'd earned today at work. What a day it was! Grace's face haunted him, and her smile lingered in his mind's eye. This type of woman usually looked down her nose at him, but she was hard up and accepted his charity.

In his stage of sobriety, he was warned away from spending hours with her that way… If he could, he'd finagle hours alone, erasing the look on her face when she dared the character in those unknown shoes to commit rape. *I want to hear my name whispered from her lips.* His chest tight, his legs trembling, he parsed his breath, to recover some balance. He leaned against the walls and fantasized her hands covering him. Remembering the sensation of her fingers glancing his forearm, a fantasy wrapped them around his sex, the other hand cupping and gripping him. Ecstasy shocked him back to reality as his orgasm cocooned him.

Why would God dangle this glittering jewel in front of me? He bargained with God. *The place is shipshape, no liquor, no drugs. I'm clean and sober. Will You hear the prayers of a punk mechanic in a cramped shower of a garage apartment?*

Gabe dried off, slipped on basketball shorts and grabbing the afghan, headed to the couch to get some sleep. In time, he woke, his sleep broken by the sounds of her thrashing. The old springs protested under her twisting, and in time Gabe heard her cry loud enough to draw him upstairs. After limping up the steps, he found her face buried in her pillow, tortured by a phantom. Sitting on the edge of the bed, he slid her close. Her eyes were shut tight, hiding from her demon. "Grace, you're okay, you're safe, it's Gabe." He repeated his quiet mantra, over and over, gently, as his auntie had when he was a child. She was soft and limp in his arms, a zephyr, a vision. Was she his dream? Only when he knew she was asleep again, did he pull back the sheet and lay her down, covering her gently.

****

Grace woke slowly in the middle of the night. The digital clock beside her read 2:22 A.M. *Tonight in a stranger's sagging bed, I feel safer than I did in my designer bedroom.* She swallowed and wished she had a little water, but she was unwilling to risk waking Gabe to get some.

The nightmare was a little too vivid, tonight. Grace had let down her guard. It must have been the shower and the safe bed. She hadn't slept in a safe bed in two years. Tonight, the dream's white caps were choppier than usual, and she was covered in dirty bay water. She was smaller than the rest of the people. The pain of Daddy's loss was more devastating.

Then, strong, gentle arms wrapped around her. Her heart raced, but it slowed as Gabe held her. Her mind cleared. The hands were rough but soothing. She smelled fresh soap, deodorant, and cinnamon toothpaste. Was it an angel whose arms cradled her, bringing her peace where there was none?

****

She didn't awake with a start the next morning; the clock radio next to the pillow woke her. Grace lifted her drowsy head and saw '6:00 A.M.' Then, she realized she was in Gabe's bed, and he must have this set for work. She reluctantly pulled out of bed and crept downstairs to wake him.

She stared at his muscled, lean form on the black vinyl sofa. He might have the most handsome face she'd ever seen, perfect from every angle. Her heart caught in her throat as she stood behind him and read the ink on his body. There was an intricate sailor's tattoo on the small of his back. The center image was a multicolored, upright anchor. Across the anchor, a net spanned from fluke to fluke, holding a delightfully, happy mermaid. Grace grinned, thinking, *Well, of course, this mermaid is happy! Look where she's sitting!* The redheaded mermaid wore ornately inked purple seashells on her generous breasts. As she twisted in the net, she displayed myriad shades of blue and aqua in her tail. Grace wondered if it hurt to prick that much ink into the expanse of his slim hips.

His legs, well defined and dusted with hair, stretched over the other half of the sofa, the afghan was on the floor. When she saw his calloused hands folded under his chin, she knew his were the soothing arms sustaining her through her nightmare.

His wasn't the hairless, smooth body of the prep school ex-sweetheart who ushered her into sex, smashing in a basement clubroom after her sixteenth birthday party. Nor, was it the fit mid-forties body, powered by steak dinners and Manhattans, who stole her innocence. This was a god, fallen from Mount Olympus, *perhaps the god of Mechanics? What's up with him?*

Breathless and wide awake now, she circled the sofa to get eye level with him. He shifted to his back. In between syncopated heartbeats she saw his nostrils flare slightly as he breathed. His dark lashes lay on his cheeks, and they fluttered in his sleep. *What is he dreaming about? That he's nuts for taking me in? Would I feel more comfortable if he was… less good looking? Is he watching me, watch him?*

She flinched at the thought of being caught, wondering if he was about to open his eyes. Grace waited, admiring his form more closely while his relaxation gave way to a hard-on under the shiny basketball shorts. *What runs through his head?* His breathing never changed.

His morning wood moved on its own. She was curious, drawn to watch, inexperienced in mornings with a real man. *I'll be mortified if he wakes up and sees me like this.* Rising, she stepped back, hoping he'd roll back on his stomach, which he did after he lowered a hand and scratched.

Grace worried all her 'admiring' inspection cost him precious minutes he needed to prepare for work. *I don't even know when he leaves.* Her chest tightened, thinking about waking him. She took a deep breath and reached out to touch his bare shoulder. "Gabe? Your alarm went off. It's six o'clock; do you need to get up for work?" His mesmerizing blue-green eyes blinked open, and he smiled at her. She melted. His gaze was crazy making. Was he crazy making?

4

"Hey." His voice was gravelly and sleep-woken. He gave her a crooked smile and then wiped at his eyes and sat up, both hands self-consciously covering his hard-on.

She was glad she was concentrating on his eyes, mostly. "I can fix some breakfast." *It's the least I can do.*

"I need to get to the store. All I have is coffee, I think." He rose, and within a few steps, he pushed open the cabinet doors. Grace saw biscuit mix, canned fruit, tuna and a jar of jelly.

"Any eggs?"

He moved to the mid-century round-topped fridge. "Six eggs, at least six weeks old, beans and a ham hock in the lidded pot." He nodded and handed the paper carton to her. Closing the door, he folded his arms over his chest, waiting.

Grace arched a brow. "Do you trust those eggs?"

"You look like somebody who can spot a bad egg. I'll trust you. I haven't heard of any young women moving in and poisoning their hosts." He winked.

His brow crooked as he licked at his upper lip and tilted his head. Her stomach flipped and fluttered at his gestures, she had to turn around to concentrate on cooking. *Where's my radar?*

"I'm going to get cleaned up for work." He took the steps up to the loft, and she heard him dressing as she wrangled the cast iron frying pan and mixed up the biscuit mix. Plopping spoons of jelly over the top, she pushed it in the oven. She broke three eggs into a bowl, whipped them with a fork, carved some of the ham off the hock and saved it for the omelet. By the time she was brewing his coffee, Gabe was in the bathroom, shaving.

****

This is too… what is it? Unreal? His gut tightened, waiting for one of them to meltdown. *What are the odds of two people meeting and in twenty-four hours amicably playing house? Not good.* He wiped his face with a towel and ambled into the living room. "So, what's on the menu, nothing crawled out from the cabinet, did it? I wasn't actually sure what was in there. I've been gone a while."

"Coffee, an omelet and coffee cake." She wiped her hands on the dishtowel tucked into her waistband. "My father and I used to cook breakfast on Sunday mornings while Mother caught her beauty sleep. It was good practice, I guess."

"Sounds better than my usual," Gabe confessed with a chuckle.

She leveled him a suspicious look. "What's the usual?"

He grimaced. "A wish sandwich."

****

"Look," Gabe continued. "I work on the other side of the wall. Mornings, I open the shop at seven. Wally's the owner, and he's a curious guy. I don't need him asking questions about you." His voice began cheerful enough, and then Grace felt a knife plunge into her gut, sure he was going to give her the boot. Her hopes dropped a few floors. "I just got out of the hospital, it's a long story, anyway, if you need me, go out that door," Gabe pointed to his front door. "And walk around to the garage door, okay?" He poured coffee and held the carafe as if to offer her some. White-faced, she shook her head no, so he drank it black and between sips kept talking. "What's on your to-do list?" His tongue darted over his lips catching the coffee that didn't make it into his mouth.

Her face was pink again, the other shoe hadn't dropped. Weak-kneed, she flustered. "I have to find a job, and I have to get on the list at the shelter." She removed the coffee cake from the oven and began the omelet.

As the eggs cooked, she tossed in the ham shreds with some ground pepper.

Gabe stood close enough to inspect her every step, and she was sure he heard her heart thumping in her chest. "You look like you know what you're doing, there's a place around the corner needs a cook, they do a hefty lunch business." He poured more coffee and spooned up coffee cake for both of them.

"I'll take anything I can do wearing the three outfits I have." She nodded at the backpack as she slid the omelet onto one plate. She cut a small corner for herself and then handed the plate to him, leaning against the other end of the counter. He dug in, smiling and savoring each bite. She watched him under her eyelashes as she ate. *Never underestimate the power of shared food, it nourishes body and soul.*

"Look, if they don't have room at the Open Door, come back here, I won't bug you. Maybe I can squeeze an advance out of Wally, and we can eat hamburgers." That wink of his punctuated the end of his sentence. He looked at his cell phone and then rinsed his dishes in the sink and nodded goodbye. She posed at the door like a TV housewife, and he slid right past her, closing the door behind him.

Grace did the dishes and rubbed toothpaste on her finger to brush her teeth. She walked around the concrete block room as she brushed out her hair. The dye-job was gone. *I'll set out with my backpack, it's all well and good he said I was welcome, I'm just not parting with my belongings again.*

She'd never gone on an interview looking quite this unpolished. She remembered Daddy talking about having a pen and being spit-spot clean. Then, she reconsidered where she could apply. She planned to hit the café Gabe suggested, along with the ones along the Harbor and even some of the market bistros. Of course, a girl with a backpack wasn't the most appealing applicant. Her cell phone was terminated, and without a phone, it was one more strike against her.

She headed for the library and signed on to use the computer. First, she made a few applications with an email for replies, and then she blasted out emails to a few friends saying she's gone for a summer in London before attending Tulane. *That will keep people from looking for me.*

***

Wally hit Gabe on the shoulder with a stack of mail. "I charge for secretary service."

Gabe turned abruptly and frowned at the envelope from the parole board. "I see I got fan mail from that stone-cold parole officer."

Wally winked and turned. "If that's the only women you attract, you need to rethink your game!" Wally moseyed back to his claustrophobic office. Gabe perused the stack of mail, weekly parole inquiries, except the auto insurance letter terminating his coverage. *Crap, this is going to drive my next insurance premium into the stratosphere.*

He headed back over to his apartment. *Would Grace be there? Maybe she hasn't left yet?* He threw open the door, and the place was silent. She was gone. *Gone for the day, or gone for good? She's not here, that means she's out looking for work; like she said she was going to.* Gabe repeated the thought as he scanned the open room, the bathroom and then trudged up the steps his right foot landing heavier from pain. His place was still as a tomb, hot and still. He wished he'd given her his cell number and money for a call. *Where is that business card with the shop's address? She probably doesn't remember where I live.* The 'if onlies' raced through his head until his ears ached. He sat on the end of the bed for a moment to think.

What did A.A. say about getting clean and factoring in a woman? *This is a bad idea, getting attached to someone who's as hard up as I am.* Thoughts boiled in a big soup pot between his brain and his heart. Was she gone for good? *I'm probably better off.* He slunk down the stairs and into the bathroom to throw water on his face. Staring into the mirror, red-faced, hyperventilating, he commanded himself, *calm the hell down. I must 'chill'. None of the guys can know about her.*

Gabe never knew anyone with that much class. Everything about her was cultured from her rose gold hair to the bright melon paint on her perfect toenails. If she hung around another few days, he'd expect the birds to fly in and make her bed while she sang to them. Grace's demeanor registered unfathomable kindness.

Her serene expressions, while she cooked breakfast from nothing, assured him she expected success from her efforts. Her kind of perfection would attract all the wrong attention. He knew he had to hide her light under a basket. That was if she returned. Surely, he was not the only man who would welcome her assets.

Gabe had to play it cool. How would he handle all the petty crap? The way he always would, with a smart-ass crack or a shake of his head. The morning dragged through radiator flushes and oil changes, things he could do in his sleep. Optimal, since his mind kept detouring to his house guest.

Juan, the detailer, came in with a bag of his wife's tamales and they sat behind the shop watching the cats pick at the field mice. "Why are you here with me today, Gabe?" Juan was a quiet guy, a family man, squeaking by on cash under the table. He had a sweet wife and two kids in diapers, a righteous guy.

"I stay here, and I stay out of trouble. Besides, you'd be jealous if Marisol brought me tamales, I hang around here, and you bring 'em to me instead." Gabe told the honest truth. He didn't need the thrill of a lunchtime ride to burn one and come back high. He was committed to his sobriety. Besides, he needed to keep a clear head. Because of his houseguest, the world was turning a little faster. *Come on*, Gabe admitted, *meeting Grace is keeping me high.* Just as they wiped the dust off their backsides, the guys rolled back into the parking lot, and work started all over again.

Gabe's mind spun back to breakfast, Grace making something from nothing, how it felt to have someone cook for him. Yeah, she had to eat too, but it was the fact she asked what he liked and took odds and ends in the kitchen to make a comforting meal. His heart and mind conversed. *Do you think Juan knows the treasure he has in Marisol? I'm out of the hospital and in, what, three days, I'm questioning everything, everything.*"

About three in the afternoon the shop slowed down. Gabe watched until Wally hung up the phone and then knocked on the door frame. Wally jumped and barked, "Yeah, what now, Gabe?"

"Can I get about fifty bucks advance on my check? I know it's Tuesday, but I need some groceries and stuff." Usually, Wally would huff and puff and then give in to his lead mechanic. It was their routine.

"Yeah, no problem. I figured you were busted. I don't want you nabbing my leftovers in this fridge." Wally's gaze scanned the tall, tattoo-covered guy. *Does he think I'm gonna blow it on booze or weed? He didn't say it if he does.* Wally unlocked the drawer and slid five ten-dollar bills across the desk.

Picking up the worn bills, Gabe arched his brow. "I got all the work on my manifest done, and I need to find a guy. Can I borrow a shop car?" Gabe could feel the pull of Wally's gaze, as he tread on his last nerve.

He was all puppies and butterflies when he barked, "On one condition, take that crap box of hose clamps back to NAPA and gas up the Impala." Wally peeled forty dollars from his money clip and handed Gabe the box of hose clamps. The mechanic picked the key ring off the hook and saluted Wally as he left.

He felt free with the afternoon sun on his face, the breeze blowing across his sweaty neck as he headed to the parts store. One job down, two to go. The Impala rolled into the Royal Farms where Gabe bought a root beer Slurpee out of the forty dollars for gas. He pumped the remainder into the tank. Coming out of the neighborhood, he searched for Grace, she'd be walking. *Maybe I'll see her, and I can give her a ride.*

5

*T*his is crap! Arthur can't be right. He said I wouldn't make it to the end of the driveway. How can I get a place without a job? How can I get a job without an address? The monologue droned in her head. *This is... unfair!* Maybe it was the backpack that gave her away, perhaps it was the lack of an address. *I bombed today.* She guessed the experienced homeless person knew some secrets she didn't.

The library housed scores of hopeless souls with empty eyes; they read it in each other's faces while they got comfortable in office chairs shoved between bookshelves. She weighed how close she was to getting on the Light Rail and heading back to her neighborhood, maybe she could crash with a couple of the girls from Loyola? Then she'd encounter a friend of Mother's or Arthur's, and that was not where she wanted to be. She'd give it another couple of days. If she could keep cooking, maybe she'd cover her room and board. A quick look in her wallet revealed five quarters, and she decided a travel toothbrush and toothpaste surpassed food; besides, dental hygiene was an investment in any career.

Looking at her watch, she thought of her Daddy. He gave it to her for her sixteenth birthday, sure a Tag Heuer would be worth something on the street, but she couldn't bear to part with it. *Where are you, Daddy? Please send me a sign, better yet, send me an angel.* She pleaded silently. How hard was it? It's called serving, not brain surgery!

Her mind mulled over the faces of the people she met on the street. Every other face was Gabe as she noticed one of his quirky expressions on a stranger, one of his half smiles, a serious gaze. Gabe's appearance in her life was so unexpected. She'd had crushes before, but this was so much more and so sudden. *Is he my angel? Did Daddy guide me to him?*

It was five fifty-five, and she needed to head to his apartment. *Where is it?* The humidity was sweltering, and she'd spent precious time retracing her steps. All the brick fronts looked the same, and she'd been too preoccupied this morning to register the street signs. Her heart thumped, and the traffic whizzed by. She remembered a funeral home and the Royal Farms, nearby. It was after six, and she was about to stop in the bar on the corner to get directions to Wally's Auto Shop. Her feet burned from the brick sidewalks and her legs ached. She paused to rest, famished. Was she confused because she was hungry? Or hungry because she was confused? *Welcome to the game, Grace. Welcome to the big, ruthless world of independence.* She fretted until she saw the Royal Farms and caught sight of the tan brick garage in a sea of red brick rowhomes. Grace broke into a run at the sight of it, lungs blazing as hot as her calves and out of breath. *Is Gabe home? Has he waited for me? Is he going to be pissed when I don't have a job? Well, at least I have a toothbrush.*

****

Gabe sat on a crate outside the garage, alone, feeling a fool because he hadn't given her his phone number. *What if something happened to her?* He worried the cops picked her up. Why were they looking for her? Probably something she wasn't anxious to share. Could he help her without knowing that? What about his craving to see those hazel eyes of hers sparkling back at him? He'd never seen strawberry blonde hair so thick and wild. She looked like a mermaid from an old sailor's sketch. He was antsy, scanning the phone, *it's 6:30, and there's no sign of her.* He got up to pace the block.

****

In the afternoon haze, Grace saw the garage sign, and kept running, she didn't see him yet, and the garage doors were closed. Then a figure came around the side of the building, she made out the coverall he left in this morning. He saw her, a block away, and waved. *Has he been watching*

32

for me? Grace returned the wave and saw he favored his right leg as he made it across the brick alley toward her. *Is he smiling at me?*

****

He remembered her run, now he appreciated it from the front, all her bright hair loose and bouncing. He waved, and she returned the gesture. He limped into the street and caught her. Even with her backpack, she was barely an armful. She squealed as he swung her around on his good leg, her feet flying. Gabe dropped her to the ground and nestled her in his muscled arms. She pressed her cheek to his chest, and he hoped she didn't mind the garage smell. Gabe felt her heartbeat, quick like a rabbit, hard like a jackhammer. Her hair was tangled, and the setting orange sun was jealous of its glow. Without thinking, his lips pressed on her forehead, and she let him. Then, in an instant, they fell apart, looking at each other with breathless grins.

"I was worried about you today." Gabe lifted a strand of lustrous hair from across her forehead.

"You were? I was worried about myself." Grace slid the backpack off and shook her shoulders. She straightened the snug teal Henley over her slim hips.

"How did you do today, did you get a job?" *She's smart, she's appealing. Who wouldn't want to see her cheerful face every day?*

She bit her bottom lip and looked up and down the street. "No. But I got a toothbrush."

"Toothbrush." *It was a rougher day than she expected,* "How'd you like to try your new toothbrush after dinner out?"

"Are we eating tuna on the back step tonight?" She smirked.

If anyone could turn one can of tuna into a meal, it would be Grace, but he couldn't mislead her. "No, Princess." That word leapt from his lips like a caress, not an insult. "You and I are going to dine on the delights of the Burger Barge."

****

Grace froze. 'Princess' was Daddy's pet name for her. Daddy *did* send her an angel, with inked wings. She ran light fingers over Gabe's stubble and hesitated over the slight mole on his right cheek, and then opened her hand to caress his jaw. He caught her hand, and they held each other's gaze, frozen. Gabe looked puzzled. She saw the curiosity in his eyes and knew she couldn't explain how they were brought together for a reason. "I missed you today."

His hand held hers as he confessed, "I came back to look for you this morning…"

"You did?" *Why?*

"You were gone like you said you'd be. I should have given you my phone number and money."

"Well, tomorrow is another day…" She fawned like Scarlett O'Hara. Gabe reached for her backpack, and she let him carry it to his apartment.

"I'm flush with cash. Let's go by the Barge and pick up a couple of burger baskets. After we eat, we can bring back some groceries, okay?"

Gabe made his way upstairs to change out of his coverall, so Grace slid into the bathroom to freshen up. By the time he was back down in a tee shirt and jeans, Grace combed out her hair and applied some lip gloss. She draped a scarf around her neck and dug out her little gold hoop earrings from her backpack.

They halted at the sight of each other. Gabe stood at the bottom of the stairs, his jeans were well broken in. They weren't pre-fab distressed; the warp and weft had comfortably worn around his hips and thighs. From the worn ivory weft brightening the indigo, she could read he habitually carried his phone in his front left pocket. His brass-buttoned fly shone brightly from use. When he straightened up, Grace thought to raise her eyes. *Who knew from his basketball pants that he dressed to the left?* His jeans were as comfortable to her eyes as they appeared on his body.

Gabe smiled his admiration, and she returned it with a blush on her cheeks and the fullness of her laughing lips. She folded her arms self-consciously around her middle.

****

They made their way on foot to a burger joint on the cusp of the neighborhood, Canton. Greasy burgers on sesame seed rolls sat on top of steaming fries and onion rings. While Gabe carried the bulk of it, Grace carried the root beer and Berger cookies. They took their bounty to the public park on the harbor and spread out dinner on a picnic table to eat. He chuckled.

"What?" She arched a groomed brow.

He sat there disarmed by her unpretentious loveliness. "It's just cute, the way you dip your onion rings." He mimicked her, holding his pinkie up while he dipped a fry into the catsup cup, and they laughed at his impersonation. The moon rose over the harbor, competing with the lights from high rise homes and offices surrounding the quiet water. There was scant conversation. Gabe hadn't eaten this much in a while, and beyond enjoying Grace's company, he savored every bite.

Once they were down to the fudgie Berger cookies, Gabe pointed to the high-rise tower across the water. "One day, I want a place, right up there on the corner, see that one on the end?" He pointed to a balcony, eighteen stories up. "Wouldn't it be sweet to call that place home?" His hopes were as lofty as the real estate.

"You never know, Gabe, things aren't always what they seem." Her ominous tone told him Grace knew things about the occupants of penthouses he didn't. *There are dickheads everywhere.* Still, he wondered what she knew. *What is her story?*

"Did you mention grocery shopping?" She changed the subject with a smile.

"Sure, or we eat tuna for breakfast…" Gabe carefully pulled himself up from the bench and held out his hand for Grace. Their fingers touched, and she popped up to her toes, almost colliding. Gabe stepped back to steady himself, and then they did bump, her shoulder to his chest. She giggled. Gabe grinned awkwardly and steadied himself.

They walked to the market. Gabe wanted to hold her hand but kept his thumbs hooked in his pockets. They compared the sales flyer to his budget. "Are you a meat and potatoes man?" She scanned the refrigerated shelves for the marked down cuts.

"You cook, I'll eat. You haven't disappointed me yet." He dug his hands deeper into his pockets and shrugged good-naturedly.

"Gabe, I've known you for what, one breakfast? What do you like to eat?" She tapped a facetiously impatient foot.

"Yeah, and it was good. So, I'll trust you not to poison me." He winked.

Her hand flew up, and she shook her head. "You name three things you like to eat; I'll see what we can do."

When he saw that hand of hers, he said. "I like ham, spaghetti, chicken, but not all together." Grace took off down the aisle, with Gabe leaning on the cart. His leg always ached at the end of the day.

They walked from the market with paltry cash in his pocket. While they made their way back home, he considered either shooting craps or playing cards at lunch tomorrow. The winnings should hold him over until he could make it to payday. It wasn't tough to win off guys who were high after their lunch break. He paused to recognize he used to be one of those guys and then wondered what the hell they'd done to the cars they'd worked on.

He and Grace dug the groceries out of their bags. Gabe wiped down the shelves in the old fridge and began to put the cold things away. They stole looks at each other. Well, he knew he was catching profiles and rear views of the new person in his life. He felt Grace's gaze on him a couple of times. Gabe tossed the box of pasta toward her with the command, "Go long!" She stepped back, caught it one-handed and placed it on the shelf below the counter.

"This is the most food I've had here, ever. I wouldn't know what to do with it all. You are planning on staying a few days, right?" Gabe pulled out a pitcher and began to make iced tea.

Grace stepped toward him with the sugar bag and their hands connected in the pass. Gabe felt the spark between them and stepped closer. He kissed her forehead, reaching for her. She stepped back and tucked her chin to her chest. Her gaze, under her eyelashes, lifted to his. "If you want me to." She said, sounding both shy and grateful.

"Yeah, of course, I do." He shut up, afraid of the awkward admission. Then, realizing their work was done, Gabe snapped out of the charm of the moment. "I don't want you to have to get up at six, I can eat cereal and then you can get up and get dressed in peace. Here are a few bucks and here's my phone number." He jotted the cell number on the back of the garage's business card after he put the money on the counter alongside his apartment key.

"I can't take the last of your money…"

"It's not the last of my money. You can't be out there alone with nothing. I won't have it." His serious expression closed the discussion.

"I'm going up to get my alarm clock, Okay?" Gabe stepped backward, savoring the sight of her.

****

Wednesday, hump-day, the day when you hope to chug up to lunchtime and roll down the other side of the day, cruising into Friday. Gabe woke up, without the alarm, every inch on high alert, extremely high alert. His boys were so tight he thought he was hefting a Louisville Slugger.

Did she do this to him overnight? He didn't remember a dream; it must be the smell of the bath gel and the scent of a woman in his man-cave. The breeze of her passing him in the confines of this room was heaven-sent. It was summer, and the lazy air conditioning unit reduced him to shorts and tank tops. He treasured any happenstance collision, skin glancing skin.

Brewing coffee, he ate fresh cereal so crunchy; he thought it would wake Grace while he chewed standing over the counter. *Does she drink coffee?* He wasn't sure if he saw her with a cup yesterday. Wanting to return the kindness of yesterday's breakfast, he left out a mug along with a spoon. He jotted down a 'good morning' on a paper towel and stepped into the shop for the day.

****

Grace took a short shower last night and climbed up the steps watching him from over her shoulder. Gabe returned her gaze from the black vinyl sofa as long as she stared at him. She held that sight inside her mind's eye, as permanent as a billboard, as she drifted off to sleep. The dream didn't terrorize her. She slept so hard; she rubbed the dust from her eyes as she made her way down the steps. The coffee smelled heavenly. *What an angel, Gabe made coffee!*

Grace crossed her legs as she sat on the sofa sipping the black brew. *Daddy, you did send me an angel. Now, how about sending me where they need a plucky yet under-experienced employee?* After washing her cup, she sprinted up to change for another eight hours of job hunting. Today, she'd have Gabe's cell number to leave, and she'd drop in at the library to see if anyone emailed her about the twelve applications she completed.

Grace's emotions embroidered flowers on her heart as she jotted a note on a paper towel. *See you around one for lunch (if you come back for lunch).* She signed it with a smilie face. Would Gabe make that pirate smile when he saw this? She pulled the locked door shut behind her and felt better than this time yesterday. She knew she was closer to a job.

****

Around noon, Gabe closed the hood of the Mercury he was working on and headed to the apartment door. He heard Juan yell, "Hey, G, you too good to use the garage head?"

"No, but your wife asked me to meet her around the corner, so I'm cleaning up." Gabe winked back at Juan, who was buffing out a Mercedes hood. Juan stopped the buffer long enough to shoot him a middle finger salute, which Gabe returned.

He sought the relative peace his hovel could provide in the middle of eight hours of engine noise. Plus, he hoped to catch a glimpse of Grace. His heart skipped a beat when he saw the clean coffee cup and her note. *You bet I'll be back at one.* He broke out his crooked smile and headed back into the garage.

"Hey, I knew you were a minute man," Juan smirked. They swapped another round of middle finger salutes and went back to work until one. Gabe's stomach was on spin cycle when he clocked out. He needed to start a conversation about who was after her. Yesterday's conversation hadn't gone so well. He needed to *know* who was after her. He didn't need another gunshot wound.

When he came through the door, Grace was at the counter, sandwich bread already in the toaster. She laid out a few slices of chicken breast and sliced avocado, carefully layering the ripe green fruit over the chicken. With a drizzle of lemon juice and olive oil over the sliced avocado, Grace layered more chicken and the avocado beautifully over the toasted bread. Adding bacon pieces and pepper, she turned to Gabe. "I should use Fontina cheese, but this will have to do." She toasted the sandwiches in the oven and poured iced tea while the yellow American cheese draped fully over the filling.

Grace put her heart into building the sandwiches, how could he not pick it up and dig in with equal enthusiasm? The truth was, he'd never eaten avocado, and it looked a little slimy. Gabe liked bacon and turkey and cheese. *Oh, hell,* he thought, he was hungry, he'd dig in with enthusiasm. *Grace deserves it.*

****

She waited for his eyes to register his reaction. Grace felt the elevator in her gut plummet to her toes. His first bite revealed nothing. The second bite was as if he'd been granted a revelation. His eyes widened and smiled although his chewing mouth couldn't. He winked and gave a thumbs up, never stopping to speak. Inside, Grace jumped up and down and clapped with happiness; outside she nodded appreciatively and began to eat.

****

Between bites, Gabe opened his mouth, about to pose a question about the more sinister aspects of her life, deciding to swallow the question with his food. *How do civilized people talk about this stuff?* When the sandwich was gone, he girded his courage and started the dialogue.

"Grace, if you've got somebody after you, I'm not comfortable with you going out alone."

"How else am I supposed to look for a job?" Her tone was almost indignant.

Gabe took a deep breath and his eyes closed as he internally counted to ten. "Okay, but who's after you? Is it one of the gangs? A dealer? The cops?"

Grace gaped at him. "You think I use drugs? That would be the ultimately stupidest thing I could do! Who would get tied up with a drug dealer?"

He chuckled dryly. "It's been known to happen in this neighborhood."

"No. I don't hang out with gangs. I don't do drugs. It could possibly be the cops if Arthur filed an assault charge."

"Who's Arthur? Your boyfriend?"

"God, no!"

"Your boss?"

She gave a quizzical look. "Would you hit your boss with a gallon of fabric softener and then kick him in the crotch?"

Gabe pondered the visual. "That might be the gentlest thing anyone ever did to Wally." He steered her back to the point. "Who is Arthur?"

Her previously jovial expression drained away. She sat up straight, both hands in her lap. "He's the bastard who married my mother. I promised myself as soon as I graduated I was out from under his thumb. Then he came home without my mother a week earlier than I expected. Luckily, I had the car packed, unluckily all my cash was in my nightstand when we fought in the laundry room. Luckily, I got away, but it's my loss he had the car picked up. Everything I have is in that backpack."

"So, you're over eighteen, right?" He confirmed. "Not really a runaway."

"Yeah, but Arthur's slimy tentacles are all over this city. I spent the day looking over my shoulder."

"Is he dangerous?"

"I think he's dangerous enough to do anything." Grace's face blanched and she pushed back from the table. "I'll understand if you don't want me here anymore." Her gaze darted to her backpack, and she leaned in to grab it and bolted toward the door.

Gabe was faster and beat her to the metal door, blocking her exit. "Did I say that?"

"I can see you travel light. No girl stuff here. You just got out of the hospital. You don't need my drama." She stepped closer and reached around him for the doorknob.

"Grace, I can't do this right now. I've got to get back to work. Don't be rash." Grace's complexion bloomed crimson. *Yeah, that was the wrong thing for me to say.* "Please Grace, calm down, Princess." His eyes closed as he winced at his words.

"Got any gas you can throw on this conversation?" Her arms crossed over her chest.

"Let's give it a couple of hours to chill. We can come back for round two before dinner." He ran his hands down her arms and caught her hands in his. "I don't want to fight. I'm just trying to help."

Grace's gaze scoured the room, and she took a deep breath, her hazel eyes brimming with tears. "I don't want to fight, either."

"Good. Tonight, we'll have a calm discussion and figure out what, if anything, we need to do to get you squared away."

6

The steam rose off the broken sidewalk as Grace avoided the oily puddles. Day three of job hunting was a bust. Not even a 'no' to the applications made online. *How long will Gabe's generosity last?* She liked him a lot, but she had never met anyone in these circumstances before, and the guys she knew always had an agenda. *When would his unknown demands raise their ugly heads?*

She unlocked the apartment door, and a gust of stale air welcomed her. Dropping her backpack next to the door, she washed her hands in the industrial sink and poured a glass of water. *By Thursday am I going to be bumming a ride North on the Light Rail?* The tap water went down as hard as her question.

With a deep sigh, Grace wondered if she'd convince her mother to believe her now that Arthur bore bruises from their scuffle? Did Arthur even alert her mother to her leaving? Grace looked at her watch. Their original return date was this Saturday. If her situation became impossible, could she survive on the street until Sunday? If she had to, could she slip past Arthur to get to her mother? Surely, if her mother understood the hand Arthur forced when he attacked her in the laundry room. She would have an ally against him. *Is this desperation talking?* An abused daughter is nowhere as fascinating as wealth.

Her spine shuddered at the thought of walking back into hell. She couldn't believe she even contemplated it. Maybe she could slip in while the cleaning service was there? Would her money be in the nightstand? Her head hurt.

Grace yanked the old refrigerator's door open and leaned on the cold metal. The smell of whatever Gabe used to clean overpowered the food. Nauseous, she couldn't even think of cooking.

"What's for dinner? Lunch was great!" Gabe's light-hearted stride took him across the room to look at her over the fridge door. "You don't look so good. Are you okay?"

"Where did you come from?" Her brows furrowed.

"Uh, I live here…"

"Yeah, but, you're like a cat…"

Gabe's gaze narrowed. "It wasn't a good afternoon, was it?"

"Bingo!" She slammed the door shut and began pacing the room. "I can't continue to impose on you. I need to be able to pay my way."

He shrugged. "I haven't asked you for…"

"Not yet." Grace shook her head at him.

"I don't need your money."

Her fists planted on her hips. "Then what would you ask for?"

Gabe threw up his hands. "Where did this come from?" He stayed on the other side of the room.

"There are no free rides in life, Gabe."

"That's true, but I want to get back to who's after you. Once we're past that, you'll feel safe." Grace was silent. "It's just a matter of days before you get a job."

Grace slumped onto the sofa. "I'm sorry, I can't even think about cooking right now. My head is killing me, and the last thing I want is to smell food."

Gabe waved her to the door. "C' mon, we'll go to the harbor, you might see a help wanted sign, and we can cool off with a snowball." She hesitated, and he waved more vigorously. "We can go together, or I'll leave without you."

She jumped at that, and they were out the door.

****

Gabe was right, the fresh air blowing cool off the water helped her headache. They sat silently on the harborside bench slurping their melting snowballs. Grace counted the number of women who slowed to watch Gabe licking the cherry red mound of ice in his hand. With a sly smile, she chuckled and shook her head.

****

"What are you suddenly laughing about? I'd say that blue raspberry has a medicinal effect."

Grace's golden eyelashes fluttered closed as she shook her rose gold mane. "You could be the poster boy for snowballs. Do you ever notice how many women stare at you?"

"Only when I give 'em a price for a brake job."

"That's not the kind of job they want from you, Gabe." She shook her head at his oblivion. His cheeks colored and gave emphasis to his stained lips. The setting sun glistened in his blue-green eyes. He smiled *with* his eyes. Her heart gave a little jerk when his gaze swept the passing pedestrians and returned to her.

"You know, this walking everywhere is a chore. I'm looking for another car."

"What happened to your last car?"

"It was seized the day I went to the hospital. I loved that SS, but it's gone."

The warm sunset glowed from around him. "So, you want another one?"

He shook his head with resignation. "Nah. Looking for something I can keep running, something trusty and… comfortable."

"Miss Lerner!" The voice came from behind her. Grace froze guiltily for a moment and turned to face the woman addressing her.

"Mrs. Spring!" Grace greeted the Nordstrom's personal shopper, whose services were worn out weekly with Linda Darby's constant demands.

"I heard you were attending The Chef Academy in London this summer. What are you doing back in Baltimore?"

Grace recovered quickly. "Uh… I leave on Saturday."

Gabe slid to the end of the bench to take in the view of the tall fashionably dressed woman. His brow rose at Grace's comment.

"When does Linda return from Bali? I do hope Arthur liked the lingerie and bathing suit ensembles I chose for her?"

Gabe's lips drew straight.

"Well, you know, we're going to miss each other. I leave early Saturday, and her flight arrives in the afternoon."

"Her flight?"

"Ah, yes, Arthur had to return home for business."

"Oh dear, all those lovely outfits just going to waste in that tropical paradise." She laid a manicured hand on Gabe's shoulder. "I do hope I'm not embarrassing your young man with discussions of lingerie." Gabe swallowed the last of his snowball with a flummoxed expression. "Do you model?" She ran her hand over his shoulder and playfully pinched his bicep. "I could use an athletic model like you for our private fall showing." She dug in her satchel, "if you grew a beard, you could be sooo hipster." Out came her business card. "Will you be leaving with Miss Lerner Saturday? I hope not."

Ignoring the proffered card, Grace checked her watch. "Oh, Ms. Spring, we have to get going. We have movie tickets." Grace abruptly rose and caught the empty snowball wrapper from Gabe's hand. Without further conversation, they left the gawking woman behind.

****

Gabe set the order of loaded fries down in front of Grace but did not join her on the bench table. He stared down at her, and she refused to meet his gaze. "Okay, no B.S., who *are* you?"

"The same girl you met at the laundromat."

"Yeah. Who is that girl, really?"

"You think I'm some poor little rich girl on a soul vacation? Gap year?"

Gabe could see the wall dropping between them as clearly as if it had been a garage door. His graduating class didn't get a 'gap year', they hit the bricks June first. She was not offering more tonight, and something warned him if he pursued his questions, she'd be gone. Were the answers a worthy trade? He decided they weren't. Grace would tell him her story when she was ready. Hell, he had a story of his own he wasn't prepared to risk telling yet.

Grace slid a portion of the fries to one side and began eating without conversation. Gabe swallowed his questions and did the same.

On the way home, they maintained their uneasy silence at the crosswalk, and the light changed. Grace stepped out into the gutter without him. Out of the corner of his eye, he saw a car corner close, nearly striking Grace. He grabbed at the shoulder of her shirt and yanked her back toward him. She screamed at the blur and the sensation of falling backward. They landed in a tangle on the sidewalk together, Grace on top of Gabe's lap. She gasped and attempted to jump off him. It soon became evident she'd twisted her ankle.

"Are you okay?" He pulled himself up, dusting off the grit, and caught her. She did an awkward, painful dance to balance on the uneven sidewalk. They recovered from the shock of her near hit, and he held her hand while she righted herself. "You're not okay. Jump on up, I'll piggyback you the rest of the way."

"What about your leg? No, really."

"Yes, really."

Something in his reflexes compelled him to save her, she realized. With his big heart and a strong back, he crouched over, caught her behind her knees and carried her the eight blocks home.

Grace giggled as she felt his muscled back against her breasts. As he bobbled her with every step, her bra-covered nipples rubbed against his tee-shirt, and she scandalously wished she was braless. His strong hands hooked her knees as she straddled his back. She was situated right over his mermaid tattoo, and with each bounce of his step, she felt the back of his belt stroke her center. She gave in to her fantasy, laying her cheek on his back and sucking in his earthy musk, all the way home.

"You saved me again," she whispered into the back of his neck. It was a statement lost in the din of the street noise.

"What?"

She spoke more directly into his ear, her words traveling on her warm breath. "Thank you."

****

"Just sit here, while I get a pan of water and some ice." He pointed to her firmly while she fought his directions. He removed her shoe and iced her ankle, "You're going to live, just as long as you stay here." His words meant more to her than anything. Once he got her to the couch, he turned on the TV and promised he'd return. "Don't go anywhere, I'll be back."

As Grace dozed on his pillow, she enjoyed sweet dreams of her 'Gabe back' ride. Sure enough, in half an hour, he was back, with a large bag of ice.

"You know how things work out sometimes?" Gabe asked as he stowed the rest of the ice in the freezer. She didn't know where this was going. She shrugged, and half nodded. "I used to work on a car for an old couple down the block. They drove this Taurus, since, I guess, 2000. When he got sick, there were all kinds of money problems. I gave them my cell number, and I'd go down there," he pointed down the road, "and I'd fix the car and she'd make me stromboli and tortoni…" Gabe went on telling tales about the Italian couple, married fifty-some years.

Grace could see the regard in his eyes as he talked about the desserts and the nights he sat on the front step with them. They were surrogate parents to him. She wondered where his own parents were.

"Frankie can't drive anymore, so Connie just called and said they have to get rid of the car. The insurance policy expires Friday, and she's afraid they'll be fined for not having insurance. So, she asked me if Wally could get rid of the car, and I told her I'd buy it." He brought two mugs of soup to the sofa. As he sipped, he talked with such affection for the old couple, her heart melted for him.

"Can you get the insurance and tag switched over easily?" Grace caught a noodle and slurped it as Gabe watched it disappear with some intent interest.

"Yeah, in fact, I can pick it up tomorrow. Wally's pissed I've taken time off, but he said he expected it, with the hospital and stuff." *There, he mentioned the hospital again... Should I ask him to tell me the whole story?*

"I've got shop business for Wally down at the tag agency Friday morning, I can do it then. Friday night, I'll have wheels!" Gabe slapped the arm of the sofa with enthusiasm.

****

Gabe's phone rang, and he glanced at the number. "Unknown. Did you give my number out for a job?" He asked before he answered it, "Hello? Yes, Grace. She's here. Hold on." He mouthed the word 'job', stuck up a thumb, and handed her the phone.

"Yes, oh, yes, I did. Yes, I can, what time? You want to see me in the morning at nine?" She made an excited face and repeated the words for Gabe's benefit. He kept nodding as she kept talking. She closed the call and let out a 'whoop.' "Their girl laid out one too many times. They fired her because of a big party, and they need dependable help. They want to see me in the morning, and if I'm a good fit, they'll hire me!" She grinned ear to ear. "Plus, they provide uniforms."

"What about your ankle?" Gabe asked.

"It's a job, I'll just have to power through it." *The girl knows what she has to do. Her first paycheck is within her grasp, and she can taste it.*

****

Saturday afternoon before the Fourth of July Grace dug her mason jar bank out of the back of the kitchen cabinet. "Gabe, I'm working the luncheon at Fort McHenry on the Fourth. I'm allowed to bring one guest for the fireworks, you wanna be my plus one?"

As he half-watched the baseball game, he looked at her perplexed. "You mean like your date?"

Grace held her life savings in both hands. She shrugged. "Yeah. Kinda. It's not like Ms. Spring has called you for modeling jobs. Wally isn't keeping the garage open, is he?"

"First of all, Ms. Spring doesn't have my number, and no, we're closed Fourth of July. What about that guy Ryan you keep talking about? Won't he already be there?"

Grace sorted money on the coffee table as she rolled her eyes. "Ryan is gay. He'll have a plus one of his own."

"As much as you talk about him, I thought I'd need to be your chaperone."

Grace's brows arched, "Jealous?"

Gabe folded his arms over his chest. "You want me to be?"

"It never hurts a girl's ego."

"Well, if he's gay, then he's no competition for me, is he?" Gabe slid further down in the corner of the sofa and chuckled.

"Not all the guys at work are gay… Sit up, pay attention, we need to talk money now."

Gabe's brow furrowed. "I told you I don't want your money."

"At least take some for gas. You always pick me up when it's a late night." She held out several bills.

He accepted them, counted the amount and folded it and stuffed them in the mason jar. "You need a better pair of work shoes. I see how worn those sneakers are. No wonder your feet hurt at the end of the day."

"I want to contribute."

"You cook our food. You do more than half the cleaning. You do the shopping. You contribute just fine. Plus, you bring home food every time you work. I have to keep you in that job for my addiction to crab cakes and Crème brûlée. Get new shoes."

****

That Friday night, one of the last vestiges of Americana, the drive-in movie, showed a double feature beginning at dark. Gabe had Juan detail his car while Grace was at work. Around 7:45 that evening, Gabe wrapped his arm around her shoulder. "Our chariot awaits!" He joked as he opened the car door. The black paint job was flattered by the waxing, and inside the deep grey leather looked fresh. "Pretty smooth, huh?" The pride of ownership shone in Gabe's smile. He closed the passenger door and jumped into the driver's seat, taking them down the road to the Honduran family restaurant for dinner before their movie.

****

"Well, it seemed like a good idea at the time," Gabe grumbled as the film droned on. "I mean, I remember all the fun we used to have at the drive-in. This is a stinker of a movie." He stretched his long legs in front of him as they lay on the hood of the car on blankets, their backs on the cool windshield.

"I remember running on the playground, eating snowballs until my tongue was frozen blue." Grace's eyes sparkled in the movie light.

Gabe watched her, his arms crossed over his chest, his hands buried under his elbows. Something radiated from her. He wanted to reach out and touch the energy. He didn't want to risk breaking the spell.

"Are you getting chilly?" She asked. He picked up the clue, grabbed a beach towel from the back seat, and she leaned forward and allowed him to wrap it around her shoulders. Their movements brought them closer together, their hips nearer, his arm around her, her head finding comfort in the hollow of his shoulder. In the summer night's chill, they enjoyed the warmth as they listened to each other breathe. Soon they tuned out the miserable film and whispered stories back and forth to each other.

Gabe heard all about her family's move from the city to the horse country of North Baltimore County when her Dad's business went global. She told him about Esther, the live-in housekeeper, who was always there for her. He understood Esther must have been warm and wonderful to put up with all her mother's antics. His heart broke when she recounted the day her daddy died. Then silence stalled any further revelations. She closed like a vault, and he wondered what kicked the door shut on her heart. Silence overtook them, and she rested in his arms.

The second movie plodded on, while Gabe opened up about his alcoholic mother and invisible father. His stories stopped with high school graduation and four years in the Navy. He bit his lip in the dark while she waited. *That's it for tonight.* He was grateful she didn't push him. *Maybe she doesn't want to be pushed, either?*

His hand found hers in her lap, and he carefully threaded their fingers together. They moved little by little, hips closer side by side, feet tapping into each other now and then. He caught the sound of her breath and wondered if she felt his heart throbbing in his chest.

She beamed up at him and dropped his hand to touch the cleft in his chin. "That's really nice." She whispered, leaving the pad of her finger in the cleft.

Is this the way people fall in love? Gabe wanted to hold this night right there, where he couldn't blunder through to disappoint her or hurt her feelings. Deep inside, he didn't think she'd react like all the other women in his life. Gabe didn't want to *ever* disappoint Grace. He caught her hand and laid it on his lips, puckering a kiss which brought a smile to her face. Her smile was trusting, sincere, and signaled for more. He placed her hand on his shoulder and leaned in for a kiss on her cheek. She moved and caught it on her lips. Her surprise was his prize.

They shared a few quick kisses, paused by an urgent need for air. He didn't expect his breath to be taken away by something as pure as a closed-eyed kiss. Gabe found the novelty of it intense. He pulled back and drew up his knees, wrapping his arms around them. "I didn't mean to put the moves on you." Something in her body language screamed 'vulnerable'. He thought about her casual comment about rape the night they'd met. *Is that it?* He reined-in his libido, and whispered, "I'd never hurt you, Grace."

****

"I think we're moving about the same speed." She admitted mimicking his posture, knees up, arms wrapped to catch her chin as she tried *not* to watch him self-consciously wrestle his hard-on into a comfortable position. *He's so cute when he works to be a gentleman.*

"What do you say we call it a night? I mean, head back to the apartment? Um…let you rest your feet, you know, get a good night's sleep, and you know, cool off?" Every verbal direction Gabe suggested sounded like a come on, and she laughed, thinking he was of the same mind. He chuckled and shook his head in mock defeat. He helped her off the hood and back into the car, gathering the blankets and towels and tossing them in the back seat.

There was nothing to disagree with. Grace knew where it would head if they stayed on the hood of the car or ducked inside. She'd want to see if his chest felt as strong as his back, and then she'd want to see it all, even in the darkness of the drive in. They had to get out of here, or she was going to act on every curious urge.

7

Sunday morning roared in with a cleansing cloudburst, and Grace snuggled further into her pillow, the grey of the day lulling her back to sleep. The hot rain overworked the wall air conditioner unit, causing a spike in its constant drone. Nudged awake, her subconscious mind relentlessly cycled over last night's confessions to Gabe. She worried she'd over-shared her story. He called her princess; was he looking for a princess? Could she trust him? Would she disappoint him in the end? A princess should be poised, beautiful, gracious, successful and have her hands on the wealth of the kingdom. She was none of those things. Maybe she'd been destined for the role of a princess at one time, but Arthur changed everything. Now, she was a simple working peasant. She didn't even have an apprenticeship. What could Gabe possibly see in her?

The loud ticking of the bedside clock called. Grace opened one reticent eye and glanced at it. Ten thirty! She groaned. *I slept my day away!* The apartment was too quiet. *Where is Gabe? Surely, he's not working.* She listened for telltale sounds from the garage, and all was quiet. With a sigh, she got up and headed for the shower, though she had no earthly idea what she would wear. Yesterday's clothes would have to do. She hoped he liked what he saw at the drive-in since it was the one near-clean outfit left.

A note stood on the kitchen counter and detoured her from the claustrophobic bathroom. *Went out for donuts. Be back soon.* She smiled at the quickly scribbled note as if she were smiling at Gabe.

With a screech, the door flew back, and Gabe surged into the apartment in a gust of wind and rain. "Oh crap!" He shook like a dog. "I tried to cover the donuts with this," he lifted a plastic bag, "but it didn't work in the storm."

"Did they survive?"

He put the bag down on the kitchen bench. "I should have bought donut holes because that's what they are now."

"Well, less to chew. Now they're bite size. But you're dripping wet." She ran to the bathroom. When she came out with a bath towel, she caught Gabe peeling off his drenched tee shirt. The inked image on his chest accentuated the cut of his muscles, glistening with rain and highlighted by the over-head shop lamp. Grace skidded to a stop, open-mouthed.

Gabe reached for the towel. "Thanks." He turned away from her to wipe at his chest and dab at his basketball shorts.

She circled him. "Wait! I want to see that!"

"What?"

"Your angel. Hold still."

Gabe quirked a grin. "O…kay…"

Grace itched to trace the angel's wings on his chest with her finger but resisted the urge and stayed back an arm's length instead. She closed one eye as if she were an artist looking for perspective. His chest bore the Archangel Gabriel, wings unfurled, in full color. The angel's foot rested firmly on a vanquished devil's head.

On closer observation, Grace recognized the artist used Gabe's features on the triumphant angel's face. He indeed could have modeled for the angel, but she was sure he still possessed a devilish side. His neck bore a crude collar of barbed wire. His muscled arms bore nautical ropes with small mermaids and compass points. The names of ships and the date he crossed the equator were celebrated in red and blue ink fit within the swirls of rope, commemorating his time in the Navy. "The angel is *you*."

He gave an ironic laugh. "I'm far from an angel. Maybe I'm the guy under his foot."

Grace looked appalled. "Don't you ever say something like that about yourself." Hot tears filled her eyes, surprising her as much as him. "You've been my guardian angel."

"Oh, Princess, you haven't known me long enough."

"I don't know where I'd be right now, without you. Probably in jail." She looked down afraid to meet his gaze.

Gabe swept her up against him, forgetting his chest and clothes. "I don't think anybody's after you. If they were, with as many job apps as you've put in, they would have found you by now." He leaned back. "You're the one crying, but look, I got you wet." She gave a watery laugh. He held up one finger. "I've got just the thing. Close your eyes."

Following his instructions, she heard a bag crinkle and then he hung two plastic hangers on her fingers. "May I open my eyes now?"

"Sure."

Grace stared in delight at two smock-topped sundresses. She glanced up at Gabe. "I thought you might need something cooler to wear. What's this color called? These would look great on you."

"This is turquoise," she held one up, "and look how happy the sunflowers are." She held up the other. "You must have read my mind." He cocked his head. "I'm out of clean clothes and cash."

"Well, here's two more days clothing. You can always wash things here." He gestured to the deep industrial sink in his quasi-kitchen. "I wash things out here all the time. It's a bitch to get them dry in this humidity but hang them upstairs. It's hotter up there."

"I was just headed in to take a shower. Let me get clean, and I'll try on one of these."

****

The rain continued to pound, and Gabe walked upstairs to look out the high windows. Grace followed after her shower, and he glanced her way when he heard her on the stairs. "Looks good."

Reaching the loft, she spun once and smoothed the paisley fabric beneath her as she sat to dangle her legs between the deck railings. "I could live in this, the fabric is delightfully soft, it's so comfortable. Thank you, Gabe, for thinking of me!"

He grinned automatically at the fabric draping her thigh. The turquoise paisley enhanced her strawberry blonde hair. Gabe longed to caress her firm thigh the way the cloth swathed her now. "I used to hate days like this, as a kid." He nodded toward the pouring rain. "Being trapped inside was hell."

"Days like this, we'd spend time cleaning tack at the equestrian center."

"Tack?"

"You know, saddles and bridles and stuff."

"The only tack I know is sailing. A bunch of wealthy people thought they'd help us city kids and take us sailing in the summers. I learned how to avoid getting hit in the head with the boom."

"Well, that's an important lesson." Grace looked down and paused. "Did I scare you with my true confessions last night?" When he said nothing for a beat, Grace looked up to see his eyes wide and wondering.

"No. I want to understand what makes you tick. Even wealthy people can be abused. It seems to me we have a lot in common that way."

"You mean, abuse?"

"Yeah."

****

Not so bright, but plenty early, Gabe opened the mechanic bays at seven. The appointments rolled in, and he wrote up the tickets while he waited for Wally, who blustered in about three hours later. By then Gabe had been under the hood of a few cars.

"Lee." Wally, a bulldog of a man, barked, holding up a stack of mail, as he stood in the doorway of his office. He handed it to Gabe with an apology, "I forgot to give this to you, one of them looks like it's important. Cops after you again?" His greasy finger tapped at the one from the State Office of Victim's Assistance.

Gabe accepted the stack and nodded a thank-you. The letter set off a blender in his stomach, he headed to the workbench, using a screwdriver to open the envelope impatiently. Something about the State address on mail flat out scared him. Slowly, he read the letter. *Hell! Holy Mother! They're paying me!* Inside the envelope was a voucher to carry downtown, where they'd cut a check for $25,000 to Gabriel Lee as a victim of violent crime. *Well, slap me and call me Susan!* He was fueled by helium; it was all he could do to keep from hitting the ceiling.

Wally called from the doorway, "You okay?"

Gabe turned off the smile and nodded, "Yeah, yeah, it's all under control."

He folded the voucher up and pushed it into the secret compartment every wallet seems to have and then walked back out to the shop. It wasn't lunch yet; he'd anxiously count the minutes until then.

He had to play it cool. He needed to handle all the petty crap the way he always would, with a smart-ass crack or a shake of his head. Now with the temptation of ready cash, would he be drawn back to Benny, his old source? No. He wanted that chapter in his life dead and buried. What had Grace said? 'That would be the ultimately stupidest thing I could do.' Nobody cares about broke Gabe, and as far as the guys in the shop went, that's how it needed to stay.

****

The traffic noise and horns honking insistently outside the garage door brought Grace awake. Monday morning. It dawned on her she and Gabe were roommates a month this evening. In thirty days, they made a little nest with a few groceries and a second-hand car. *I should cook something special tonight.* The work schedule on the nightstand excited her. She was employed because she was the right person, at the right time, not because she was someone's daughter.

A glance at the clock told her Gabe let her sleep. It was 8:44 A.M. She'd have to leave in an hour for work, but right now, she was going to stretch out in the old lumpy bed. She wondered what kind of girls shared this bed with him. What sort of girl turned Gabe on? Where were the old girlfriends? He kissed her hotly at the drive-in, and she admitted to herself with surprise, she wanted more.

When he kissed her, his next move was rearranging his package. She knew she was getting to him, and he was getting to her. *What's stopping him? Is he waiting for some signal from me? I've always expected the guy to make the first move. Was that because the prep school guys didn't turn me on? That's not a problem with Gabe. He's heart-stoppingly handsome, and his body is art in motion.*

Grace remembered the clutching, low in her belly when they made out at the drive-in. Saints alive, if he hadn't put on the brakes, she would have pulled him into the back seat. Her admission shocked her. She'd never had sex in a car. Prep school sex was in cushy club basements where parents ignored their teenagers. His muscular physique and classic features woke every urge in her body. *I wish I had the guts to ask if something is standing in the way of our sleeping together. He told me he'd never hurt me. Why would he even mention that? Prep school guys are too selfish to worry about hurting a girl. Maybe caring men are different.* She sighed, wishing they were already over this hurdle and rose for the day. Smoothing the flat blue sheet over the green fitted sheet, a detail she hadn't noticed until right now, she laughed. Maybe they could exploit this into a fashion trend? Then she wondered, as she left the loft area, *will we ever share this bed?*

She looked at her birth control packet peeking out of the top zipper of her backpack. She needed to get by the pharmacy in two weeks, or she'd have a terror of a period. With her insurance, the pills were free. She'd run around the corner on her break.

Having her period always brought back intrusive memories of Arthur. Before she took the pill, his first attack was in the middle of a horrendous flow. He dismissed her fears of pregnancy saying it was "virtually impossible to get pregnant during your period." Typical of him, he ended the bloody experience by wiping himself with the bed skirt and a flippant comment. "Think of this as a cure for cramps." From then on, she asked for the pill that ran as long as possible between periods.

****

Gabe got to the State Department of Revenue Office around four in the afternoon. The lady behind the glass looked bored handling the letter. She asked the usual identification questions and then took the voucher and told him to have a seat. He waited patiently, considering there was no television, radio or magazines, just some pamphlets about disability and jobs. *Hell. How do I get one of those jobs where everyone sits on the other side of a Plexiglas barrier drinking who knows what out of a travel mug at four fifteen in the afternoon?* He sat with his chin on his hand and reran the past twenty-four hours. *I haven't used, I haven't stolen, I've stayed focused. I feel pretty good about that.*

He was just about to zone out when he heard a flat voice. "Lee? Gabriel Lee?" The tired woman waved him back to the window and pushed a stack of papers toward him. She used a pen as a pointer and emphasized the little red X's. She nodded to the pen on a chain and in a few seconds, Gabe traded papers for a manila envelope and a green check. Stunned, he stood, counting the zeros and where the comma fell, twenty-five thousand dollars.

"Any questions, Mr. Lee?" Her voice rose and broke his concentration on the check.

"Do I have to file taxes on this?" He shook the check.

She inhaled, the breath whistling through her narrow nose. "Read page three or consult your tax professional." She pushed the envelope through the slit in the Plexiglas window and reached a pudgy hand up to slide the shade down. She cut a look at the clock, it read 4:45. He nodded and got the idea. *I have their money; it's time to go away.*

In the afternoon traffic, he tried to make a list. He could pay off the car. His rational mind screamed, bank account. To cash the check, he needed a bank account. *I can't keep that much cash at my place, not even inside the box spring. I need to get a notepad and write things down.* He felt like a frog in a blender, but the sound of the motor was a song. "Nobody can know about this money, because nobody cares about broke Gabe, and that's the way it needs to stay." What a song!

****

Gabe realized he had another month's sobriety to celebrate. Ten weeks in total. Since he'd been out of the hospital, he hadn't used, hadn't drunk, and hadn't stolen. Each day sober was a banner day. Thus far, the guys left him alone. *Guess they don't want to mess with a man they think shot and killed his girlfriend.* He was satisfied with their lack of attention; he didn't need the complications. He breathed easier, knowing his freedom was supported by a clear head. Tonight, he'd known Grace a month.

61

Would it be presumptuous to bring home root beer and ice cream to celebrate? Would this be the night to show her the view from the roof at sunset?

When he needed solitude, he'd climb the metal steps to the flat tar paper roof and step over the two-foot gap to the building next door. It was a haven built with recycled patio furniture and a cobbled together pergola covered with grape vines. The tiki torches stood out of used whiskey barrels over-flowing with purple and white petunias. Once you got past second-hand appearances, you could take in the panorama of downtown Baltimore and enjoy the setting sun. If you stayed long enough, it was a poor man's planetarium.

Tonight would be a good time to divulge a little more about himself. Gabe had to tell Grace sometime, he was a felon. On hearing his news, would a girl like Grace jump the three flights off the roof? But he figured it was better to know now, instead of losing even more of his heart and then watching her take off.

Grace asked if she'd told him too much. *What a joke.* Anything she could have done paled in comparison to his life. Maybe, if they got past his story, Grace would return the favor, and he'd understand her better.

The fear of his confession made his mind gravitate to booze instead of soda. He jittered the entire way to the convenience store for root beer and ice cream. He knew he had to stay sober. He'd made a vow to his son, and he needed to keep it. Sober, maybe one day, he'd have living children to make promises to. He'd never be able to fulfill his dreams if he backslid. Was he kidding himself about hoping Grace would be there with him? Without her and sobriety, even with twenty-five thousand dollars in his wallet, life would be much less satisfying.

8

The roast chicken with garlic smashed potatoes was a hit. Esther's recipes were locked inside Grace's mind. Because of the nurturing black woman, she would forever know how to make the best-tasting comfort foods. Esther was a shelter from her Mother's moods. She served up love on a plate, or insightful words with a cup of tea. As Grace cooked, she offered up a silent prayer for Esther, furious all over again at the thought Arthur rewarded her years of service with a small check and a pat out the door.

"You learned to cook from watching?" Gabe snooped.

"Uh huh, I did."

His gaze followed her in the small kitchen as she assembled their dinner. "How do you know what seasoning to use?" He leaned his chin on his palm sitting at the Formica table.

"It's science. Cooking is chemistry. The right seasonings bring out the natural flavors."

"And you know this because…"

"I spent exhaustive afternoons in the kitchen doing my homework as Esther cooked. And eating, we did a lot of kitchen experiments." She giggled.

"Did you ever mess up? All the comedies on TV show hilarious mistakes with food."

"Well, tonight I hope this isn't the Crazy Cook of Fell's Point."

Over dinner, she shared fond memories of the conversations she'd treasured with Esther during the week, and with her daddy on Sunday mornings. Gabe listened indulgently, but there were no experiences of his own to offer.

"I was damn lucky when anyone made peanut butter sandwiches. Who could afford jelly?" He swept his bread around the plate, catching gravy and chicken shreds. "Do you like root beer?" Grace smiled at the sight of his long, lowered, eyelashes as he regarded his dinner plate. He enjoyed every bite!

She thought with distaste of her Mother's admonitions to her father. She mocked him as 'common' for sweeping his plate with his bread. Her censure of his simple enjoyment made him feel small. Grace's lips curled into a smile of defiance as she followed Gabe's gesture with her own, sweeping mashed potatoes into the remaining gravy.

She nodded "Yes, I love root beer."

"How about floats, vanilla ice cream?"

"Love those too, but I'm going to be a cow if we keep up the treats." She stopped sopping up the gravy at the mention of root beer floats.

"Naw, I don't believe that." He winked and carried his nearly clean plate to the sink. "Somewhere inside, I know about women and their weight – time for me to shut up."

Gabe grabbed two football-themed Big Gulp cups, and they watched the root beer fizz as he poured it over the ice cream. Stabbing straws into each of the sweet-smelling cups, he picked them up and led her out the door. "Come on, follow me." They climbed up three flights of metal stairs leading to the tar paper roof. The two-foot gap between his building and the one next door was swallowed up in one of his long strides. He left Grace momentarily staring down at the three-story drop, while he put the floats on a picnic table and grabbed the wide plank used to span the buildings. She didn't like heights, but she let him help her across the gap just the same.

The view of the high rises in the distance made a breathtaking panorama behind the shorter neighborhood buildings. The sight was cloaked by the golden hour of the sunset as it cast a glow of oranges and purples in the sky. "I was stoked when the company next door to the garage fixed up their roof. How do you like the grape vines and plants?" His brows rose. Grace turned in a slow circle, admiring the full effect of the garden.

"It's certainly a break from the sidewalk! It's very relaxing once you make it over that plank. Any plan for a bridge with handrails?"

"I'll consider that. It's all good, the employees like the get-away, and in the evenings, it's my own private park. Now, I can share it with you." He sat at the picnic table and slid the float to her.

She used her straw to blend the ice cream with the root beer. "This is very quixotic." Grace smiled.

"Whatever that means." Gabe paused. "I always think of it as my great escape." He got comfortable at the picnic table, stretching out his right leg. "I can't get my mind off those high- rise condos over there." He pointed to the same one he indicated a month ago. "What would it be like, to live in a place like that?"

The sight of the sand-colored brick building plunged a knife in Grace's heart. Arthur's business condo was over there, it was a one-bedroom apartment he kept for 'monkey business'. Grace cringed at the memory of being forced to attend football games downtown with him. It involved staying there after the game because Arthur liked to enjoy a 'drink or two' in the stadium suite, and it was a long drive to Hunt Valley. Mother hated football, so Arthur nabbed Grace to act as hostess in his business suite. Grace tried to decline, and failing that, tried to arrange activities to excuse herself. Before long, Arthur nixed that. "The young lady needs to learn her place in the business world. If horse shows are keeping her away from those lessons, we can always sell the horse." Grace loved her horse and grieved with everything in her when Arthur sold him.

Grace slowed down on the float, but Gabe wasn't letting go of his dream. "Someday, someday, Grace, working hard will pay off, and the money will be there to get out of this grind." Her shuddering inhalation drew his attention. "You okay?" His brows rose in the center.

She nodded, licked her lips, and then raised her gaze to his. "Do you have any idea, what sordid hell exists up there? I mean…" she drew a deep breath to continue. "I know a girl whose family has a place over there." His gaze followed her sudden animation. "Her stepfather molested her there, over and over. When the girl ratted out the bastard, her mother wouldn't help her. She let it go on for two more years."

****

Grace's face was ashen with the torment of first-hand knowledge. "That's gotta be tough," Gabe began tentatively, "knowing that's happening to a friend. Not being able to do anything about it." Gabe watched as her lips paled, and a sad pout overcame her expression.

"She told me… she, she said… she'd lie in bed at night shaking… waiting for the pervert to come into the room…" He tasted the venom in her words. "…Waiting for his disgusting hands to cover her, touch her in all the wrong places." Her voice grew so faint, Gabe leaned forward to hear her. "Finally, she left. She ran." She stared down into her cup-- avoiding eye contact with him.

"When things are bad, some people push it down, deep inside themselves, so they can pretend it happened to someone else," Gabe suggested gently.

"Well, what does that mean?" Her gaze flashed up at him. "You think it happened to me?" Grace twisted her hands in her lap so tightly she winced.

"None of us are safe from that kind of thing, Grace. Especially kids. It's not something they ask for, and it's sure as hell, not their fault." *Dammit, I should have known.*

"Safe? I was only safe when Daddy was alive. Now I'm… that pervert… now I'm just used and broken…" She crossed her arms on the picnic table and dropped her head into them, her wails of anguish muffled and distorted in their depths.

He reached across the table to calm her, wanting with all his heart to gather her into his arms, but knowing instinctively she had to cry this out on her own. His hand rested gently over her clenched fist, and she grabbed it as if he were her life-line. He could feel her sobs reverberating through her and into the picnic table. His heart broke for the sweet, terrified kid she must have been. He fought bawling right along with her. When finally, her shaking sobs gave way to stuttering hiccups, he figured it was safe to embrace her again. He circled the table and pulled her into the comfort of his arms. She sighed as she rested against the strength of his solid chest.

"Grace, Princess, you are not broken." He whispered huskily. "Bad things happened to you, but you're better than he is, you survived it. You did something about it. You're gonna be okay." He hugged her tightly as she wrapped her arms around him and clung on.

"You want to know broken? I'll tell you a story about someone who's broken. I mentioned when I met you, I just got out of the hospital?" He nodded to her, and she nodded agreement. "You're a smart girl, you read much news? Watch it on TV?" He was aiming for disclosure about Carla. Grace shook her head no, and he nodded. "I knew a girl named Carla. She started down the wrong path before I met her. She came from a rotten family, and she was out of control. She hung around me for the high." Gabe looked out at the harbor, as he ran his hand over his bullet wound. Grace's hands went to his knee. He saw those clean, soft hands and knew they were there to comfort him.

"About Carla, where is she?" Grace's question was quiet and direct.

Gabe drew in a deep breath and bit his bottom lip as he picked at the small gold charm on his chain. Holding it, he worked it side to side. "We made a pact when she told me she was pregnant. We agreed to get clean. I did, but she kept using behind my back. I couldn't trust her if she out of my sight." Gabe jerked up from the table and paced the tar paper roof, his hand covering his face. "She was six months pregnant when I caught her. She was making a drug deal, trying something new. She was gonna ride the white horse." Grace wrinkled her nose and shot him an uncomprehending expression. "She was looking for heroin."

"Oh, no!"

"I got to the buy just in time to see her pull a piece on the dealer." Gabe stalked back and forth, recounting those last minutes. "The guy pulled a bigger gun, and she shot, and hit me instead."

"Did she go to prison? Where is your baby?"

Gabe's head dropped back, his hands on his hips. "The dealer killed them both with one shot." He looked at Grace. "The cops thought I did it until they did the CSI thing that proved I hadn't handled the gun. I gave them the dealer's, name and description. They knew him, and since I was clean, they figured I wasn't in on it." Gabe rubbed at his stubble and arched a brow. "If you hang around me long enough, someone is gonna tell you, I killed Carla and our baby. I let the characters around here think that just, so they stay out of my way."

Grace shook her head. "Wha…"

"That's broken. Carla was broken, and in a way, I suppose, she was suicidal. I mean, no one, even messed up on dope, would be stupid enough to pull a gun on a dealer and think they'd live through it. Yeah, Carla was broken."

"Oh my God, Gabe, I'm so sorry. But, why would you let people think you killed her?"

"There's more…" He waded into deeper waters.

"I didn't know my father; my parents were never married. My mom was around when my gran got our assistance checks, other than that…well, her drug of choice was booze…and she got plenty of booze dancing…and other stuff." He let that gem hang out there for a second. Grace swallowed hard. "I went to parochial school and got basic morals drilled into me by the nuns. I went to Polytechnic High. I was good with my hands, so I took the mechanics program. My gran knew Frankie and Connie, you know, the couple who sold me my car? They were big influences on me. Frankie suggested the Navy when I scraped through to graduate high school at seventeen. Those four years were the best thing I ever did. Check this out!" He turned and looked over his shoulder. "I hope this doesn't freak you out." He dipped the back waist of his basketball pants and lifted his tee shirt to reveal his mermaid. "I got this when I crossed the equator."

Grace inhaled deeply and smiled. "Ooh. That's beautiful! Did it hurt?"

"Nah. Sailors know where to find great artists. Look at this one." He flexed his forearm, moving the inked rope over his muscles. "Here's the first base I served."

"It sounds like you liked the Navy."

Gabe nodded agreement. "Yeah, I really did. Nice quarters, three meals a day, medical, dental, uniforms. And they let me work on cars! Shit, I thought I'd died and gone to Heaven."

"Why did you get out?"

Gabe shook his head in self-disgust. "I don't know. I was a stupid kid, I thought I'd get out, go to college on the G.I. Bill and then maybe go back as an officer. I didn't know how to be successful in the civilian world. I messed up, and now I can never go back."

"What did you just tell me about being broken?" Grace's gaze was piercing.

"I'm not exactly broken, but I'm a little cracked. I got out of the Navy, I got a part-time job, and enrolled in community college. I rented a little place north of here near the college. I met a few guys like me, and we…ah, you know, would get together and burn a joint or two every now and then. You don't smoke dope, do you, Grace?"

She shook her head, her eyes wide. "I couldn't risk being drunk or high around Arthur."

Gabe nodded knowingly. "One night, I was driving for a twelve pack, when Monty and Jack waved me down a block before the beverage barn. They were out of breath and looked a little shook, so I ask them, 'what the hell are you doing'? They were all hopped up, and they say they went out for a run. And I say to them, 'a run'? And they say, 'keep driving'. So, I didn't think anything about it, the next thing I know, there were lights and sirens and about a million squad cars all around me. I got fingered as the getaway driver for their little experiment in how *not* to hold up a convenience store. They carried a gun, and they got sent up for a while. None of the victims could identify me, and with a decent attorney, they should have let me go. But my green Public Defender looked at me like I was a stone-cold killer, so I got two years. I earned time served and what they called 'good time'. Since I was such a choir boy, it reduced my time inside to about six months." He sat on the picnic table, looking down at Grace, his elbows on his knees, bent toward her on the bench. She didn't move through any of his confession. Gabe sat still as he awaited judgment.

"That's it? You gave friends a ride, you weren't even near the place, how could they call you the getaway driver? Oh, Gabe, if I'm frustrated by the charge, I can't imagine how furious you've been!"

"Yeah, there's an old saying, 'fly with the crows, get shot down with the crows.' My auntie preached that when I was this tall." He held his hand out to measure a six-year-old. "I got shot down -- way down."

"Gabe, our two situations, they just seem as if we got railroaded."

"The contrast here is, you were knee deep in money, but it didn't save you, and I was flat-ass broke, and it penalized me. No one ever said the world would be fair. I was sent up on a felony charge. I can't go back to the Navy." His breath was deep and slow as he chewed on his bottom lip. He raised his head abruptly and shook it as if to whip off some invisible mantle of guilt.

"So… you decided to work as a mechanic." She said, seeking eye contact with him. As she sat listening, her body language closed up. Her arms wrapped around her torso as she nodded for him to continue.

"Yeah, I've been working here since I got out of prison." He sniffed and assumed a more assertive stance. His muscled forearms were roped with healthy veins and ink, he crossed them defensively over his well-developed chest. "I started using again, cuz I was pissed at the world, and bored. Then Carla came along, and you know how that ended." He took in a deep breath, his nostrils flared. "As bad as the experience was, I learned something about myself, and about life, finally. I know I have to stay clean and sober. I have to stay honest. I have to live up to the expectations of the people I admire." He got off the table and sat beside her. Pulling the charm out of his tee shirt, he held it for her inspection. "I gave this to Carla when she told me we were having a boy."

Grace took it from his hand and turned it to read the name. "Gabriel Carlos." Her breath caught. "That's a beautiful name. With what you've said, you'd make a wonderful father."

"I swore to him I'd live for both of us, now. And that's what I'm going to do."

His gaze bore into hers, still awaiting judgment. His posture belied his pessimism. Gabe felt he'd rolled snake eyes. *What a crap out.* He expected the loss of everything he and Grace worked for in the past weeks.

****

"Will you give me some time alone?" She whispered. A rush of air left her lungs, and she buried her face in her hands, her elbows on the picnic table.

"Do you want me to leave for a while, so you can have downstairs to yourself?"

All she could do was nod without looking at him. Grace waited until the sound of his boots faded to silence and then left what should have been a beautiful scene on a stellar night.

Her backpack was under the bed, and she pulled it out, unceremoniously dumping the few contents and sifting for the waterproof makeup bag. It held Daddy's letter. Carefully peeling the flap back, Grace held the envelope to her nose. The scent of his pipe tobacco was still faintly evident. She opened the letter and skimmed the handwritten epistle.

> *Dear Princess,*
>
> *By the time you get this, my journey will be over. Will it be years before you can forgive me, probably? Your Mother and I are such different people, she sees things in black and white, I see black, white and a million shades of grey.*
>
> *Lately, for your Mother, my black wasn't black enough, and my white just wasn't white enough. Nothing was ever enough, and I can't take it. I'm cracking. I hope you'll be stronger, and soldier through to make your own life.*
>
> *I ask you one thing, especially while you're young and it's easy to be judgmental. See people in their totality. Consider the good they do, not just your mother's idea that financial success is everything.*
>
> *We all find our bliss in different ways, and we need each other.*

There will come a day when you'll meet someone special to you. Keep your heart open to the fact no one is perfect. Then, the two of you will have a perfectly imperfect life.

I love you, Princess. Please remember your name was the last word on my lips.

Daddy

Grace couldn't even cry. She wondered if this was all a test -- to see if she was worthy of love. Countless times, in the last week, she heard her daddy's voice in the wind, in some form of heavenly counsel. Confusion washed over her, leaving a thin layer of sweat that chilled and dried. She felt clammy and foul. She wanted to float, she wanted to be absolved from all confusion. She reached for her sunflower dress but the evening chilled, and she needed more. One of Gabe's long-tailed shabby dress shirts would work, and grabbing it from the makeshift clothes rack, Grace headed for the shower. She'd not shaved her legs or underarms for weeks. Sometime around when Gabe was released from the hospital, Grace hit the streets. Now, when he reminded her, she remembered the news. She was struck by the tragedy of a young, pregnant women shot during a drug deal and left for dead.

She ran the shower as hard as its weak water flow would allow, furiously scrubbing and shampooing, and then shaved her downy hairs. When a communion of soap and water failed to absolve her sins, she slid down to the floor and held herself until she shivered from the lack of hot water. She turned off the faucet, dried herself with the thin towel, and dressed. In the tiny bathroom, in the discolored mirror, she stared at herself and accepted her decision.

Slipping on shoes, she headed to the front door. "Gabe," she called. The apartment was silent. She opened the door and saw the odd peace of a city street at midnight. She walked to the corner and looked both ways. He wasn't within sight, and she leaned against the light pole resorting to her only option. She summoned air into her lungs, cupped her hands to her mouth, and bellowed, "Gabe." She listened for the echo and an answer and then bellowed again. "Gabe." She folded over in resignation, and then drew in one more breath for an extended, "Gaaabe!"

****

Around the corner and down the street, Gabe sat on milk crates while he drank a root beer, beating down the demon demanding something stronger. At first, it could have been his imagination. Then, it was louder, and he pricked up his ears as he bounded for home. Under the light she stood, hair wet, wearing his shirt like a dress. She swung to gaze down each road, a desperate woman. Her anxious cries were met with his heavy footfalls, and they collided. He reached out for her shoulders and sought absolution in her eyes. Gabe recognized her raw acceptance.

9

Her voice was clear, her words distinct. "I don't want us to stand alone. I want to be here, with you." They drew together in a tight embrace and held each other as they moved inside the apartment.

He breathed, "Princess," drawing her close in a little dance. There were whispered words and the tenderness of his fingers through her hair as he moved them to the sofa. Her hands clutched at his back, and she hung on for dear life. Gabe dropped into the corner of the couch and held out his arms. In that split second of invitation, her breath and her sigh went on forever. Gabe nodded and patted each side of his hips, and she dropped to her knees to envelop him in her embrace. She was heavenly weight as she wrapped her fingers softly around his neck. He smiled slyly, and she came in for a glancing kiss only to break away and gaze into his lusty blue-green eyes. Gabe's thumb gently stroked her full bottom lip.

"Your lips are hungry, mine are too." He murmured huskily.

Grace melted against him, braless behind his worn dress shirt, she felt every muscle as he quivered beneath her. Chin to chin, their anxious mouths, close together, breathed as one. Without actually kissing, their lips danced back and forth, igniting their desire.

If Grace was anxious about her kissing ability, his immediate response beneath her quelled her anxiety. His hips rose to her warmth, and she caught herself counting to keep from rushing. Which part of him had Grace wanted most? Hadn't she wondered about the control in his hands? What could a man with his experience do?

His voice rumbled deep within his broad chest as she pressed herself against him. Now, with a hand on the back of the sofa and another on the arm, she felt like a tease with his shirt hanging away from her inviting flesh. His hands claimed her thighs as he drew her closer to his lap, with a heady inhalation, his hands disappeared under his shirt and up her hips. His thumbs met at her belly button, and he tickled her, waiting for her to collapse even closer.

"That's not fair."

"What's not fair? It's my shirt. I like the way it looks on you, but it's too big. You should take it off. I could loan you my tee shirt."

Grace pressed his cheek to her covered breast. "If you take off your shirt, and *I* take off your shirt, then we're down to my underpants and your jeans."

"Sounds about right."

"Am I too aggressive, being on top like this?" She let her full weight rest on his hips, and he moaned. With a quick embrace, Gabe topped her and flipped her to her back at the other end of the sofa. With one foot on the floor and one knee by her hip, he spread her luscious hair around her face.

"I've always loved the way you move." His perfectly shaped lips pressed lightly against her, his stubble brushed sensual frisson as he moved upward to her cheek. "I didn't want you to think I was some sort of monster."

Grace's lips parted slightly, her little pink beast of a tongue resting on her full bottom lip, and she gave him a saucy smile. "I was sending you all my signals, and I wondered if you'd ever get them?" Her arms wrapped around his broad back, insistently pulling him closer.

His grin spreading ear to ear, Gabe slowly unbuttoned the shirt she wore. "You're coming in clear tonight." He held one side of the shirt up to reveal his prize, and as his lips descended to kiss her cleavage, the metal door rattled on its hinges.

"Anybody in here? Nobody's answering the tow number! I've got a G class stuck in Howard County, and I need it in your shop asap." The voice was booming and angry.

Gabe's eyes closed solemnly as he withdrew his body from over Grace's. "Princess, I'm on call. I am…"

"I can see the lights. Somebody's in there!" Bang, bang, bang, the man's hammy fist beat the door repeatedly.

"Hell's Bells!" Gabe tucked his tee shirt into the front of his jeans to tame his excitement. He walked awkwardly to the door and hid behind it as he answered the man. "Sorry about that. I was napping. I'll meet you around at the garage door. Give me five."

Grace was at the top of the stairs. "Do you have to leave? Isn't there someone else to call?"

Gabe frowned. "It's part of my rent. Wanna go on a run with me?"

Grace pouted and dug for a pair of Gabe's basketball shorts. "Well, that's my second choice. Sure."

Within seconds Gabe was upstairs lacing up his work boots and grabbing his leather gloves. With a tender arm around her shoulders, he whispered. "I swear, I'll make it up to you."

****

What technically should have been forty minutes out, thirty minutes to hook up and forty minutes back turned into a five-hour para-military maneuver. The spoiled rotten college kid took mommy's hand-crafted AMG V8 Bi-Turbo into the woods in Howard County's Centennial Park after a downpour. All six thousand Designo pounds of the SUV sat up past its wheel wells in the muck. Grace sat inside the tow truck aghast at the liquor and beer bottles in the picnic area. She slunk down behind the wheel when she spotted her prep school, hoodies on a couple of the girls.

"If you guys don't clear a path from the car, I'll never get my tow truck back there." Gabe preached to the stumbling students. "If I don't see a path in three minutes, I'm calling the Sheriff's Department." He held up his cell phone with a military frown. The ablest of the partiers stumbled in the headlights to clear the rubble and avoid arrest.

The dozen or so students cussed out the guy passed out on the picnic table. One snooty debutante circled Gabe and huffed. "He has the fun, and we do the work."

Gabe drew on his work gloves and shook his head. "That's life, darlin'." When he got back in the truck, he snickered.

Grace bumped his shoulder. "You do have clothes on under that cover-all, right?"

"Sure, Princess. And you can find them when we're done."

"You were such a badass to those kids." She made an astonished face.

"Those kids are your age."

She shook her head. "I was never like that."

He kissed her on the cheek and sighed. "No, I don't expect you were."

****

As the sun cracked the horizon, Gabe carried his sleeping Princess up the stairs to bed. She stirred momentarily, and her nose wrinkled at the noxious smell of stagnant lake water mixed with frustration. "I'm sorry about tonight."

"Will you hold me until I fall asleep?"

"I would if I could. I've got to shower and go open the garage. It's almost seven."

Gabe pulled back the blanket and top sheet, and she slid into bed. For extra torture, he saw close up those nimble legs that ran to him. Her graceful curves ended just out of his sight, and he paused to breathe deeply. She watched him pull the covers over her, and then step back.

****

It wasn't the smartphone she was used to, but having the pre-paid phone gave her the ability to text and talk to Gabe when she was at work. Today she was working a split shift, and she had Italian meatball sandwiches to share.

> *Meet me at Harbor Bridge Walk at 2pm. I have meatball sandwiches and garlic knots!*
>
> *Okay.*

Grace slipped the small phone into her apron and went down the counter re-filling coffee cups. *When did that woman slide into the back booth?* The woman tore sugar packets into the full water glass left by the last guest and picked over the abandoned plates. Gobbling the rye toast, she washed it down with the sugar water. Grace wrote a ticket for two eggs and toast and asked the cook to "step on it".

Anyone could see the woman was destitute. Despite the grueling heat and humidity of the Baltimore summer, the woman dressed in multiple layers of mismatched clothing. The plastic shopping bag under the table bulged with a sleeping bag and raincoat. Her graying hair was braided and becoming dreds past her shoulders. The nails that adorned shaking hands were chipped and dirty. Grace needed to get her fed and out of here before the customers complained.

"Order up!"

The smell of scrambled eggs followed Grace to the back table as she quietly placed the plate in front of the woman. "Please, this is fresh. Eat this." Grace swept away the used plates. "Would you like juice or coffee?"

"I can't pay for this. This isn't mine." The woman's hands trembled as her words quaked from furrowed lips.

"It's been paid for. The man just left," Grace whispered as she looked around the emptying café. "He does this all the time. He believes in paying it forward."

The woman's red-rimmed blue eyes widened at the offering. "I'll say a prayer for…" She shoveled eggs into her mouth while Grace moved a jam caddy and a full coffee mug before her. Grace observed her from a distance, as the woman squinted at the plastic creamer cup and then drank the half and half. Grace appeared rapidly with a tall glass of cold milk. Still chewing, the woman put out a gaunt hand. "Ah, honey, you are my angel today." Grace's smile wilted at the woman's physical condition. Her freckled and wrinkled complexion resembled a worn paper grocery bag. Under the avalanche of clothing, she was only skin and bones. "What's your name, honey?"

"Grace. What's yours?" All the while Grace watched for the other servers and the manager.

"Myra. Just Myra."

"You know, Myra, there's a pretty nice shelter I know about. My name was on the list. I'd be glad to give you my place."

Myra chugged the glass of milk. "Oh, honey, but where would you live?"

Grace shook her head. "I'm okay now. I'm set. I've got a place."

"While the weather's warm, the churches generally feed us a couple of times a week and sleeping outside isn't bad. I'm okay."

"But you're so hungry today."

"Yeah, my money gets posted at midnight. I'm hungry now." She fingered the lanyard around her neck with her bus pass and EBT card. Nervously, she pushed it back under her clothing.

The door chimed as a customer approached the counter. "I've got to run, Myra. Take care."

****

Gabe already scouted out the shadiest bench on the walk and had the cooler holding ice and root beer set like a small table. He looked up and waved. "Grace! Over here!"

"Aren't you gallant with this lovely spread table?"

Gabe rose and bowed from the waist. "And it doubles as a cooler!"

"Em! Form and function!" She sat and accepted the sweaty bottle of root beer, and then she unwrapped the two footlong sandwiches. "Dig in!"

Gabe waited as she picked up the sandwich and began eating immediately. "What, you aren't going to pull stuff off it?"

"No, silly! I had them make it the way I wanted it."

Gabe shook his head as he looked at his sandwich which contained the works. After he balled up the wax paper, he wiped his lips and stretched. Sitting back contented, Gabe extended both long legs before him. After watching the seabirds for a few seconds, he shifted to sit sideways, drawing up his knee to face Grace on the bench. Hesitantly, he began speaking.

"If you came into some money, what would you do with it, you know, to make it last?"

She swallowed her bite and thought for a second. "Daddy always said you need to save three months' salary in cash, so… maybe put that in an interest-bearing checking account. The rest, in a balance of stocks, bonds, and retirement investments. You'd want…"

Gabe nodded along with her until his laughter grew from a chuckle to a full belly laugh. Her serious, instructive expression melted. She flushed red with uncertainty. "What? What's so funny?" Grace stammered.

He froze, seeing her pain, and then threw his hands up in surrender. Losing the smirk, he asked earnestly, "How much money do you think I was asking about?"

"Five hundred thousand, to a million dollars." Grace's expression was serious while she seemed on the verge of shutting down. She shrugged and flipped her hair back from her face.   "What   about   twenty-five thousand?" He licked his lips and waited to be laughed at. It was his turn.

"It would depend on the lifestyle, but the same basic principles apply." She was less enthusiastic now, and less authoritative.

"My lifestyle." He sat back, hands on his thighs, his back squarely against the bench.

"That's a lot of money. How's that possible? I mean, for a…" Her stammering continued.

She was saved when Gabe broke in. "For a mechanic? A broke mechanic? Yeah, I know. Although mechanics can make decent money if we get a couple of good breaks." He rifled through his wallet, while he defended himself. "It's all legal; I know what people think about how I live. I mentioned I was in the hospital, right?" She nodded. "When I was shot, and my car was seized, this is a victim's compensation check. Somehow, they think the hole in my leg and my car are worth twenty-five grand."

Grace's face darkened. "I've watched you limping sometimes. Are you getting better now?"

"Better than some, not as good as most." He cocked an eyebrow and shrugged, and then scratched his head. "I need your help. I've never been great with money, and I don't even know the best bank. I need to tie this money up, so I can't get to it easily."

"Why me?" She asked nervously. "I don't think I'm the person you should turn to for financial advice."

"When I go into a bank, they look at me like I'm going to hold them up. They just give me the willies. I need, I mean, I'd like you, to go with me." That was it, he asked, and with a nod, she agreed to go with him tomorrow morning.

10

The bank was one hundred and ninety-seven years old, initially serving the sailors of the port. The marble edifice defending the cash and notes against the elements of the harbor also intimidated the impoverished residents who now occupied the surrounding neighborhoods to the south.

At the start of business, Thursday, Gabe and Grace set out on foot toward the Maritime Bank. They signed in at the front desk and sat in the cavernous waiting area watching customers approach tellers behind ornately carved brass screens. Business customers strolled in with their zippered bags and made small talk with the tellers while Gabe took in every detail built by old money. Grace chewed on her cuticle and read pamphlets about bank services. The priggishly dressed middle-aged woman at the back desk approached them and spoke to Gabe. "Mr. Lay," she mispronounced his name as she extended her hand to him.

"Lee." He quietly re-pronounced it for her.

"Ah, yes, Mr. Ley, I'm Ms. Fenton. I see you'd like to open an account, please come with me." They rose and followed her to a desk in the rear of the office. Grace cast her eyes upward to the thirty-foot ceilings as she walked. The floor to ceiling leaded glass windows amplified the sunlight over the desk.

The 'bank-speak' was flowing, as Ms. Fenton outlined the benefits of their institution and the variety of services. When Grace detected a bit of condescension in her tone, she sat further forward and touched Gabe's arm to get into the conversation.

"Mr. Lee, not Lay, would like a money market account and a few certificates of deposit. I see the interest rates posted are from Monday, where are your current rates?"

Ms. Fenton recovered quickly as her fingers flew over her keyboard. "Mrs. Lee, I'd be happy to get that." She wrote the percentage rate on a sheet of paper and slid it toward them.

Grace pulled herself up to her best posture. "Mr. Lee and I believe you can do better." Gabe looked at her with astonished admiration, his mechanic's hands folded in his lap, while he watched the women verbally spar. Ms. Fenton excused herself, leaving for an office further back. Somehow, Gabe felt starting a conversation here would be like talking in church. Instead, he gave Grace an impressed but incredulous look. Grace gave him a serene smile and patted his thigh. He got the message, I've got this.

Ms. Fenton returned with a different portfolio; precisely what Grace expected earlier. When their licenses were traded for signature cards, Ms. Fenton sought Grace's eyes. "Ms. Lerner of the Hunt Valley Lerners?"

"That's right. Now of the Harborside Lerners." She chided herself for being part of the moneyed class, identified by their community.

"Ms. Lerner, what brings you to…?" The clerk read the address on Gabe's license and then gulped in astonishment.

"A change of pace, a fresher outlook. Mr. Lee gives me that." Grace sat back; her fingers laced over her kneecap. Gabe began to perspire in the bright sun. He looked sideways at Grace and forced a quick smile. She could tell he was uncomfortable. "So, what are you going to do for us and his twenty-five thousand dollars? Mr. Lee would like to pay his car off." Grace turned to Gabe. "How much do you owe the DeRosas?"

"Three hundred dollars." His throat was dry, and he croaked.

Grace turned to the woman. "He needs at least that much cash today."

"Yes, Miss Lerner, of course. Mr. Lee, how much did you want to deposit into the inflation-protected security fund?" Gabe and Grace put their heads together over his notepad, and he answered, "Ten thousand dollars."

Grace volunteered, "Five thousand dollars to the interest-bearing checking, and the remaining balance will be deposited into CD's with staggered periods allowing you some variety of liquidity." Gabe's eyes glazed over at the bank-speak. Grace read his drained expression, even this early in the morning. The remaining papers were completed and secured in a folder handed to him.

"If we need further service, who would we call?" Gabe asked.

"Ask for me, Mr. Lee." She handed a business card to each of them, and Grace caught her stare at Gabe's hands. The stare lingered on oil darkened nails and calloused skin. Ms. Fenton's tight smile straightened as she withdrew her hand.

Grace's gaze burned through the spinsterish woman. "Mr. Lee is a certified auto mechanic. Do you have a good one, Ms. Fenton?"

"I do not. Perhaps I can't appreciate a good mechanic. I ride the Light Rail." Her tone was of a woman who needed her front end aligned. "If that situation changes, I will certainly keep you in mind, Mr. Lee. Thank you, for choosing Maritime Bank." She extended her hand to Gabe and let it linger.

****

"What was that in there?" Gabe asked on the walk home, his wallet a few bills heavier, his strut a little lighter.

"What was what?" Grace avoided the question all the way home. She shifted the direction of his conversation and left him smiling at the parry and feint. "They have the Pink Floyd Experience with dinner in the park tonight. I'm excited."

"That means we'll be home tonight. I wanted to visit Frank and Connie Monday night. I want to take them this money. They can probably use it." He grinned at her. "You wanna come? They'd love you."

"Of course. I'd love to meet your friends."

****

Grace was in a foul mood. A group of young men in expensive suits walked on half the bill leaving her with half her usual cash. She did her best to pink up her cheeks and put on a smile before she met Gabe at the pier, no reason he should suffer for her lousy lunch shift.

The dock opposite the concert site began filling around three-thirty with folk who skipped paying the hefty ticket prices for the Pink Floyd Experience. At show time they would get the sound and be left imagining the psychedelic show.

Sometimes it was a pleasure just to watch Gabe from afar. Without mutual friends to interact with, she was not sure how Gabe behaved around other people. Who was the 'other' Gabe in society? She saw the confident mechanic and the pleasant Gabe in the neighborhood grocery store, everywhere old women loved him. He'd introduced her to his friend Lamar at Royal Farms, who was a good-natured guy and seemed to bring out the street Gabe. Tonight, she saw him fifty yards away while he stood at a food truck. She paused behind a thick tree trunk and enjoyed watching him fend off female attention.

Three young professional women who cut out of work very early, doffed their suit jackets to reveal silky halters. They were probably heading for happy hour around the corner. Grace smirked as they surrounded him, all smiles and welcoming body language. Meanwhile, Gabe kept retreating until his back was against the food truck. His shrugs were answered with more animated invitations. She supposed she should be jealous, but he was so adroit at gallant refusal, the girls kept grinning.

Abruptly, he held up one finger, looking over the head of the girl to his left. With a polite wave goodbye, he headed toward a woman on a blanket on the grass. Curious, Grace followed at a safe distance, and to her surprise, saw that he stopped in front of Myra, the woman Grace had fed the day before. Myra sat, wearing the same clothing. Gabe bent at the waist to speak to her quietly, his hands in his jean's pockets. Grace moved closer, feeling guilty at eavesdropping, but wondering how he treated street people.

"Hey, did you get any of my messages?" He asked defensively.

"The last one, you got a girl pregnant." Myra's tone was flippant. "How'd that work out?"

Gabe straightened up, frowning. "Then you didn't get the message from the hospital. I nearly died."

The woman rose to pace around Gabe. "Did you have the good sense to claim disability?" Her voice became more strident. "You're up right now. Are you working again?"

"Always. I've been back over a month."

"Good. Got any spare folding money?" Gabe sighed and reached protectively for his back pocket. "I'm sure you've got a few twenties you can spare."

Gabe's hand dropped from his wallet. "How are you doing on disability? Are you making your money last?" His penetrating gaze swept her from head to toe.

"Don't you judge me, you little bastard."

"That I am." He closed his eyes and shook his head. "Have you been drinking today, Mom? You know the doctor said it would kill you."

She turned from him and gathered her belongings. "Doctors say a lot of things. They don't know."

Gabe dug out his wallet. "I'd feel better if I was giving you food, but here's twenty. It's all I've got on me. Please don't spend it on junk." He held the bill out.

She looked at it scornfully. "That's all you've got?"

Gabe pulled it back. "If you don't want it, I can use it!"

She grabbed the twenty, and he let it slip into her grasp. She walked off with an unsteady gait leaving Gabe with his chin tucked to his chest.

Grace's heart ached at the drama between the man she loved and the mother who gave him life. How could she be so soul-sucking? Grace's opinion of her self-absorbed mother was suddenly elevated. She thought she knew what lousy parenting was. She had no idea.

Grace retraced her stealthy steps and got in line at the food truck. Gabe could never know what she overheard. She heard her name called cheerfully a few yards away.

"Hi, handsome! You are *my* date this afternoon. I'm surprised women around here didn't carry you off, as good as you look." She leaned in and nibbled his earlobe. He blushed and caught her around the waist.

In a breathy whisper, he murmured, "Don't we have some unfinished business?" He nuzzled her in return.

She collapsed against him. "We do, and you're going to hate this, but I'm one of four servers who aren't contagious. There's a big wedding tonight, with a reception at nine and we're already three servers short. I have to work, it's mandatory." Gabe groaned. "You want to steal kisses in the alley between courses? I could get you a gig as a busboy. Your hands would get really clean."

"This is the only night I'm not on call!" Gabe spun away in frustration.

"I won't be home until about two in the morning, and according to the calendar we don't have a night off together until Monday."

Gabe growled low. "If you didn't need the nourishment," he gestured to the food truck, "I'd carry you off right now."

"I don't want it to be like that." She pouted.

Gabe embraced her softly. "I know... It's gonna be a long weekend."

****

Saturday morning, Wally's voice had all the charm of a drill sergeant. "Gabe!" Gabe dropped the shop rag and headed for the office. "Have a seat, Ace." Gabe expected the worst when Wally kicked the door closed on the closet-sized office. "I need another Mercedes E Class." Wally pursed his lips as he sat back in his office chair.

"Yeah, the market is brisk for them. You should be able to get one cheap at the auction. What year?" Gabe purposely missed Wally's meaning.

"Naw, not at auction. I need one for a special client, no paper trail." Wally looked at his desk, pushed papers around as his stipulations echoed around the room. Gabe's heart sank.

How many hours had he dreaded this moment? How could he stall Wally? There was no way to get around this. He needed a way out of the equation. Who did he know, who wouldn't bat an eye at boosting a car? "Any special requests, color, year?" Gabe put on his best poker face. "What's my cut?"

"Something average…no distinguishing colors… How about Desert Silver, they're everywhere? Hey, no diesel, they make too much noise. Quarter cut, and a bonus if you get it by Monday." Now, Wally made eye contact.

This is a big client for that kind of cut. "Let me do some digging." Gabe calculated these words, to mean 'digging for a thief'. He hoped Wally interpreted them as, 'digging for a car'. Gabe scratched at the barbed-wire tattoo on his neck, and they nodded in agreement. Wally rose to open the door, and Gabe took off.

The rest of the morning in the garage, the digging Gabe did was the painful examination of his conscience. It took him all the way back to the little classroom at St. Mary, Star of the Sea parochial school. Back then, Sister Anne Paulette peered down her nose at him and pointed a finger to reduce him to the obedient second grader she expected him to be. Those answers were simple -- sit down, keep your mouth shut, and print neatly. *What did a seven-year-old have to confess? A lot less than a twenty-three-year-old. "Bless me, Father, for I have sinned. This is my first confession. I hit my cousin and stole chocolate from my gran." If it were only that easy today.* His digging consisted of finding a thief for hire. Which meant lying to Wally. It plausibly meant losing his job, and his crummy apartment. *Too many things to face this morning,* he'd think about it after lunch. Right now, he'd make plans to take Grace over to Frank and Connie's Monday night. He wanted them to meet her.

****

Grace was exhausted. The money from working lunches for the catering company's diner was steady. The bulk of her income was from the splashy event and weekends. She'd finally gotten those new work shoes Gabe nagged her about. She thought she would run through the first pair in a month, at this pace.

On her lunch break, she turned into the chain drug store to pick up her birth control pills. She wanted to be prepared. They called her name, and she walked to the register. The pharmacy tech looked bored.

"I'm sorry, your prescription has expired."

"But I have a refill left."

"The prescription expired last week. You need to watch the dates on those things. They get away from you. And, do you have a new insurance card? Your insurance is terminated."

"No. Well, when I get a new prescription, how much are the pills?"

"One hundred and ninety-eight dollars."

"What?"

"When you get a new script, we can help you."

My insurance is canceled. Grace was livid. *That bastard! Oh, damn it, I'll stop at the family planning clinic Monday.*

She slogged back to the diner wishing she could see Gabe and snap out of this mood.

****

Being creative, Gabe found a thief, knowing full well it could lead back to him. It was a chance he took. It would buy him time to get out from under Wally. The boost went down Saturday night, and by Sunday the Mercedes was already moved to the next pair of hands.

Monday morning, the dry toast refused to settle his stomach. The coffee brewed a dark melancholy within him. He couldn't face Grace, and he was glad she slept until eight every morning. This was going to be a burn-out of a day, and it was only ten.

Wally was unctuously friendly as he slipped him the envelope with several worn and tattered hundred-dollar bills inside. Gabe exchanged hot words with a guy in a BMW. They argued briefly about the cost of brake pads, and the car backed out, spinning rubber. It looked convincing enough to everyone else, and it transferred the cash from Gabe to the thief without having to walk back into the bar where the guy hung out. Gabe couldn't spend another minute in a bar.

11

On Monday Grace only had to work the diner and she delighted in being home with Gabe for dinner. Sadly, ham night didn't hold the magic chicken night held. The honey glaze was just the way Esther always made it. The potatoes au gratin could have been a little salty, she thought. She watched Gabe push the food around before he chewed it too long and swallowed glumly.

"I want you to meet Frankie and Connie. You free tonight?" His eyebrows rose at the question, the first bright expression he'd worn since arriving home.

"Free?" *Is he being funny? I was looking forward to being seduced. I shaved this morning.* "Sure, why not?" She agreed uncertainly. She leaned an elbow on the table and rested her chin in her palm, giving her best confident smile, hoping to soothe whatever bug was biting him. *We might as well go out, he doesn't look ready for a romantic night in. What is going on?*

"The DeRosa's. The people I got the car from. I haven't been around since I picked it up, thought we'd go by, pay them off and tell 'em how great it looks all waxed up." He looked more relaxed, talking about the old couple.

"I picked up some fruit, it's deliciously fresh, would you like to take it over to them?" Gabe spoke with such love and respect for this couple, she had to meet them to know him better.

The walk was leisurely in the dusk, the sounds of the city reverberating off the tall rowhomes, as Gabe told stories about the old couple. The front door was incongruously wide open, boxes on the porch, and rolls of bubble wrap on top of the console TV. Gabe stood in the doorway and wrapped his knuckles on the open door. Grace shadowed close behind him. "Hello? Frankie, Connie, everything okay?"

They heard a thunder of footsteps from the basement, and a man in his fifties stood before them. "No. I'm Frank Jr., and you are?"

"I'm Gabe Lee. I do odd jobs for your parents." Gabe felt immediately leery of the scenario.

****

Grace's eyes scanned the small living room, viewing the faded areas where photos were removed after a lifetime of hanging in the same spot. She saw the ornately carved mahogany sideboard, the doors wide open revealing the family linens and silver. The Oriental rug cushioned the carved ball and claw legs of the dinner table where twelve chairs circled. At one time, there was a big family in this little house. She spied a stack of mail, and on top, Gabe's one-hundred-dollar bills. The cash hadn't been spent. *This isn't good. Something bad has happened.* Her heart sank.

"Oh, yeah, you're the guy. Dad talked about you, he talked about you a lot. Thanks for putting up with them." Frank Jr.'s laugh was almost a sneer at the task of humoring old people.

"We brought them some fruit, are they here?" Gabe hooked a thumb at the basket Grace held, she smiled on cue, as she stepped forward.

"You don't know?" Frank Jr. stepped closer, shaking hands with each of them, and leading them to the sofa. "Have a seat. Can I get you a beer or something?" Grace recognized the shoes, the shorts, and the shirt -- all of it bellowed wealth, new wealth. He was one of the nouveau riche, the next generation of immigrants, who balked at their parent's humility and left the immersion of their culture. Grace's mother abandoned her Irish roots, returning solely for ceremonial St. Patrick's Day bouts of drinking.

"We don't know what?" Grace piped in hesitantly, as Gabe sat stunned. What a difference it is when an estranged relative comes into a home and begins the task of sorting the valuables out of a lifetime of belongings. She knew it was coming, but she flinched, anyway.

"Dad died Friday night, and within hours Mom followed him. I flew in Sunday morning and handled their cremation. We don't have family around here so…" His voice trailed off as Grace looked over at Gabe. He looked like a man who wanted to turn back time.

****

I was so excited about the car, I just waved a hasty goodbye and left. I never fully expressed my gratitude. I always thought there'd be time…

"How would I know? You didn't even go through their phone list? Connie saved all the numbers on the board next to the telephone." Gabe pointed to the kitchen. He was angrier with himself than he was with Junior. His voice shrilled, and then it wavered to near cracking.

"You were the only person they ever talked about. Gabe this, and Gabe that. Man, you certainly put up with their stories and their nitpicking. I figured you wouldn't have time for a funeral, you being a working stiff and everything." Junior picked the eight by ten sepia photo from the mantle and held it out, sharing the view with them.

Gabe wiped at his eyes, running the back of his hand under his nose to keep a drip from escaping. His chest tightened, and his head spun. He felt the fury of near-family breaking his heart.

"Working stiff? Me, not have time to say goodbye to these good people?" Gabe's voice rose in indignation. He sat forward, his jaw jutting as he leaned, palms on his knees. Junior stepped back and looked perplexed at the reaction.

"I see the bill of sale -- that he sold you the car. He was so damned worked up with me about not being able to drive. I must have taken three telephone calls over it. I was about to move them into an assisted living, they needed full-time care, but they hated the thought of leaving this house."

"Anyone would," Grace interjected quietly. Gabe said nothing but fumed beside her.

"Do you want this?" Junior blankly held the portrait out to a frozen Gabe. Grace stepped between them and received the offering.

"Of course, we do, it will always be special." Grace's soft thanks covered where Gabe's heart screamed for more choices. He wanted to be there for them, to sit and reverently pay his respects to their lives. "Gabe wanted to pay them the balance on the car. We came over tonight with this fruit to thank them."

That opened a new vein on Junior. "It's a 2000 Taurus, how did he have the nerve to charge you?" Grace nosed to the deposit money on top of the mail, and Junior picked it up eyeing the amount. He scoffed and shook his head. "All you did for him, and he had the nerve to charge you?" He held the money in his hand and folded it in two, stuffing the bills in Gabe's shirt pocket.

"I wasn't going to take it from them for nothing, they could have used the money for a bill or something." Gabe was indignant, now. "I did things for them because they didn't have family around. When I was done, they invited me into their home, and your Mom cooked for me and sent me home with food." Gabe paced the small path in front of the sofa, and at one turn he came near chin to chin with Junior. The testosterone flowed, and Junior backed up until his calves hit the wing chair catching his fall.

The older man looked up at Gabe. "Just keep the car. As hard as you worked to keep it running, you deserve it."

Gabe bit at his bottom lip and cut his next words off. He looked at Grace, and she rose to join him. She crossed Junior's path, and turned to stop and say, "I'm sorry I never got to meet your parents, and I'm sorry for your loss."

****

Though Grace was tall, she jogged to keep up with Gabe's long strides. He practically ran from Junior's indifference. He looked down at Grace and slowed his pace. "They didn't do it on purpose. I can tell you right now, their love just swept them up, and when Frankie died in his sleep, Connie lay down beside him and passed within hours." They walked in considering silence. "What would it be like to earn such love and devotion over a lifetime together?" *How lucky was Frankie?* Gabe thought he was pretty damn lucky.

As they continued their short walk home, he and Grace seemed disjointed. Their strides were uneven, and they couldn't keep a conversation going. Grace's head hung, and she was silent. They got to the door, and Gabe unlocked it, holding it open for her. Once she was inside, he stepped back. "Princess, I gotta get some air, I swear I'll be home real soon, I just have to take a walk."

****

Grace felt a powerful physical loss as he stepped off the curb and ambled away. She sorted the mosaic of emotions she'd walked through in the past couple of months. It would take another marathon shower before she sat in a trance, cross-legged on the sofa, combing out her hair. The eleven o'clock news began before she heard the key in the lock, he came in head down and covered in the damp night air. She ran to him. "Are you okay? I mean, of course, you aren't. I was worried…"

"I had to clear my head. Frank Jr. was a dick; I mean a grade-A dick. How could two decent people have such a dick for a son?" Gabe shook his head while he ran his hand over the short stubble covering his jaw. They faced each other; another awkward moment fueled by his anger with Junior.

"I already got mine, why don't you catch a good hot shower, and then we can have a chamomile tea, okay?" She stepped out of his path, and he nodded.

****

How does she always seem to have a solution? Or, at least she tries. He slid off his windbreaker and untied his boots. While he walked the remaining way to the bathroom, he watched her begin her steps for making tea. He considered the thought she needed a teapot. *Yeah, a teapot.*

Gabe leaned against the bathroom door and ticked off the list of the day's casualties. Sure, the anger he felt at Junior, was part of his terrible day. Satisfying Wally's demand was another factor. His walk tonight topped it all. It was a trifecta of crappy conversations, and they'd all caused pain.

How bad is your life if you can't even show the person you love how much you love them? Gabe sagged into the dinette chair and leaned his cheek on his palm. "I don't think I need any Chamomile tea. I'm exhausted. I think I might be getting that flu you've been talking about."

Grace reached across the scarred table to feel his forehead. "You are a little flushed. You want some aspirin or something? You wanna sleep in the upstairs bed where you can stretch out?"

"No, Princess. I don't want you to get this too. If you don't mind, I'm headed for the sofa. Goodnight."

****

At dinner the following night, the plate of tacos sat uneaten, while Gabe gulped mouthfuls of sweet iced tea. Grace watched as she picked at the avocado on her salad. "No appetite? Still feeling bad?"

He grunted back at her, dropping his head to his chest. "You know what was wrong about last night?" His voice was soft, his head still down.

Grace leaned closer to hear his deep voice. "Hum?" She asked, across the table.

"You know what was wrong about last night?" He repeated.

"What do you think was wrong?"

He opened his mouth, and raw emotions boiled out. Yes, it was to be expected, his feelings were sold short with the DeRosa's passing. Everybody wants to be loved, and he knew they loved him. Grace watched as he pushed away from the table, came to her, and knelt, looking up. "Their life was built on love, and their love built their family with their hard work. You know, he was a mechanic too?" Grace took his hands into her lap and held them, and then shook her head and waited. "They were married out of high school and had eleven children. One died as a baby. Miss Connie was the total mother, everything was homemade. All their kids went to college, and that asshole, Frank Jr., he's a lawyer."

She gently squeezed his hands. "Then you saw firsthand how a real marriage works." She attempted to soothe him with the look in her eyes, the tilt of her head.

"I know, if I'm going to earn any love in this world, I have to be drop-dead honest with the one who means the most to me." He moved closer to her, dropping his head in her lap. As her hands found a place on his shoulders, the flat of her palm brushed the silky hair on the back of his head. He trembled at her touch, and her hand trembled in response. "I haven't been honest with you, Grace. I need to be honest." Gabe raised his head and stood, holding out his hand for her to join him. Once they were face to face, sitting at opposite ends of the squared vinyl sofa, he began sharing his truth.

"Carla used to ride with me while I was boosting." He grimaced. "I was stealing cars." He waited to hear her gasp or pass judgment, but she sat stoically. "Saturday, Wally asked me, no, he told me, he needed another car. I didn't want to be involved. I found somebody who would do it, and I gave him the money Wally paid me. I was in a shit mood because it bothered me. I shouldn't be short with you. The way I treated you last night, wasn't right. I was wrong not to tell you, right off the bat, what was going on. Now, knowing the truth, and acting on the truth-- that's two different things. I'm going to lose my job over this, and there aren't too many places I can work."

"Gabe, it's a job, and this is an apartment. We can find other jobs and other apartments. You have some money, and I'd bet if we left tonight, you'd never have to face Wally again."

"I wish I could feel confident about that. Wally has a mean streak. He could ignore me, or if he can't find another stooge like me, he'll come after me." *She's so young, she doesn't understand his reach.*

Gabe and Grace gathered up their few belongings and loaded the trunk of the car. Gabe left the keys on the office desk and pulled the locked door tight. If it was an escape, it was a solemn one.

The kindness of strangers was not a myth. On any other day, would two people from opposite worlds come together so well? In their silence, Gabe drove, believing they would find their answers together. Rolling into an extended-stay motor court on Pulaski Highway, they traded one trap in hopes of higher, safer ground. Living there would be an adventure in itself. Tonight, the price was right. They unpacked the car and moved their few things into the room at the end of the mid-century motor court.

12

G abe, worn ragged, mutely excused himself to take a shower. Stripping off his clothes, he ran the hottest water he could draw. The last forty-eight hours were a dark hole, and Grace was the sun and the moon to him. Their reality, as he knew it, was changing, he mused. He soaped himself with the generic motel sliver. Despite carrying sexual tension since their first embrace, lousy timing had continually delayed their first experience together. He knew their eventual reward would be worth the wait. She was ready, he was ready, but the situation was never right.

He wanted to feel her naked against him, hair undone and stuck to him with their sweat. Nothing would be more satisfying than to bury himself within her. His fantasies of giving her an unhurried night of tenderness grew more vivid daily. Wouldn't their love replenish the innocence lost? His deliberate strokes on himself drew the pleasure to rise out of him. The slip of the soap and the rhythmic tension of his hand performed the relief he couldn't ask of her. His fantasy of Grace exploded in white light as he leaned his head into the back wall of the shower.

****

Anxieties hung heavy in the air. Grace knew Gabe would crave a root beer. The Royal Farms store was a few steps from their door, she pocketed the key and walked to buy a six-pack. Once back in the studio, Grace set about making the shabby room feel more like home. Grabbing candles from her shopping bag of belongings, she placed them on the desk and the nightstands. Carefully, she lit each one and whispered a prayer for her, and for them. Her attention was drawn to the half-open bathroom door, where the steam rolled out, inviting her to spy on him.

Through the clear shower curtain, she watched his muscular back flex with the movements of his arms. She watched his glutes contract as he balanced from foot to foot. Deep inside, she felt the stir and warmth she remembered from the last time they kissed. As she concentrated on his ink, and its details, it felt as if she only imagined moving closer, removing item after item of clothing. Her fingertip pushed the curtain aside without disturbing Gabe. He stood; eyes closed as his fingers worked bubbles through his thick head of hair. Her breath hitched at the idea of being naked in the same city as this inked angel. Now, she was two feet away from him, and she tingled. Heart pounding, she took a brave step nearer and moved into the tub. She pressed behind him under the flowing water and wrapped her arms around his waist.

****

He gasped when her flesh glanced over his back, and he felt her flat belly at his buttocks. She snaked her hands around his six-pack, and he huffed out a breath. Gabe prayed for control. "I think you need to know; my girl just went for ice." His voice rasped over his shoulder.

Her eyes caught him, and she kissed his shoulder blade. "Well, you can have ice, or you can have all this." She gestured to herself like a demonstration model.

"I would be honored to have all this!" Gabe turned slowly into her embrace and ran his palms down the hourglass of her figure. He stepped back to balance himself, amazed. He watched the water sluice from her shoulders to her thighs and everywhere in between.

She handed him her gel soap. "I have a feeling the pleasure will be ours." Grace smiled as she ran her fingers over the ink on his arms, engrossed in the man and his body art. "Are these things, ah, flavored? You know the red is cherry, the blue is blueberry?"

He was one huge smile. "I'm pretty sure they're not, although you are the very first person to ever ask me that." He reached for the washcloth and for the first time, she got a genuinely close look at the angel inked across his chest.

"This is a work of art; it must have taken hours!" She wiped the bubbles off and turned him toward the light. "I can't believe how perfectly the artist captured you!"

"Well, yeah, in another lifetime when I was feeling cock-sure, I was going to right all the wrongs in the world."

"That's a big job for one angel."

"Well, he is an *archangel,* but I'm not."

"So, I have my angelic bad boy?"

He stepped closer and snaked an arm around her waist. "How bad do you want me to be?"

"You've already stolen my heart…" She laid her palm over his heart.

He was mesmerized, watching the trail of bath gel make its way from her shoulder to her breast. "I didn't steal it. We just traded them." Realizing he didn't want the cotton barrier of a washcloth between his hand and her body, he made bubbles chasing the water down her curves. She surrendered to his gentle strokes.

"I don't know how to please you." She confessed, as his gentle fingers washed the other world away.

"What feels good to you?" Gabe murmured into her ear as he drew her closer. "Chances are, that would feel good to me, too." She blushed. He was hypnotized by the sensations they shared, and by the look in her eyes. He was going to test every theory of pleasure until they were exhausted. Gabe held out his arms, and she fell into them. Their lips locked in a deep kiss, while their hands blessed each other. He caught her bottom lip in his and sucked at her sweetness. She pressed her tongue to his lips and begged entry. "You're catching on pretty well." Gabe rumbled in his chest.

"You're a good teacher."

"Do you want to get out of the water, so we can be more comfortable?" He kissed her forehead, then her nose and her chin. Smiling at the water drops on her long golden eyelashes and how the water welled up between them as they embraced tightly. He turned off the water. They took turns drying each other. Grace took a step back and stared as Gabe put a foot on the edge of the tub to thoroughly dry his thigh. "You know, Princess, I have to be a responsible partner. I have to protect..."

"Oh! I'm on the pill."

Gabe nodded. "Good! But you know, that's not all a girl should worry about. I'm clean, and I know it because they did all the STD tests on me in the hospital. Nobody knew where Carla was or who she was with..."

"I felt the same way about Arthur. I went for testing every month because I don't think even Arthur knew where he was putting it."

"Well, at least you were the responsible one." He frowned and dabbed the towel to his chest. "I can go to the store and pick up some condoms right now. I'll totally understand if you want me to."

"Two negative tests, six weeks apart, I think you're clean."

Gabe shrugged. "That's what the doctor said, but I'll still understand..."

"Let's trust the doctors."

Gabe picked up her hand and gently kissed her fingers. "So...I'm a mechanic. Do you want a mechanic's explanation of... all this?" He gestured to his male equipment.

She looked at him through her eyelashes. "Uh-huh." She nodded, as she bit at her index finger cuticle. He caught her hand and drew her closer.

His hand held hers softly as he started his 'instruction'. "Treat these with care, this is my most sensitive spot." His fingers closed around her hand as he led her to caress him. "Ah, you have the right touch." His head fell back, and he winked at her.

"Could I kiss them?" He watched with amusement as his body immediately responded with a twitch. A sly smile quirked her lips. "I'm guessing, yes?"

"As you can see, parts of me have a mind of their own."

"It's so fascinating." Her hand slid out of his, and she pressed a gentle fingertip to the topography of his body. "It's hard, but you're silky smooth." Her breath hitched as she processed the effect of her touch.

Gabe shuddered with ecstasy. "The better to stroke you with, my dear." His lopsided smile grew as she wrapped her fingers lightly around him. He folded his fingers over hers and gripped firmly. "As sensitive as his two friends are below, you can get a good, strong grip here, and stroke all you like." He slid her hand up and down his length.

She giggled.

"You know, in those corny movies where they imply sex and show a train going into a tunnel?"

She giggled again.

"If you want to talk mechanically, think of it as an amorous piston and an inviting combustion chamber."

Gabe laid-on one of his deep, wet kisses weakening her knees. "This is the spark, your lips on mine start the burn.

His hands caressed her shoulders. "We build up a little steam," he pressed tightly to her, breast to chest. His splayed fingers traveled up her neck into her strawberry blond hair, and he held her there tightly. He kissed the top of her head and tucked her under his chin. "Before you know it, everything's warmed up." Grace moaned at the sensation of his flesh against hers. "And the engine purrs." His fingers found their way to the delta of her thighs. He nuzzled her, as his fingers ignited her. She hungrily leaned into his grasp. "And my piston finds it's very tight home, and together, we make steam."

Breathlessly, she confessed, "this is not the way Sister Irene said it worked."

"Did Sister Irene teach mechanics?" Gabe leaned back to see the excitement in her face.

"We didn't have that. Sister Irene taught health class."

"Did she explain to the young ladies how beautifully the female body responds to engines like mine?" Grace shook her head. "You see, the physical part of love gets a bad rap from some women because they've never known a man who spent the right amount of time with them. If I knew in high school, what I know now, I'd be the big man on campus."

"Yeah, high school boys are…"

"Selfish? Hasty? Bad lovers?"

"Yeah, pretty much."

"So, you don't even know, what you don't know."

Breathlessly, she made a face. "I don't?"

He held her tightly with one arm, as he drew lazy figures over her collarbone to the demi-lune of the top of her breast. His hip pressed hers, and he felt her spark of anticipation. "Not yet, but you will."

****

She watched his muscles move under his inked skin as he hung up their towels. "We're going to need these later."

When he turned from the bathroom to the candle-lit bedroom, he stopped in his tracks. "Wow, Princess, this is something! I'd have left the old place sooner if I knew we'd be here like this."

Grace blushed. Who knew a few dollar store candles would have this effect? The rose scent filled the room in a delightful way for her, too. He pulled back the coverlet, and she climbed into the crisp, white sheets. He followed her. "Please, continue the lesson, master mechanic."

"Very well, class, listen up. Ms. Lerner has kindly agreed to be my demonstration model tonight. I'm going to begin with the tender patch of skin in front of her ear…" Her body arched nicely against his.

****

"Ears are so delicious…" His tongue traced the shell. Gabe felt the heat between them and grinned at his good fortune. What more could he say to her? He took her hand in his, kissed her fingertips and ran her hand down his chest, following his treasure trail. "Touch me here." He watched her expression. Her hands skimmed his sex. For her, he was hard and alive. Her eyes closed with a whimsical smile. "You can touch me, *harder*," he begged. He wanted to dive into her with everything he was. There was a fire in his belly to make hard, fast love. Yet, everything in their future hinged on his next move. At what touch might she turn off? *What if I do or say something that scares her?* He couldn't risk it. He moved deliberately and with her permission. He glided over her, drew his head up and took a deep breath of the musk they generated.

"Gabe, you're quiet all of a sudden. Is everything okay?" Her eyes went wide.

"I don't want to spook you."

She hungrily kissed his earlobe, "You won't. I trust you."

"Tell me what you want." His breath was hot.

"I want you." She nodded, "Yes, I want you." She smiled, breathing deeply. They giggled and kissed. Something Gabe expected to be solemn and serious was becoming a sensuous and happy give and take.

Wrapped in each other's arms they fused front to front, legs entangled, her tender toes running up and down his calf. He flipped her over him. She rested her hands on the pillow on either side of his head. Pinned, he hoped she'd keep him like this – letting her red-gold hair dance over him. *How long can we stay like this?* He curled his legs around her and whispered, "Gotcha!" Grace kissed her two fingers and placed them on his lips. He kissed them, held her hand to his chest, and then winked at her and returned a blown kiss. They rolled together, spooning. He kissed her neck and whispered, "Princess -- it doesn't bother you if I call you Princess, does it?"

"No." She murmured. "I like it." She ground back into him. *Does she want me slow and gentle from behind?* He pulled her hips back to him. She flipped on her back and declared, "I want to see you when you make love to me. I want to see your face." She lowered her gaze, fluttering her lashes, and that was it.

Gabe knew they'd have the rest of their lives to kiss each other or play with the many positions of love. His Princess asked for an old-fashioned face to face love-making, and he would please her. He drew back to caress her with gentle fingertips. Together, they took a small breath.

****

Grace committed this moment to her heart. She watched him move with care and tenderness. She counted on his control to shepherd them through the love she deserved. Grace's eyes widened, and he hesitated and retreated. "Ah, Gabe, don't stop." His movement began their dance. It was all natural, and she felt some silent guide overtake her as a part of her flew to heaven. She felt treasured, loved. Grace's eyes widened at the shared sensations. His eyes closed for a moment, while his tongue escaped his lips. *His eyelashes are divine!* Her energy met his and enjoying his tenderness, she glowed sensuously.

****

This was sheer ecstasy, and he hoped she was feeling it, too. *It's so difficult to know about women. How will she know when she's coming if she's never come?*

"You have me dancing on clouds."

Gabe's lips measured tiny kisses at first and then built in pressure and tempo. His tongue caught a sleeping part of her, and he loved her until she arched into him with shuddering sighs. Grace's mewling deepened and lengthened until she moaned his name. The candlelit room brightened, and he knew he gave her the world within their embrace. He cast her to the stars. Delicate hands grasped the sheets, and she sang his name like a hymn.

Gabe wiped at his lips and kissed a trail up her torso. She reached for him, "Got *you* this time." Grace held him so close, he could barely pull back to thrust. Her nails drew heavily up his left thigh, marking his inked body. Her splayed fingers caught his neck and delved into his sweaty waves. He felt a defining sensation crawl up from inside his gut and force its way out. The sweat rolled off his sharp profile, and she caught it as she held him close. He didn't want her to let go. He didn't want *this* feeling to end.

****

Grace reveled in the sensations he gave her. She was still reeling from the thrills of his tongue and lips. *Does it feel like this every time? He did say he wished he knew how to do all this when he was in high school.* Grace watched his flesh color with arousal. The male beauty of his face was glorious in the throes of passion. It was everything she dreamed of the past few nights, but it was more. It was the total adoration he gave her body; it was his unerring focus on her pleasure. She wished she knew how to make this better for him. She kissed his shoulders and dug her fingers into his back. *Never let me go!* Gabe's resolve burst like a dam, and he shuddered with release.

With the little amount of strength left, he fell onto his back and pulled her to him. "Grace, Grace, oh, my, Princess." She licked at her lips and grinned in the afterglow. She stroked her fingers through his wet hair. With a single heavenly breath, she whispered, "My Gabriel," and sank into irresistible sleep.

Their slumber was punctuated by her cupping and smoothing her hands over his body. When Grace did this, Gabe responded the same way. Her body and soul were finally sated.

****

Turning over in her sleep, Grace felt a man's arm, heavy across her waist. She was stunned by the weight. Arthur never stayed after his plundering. If she shuddered, would he grab his boxers and take off? Rubbing at her eyes, Grace squinted in the half-light leaking under the curtains. She saw ink, and immediately awoke, knowing it was Gabe, and Arthur would never find his way into her bed again. She rolled over to watch him sleep. His aristocratic profile, with a dimpled chin, fascinated her. She smiled at his nostrils flaring with inhalations, lashes fluttering on his cheeks. *He is such a rush.* She closed her eyes and fell back asleep on his chest.

****

His body woke at this hour every morning. It was one of the good habits he'd acquired in rehab. The sight of his woman, sleeping next to him, gave Gabe a breathtaking thrill. He called her his Princess, but in reality, she was a warrior princess. She took on the bank lady, wagering a better deal for him. Grace compassionately dealt with his confessions. She was in his corner when his grief over the DeRosa's deaths could have sidelined him. Whatever spell overcame him when they first met, overwhelmed him still. It confused him, and he could not block the thoughts of her dominating his mind night and day. Her exacting gestures and charming expressions replayed in his heart. Many times, during the day, a thought hijacked him to something she did or a look she gave him. From this day on, he wanted to be the first thing she saw every morning.

Princess, Sleeping Beauty, come out, come out. Gabe wished her awake by staring at her.

Grace winked one eye open. "Gabriel, are you trying to will me awake? I swear I felt your eyes on me in my sleep." She rolled on her side

107

and propped her head on her hand. She ran a finger against the grain of his whiskers. "Aren't you dark and handsome this morning!"

He rubbed at the stubble on his cheek. "A little scruffy, too. I don't want to give you beard burn."

"Your eyelashes…that was it…you woke me with the breeze from those things!"

He blinked a butterfly kiss on her cheek, and she snuggled closer and spooned to him. Looking over her shoulder, she pouted. "How about your Princess comes back in an hour?"

"But my day began so great! Seeing you in this bed with me!"

Grace turned to read the digital clock on the nightstand. "Is it sex o' five?"

"I like that time!"

"How can such a tough-looking guy be so sexy and gentle?"

"Well, I don't know about that! I do know, I have to get up and find a job! But, I do not want to leave our bed." He stroked her back with light fingers.

"Then stay in bed, and do *not* get dressed." She smiled back at his touch.

"We've gotta get breakfast, coffee, and wi-fi." He was up and out of bed, pacing to find his jeans and shirt. "Truth be told, I would love a cigarette, and I'm rethinking my oath to quit."

She stretched invitingly. "Oh…you're so kissable with those sparkling white teeth. You don't want to taste like an ashtray. I don't like ashtrays."

He clapped his hands together and raised them in surrender. "One more bad habit forgot."

****

"Yeah, I should get up with you, it will take longer to get to work." Grace swung her legs over the side of the bed and felt the gentle ache between them. She blushed, as her hand covered where the sensation of her climax settled. His eyes fell to her, and he followed, dropping to his knees between hers.

"I didn't hurt you, did I?" His look of concern scared her. Would he stop taking her twice in a night if she admitted she was feeling it this morning? She'd gladly feel like this to have him love her every day. His face buried in her embrace, and just with her eyes, she let him know it was magnificent to feel their afterglow. "Do you want breakfast in bed?" She whispered.

"What did we bring, I left the milk..." Gabe missed the point until her fingers walked down his back to grab his buttocks.

He chuckled. "Okay, Princess, I'm just going to drink you up if you don't let me go." Gabe's resolve to eat breakfast and check the help wanted crumbled. He raised his head and pulled her closer to the edge of the mattress. His eyes spoke of what he was about to do, and she fell back, surrendering. She felt her body surfing the waves he pulled her through with his lips and tongue. His calloused hands held her loosely, and she grabbed at his wrists. She asked herself if she could ever discipline herself enough to get out of bed with Gabe beside her? She tripped through the same sensations he introduced her to last night. *Ah! This is what an orgasm feels like!* She knew where he was taking her, and she gave herself to him. His lips coaxed her down a rabbit hole, and like Alice, she fell into a white, hot explosion.

Her sweat cooled as he posed at the end of the bed and teased her. Her body tingled with aftershocks. She arched herself closer to him.

"If you tease me, I'll pout." She confessed cutely.

"I can't have a pouty princess." Gabe's early morning rasp of a voice reverberated through her. He moved on her to his own beat. She met him and embraced him. He couldn't hold back this morning; she flipped his switch holding him this close. His legs shook as he ground out a moan in her name.

"Ohhh, we'll be fine as long as people bring us food, right?" His laugh rumbled in his chest. "You are wearing this old man out." He lay beside her and smoothed her hair back from her face. "I don't know what to say. Usually, I'm a smartass...but...right now -- I have no words. Anything I could say...would not be good enough." Grace knew this was his humble pillow talk.

"Well, I need to say something!" He looked at her curiously, *those huge blue-green eyes, are his tell, he's expecting something ominous.* "Uh! You've confirmed something this morning." His head bowed, and he looked at her through those killer eyelashes. "It was unexpected last night, and the second time it happened, I still wasn't sure…"

"Did I hurt you?" His voice was husky and deliberate.

"No, silly!" She swatted at his head playfully. "I know what an orgasm is now!"

A lopsided grin spread across his handsome face, "You have to watch out for those things! They're addictive." His eyes twinkled.

Grace rolled over to straddle him. "I think you're addictive."

His chest expanded with male pride. "Yeah?" There was a cocky note in his voice. "If we make plans for three meals a day, I'm sure we can squeeze in at least one of those a day."

"We'll just watch less television."

"I love a practical woman."

"You might not like me in the next few days…"

Gabe laid there sated and smiling. "Impossible."

"No, seriously, the pill I take goes for eighty-four days, and I take them all year without a period."

"So?"

"So…I went to get my pack refilled, and my script is expired. They wouldn't give them to me. Plus, Arthur's terminated my insurance. The damn pills are two hundred dollars. I have an appointment at public health in three weeks. They're free there."

"Three weeks? Seriously?" Gabe slithered out from under her warmth.

Grace grit her teeth. "Perhaps till then I can kiss everything like last night?"

Gabe rolled on his side and shook his head. "Do you know how much tires cost?"

"What? Why?"

"If I can buy four tires for the Taurus, I can buy three months of pills, but if it's three weeks until you get a prescription, then it's three weeks of condoms."

"Oh, I've heard it takes months for women to conceive after being on the pill for two years."

"Are you sure? I can time an engine, but I can't tell you anything about women's bodies. I don't want to play games with you, Princess."

Grace shrugged. "That's what everybody says. But, in about two days, I may turn into a psycho woman from hell, and bleed like I'm dying. You might just leave me in the tub and throw me chocolate and raw meat."

Gabe grimaced. "You clearly aren't looking forward to this, are you?"

"You shouldn't either if you're smart."

Gabe gathered her up and kissed her ear. "This'll be a good test…"

"What, you had survival training in the Navy?"

He laughed. He had the cutest man-giggle. "I wasn't a SEAL, but I'm pretty rugged. Just don't shoot me." His eyes creased with his smile.

He's still warm from our loving, and he's got the best sense of humor!

They fell to their backs on the bed and lay side by side, their eyes to the ceiling, laughing. "I love you!" Their gazes locked immediately. Her words changed the room's vibration. *Oh… I just said that out loud!*

In any other context, she wouldn't have trusted an "I love you." They knew each other for two months. She imagined while his heart broke down the stone barriers from his childhood and his addictions, love was still a mystery to him, too. Could the longing she held for him be love? Grace knew blind love. Her father's love for her mother was such a love. She never wanted to love a man that way or hurt a man like that. She wanted it all, to give her heart to a friend, a partner, and a lover.

****

"I can feel that, right in here." Gabe patted his heart. "Is it too crazy for me to say everything about you is inside of me twenty-four-seven? Every decision I make, I want to do right for you."

"No one has ever told me anything like that."

"I needed to make sure I got the steps right before I told you what you mean to me." He took her hand and kissed her palm. "Grace, you're the love of my life. You're my gift. I love you."

Her hazel eyes widened with her smile, and she bit her lower lip. "Then I'm the luckiest girl on earth."

Their romantic cocoon was split by a raucous rock song. "That's the damn alarm on my phone. I set it last night before I got in the shower. I wasn't sure if I'd oversleep this morning, but, you seemed to wake me up just fine."

13

Grace pulled herself together for work, squelching an insistent smile. Gabriel, too, looked like a man reborn. He shaved and dressed in his least shabby blue dress shirt, and best jeans. She could tell by the scruffy washcloth on the sink, he tried to wipe his steel-toed boots to some semblance of a shine. He was an effort in the making. As they left the apartment, he asked, "You have the debit card?"

She was holding the card at his request, carefully dosing out cash as necessary. "Sure do, what do you need?" She asked precisely the way he told her to.

"Nicotine gum, a razor, deodorant…body armor, a whip, and a chair."

"Now, I see, you love *and* understand me. How about this, when you pick me up after work, we'll hit the store, and do a little retail therapy."

They rode in silence the short way to the restaurant. She watched Gabriel; he was hypervigilant at each intersection. At stoplights, she followed his gaze into the rearview mirror. *Should I be looking for cars tailing us? Otherwise, life is terrific. He loves me!* She hugged herself.

He pulled the car to the curb and put it in park, and then leaned over the console to kiss her goodbye. He made their first kiss good-bye long, and slow and wet. When they came up for air, she sighed deeply. "I can't get enough of you."

His male pride gleamed. "That goes both ways, Princess! Now get out there and have a great day."

She left the car floating on a cloud.

****

The word was out on the street. Every contact was a dry well. Garage after garage shut their doors in his face. Evidently, Wally wasn't thrilled his lead mechanic, and number one auto thief flew the coop under cover of night. By two forty-five, Gabe wilted and headed closer to home, to a heavily air-conditioned café within walking distance of their studio. He stepped through the door and nodded to the waitress behind the counter. She bent over pad in hand, for his order.

"Root beer, light ice, burger, and fries." He said as he peered into his wallet at the single twenty-dollar bill. His foot tapped to the Muzak, as she served his root beer. The waitress watched him watch the regulars at this nontraditional hour. There were businessmen hunkered over tablets, returning calls over half-eaten food, a school girl doing homework, perhaps a daughter of an employee.

As he squirted ketchup on his fries, the doors swung open, and two impressively built men in suits entered with clipboards in hand. They looked too fancy for the Board of Health; Gabe observed. He ate leisurely, extending his meal. The taller guy leaned over the counter to bump fists with his waitress and Gabe saw the handcuff tie tack. He breathed deeply and checked himself, then relaxed. *I'm doing what I'm supposed to do. I'm job hunting, I'm sober, and I'm not holding drugs or firearms. I've checked in with my P.O.* One of the guys caught his eye and nodded at him, Gabe nodded back, his hand over the tattoo on his throat. He took a long draw on his drink and licked the foam on his upper lip.

The waitress looked at Gabe's glass. "Refill?" He nodded with his mouth full of burger. *Why do servers wait until your mouth is full to ask a question?*

Before she got away, he swallowed and asked, "No ice this time, more foam, okay?"

"One root beer with head coming up." She snorted, returning with an inch of foam on the top of the soda and a smirk on her face.

Gabe grinned at her comment and raised the glass to her before taking a long draw. He watched the two detectives eat lunch over the report they debated. All he wanted to do was find a job, blend in, and earn Grace's love.

****

Six minutes after six, Grace pushed out the front door of the restaurant, carrying a bag of Philly cheesesteaks and sodas. The fragrance of onions and peppers hovered as she floated toward her Gabriel, leaning against the bumper of the gleaming black car. His face lit up as he caught the first sight of her. She held up the bag and entered his outstretched arms. There was a kiss, a wet kiss, and a clutching open mouth kiss.

"Umm. You delicious kisser, you." She pulled away to see his smile.

"Must be the root beer." He rolled his eyes and licked at his lips as he opened the car door for her. He took the bag of sandwiches to sneak a peek at them. "What's this?"

"Dinner, so we can drop in at the second-hand store and the drug store before we go home." She buckled in, and they headed for the neighborhood park across from the Goodwill Superstore.

"How was the job hunt, Gabriel?" She asked gaily, picking the peppers off her cheese steak and pushing them over to him.

He flinched. His hands left his sandwich and balled into fists on the wooden table. "I've been black-balled. Wally's word is out. Between him and being an ex-con, I'm hung out to dry."

Grace reached across the table to cover his fist. "Oh, Gabriel, you're doing the right thing. It will pay off, eventually." She pushed her sandwich aside and threaded her fingers into his. "I believe in you, I have from the moment I met you, and other people will too. Everything is going to be alright. You'll see, and until then, we have my job, and there are some savings in the bank. We will be fine."

****

Gabe thought the last time he'd heard supportive words was from his Aunt Marla. That time, she'd been right. That was just before he went into the Navy. It was one of the best times of his life. When everyone was still proud of him. When he was still proud of himself. "I must have done something good to deserve you." His smile was more relaxed, and his kiss on her hand was soft. With a grin, he looked at the peppers she'd pushed his way. "These are for me? I love peppers."

"Yuk! You're welcome to them."

"You have never been hard luck hungry. I can remember onion and butter sandwiches."

"Oh, Gabriel, that sounds desperate!"

Gabe shrugged. "Actually, they're tasty and filling. But, yeah, there wasn't much to eat."

****

After eating, they sifted through racks of clothing and Grace found most of the brands she was familiar with for a few dollars. *Do I miss cruising Nordstrom's with Mother? No.* Gabe winced at some of the fashions she held up for him, and she returned the favor when he came back bearing four tee-shirts and three pairs of work pants.

"Gabriel, would you consider something for me?" She winced comically, as she held the clothes behind her back. He looked at her with a 'do I have to?' expression and then took the clothes into the dressing room. A new Gabriel emerged. He did a parody of a model's walk to the three-way mirror and surprised himself. The outfit wasn't as lame as he expected.

"Where am I going to wear these?" He asked as he fingered the polo player on the black Polo shirt and the blue striped dress shirt.

"Wherever you want." She was a little flip in her answer, then again, she thought he liked the way he looked in the mirror. "Plus, these are the kinds of clothes I love to pull off you." That sealed the deal on the clothes.

Grace picked out a few items she almost swore she owned a lifetime ago, and they left the store feeling like they'd spent a few thousand dollars.

Gabe stopped on the sidewalk, saw the snowball shack and asked. "How about something sweet?" Grace accommodatingly pecked him on the cheek, and he chuckled as he pointed to the people sucking down the snowballs. She faux pouted when her kiss wasn't the sweet thing he sought. He stopped on the street, wrapped his strong arms around her, and pressed his lips to hers. She tingled from his public display of affection.

The snowball vendor took Gabe's order for a cherry cone and winked. "And what for the little missus?"

Grace and Gabe exchanged a wry smile. "Well, woman, I suppose you want marshmallow on top?"

Grace blushed. "You know what I like on top." She hid her blushing face in his shoulder.

Gabe nodded to the vendor, "grape with marshmallow, please." He looked down at her. "You are so frisky tonight!"

Her eyes sparkled up at him, as she received her treat. "Thank you, Gabriel."

They headed toward the car. "When did I become Gabriel? Last I knew, my name was Gabe."

"That was before I met your angel up close." She tapped his chest and winked.

A grin split his face. "Oh, so, my horizontal talents convinced you of my sainthood?"

She poked him in the ribs. "I do remember you calling God's name a few times last night. But, seriously, you've elevated me to Princess. Certainly, you are my guardian angel. I think, from now on, you should be Gabriel."

He ducked his head shyly but wore a grin from ear to ear.

****

Monday, Gabriel sat at the diner's counter, his tablet open to the skilled trades. He favorited the positions matching his skill set. A Sun's columnist spouted off about companies making jobs available for ex-cons, and Gabriel was ready to call the guy to see if anyone stepped up to offer one of those jobs. By now, the server, Audra, knew he liked his root beer with light ice and a full head.

He gnawed at his knuckle as he calculated the weekly rent and their expenses. Sure, Grace brought home good tips, and her check would cover most of their living expenses, there were savings for the rest. He still felt like a chump for taking a ride while she worked. He was ready to leave when a guy in a Minute Lube shirt held the door open for him. "Thanks." Gabriel nodded, and the guy mumbled a reply. They ambled down the street in the same direction, and the guy turned right into a small shop on the side street. Gabriel missed the place before, and he could see why. Tree limbs covered the signs. The concrete was cracked, and weeds flourished.

The parking lot and sorry-ass grass easement were over-run. The building wore patches of the previous color peeking through the blue paint.

How easy would that be? Gabriel asked himself. *Minute Lube?* He crossed the street and walked into the office. "Hi, is the owner here?" He straightened himself up and presented his hand, "My name is Gabriel." The lethargic pair of technicians in the shop worked on the sodas the one tech brought back from the cafe.

"I am, what is it, son?" An unglamorous older woman stepped up. She removed her glasses, hanging on a chain and let them drop onto her ample bosom.

"I'm looking for work, I'm a certified mechanic. Plus, I could get those trees trimmed, and the parking lot weeded. You need some general maintenance." His eyes smiled; she didn't look like too many people smiled at her.

"Son, I've got all the mechanics I need. I need customers." She cranked back at him.

Gabriel leaned his elbow on the counter conspiratorially and gave her his most winning smile. "I've been up and down this street for three days, and never noticed your business. You need those trees trimmed, and the parking lot weeded. You want customers, people have to know you're open. Maybe I could spruce up your sandwich board– it's pretty faded – and move it to the sidewalk." He listed off the chores that would spit-shine the garage's curb appeal.

"And, you'll do it for what, twenty-five hundred dollars? Take your gypsy-ass down the road." Although she dismissed him with a wave of her hand, he stood his ground.

"I'm no gypsy. Hire me as a mechanic, and I'll do it between jobs." His shoulders squared, he stood tall. He wasn't too proud to beg. That afternoon, he put on the Minute Lube tee shirt and weeded the parking lot, rendering the place almost clean. That week, while the other, less motivated mechanics, lounged around between jobs, Gabriel sorted and oiled all the tools, mounting them back on the pegboard where they belonged.

By Saturday at six P.M., the bathrooms were pressure washed, the trees trimmed, and the sorry excuse for flowerbeds mulched. Mae, who was once a grouch, accusing him of being a gypsy con, *had* experienced an increase in customers and was now as friendly as an Aunt. "Gabriel." She exhibited a pit-bull presence over the mechanics. "Get in this office." Her stout shape filled the doorway as he approached her with a smile.

"What do you need, Miss Mae?"

"Suck-up," Norman called from the back.

"But I'm Mr. Suck-up to you, Norman. Have a little respect, this is the woman who signs your checks."

Her face was grim, and Gabriel began to doubt… "Shut the door." In a softer voice, she added. "Please."

"Yes, Ma'am."

"I don't like when I'm wrong. Norman is my nephew, and he's the biggest mistake on this planet…"

"A little time swabbing decks wouldn't hurt him." Gabriel stood at parade rest.

"You're a good boy, Gabriel. You've done a hell of a job this week."

"Thank you, Ma'am, I appreciate the opportunity."

She slid a worn twenty-dollar bill across the desk blotter as a bonus. "I wish it were more. But, you were right, and business is picking up. People know we're open. Now, get out and don't tell a soul about this."

Gabriel folded the bill and slid it into his front pocket. "Yes, Ma'am. See you Monday."

"Don't spend all that on fancy women."

"Oh, no, Ma'am. My Princess is a keeper."

****

Grace saw a fulfilled man beside her. Gabriel was a new name for a man who worked hard and loved her harder. The honest physical work he did during the day fueled his good humor. In the early evenings, they'd walk, or they'd indulge in whatever cheap entertainment they could find. Last night they saw a children's movie in the park, the night before, it was a concert in a different neighborhood. The previous weekend they'd gone swimming at the public pool, and she caught him scanning the parking lot while she read a second-hand paperback.

When the lights went out, they worked each other into possessed sessions of moaning, sweating love. Each morning, he woke up reaching for her and she met him, wanting every bit of him. He said if he died in bed, it would take the undertaker a week to wipe the smile off his face. His satisfaction tank was on 'full', waking up to the most gorgeous girl in the world. She pinched herself before she got out of bed each morning, thinking she was still dreaming.

Grace drove the Taurus to work. Gabriel walked the few blocks each day and returned to the studio for his lunch. She'd return from work and find the Igloo outside, set like a table, with their dinner waiting. Sure, it was guy food, hamburgers or prepackaged ribs from the market, but it was his gesture speaking to her heart.

****

"Gabriel", she said, "you up for a drive? There's something I just remembered. I want you to see it." She wrung out their socks and spaced them along a wooden drying rack.

"Sure." He folded the Sports Illustrated and slid it on the shelf of the nightstand. "What's on your mind?"

They buckled into the car, and she glanced at the gas gauge. "Do we have plenty of gas to get to Towson and back?"

"What's in the suburbs for us?"

"Something I think you'll enjoy!"

****

Gabriel drove with his ball-cap pulled low. "You never mentioned anything good up here."

"Oh, but *this* will blow your mind." Grace gave him directions and a code. "When you pull up to E-Z Storage, the gate code is, 0-2-2-1, my birthday."

"That's your birthday? I did not know when your birthday was. I can't believe we never talked about birthdays! At least I have a few months to save for a gift."

"I know! When's your birthday?"

"Halloween must have scared me right out of my mom. I was born on November first. The nuns loved to make a big honking deal out of the fact I arrived on All Saints Day."

"What irony, we know each other's hearts, but not each other's statistics."

"That's true, you keep trying to convince me you weigh a ton, but I'm not feeling that. I still don't know how much you weigh."

"And you never will!" She pointed, "Turn down there. It's the last garage door on the left."

He watched her excitement build, the closer he drove. "Do we need a key?" Gabriel parked the car and scanned their perimeter.

"No. It's another combination lock. Same numbers." She trotted to the garage door and flipped the cylinders. When the door went up, she turned on the light.

Gabriel stood back; his arms folded over his chest. He blinked at the full storage unit. Far in the back of the twelve by thirty-foot aluminum unit, were shelves of auto parts and accessories. By the look of the tool chest and hanging machinery, the item hidden under padded blankets must be a boat of a car.

"Gabriel, c' mon in!"

"It's sort of a thing, Grace, men don't touch other men's machines. Whose is this?" He paced around the car without removing the blankets.

"It's mine."

"Seriously?" He crouched to look at the wheels. The car was up on jacks to keep the pressure off the tires.

"It was Daddy's. I inherited it when I graduated. I just don't know a thing about getting it running again. All the equipment and supplies are back there, but I'm no mechanic."

Gabriel rubbed his thumb across his lower lip, his excitement building. "Then it's a good thing I am. Let's see what's under this baby!" He reverently folded back the blanket. "Wow, Princess, this is a 1968 Hearst/Olds!" His thumb ran under the logo at the rocker panel. "The Peruvian silver paint job isn't in too bad a shape. Where did he keep this?"

Grace leaned back against the tool chest, giving him room to walk around the car. "It was garaged once he brought it from his family home in West Virginia. It was his father's originally."

Gabriel opened the hood and ran his hand over the fire panel. "How many miles on this thing? Is this the original engine?"

Grace opened the driver's door and slid into the seat. "68,782 miles."

"You can't be serious!" Gabriel blinked.

"That's what's on the odometer." She crinkled her nose and shrugged. "Do you think it'll run?"

"When I'm done with it, it will!" Gabriel took inventory of the tool chest drawers, seeing everything he would need for the restoration. "My only question is, why didn't you tell me about this before?"

"I didn't want you to love me for my vintage car?" She got out of the driver's seat and held the door for him. "Frankly, at the time I took off, this was not the most pressing subject. I waited on a party of four guys bragging about their cars, today. They were about my dad's age, and it made me think of this. Do you think it's worth anything? We need money…"

"Oh no! Princess, you should never let this go! You'd need a high-end auction company to get the right price. But it could never be replaced. I know you'll want to drive it. It's not a trailer queen. Enjoy it!" He slid behind the wheel and played with the gear shift, moving the mirror, adjusting the seat. "The power this thing has will blow your mind! You will want to drive it, but not in Baltimore. Wally's goons will use it for target practice."

Grace made a face. "But that's where our jobs are…"

"I feel the clock ticking. Princess, we need to get out of town."

"Out of Baltimore?" She looked up at his serious expression. His blue-green eyes squinted into the sunset as his gaze swept the parking lot behind them. "Where would we go?"

"As far as my parole officer will let me. The faster I get this car finished, the quicker we can leave. If I get it running, we can finish the job somewhere safe."

"Okay, but our jobs…"

Gabriel's hand sliced the air decisively, filled with excitement. "Princess, your dad left great equipment here, I could load this up and have enough to open my own shop!"

"Wow, I had no idea…Gabriel, what's wrong?" She shielded her eyes from the sunset and drew closer to him. He still watched the parking lot. "You're getting jumpier the longer we're at the motor court."

Gabriel nodded his head and got out of the car. He dug his hands into his front pockets. "No, I've had bad vibes in general since we split the garage." He combed back a wayward hair from her face. She was radiant at this golden hour. "How can you look so gorgeous all the time?"

Grace folded her hands in front of her and shrugged. "It must be love."

The 'L' word. The word that drives me to get out from under Wally's thumb. "I think you're right. But most of all, if I cannot protect the one I love, what good is love?"

"Don't you think you're exaggerating the threat?"

He barked out a regretful laugh. "Not one bit. Why did I tell you to take different shifts at the restaurant? Why do you think I told you to drive on the main roads and change it up every day?"

"You're kind of scaring me, babe." Grace drew in a stuttering breath.

****

"I wish I didn't have to. I'm serious about us leaving town." He drew her into an embrace and kissed her forehead. "I figure we have one week, tops."

"Let's get a root beer and sit down and talk. If we need to move, we have to make a plan." Grace watched him through half-closed eyes, frightened she was the cause of his trouble. She wasn't sure if, in trying to get them to safety, he was fighting off a breakdown.

14

In the middle of their fourth week at the studio, unexpectedly, he felt cornered, jumping at every shadow. His addictions cried out to him. 'I can make it better…' The pressure to get the Olds running closed in. He worked until his eyes were crossed from fatigue. Each night, he came home completely exhausted, even though Grace was the best mechanic's helper he could ask for.

She cleaned tools, re-sorted already sorted accessories, and kept him amused with stories of a privileged childhood he couldn't imagine. Close to finishing the engine test, he planned on renting a U-Haul, which led to feelings of elation and anxiety at the same time. Gabriel tossed and turned in their bed. He lay sweating, wide-eyed and apprehensive. His closed eyes brought nightmares jolting him straight up in bed, his arms around a pillow.

He warred with himself, take a shot or *be patient.* The doctor told him at the hospital, the road to recovery could take as long as two years. Two years was a lifetime when you're in a rush to get it done. Intellectually, he knew he couldn't blast through recovery. Recovery was one day at a time, isn't that what A.A. said? *They've been telling you that, you idiot! It's the truth.* He still wanted a drink.

****

Gabriel came in from working on the Olds. Grace was serving at a wedding reception. It was late and as exhausted as his body was; his brain ran like a highly caffeinated hamster. He locked the apartment and slipped around the back of the long motor court. Kids tore the chain link from the six-foot fence, and it opened on a path to the dark public playground. The first thing he did was aggressively work out forty plus pull-ups on the monkey bars. *If my physical therapist could see me now!*

His *two* minds ignited the battle. *God, I'm so tired.* The sweat ran down the center of his muscled chest, and it appeared the angel, Gabriel, wept.

And what is it A.A. says about triggers for booze and drugs?

'Never get too angry, too tired or too hungry'.

Seems about right, and tonight I'm all three.

I can eat, no problem, but I'm so wound up I can't sleep, even with everything Grace does to relax me. Some weed would mellow me out.

He climbed onto the top railing and hung upside down from his knees. The night air was humid and thick, the slight breeze cooled the sweat on his shirtless body.

And what about that anger? This was a particularly incendiary question.

He answered as he curled his fists up to the sides of his head and began doing sit-ups to the bar. *Yeah, what about that? I'm angry at my mother. I'm angry about leaving the Navy. I'm angry about going to prison. I'm angry about losing the baby. I'm angry about Wally's shit. How do I absolve all the anger?*

His heart pumped madly; his breath heaved in short gasps. He felt every muscle in his body burn with exertion. He flipped off the top bar and landed resolutely. Picking up a handful of large gravel stones, he pitched them at the tire swing as he ticked off his mental responses. *Even if I could find you, Mom, I have nothing to say to you. The best thing I can do is be a better man.* He took a pitcher's stance and wound up. *No time machine, so I am shit out of luck on going back to the Navy.* He bent over to catch his breath. Perspiration ran down his back, matting his basketball shorts to his sweaty flesh. *If I ever win the lottery, I can get a lawyer, and clean up my record.* He stood up straight. *The baby is gone, kids deserve two loving, functional parents. I'll work every day to earn Grace's love, and we'll build a life together.* Gabriel dragged his wet and spent body toward his apartment. *There has to be a way to stop Wally.*

Inside, the fridge held lots of cold root beer. Tonight, Gabriel's addictions rolled over him like a paving machine. For days, he'd slept poorly. He barked. He was in a dark frame of mind. It happened at the worst possible time. Was it what they called 'magical thinking' that made him believe he was past the cravings? It was now apparent; he wasn't different from any other addict. Grace was not some magic charm, and it could be as turbulent for him as it was for everyone else.

He ran the shower hot and hard and scrubbed his aching muscles. He didn't know what to expect from Wally and his mob. He was worried they'd catch up to him before he could get Grace out of here. The closer they got to moving, the better he felt, and when they were two days away from departure, he bounced out of the funk. As his mood brightened, Grace joked they'd never rehab another car…it wore him out.

****

On a tawny fall evening in the storage garage after the last item on the repair list was completed, Gabriel dug in the tray on the top shelf of the workbench. There it was, the small tan O-ring. He smiled to himself and turned to face a curious Grace. He held the silicon ring on his pinkie and raised a brow. "This is an O-ring. These rings are commonly used to help to ensure a tight seal between two objects."

Grace, sitting in the passenger front seat, leaned forward on her elbow. "Uh-huh."

Gabriel took a long step toward her and dropped to one knee in front of her. "This is only temporary, but in my line of work it has great meaning." Grace looked stunned and confused. "I love you, Grace. I've loved you from the moment I saw you banging on that washing machine." Grace's mouth dropped open, and her eyes widened. "I don't know if I deserve your love."

"Gabriel…" The word was a protest that he spoke over.

"Let's put our hearts into each other's hands for life. I promise you no one will work harder to make you happy. No one will treasure you more than me. Will you marry me?"

She looked at the flexible little ring he'd placed on her left hand and giggled. She reached her arms around his neck. "I love you, Gabriel! Of course, I'll marry you! I thought you'd never ask!" She looked at her watch. "Ohhhh. It's too late tonight. Let's go tomorrow morning!"

"Just can't wait to collar me, huh?" Gabriel laughed.

"That's right! Life sentence! No parole!"

"Take me to the judge!"

****

They spent half the night giggling and making plans. Gabriel looked up the hours of the courthouse. They needed to apply for the marriage license, but that would have to wait until nine A.M. They celebrated their plans to marry exercising several positions as a preview of the honeymoon.

Grace pushed him over on his back and climbed on to straddle him. "What's on your mind, Princess?" She snickered and shook her head, retreating down his thighs until she crawled between his legs. "Oh, there you go, in the driver's seat about to make me crazy…"

She knew he loved it when she took the first step, especially for this. She caught her breath as she began. The more he watched her work her magic over him, the faster he surrendered to her lips, her tongue and her fingers. When he full-on exploded, she brought back a warm wrung out hand towel and ran lazy, comforting swirls over him. She wondered if either of them could sleep, waiting for their official future to begin.

****

Grace had already decided she would be calling out from work after their ceremony. She pulled out her best ivory lace dress from the Goodwill designer rack. Gabriel hadn't seen it; Grace was saving the sheath for his birthday celebration in November. Before she slipped into the bathroom to dress, she left his black jeans, the navy striped Polo dress shirt and black vest on the end of the bed.

Once Grace had the bathroom door half closed, Gabriel wisecracked. "When we're married will you always lay out my clothes?"

Grace made a face in the bathroom mirror and quipped back. "The license means I can legally remove the clothes."

"So, I still get to dress myself, right?" He slipped into his wedding wear.

"Just trying to be a good wife."

Gabriel straightened his collar in the bedroom mirror and heard the fan turn off in the bathroom. "Sure, dear." He turned to see Grace shyly ducking out of the bathroom with an innocent smile. "The most beautiful girl in the world is going to be my wife."

****

Grace sat dejectedly in the passenger seat, Gabriel looking glum beside her. She stared at the date. "Well, it's not so bad. We weren't planning to leave town until Saturday anyway. We can get married on Friday evening; we can go to the Honduran restaurant for a nice dinner afterward."

"Pack up the U-Haul and leave for Frostburg first thing in the morning."

Grace pinched his knee. "If we have the energy." The closer they got to their apartment the more they agreed to make this a workday since it wasn't their wedding day. Festive clothes were hung back on hangers. Tuesday went back to normal.

****

Mondays were usually laundry night, but this week it was on Tuesday. Gabriel passed her coins and urged her to "feed the washer." She gave him a sideways look and stuck out her tongue.

On their walks to the laundromat Grace paid close attention to the jewelry in the window of a pawn shop. She eyed the row of glittering diamonds and stones, tilting her head up and back to appreciate the settings. They took their pizza to the Sudsville and ate while their clothes spun.

When the dryer stalled, Gabriel nodded to her, "I'll pull them out if you sort and fold."

"What kind of a deal is that?" She asked, sauntering over and making a face while he walked back to the car for hangers.

She sorted underwear and began to smooth out their tee shirts. She got to Gabriel's jeans and felt a weight in the pocket. "I can't wait to see

129

what you left in your pocket." Grace fished into the front pocket. The object didn't move. Grace found a large safety pin, and on it, was a ring, a small diamond ring.

He stood across the room, watching her expressions as she discovered her prize. She shook her head, holding up the ring.

"I wanted you to have something nice… I know you deserve more… I mean…" His words faded as she took a run toward him to jump into his arms. It was three months since they shared their first sandwich.

****

"Gabriel, you going home for lunch today?" Bernie asked as he hung up the air hose.

"Yeah, leftover ribs, you need something?" Gabriel was at the sink rinsing the GOJO from his hands.

"Could you bring back sodas?" Bernie was kind of a freeloader, but if you asked up front, he generally ponied up.

"Yeah," Gabriel held out his hand, and Bernie shook his head but relented by digging into his wallet for the cash.

"I'll be back in an hour, okay?" Gabriel clocked out and headed to the studio.

He slid the key in the door, pushed it open, and then pulled back the drapes in the dark room. He gawked at Wally. "Of course, you were expecting me, Gabe." Wally sat comfortably on the sofa, his feet on the coffee table. "It took me a while to find out you didn't boost that car. The little jackass who did the job for you, came back last Thursday, wondering if *you* had more work for him." Gabriel stood frozen. "So, it all made sense that you took off in the middle of the night. What's your problem? You get a straight woman, and you get too good to work for a living?"

"I do work for a living." Gabriel threw the door open and stepped aside. "How did you get in here?"

"Yeah, I made a visit to your parole officer. Terrible thing about her accident." A chill shot down Gabriel's spine. "Did you forget I dug your maggot-ass out of the dumpster when you got out of prison?" Wally ground his fist into the palm of his other hand while he spoke, which was his usual intimidation move. It worked in the past; it just wasn't working this time.

"I won't steal for myself now, Wally. I won't steal for you." Gabriel took a step forward and rested his hands on his hips, squaring off in front of Wally.

The thug pulled something from his pocket and held up a snapshot of Gabe and a girl taken at a street fair. "Would you steal for her, Gabe?"

Gabriel's heart lurched, and he felt the prickling of an adrenaline surge. That was last weekend's street fair.

Wally waved it under his nose. "She's a pretty little thing, what eighteen, nineteen years old?" He slid it back into the breast pocket of his gaudy sports coat.

Gabriel lunged toward Wally. "She's none of your business." Gabriel's chin thrust forward, chest heaving when he hauled the fat man to his feet. "Wally, get out of my place and don't come back. I've settled any debt I owe. Find someone else to steal for you, understand?" Gabriel felt the boil of his anger roll up from his toes.

"Oh, I was planning to leave after I spoke with you." Wally straightened his jacket around his pudgy frame and edged around the coffee table. "Your debt will never be settled, by the way. So, when you're thinking about how pretty this one is," Wally tapped over his breast pocket. "Think about how she'd look if there were an accident." The intruder took a few steps toward the open door. "How would you look at her if something happened to her face, you know? Could you shave your handsome mug every morning knowing you ruined her life?" Wally dug for the car keys in his pocket. He saluted Gabriel on his way out and then paused before he exited the small studio. "I'll need you Saturday. Be ready, I'll be in touch."

After Wally made his ominous exit, Gabriel was driven to take a seat. His knees went weak and his chest imploded. All his thoughts collided, and survival became his prime instinct. One name came to his mind, Esther. He would figure out a way to deliver Grace to Esther until this was all over. His Princess wouldn't be safe beside him. He went into the bathroom, closed the door, sat on the commode and cried like a child. *Where I am today is the result of exceptionally poor choices.*

He cleaned his tearstained face and looked in the mirror. *Starting with Grace, I've been making the right choices, and I'm not going to stop now.* He forced himself to eat. He picked up the sodas and returned to work, keeping everything on the down low.

15

"You talk so much about Esther, have you ever thought of visiting her?" Gabriel posed it as an innocent question while they picked the roasted chicken apart on the front porch.

"I know exactly where she lives. Her granddaughter, Kendra, just moved back in with her while she's in college to become a dental hygienist. She brought her baby with her, it's just the three of them now." Grace's expression relayed her love for Esther and all the decent things she stood for.

"Why don't we give her a call and drop by tonight?" Gabriel steeled himself to move Grace out of the danger of Wally's treacherous threats. "Does she like flowers? Those pink things are pretty, you like them, what are they?" Gabriel watched her spin her engagement ring on her finger as they talked. She looked relaxed and casual, sitting back in the lawn chair, one foot up on the chair's edge. He could see the delicate hollow where her shapely leg met her buttock, and he bit his lip.

"Gerbera daisies." She smiled and jumped up to clean away the dishes. She dashed into the shower, and he followed her into the bathroom, closing the door behind them. This intimate time together needed to last for a while, he wanted to remember everything about her.

****

"Hey, Princess, would you walk over to the market and pick up those flowers? I want to check the tires, okay?" Gabriel peeled a bill out of his wallet and retreated inside. Shoving her belongings into a duffle, he was careful to wrap Frankie and Connie's wedding portrait in her tee shirt. Everything she owned fit in a duffle and two shopping bags. He watched for her as he opened the trunk and piled them inside.

Grace co-piloted him through the warren of Charles Village's narrow one-way streets. He kept an eye out for tails in his mirrors and pulled the Taurus onto a slab parking space in a shrubbery obscured alley. The Victorian painted lady stood proudly in the sunset glow as they walked around the corner to the front of the house. Residents sat on porches while kids rode bikes on the sidewalks or tweens jumped double-dutch in the empty street.

Gabriel could feel Grace's excitement as they drew closer, and although it killed him to do this, he was sure she'd be safe here. Her security was his immediate priority. Esther answered the door. She was an attractively round woman in her sixties, with glowing cheeks and expressive ebony eyes. Her hair was drawn back into a smooth chignon with emerging grey at her temples. She whooped a hello of pure joy. "Cici! You look like heaven to my old eyes!" She levied a suspect look at Gabriel's tattoos.

Their conversation on the front porch covered how good the lemonade was, the beautiful flowers, and her newest grandbaby, a boy, Antwoine. When Grace mentioned Gabriel was a mechanic, Esther's eyes widened. "Oh, Kendra has some questions about reliable used cars, Gabriel. Can she bend your ear?"

He nodded agreeably. "Sure. Especially if I get to hold Antwoine."

Grace followed Esther back into the house. "Once they get talking, may I speak with you in the kitchen, privately?"

"Well, sure, Cici."

****

Grace leaned on the butcher block counter, staring out the small back window.

"What's on your mind?" Esther snuck up behind her and put a welcoming arm around her waist.

"He's a genuinely good man."

Esther nodded. "He seems to be."

"We're getting married."

"How'd you come to meet him, honey? I'm guessing he's not from Hunt Valley."

"No. Gabriel isn't, but he's a good man. The reason I know good men from bad is because I endured two years of Arthur. He *is* a bad man."

Esther guided her over to the small kitchen table, and they sat. "What are you trying to tell me?"

"Arthur raped me, many times. Mother wouldn't believe me."

Esther shook her head, "That devil..."

Grace poured out the story, "Finally, they were in Bali, and Arthur arrived home early. He came at me, I fought back, I got away." She giggled at the memory of the executive on his backside cursing. "I kicked him in the crotch, left him on the floor, and I ran. I took my car, and I was sure he'd report me for auto theft. I hid out until the police found the car and towed it. I lost my hide-out. That's when Gabriel found me, desperate, no money, on the street. He took me in, and somehow, we just clicked. I love him. I see my future with him."

Esther sat silently with her hands folded, her eyes closed in prayer. She raised a hand and opened her eyes. They were clear. She laid her hand on Grace's shoulder. "Heavenly Father bring this child knowledge and wisdom. Give her the strength to walk the right path." Grace was silent through the prayer. "Honey, are you crazy? Do you see the tattoo on his neck? Don't you know the kind of things those men do? Has he been on you?" Esther turned from prayerful grandmother to fierce protector. "Arthur was bad, and I could see it. You should have driven right here the very first time that predator set his hooks on you."

"I know you. The first thing you would have done was call the police."

"Damn right!"

Grace nodded. "That would have blown our family apart. Mother would have disowned me."

Esther's eyes burned. "She disowned you when she didn't believe what that devil did. To my mind, you don't owe her a damn thought."

"Maybe not, but I think a trial would have killed her. That's assuming they could have gotten a conviction, it's my word against Arthur's. I think she might have followed Daddy into suicide, and I couldn't drive her to that."

"So, you run off with nothing?"

Grace held up her hand. "He bought me an engagement ring!"

Esther peered at the ring with concern. "Where are you living?"

"I told you, Gabriel found me. He took me home to live with him. We were forced to leave that place, and right now we're in an extended stay motor court." Esther put her face in her hands and groaned. "Gabriel says we need to leave town, so we're moving to Frostburg Saturday."

Esther's face tightened into hard lines, and she raised her head. "You are living like gypsies. Why does he need to leave town? What has he dragged you into?" She wiped at her mouth with the corner of her handkerchief.

"I know what it sounds like, but it's not like that. We both have jobs, we have money in the bank, we're trying to get re-established…" Grace's words were halted by the sound of Gabriel's boots approaching through the dining room.

****

Gabriel filled the small doorway. "May I trouble you for another glass of lemonade?"

Esther turned, and her face softened at his manners and his smile. "You can pay for the lemonade with the truth, young man!"

Gabriel gawked. "O…kay… What do you wanna know?"

"Your young lady, here, has been telling me what a good man you are. Is that just because of your pretty face and that magic wand men wave at young girls? Is she blinded? I am not blinded, so you tell me about yourself."

"Oh, Esther…" Grace interrupted, placing her hand over Esther's plump fist.

The experienced woman patted her in return but was undeterred. "You've had your say, this boy is so good, he should be able to speak for himself. So, speak up, young man. Why are you dragging my Cici from

136

place to place? Who's after you?" She scooted out a chair with her foot. "You sit here and tell me the truth. Not your truth, *the* truth."

Gabriel sat down with a heavy sigh. His gaze passed from Grace to Esther to the framed photo of the praying hands over the doorway. "Yes, ma'am. I never wanted Grace to be in the middle of this. I love her. I'd never put her in danger, and to tell you the truth… that's why we're here."

"Here? Now we're getting somewhere. What's chased you here tonight?"

She watched Grace's mouth drop open at his words. "You said you wanted to meet Esther. This was just a little visit."

"Please Grace, one thing at a time." He faced Esther and drew in a deep breath. "I was raised by a good woman like you. I didn't have the best life, and I'm fighting to get out of an auto boosting ring. They won't let me out. They've threatened Grace if I don't keep stealing for them. I'm going to the cops with what I know, but I can't keep her safe. She needs someplace away from me…"

"Were you going to just leave me?" Grace stood so abruptly the chair fell back. Tears sprang out of her wide eyes. He looked up at her.

"Wally broke into the apartment today. I went home for lunch, instead of left-overs, I got an ultimatum. I steal, or you're disfigured."

Esther rose and circled him to embrace Grace. "Child, this is serious. Only a weak and evil person would threaten a man's woman. I *do* need to keep you safe." Grace wept on her friend's shoulder. "The less we know about those criminals, the better off we are. You may just be right; he is a good man."

Gabriel slumped, his face in his hands. When he lifted his gaze to the women, his eyes were red.

"What do you aim to do now?" Esther continued hugging Grace.

"Tonight, I packed your things." Gabriel stood and faced Grace. "They're in the car. I need you to stay with Esther. If they have me, they won't be interested in you." He looked over to Esther. "If that's okay if she stays with you? I love her so much, if they hurt her, I will die. I can't gamble that." Gabriel opened his wallet and reached for his accumulated rainy-day cash. "I can give you more, I can, Grace has the debit card. There's plenty of honest money. Please keep her safe."

"I have a job. I don't need your money." Grace challenged him.

"If anything happens to me, you should have it."

"Good God, what do you mean?"

Esther watched emotion swamp Gabriel and answered for him. "He means if he doesn't come back, he's dead."

Gabriel nodded, and Grace wailed. "Can't the police protect you?"

"Right now, Princess, it's my word against a business owner, and I'm an ex-con. I'm hoping they'll believe me. I'll give them names and dates, but, they don't spend a lot of resources on guys like me."

Grace collapsed back on the chair, breathless. Esther got her a glass of water and dampened a dishtowel to wipe her pale face. "You left a world of privilege. Welcome to the real world. Now, you've got to be a good woman, and give your man the room to do what he has to do. He doesn't need to be worried about you." Grace looked up at her, and Esther could see the young woman understood.

"You're right. I'm sorry, Gabriel. I love you, and I'll be here when you come back."

Esther receded from the kitchen, leaving them in their dark cloud.

****

Grace was terrified for Gabriel. If he was shot months ago what could happen next?

She found herself within his strong embrace. "Princess, I love you with all my heart. I do, I truly do." Gabriel whispered through their tears. They trembled together. He took her hands and saw she wore her class ring on a necklace. He reached for the clasp.

"What are you doing?"

Without answering, he opened the chain and slipped the class ring on his pinkie.

"Gabriel, what?" She sniffed. "Wha --"

"There now, I have your ring, and you have mine." He kissed the engagement ring on her finger. "When I come back, I'll have a wedding ring for you." He crushed her into his arms, and they sobbed together.

"I must truly love you, or this wouldn't hurt so much."

Gabriel's hand covered his own heart. "I'm feeling ya."

"We have so many things left to do. You have to come back to me, Gabriel."

"You can bet on it." He kissed her soundly, and she hoped it wouldn't be their last embrace.

16

Gabriel wore his devastation like a wet cape. His shoulders withered from the weight of leaving Grace with Esther. His lips curled down, his movements were measured, alert to any suspicious new stimuli. He'd go back to the studio because Wally would expect him to run. He had three full days, and he had to maintain an image of normalcy.

There in the bed, he smelled her scent, the fragrance of her shampoo on her pillow. He forgot to pack his Led Zeppelin tee-shirt. She slept in it every night, so he clung to it and tried to sleep.

Everything about the four walls screamed *Grace*, and it took all the control he could muster to shower and go to bed. In the shadows of his dreams, demons rounded him up and ceremoniously tied his limbs. They peeled the flesh from his bones as he writhed in pain. The gallery of faceless onlookers screeched for his torture, and then cheered at his cries. He woke at 3:33 A.M. and shivered in the sweat-drenched bed. He showered again, thinking warm water would wash the wretched stink away. When that failed, he was left awash in memories of their last shower together. He dressed, thinking of picking up a pack of cigarettes and chain smoking all of them. Dressed in the clothes Grace chose, he got into the car and cruised the lonely streets.

He chewed three pieces of nicotine gum while spinning Grace's ring on his pinkie. The cafe was open, and he entered cautiously, evaluating the different set of players from his usual crowd.

Nodding to the waitress at the counter, he asked for, of all things, chamomile tea. *Doesn't Grace drink that to relax at night?* The teabag colored the hot water as it steeped. His muscles felt as if he was torn apart, his every thought was wild. Fantasy argued with reason. Would the police listen and have the power to stop Wally? *Will anyone care enough to believe me?* He finished the tea and felt the tension slip enough to drive home and catch a couple of hours of shut-eye before work.

****

Wednesday, Gabriel calculated his lunchtime to catch the detectives. He beat them to the cafe and slid into the booth across the aisle from their usual spot. Sitting with his back to the wall, his focus riveted on the front door. By the time his root beer arrived, the detectives rolled into the cafe with their same confident swagger and greeting to Audra. They slid into their booth without acknowledging Gabriel and began their lunchtime conversation.

At a break, when the waitress left with their order, Gabriel turned to them and got their attention. "Could I have a word with you?" They both shrugged, and the shorter guy slid toward the wall to make space for him.

"So, sport, what's on your mind?"

"I need to talk to someone about stolen cars." Gabriel maintained his calm, quiet demeanor.

"Not us, guy." The taller detective deflected.

"Okay, who?"

"Call the department's non-emergency number." The alpha male reached for a business card and slid it to him. Gabriel picked it up and stared. *These guys are blowing me off! Will their light-bulb flicker when my body is found in an alley? Probably not.*

"Look, I've been threatened. My girl went into hiding because of their death threats. They beat my P.O. until she told them where I lived. I have names and dates of auto thefts. I know these have to be open cases." Gabriel jammed his index finger on the Formica tabletop to make the point as he spoke in a hard whisper.

"Yeah, they'll take care of it at that number." The big guy apathetically poked his finger at the business card.

142

"So, I just try and make an appointment to save my ass?" Gabriel shook the card at the bigger guy in disgust. He sat there, his muscles quivering, his hands beginning to shake.

"Call now." The guy pointed to the pay phones behind the booths. Gabriel got up, flustered, feeling for his cell phone, no need for a pay phone. What he did need was a receptive ear and maybe a shoulder to lean on. He went back to his lunch and pushed down the food. Being desperate and hungry was a dangerous combination. He ate staring at the door as if Wally and his goons would burst in and carry him out at any moment.

His phone vibrated, and he looked at the caller I.D. It was Wally's garage. "G, it's Juan. Wally wants you here Saturday night at nine, you got it?"

"I got it." Gabriel cut off the call and attempted to finish his meal. The next few bites tasted as foul as ash, and he pushed the plate forward, resting his elbows on the table. Gabriel buried his face in his hands. He needed to think straight, it was vital that he make good decisions, he needed to make that call. Time elongated. The detectives ate their food and his server, seeing his 'funk' dropped off a new root beer without speaking. He cut a sharp glance at the detectives as he got up and left the diner. *Bastards!* He pocketed his change.

****

Dates and car models danced in his brain and he supposed sitting down and listing every boost would lend credence to his confession.

"County Non-Emergency." The operator was all business, speaking in precise, clipped words.

"I need to speak with someone about auto thefts, I have information on open cases." He didn't want to sound cocky; he just knew they were unsolved.

Her calm, collected attitude upset Gabriel. These thieves were dangerous people who shouldn't be ignored. Then, there was a cool, attentive voice in the grand theft auto division. Gabriel made his best pitch and earned an appointment at eight on Saturday morning.

He was insane with frustration. They were putting him off. That meant if they took him seriously, they'd have only thirteen hours before

Wally expected him to show up at the garage; thirteen short hours to do something to trap Wally.

Gabriel went to the store and bought a composition book. He returned to the studio to list his transgressions to the best of his memory. He wanted to drive to Esther's. Would Grace be in front of a window? *Maybe, I can catch a glimpse of her.* He decided it would hurt way too much to see her and not be able to hold her and stay with her.

Friday was a glorious Indian Summer day. It would have been a perfect wedding day. Gabriel would have been antsy to get out of work and make Grace his wife. Instead, his guts were a churning bag of snakes. All his energy went into keeping an appearance of normalcy.

When the last job order rolled out of Minute Lube, Gabriel prowled the shop closing for the week. They shuttered the garage and went their separate ways. He slipped an envelope under Mae's door thanking her for the opportunity given him and apologizing for quitting without notice. He couldn't tell her why he was leaving, but he directed her to use his last check to get better locks and a security camera.

Once all the details of the thefts were reconstructed, he looked at the composition book and assessed his life. It was too much to think the authorities would believe him. He had everything to gain by getting out from underneath Wally, but would the police give him a hand up when he couldn't climb out of the cesspool by himself? Finally, he ripped a page out of the book and wrote to Grace. He'd find an envelope somewhere; this would be more personal than a postcard.

> *Dear Princess,*
>
> *You're the best person I've ever known. Every decision I'm making is for our future. If we don't escape this threat, we'll never have the life we want. Once I mail this, I'm deleting any record of you and Esther from my phone.*
>
> *I can't chance it falling into the wrong hands. Keep your eyes and ears open, I think this is going to make a lot of noise. If you don't hear from me within a month, believe I am dead. For your safety, don't admit knowing*

me. If someone approaches you asking about me, you have no idea who I was.

I'll love you until the end of time.

-Your Gabriel

****

His parochial school upbringing told him to 'believe'. His broken spirit hovered in despair at being the lowest guy in the chain of command. He was the bottom of the food chain, and he knew the heartless bastards at the top believed he was going to taste great on a cracker. He needed a meeting.

The community room at the church filled quickly on a Friday night. Gabriel grabbed a seat in the back and listened to the third step study. He did long to turn this whole situation over to God because God knew he didn't have the answers. He was convinced only divine intervention would help him now. When it was his turn to speak, he stood, trembling. "Hi, my name is Gabriel. I'm an alcoholic."

"Hi, Gabriel."

He acknowledged the crowd's greeting with a nod. "I've been sober one hundred and forty-eight days. I could never have done it without the support of the Program… and my Higher Power." There was sporadic applause, and he stumbled for his next words. "… I know what the third step is. I've decided to turn my will and my life over to the care of God as I understand Him. But, tonight, I had to feel it by being with like-minded people." His shoulders squared, and a placid smile returned to his face. "Thank you for being here tonight." He dropped back into his seat and inhaled deeply.

****

Grace pushed herself through Friday. She told herself sacrificing her wedding day was doing the brave thing, *the right thing*, even though it hurt terribly now. When she wanted to give way to her broken heart, a spark inside told her, *he's not going to die. He's doing this so we can be safe together. This isn't like when Daddy died.* She held the DeRosa's wedding portrait and visualized herself with Gabriel in their place. *In forty years, will anyone cherish our wedding portrait?*

Esther and Kendra welcomed her. That night, after she cried herself out, she realized if she could go to bed and remember his smile, the feel of his lips, then her dreams would carry her to tomorrow. One day, Gabriel would call and give her the 'all clear'. Yeah, that's the way she'd go to bed tonight, believing tomorrow would be the 'all clear'.

****

Saturday morning's appointment allowed the police to pick a former criminal's brain. They read what he offered, they even copied it. They gave him no indication of any interest. By midmorning, he waited for the next round of questions. The room shrank with each hour, his legs fidgeted, and he wanted to pace. He stared at Grace's ring on his pinkie. His addiction whispered it could soften the blows of being alone; it could ease this interview. His craving reduced him to a cowering shell. *How long would I be there?* They could talk all day, but would they have his back when he left?

"Gabriel, we need to get this info cross-referenced. You have a lot to process here. When did you say he expects you?" Detective Barbaran tapped the book confidently.

"Tonight. Wally expects me tonight at nine." Gabriel gnawed on his thumb, folded into himself.

****

Detective Kerry, a round-faced nearly bald guy, watched Gabriel's confident persona deteriorate as the day continued. The close confines, the repeated questioning, woke up old memories of the sordid type. Kerry understood that. He'd spent time undercover, and the tension and proximity to drugs led to his time in a drug treatment program. He knew Gabriel's pain, and he saw the future collapsing for the well-meaning tattooed guy.

"We need you to go in relaxed, you can wear a wire, and we'll watch, okay?" Barbaran threw down the offer.

****

Gabriel sat and stared at the reflective glass. *Finally! Is my shit together or is my shit together?* "Not with a wire. If they find a wire on me

– and believe me, they'll frisk me – I'm a dead man. Without a wire, how close can you be?"

"We'll keep you under surveillance…"

****

When Gabriel left the back door of the precinct, he wondered if he needed to go to confession. All his stewing centered on wanting to bust Wally's head wide open like a Halloween pumpkin. It was a quiet drive back to the studio with the radio off. He needed to think. First, he had to pack up his gear, settle his account at the rental office, and check out.

He did go to the church in his old neighborhood. Sitting in the back pew, Gabriel watched as the neighborhood women genuflected and crossed themselves with holy water before disappearing into the confessionals. He spun Grace's ring for the last time today. His high-top boots had thick laces which he loosened to secure the small gold ring inside the padded tongue. He tied a double knot praying he would be as safe as the ring.

Gabriel spied his namesake's statue over a bank of candles flickering in blood red votive cups. He dug out a dollar and dropped to the kneeling bench. With Grace's name on his lips, he lit the fresh white candle. As the wick quivered and burned, he folded his hands and earnestly prayed. Eyes closed, Gabriel's mind opened, throwing away his fears in the hope a revelation would overcome him.

Gabe, buddy, we haven't talked for a while, but I need your help tonight maybe more than ever. Please, show me what to do and give me the strength to do it. I don't know if I deserve your protection, but I'm asking for it, especially for Grace.

Gabriel made the sign of the cross and bowed his head in true humility. His elbows rested on the rail as he buried his face in his folded hands. *I'm ready when you are.*

He couldn't make his feet carry him behind the ruby velvet curtain separating the repentant from the unremorseful. He sat through the Saturday evening mass and felt like a heretic when he walked to the communion rail for the Body of Christ. He needed the reinforcement of someone bigger than Wally or the cops. He wanted to believe Heaven was on his side.

The priest intoned, "The Mass is ended, go in peace."

The elderly woman in Gabriel's pew rose and turned to leave. Gabriel still knelt; his face buried in his prayerful hands. After a beat, the woman turned and exited by the side aisle. The church emptied, but Gabriel remained as he was, filled with a joyous peace radiating from dazzling white light. Slowly, the light faded, and he found himself under the gaze of a kindly Priest. "Son, do you need help?"

Gabriel stood, with a shy smile. "Thank you, Father, I think I got it."

The old man performed a blessing as he spoke. "May the Lord show you his favor and give you peace."

****

Gabriel made his way back to his car with a renewed sense of protection. His serenity shattered when he heard the jagged sound of a woman shouting his name. "Gabriel James Lee!" He froze with his keys in his hand and scanned the street corners. She bellowed again. "Boy!" His spine tingled at her scolding tone. It all came back to him. He turned his back to the car and pocketed his keys. A woman, ravaged by cigarettes and alcohol over time, rose from a slouch and waved a bony arm at her son.

"Mom. Where have you been?" *Why tonight, of all nights, does she magically appear?* Without a conscious decision, he headed in her direction.

She fumbled with a light windbreaker, reaching for her customary pack of smokes as he stood in front of her. "Take a load off." She shook the half-empty cigarette pack at him. "Here." She held out a cheap lighter.

He waved a declining hand. "No thanks. I quit."

"And you go to church now? Grannie would be so proud."

Gabriel frowned. "I don't go as often as I should." His gaze swept the homes on the street. "Are you living around here now?"

She lit a cigarette and turned her head to blow smoke rings. "I don't live anywhere in particular, unless you call the Salvation Army Shelter a place to live. Where are you living?"

The smoke irritated him, and he sniffed in defense. "I'm heading out of town. Don't know where I'll be living." *Or if I'm going to be alive after tonight.*

"You have a kid now. How old is he? Is that girl treating your baby right? Are you on the run from her?" She pushed her disheveled hair out of her eyes.

"The baby died. Carla died."

His mother gazed at the sunset over the church spires. "This city doesn't need more babies that way. No wonder you're back to church."

Her comment drove a stake into his heart. "I was one of 'those babies'!"

Her lip lifted. "And look how you turned out. I was hoping you'd take care of your mother in her old age. Instead, you're 'leaving town'."

Gabriel's hand drifted into his pocket, and he scuffed the toe of his boot absentmindedly. *Old age? You aren't even forty.* "Really, I was hoping you'd develop the will to take care of yourself."

"You just run on out like you did when you joined the Navy. Don't give me another thought. I'll mention you to St. Peter when I wind up dead on the street. My son, the churchgoer, could have helped his mother, but he was 'leaving town'…"

"Have you eaten today, Mom?"

She stared at him, sucking on the cigarette. Her eyes moved right to left to right in thought. "I think I did." She scratched chipped fingernails over her neck.

"Are you coming down, now? Are you hungry?" *If I give her money, she'll score anything she can buy. I've got less than two hours until I'm due at Wally's.* He sighed with resignation and patted his back pocket. "Get in the car. I'm taking you to Motel Six for the week. On the way, I'll pick up some food. The hotel is close to some A.A. meetings. Talk to them, they can help you."

Her lips turned down. "A.A. is for quitters." Her laugh was derisive. "I'm not like those people." Her laugh petered off in a wet cough.

I am but arguing with you when you're on a drunk is useless. "C'mon, Mom." He picked up her tote bag and hoped it wasn't riddled with bed bugs.

She shifted on the bench and gathered her balance. "This is nice of you, baby."

"Yeah. I'm a nice guy, now."

17

The shop was filthier than Gabriel remembered. He entered the garage's semi-darkness and saw Wally's face in the bilious glow of the desk lamp. Gabriel stood a good five feet outside the office. "Okay, man, you got me here, why did you need me so bad?" He spoke quietly to his nemesis when he heard feet shuffle in the shadows. His spine went tight as a bowstring. "Who's in there with you?"

Wally cast a censorious gaze sideways and returned his gaze to Gabriel. "None ya."

Freddy and Conrad bumped Gabriel from behind, thrusting him to the edge of Wally's desk. A short man in a snazzy suit leaned against the one tall file cabinet as if he were trying to blend in with the black metal. His blonde hair glowed like a torch in the dark. His tan contrasted highly against the heavily starched white collar and cuffs. A gold chain glittered as it led from one vest pocket through a buttonhole and into the other pocket. From that pocket, a gilt chain and a Phi Beta Kappa key dangled conspicuously throwing spears of light in the darkness.

Wally cleared his throat. "One more job. Well, if you can believe it, one more job. Then you can run off with your little redhead." Wally withdrew papers from his desk drawer, a list of addresses, and passed it to Gabriel.

Gabriel shot a gaze to the silent stranger and back to Wally. "Great, peachy keen. Tonight, we're done. Through. No more jobs." Gabriel countered as he accepted the list. "I've got till six in the morning, right?"

Gabriel stood still while Freddy and Conrad frisked him, pulling up his shirt, checking for wires.

Who the hell is that guy? The buyer? Wally's boss? Where has he been all this time?

"I can't be too careful, Gabe, you had a few days to go crying to someone." Wally came around his desk and cupped Gabriel's crotch, feeling for more wires or maybe just to mess with him.

"Right." Gabriel shook his head in disgust and turned his face away from Wally, noticing the surveillance photo from the street fair tacked on the wall amid insurance claim photos and to- do lists. He tapped the picture. "I want this." The blonde man bit hard on the stub of his unlit cigar when his gaze landed on the photo.

"When you get back with the cars, it's yours. It's the least I can do."

"Yeah." Gabriel's contemptuous glare swept over the stranger.

He left the garage in the Impala. Freddy sat against the passenger door, alternating a malicious scowl at Gabriel and then a smirk toward Conrad in the back seat. *Juan isn't involved, thank god.* Gabriel hoped Juan wouldn't fall into Wally's crap trap as he had. They parked a few blocks away, and Gabriel approached the first car on his list.

Advancing from behind, Freddy smacked him at the back of his knees with a telescoping baton, driving him down. Together, Freddy and Conrad rained hell in a barrage of kicking and stomping. Gabriel's recently recovering bones were in no shape to fend off two determined street fighters. On the potholed bricks, the blows to his reconstructed right hip were paralyzing. He curled inward while four steel-toed boots punished him relentlessly. When there was no resistance, Freddy shoved a foot into Gabriel's center and flopped him on his back. He laid eyes open and motionless, and they left him. A bloody body in the gutter, in this neighborhood, wasn't much news.

****

Gabriel's consciousness left his body. Lying broken on cold pavement again, his mind was blank… he seemed to think it all felt better when he was numb and cold…or so he thought... The unmarked police cruiser dispatched to follow Gabriel got waylaid by a shootout on the wharf. A cadre of auto thieves with automatic weapons, loading containers of car parts, outdid one confidential informant. Besides, their brothers in arms were under fire. By the time the police found Gabriel, all they were suitable for was an escort to the trauma center.

Harbor Health Trauma was impressed a police car preceded the ambulance. Their presence bought Gabriel immediate attention. He was dashed in and treated for multiple contusions and abrasions, a concussion, broken nose, dislocated shoulder, broken ribs, bruised liver, spleen and kidneys, and too many stitches to count. The admitting clerk kept badgering the officer for a "next of kin" on the John Doe until they could get his blood-soaked wallet off him.

"Detective Kerry, this is Harbor Health Trauma, we've got a police escort who brought a Gabriel Lee into the E.R., can you get out here? We don't have a next of kin." The sympathetic clerk asked in her kindest, almost midnight voice. "He's coming out of a shit-kicking, and you may want to be here."

****

Gabriel lay devastated by the pain, as they manipulated his left shoulder back into the socket. The shock threw him into a rush of sound, light and confusing agony. He fought for an understanding of where he was. While he was unconscious, the E.R. staff was able to start his I.V., insert the Foley catheter and get his C.T. scans done.

The tearing sensation of his shoulder drew him back into the land of the living, screaming. "What are you doing to me?" He spied the I.V. and the hanging bag, saw his clothes were cut away and tried to rip out the I.V. line. He froze when he saw the nurse with an injection moving toward him. She sat the hypodermic needle on a tray and went to him immediately.

"Calm down, Mr. Lee," she soothed. "You need the fluids we're giving you. Let's get your blood pressure." She deftly wrestled his hands while placing the cuff around his wrist and waiting for it to yield a reading. "You were badly beaten. We've been treating you for a variety of injuries." She spoke pleasantly, as though nothing critical happened. "Can you tell me where we are right now? What city is this?"

"Baltimore." His head was fuzzy. "It is Baltimore, right?"

"That's right. And, what year is this?"

"Um…can I answer later?"

"Sure. Do you know what this place is? Where are we right now?"

Gabriel glanced around. "A hospital ship?"

"I'll take that for now. I have some medicine for you. We have to fix your nose, it's been broken. Please, lie still, we don't want you to displace your ribs." She didn't talk like a military nurse. A military nurse would make it an order. Still, he was inclined to follow her instructions. Moving hurt. "So, now, you mustn't touch your I.V. You don't want me to have to start a new one." She smiled. "Okay?"

"What are you giving me?" His voice was ragged from the pain. Even with that, the fear of being shot full of drugs he'd crave for far too long afterward loomed more significant than the fear of the discomfort.

"Well, nothing but fluids. I have some morphine for you so we can set your nose and…"

She was cut off by his loud insistence. "I don't want anything for the pain, nothing, ya hear me?" The tremors in his voice belied his claims.

"We do suggest fast-acting pain medication. It will wear off quickly. You're pretty torn up. You'll have some significant discomfort." She wasn't kidding he thought, as he felt the broken nose with each breath. "I can't force you to take it. You have the right to refuse, but…"

His voice tore out of him. "I can't take anything, you don't understand." He cried out, shaking his head and squeezing his eyes closed.

"Okay, okay." She leaned over him, and her hands rested lightly on his arms. "Just try not to move. I won't give you anything you don't want. I promise." She bit her lip, clearly at odds with his decision. "Right now, Mr. Lee, let's get you treated, okay?"

****

From the other side of the curtain, Detective Kerry heard it all, the rasp in Gabriel's voice, and the anguish of the physical pain. He knew the fiend Gabriel fought, and it wasn't a battle to fight alone. Gabriel had done a great job staying clean and sober with the help of his A.A. group, but he needed more. He needed an actual alcohol recovery program where they could focus on his addiction triggers while tonight's wounds healed. He had deeper emotional problems to sort through, and he needed professional help.

Kerry blamed himself for the beating if he'd only insisted on more backup. What would have made his partner take Gabriel seriously? Now, Kerry relived his own withdrawal, his slide into the belly of the beast. He needed to make up for their apathy. Gabriel needed treatment. He needed to be released from this physical suffering and immersed in recovery.

****

The harder you try, the dumber you look. Memory trickled back to Gabriel now. The simple act of trying to save his ass got that very same ass kicked. Conrad and Freddy worked him over pretty well. He hoped they broke out in boils. There he lay, on a gurney in the E.R., the sun rising, and he was supposed to be driving to Esther's. His plans included their blowing town. He fought off the medical staff pumping him full of whatever poison would drag him back into addiction. That was his one success in the past twenty-four hours.

The nurse returned with 'a muscle relaxer'. He stubbornly insisted to himself once he soaked in a hot tub of water he'd feel almost human again. Just when he wanted to get out of the bed and leave, Kerry pulled back the curtain and announced himself.

"What?" Gabriel shot back, as he pulled the drape over his bare legs. *This character has a lot of nerve coming in after the beating they allowed.*

"Detective Kerry," he announced to the nurse, presenting his business card. An infuriated Gabriel turned his face away. "I think I can get you some help, Lee." Kerry lowered his voice to a near whisper.

"Is this where you bait me into taking out a contract to kill Wally?" Gabriel accused the Detective.

"What?" Kerry stood back and looked around the room. He repeated his comment and Gabriel's face twisted in confusion as he repeated his response.

"No, this isn't a sting on contract hits, and if I'm speaking out of turn, I'll leave. I want to maybe offer you some help." Kerry treaded delicately, Gabriel was already agitated.

"Help? How about you guys pay for this little vacation I'm having, along with a one-way ticket for me and my girl to someplace warm and safe?" Gabriel attempted to sit up and fell back in pain. He reached for the bed control; he wasn't going anywhere fast.

All Gabriel's defenses were heightened, he protected what little sobriety he thought he had. Kerry leaned close and bent to Gabriel's ear. "I've been where you are, I've held on to the last thin edge of sobriety, and it felt pretty lonely." The cop changed the slant of the blinds to block the morning sun. "You can try to white-knuckle it, or you can get help. I'm not a betting man, I gave that up a while back." Kerry drew closer to Gabriel and scoped the foot traffic before he continued his monologue. "You have a problem, and as long as Wally has you by the short hairs, you are going to have many more problems." Kerry's eyes narrowed, and Gabriel followed him. "If you kicked being Wally's bitch, you can kick your drug of choice." His rising eyebrows punctuated the end of his sentence.

"What's your interest?" Gabriel retorted.

"I was in your position – just like this. I was a cop on the inside, using to fit in, got the job done, and the job nearly finished me. I lost my wife, my house, damn near my life."

Is Kerry's crust chipping away? Is this guy for real? "So, you think we can get to be buds, play some cop and C.I. games and I'll be healed? You just want your pound of flesh, too."

"Nope, I'm going to be your brother. I'm going to offer you tough love, ever had tough love?"

"I used to have a girlfriend, she shot me." Gabriel pushed back.

"Ooohh, that wasn't the kind of tough love I was thinking about." Kerry shook his head as he spoke. "Let the department get you some help. Get clean the right way, make some new friends, move if you have to."

In Gabriel's heart, he wanted to be clean. He wanted Grace with him every morning and evening. He needed a straight job. He sought to make her proud. "What's it going to cost me, my left nut?" Gabriel shifted in the bed at the thought.

"Let me pull a few strings. If it's a go, you have to be ready." Kerry dipped his head and looked over the top of his glasses. "Where can I get a hold of you?"

"In this bed, until they throw me out." Gabriel realized he checked out of the studio and his car was at Wally's garage.

"And then?" Kerry pushed.

"On the street," Gabriel explained his situation.

"Then, let me see how quick I can work this up." Kerry turned to leave, and then returned to Gabriel. "Don't let them discharge you. Tell them about your issues." Kerry was invested in Gabriel, now. Gabriel nodded and blinked, even that hurt.

****

Gabriel rode the wave of nerve plucking pain by returning his heart and mind to his first time with Grace, how she melted around him. He drifted in the memory of a mind-blowing climax again and again, until he willed himself to sleep. Within that sleep, he dreamed of climbing Grace's body like a mountain range. Her pale skin rose out of the sheets as a dune on a beach. He climbed, small and nimble over her length, finally close enough to her ear, whispering, "I love you. Wait for me. I do love you."

"Mr. Lee," the new nurse tapped her ring on her clipboard. He jumped at the sound of her voice, and rubbed his swollen eyes, blinking to focus. She smiled at him kindly. "We have a room for you, Doctor wants to admit you for a few days."

Sure, whatever. "What time is it?" He was exhausted.

"7:45, Sunday morning."

It was all he needed to know. He digested the current time and tried to figure out when he'd last seen Grace. *What night was it?* They rolled his gurney to a room at the end of the hall with a view of the harbor. The images of the meals he and Grace enjoyed on the waterfront played in a loop. He thought of the night she described her experiences with Arthur. He tried to doze and ended up using his one pain-free finger to work through the T.V. channels.

"Mr. Lee." a new voice preceded Kerry into Gabriel's line of sight. A pretty face with soft blue eyes and blonde hair the color of corn silk. He thought about white sweet corn and that he was hungry, and then he blinked into the present.

"Yea, it's me, who else wants to be here like this?" Gabriel regarded his injuries and the room before looking at the woman.

"I'm Beverly Dawson. Detective Kerry's told me you want to stay sober. I hear you also have reason to avoid someone while the police sweep up. We thought you might want to come to inpatient rehab, it's confidential. I think we could help you, Gabe."

Gabriel's head began to swim. *Hide and clean up? What's going on?*

Kerry stepped closer. "You blew the top off that boosting racket. Your former employer was a little showy with you, and it's a good thing you wrote everything down." Gabriel closed his eyes – nothing made sense. He held up the remote and turned off the TV, its chatter was too much. "Turns out," Kerry continued, "he's connected to the Russian mob, been moving product for the past three years. You didn't realize that, did you?" Kerry grinned. "Your statement is truly panning out. Right now, we want him to think you're dead. You sure could have been." He idly picked up the cover on Gabriel's untouched breakfast of warm Jell-O and cool broth and made a face. "We'd have towed your car, but Wally torched it. We'll be moving you to a safe house when you get out of this four-star joint unless you decide to go with Ms. Dawson, here. No matter where you land, you'll be in for some interrogations. They'll grill you on each detail."

"So, the car was a total loss?" Funny how insignificant things meant everything at odd moments.

"Pardon the expression, but, it was a car-beque. You came out of this better. You don't want to be connected to that car, anyway." Kerry waved his hand at Gabriel. "It's a sure bet someone will be watching your old haunts. The best thing for you, while all this is going on, is to get help from Beverly."

Gabriel felt a rush of new responsibility thrown at him along with the pressure to clean up his act. Even he admitted it was a good plan. "Yeah, I appreciate the offer. I just need to contact my girl, and let her know where I am."

Kerry shook his head with finality. "Can't let you do that, Lee."

Gabriel was deep into irritable at this point, between the pain and the aggravation. "Why the hell not? She's the reason I did all this!"

"And I'm assuming that means you want to keep her safe, right?" He cut Gabriel off before he could voice his objection. "You don't think the Russians have people watching her day and night? You contact her, even if you don't see her, she starts looking different, maybe a little happier? Lee, I don't think you get they need to believe you're dead, or nobody around you is safe." Gabriel brooded, but even he couldn't argue with that. Kerry drove his point home by adding, "You need to know your former boss is in protective custody after a Ruskie hitman damn near blew his head off, and they still remember what you look like."

"They almost got Wa..." Gabriel caught himself, and looked up at Beverly Dawson, "...er, him?"

Kerry nodded emphatically. "You know, your name is on the toe tag of a sad, homeless man who left here feet first. That's the only reason you don't have a set of guards on your door."

"Shit." Gabriel considered. "Is that on the news? It will freak out Grace!"

Kerry shifted weight uncomfortably. "We kept it on the down low. It didn't make the evening news or the papers, but I'm sure it's in the obituaries. If she was looking there..."

"I'll do whatever it takes to keep Grace safe, but can't we get word to her that I'm alive?"

"No, son, you would get her killed doing that."

Gabriel hid the hot tears by pretending to rub his eyes. He probably wasn't fooling anyone.

Kerry made to put a friendly hand on his shoulder and drew it back. He glanced at Beverly. "So, Dawson, when do you think Gabe, here, can be discharged to you?"

Beverly smiled reassuringly at Gabriel and turned to Kerry. "First, I'm not a doctor, though we do have a medical program at Loch Raven Recovery. It's meant for folks who are more in withdrawal than physical injury. Let's wait a couple of days until the physicians say he's ready for discharge, and then you'll have a home waiting with us, Gabe."

Gabriel gave her a genuine smile. "Thanks, Ms. Dawson, I appreciate that."

****

Sunday dawned grey. Grace woke to a silent home, Esther and Kendra left earlier for church. They hadn't badgered her, but before she went to bed, Esther asked if she had church clothes. Not having them bought her a chance to sleep in with her anxieties. Today she would be on high alert for any call.

How long did he say it would be before I considered him dead? She rolled back over in the twin bed and put the pillow over her head. *Can I hear him on the front porch from here? No.* She reluctantly rolled out of bed and dug out sweatpants and a sports bra, and then enjoyed ten minutes in the single bathroom without hearing a knock on the door. The coffee pot was still warm, so she poured a mug and headed to the front porch for the newspaper. She wanted to see Gabriel bounding up the walk, telling her they were free to live their lives together.

The Sunday paper was stuffed in a plastic bag on the cracked sidewalk. She scampered to get it and shook off the heavy dew. Spreading the ads out on the glider, her hands trembled as she read the obituary page. Nothing in the Sunday Sun, *but it would be too soon, wouldn't it?* She said a prayer Monday's paper would be equally kind. She reached out into the universe, could she feel his loving vibration out there? She felt *pain,* and she couldn't discern his from hers.

****

She ran for the waiting train and shoved the newspaper under her arm. Should she gamble and open the paper here, on the train at rush hour? Or, should she put it off until she was safe at home? *I can't stand not knowing.* It seemed fitting, she'd met him on a Monday evening, and now, this Monday, she read his lonely obituary.

Lee, Gabriel

Aged 23, died Sunday. Survived by loving brother,

Alejandro Santiago, and nephew, and niece, Diego, and

Marylee Santiago. Predeceased by his parents and

grandparents. He was a proud graduate of Polytechnic High School Mechanics program, served in the USN for four years and was employed by Wally's Garage as a mechanic. There will be no service. Interment at Most Holy Redeemer Cemetery.

No photo, no service, not even a time of interment. Gabriel spoke of his Gran to Grace, and she knew his mother was alive on the streets. They wouldn't have known to mention his unborn son. She'd never heard of a brother. Grace bumped along on the train, her tears streaming as the other harried riders dealt with their Monday.

When do they bury people without services? Was it the first thing in the morning? The last of the day? Can I borrow Esther's car to ride out to the cemetery?

****

Grace sat at the kitchen table staring at his letter, atop the newspaper obituary. "He told me he might die, but the newspaper says there was a brother. Gabriel never mentioned a brother and his mother *isn't dead*. How do I know if this is even *my* Gabriel?" Grace shook the notice, one hand gripping the rolled-up newspaper.

"Cici, what did he tell you before he left? He tried to prepare you for the worst. How many Gabriels do you know at Wally's?" Esther worked the paper out of Grace's hand. The dance began with a motherly embrace moving Grace to the sofa and ended when her face fell into her hands, and the newspaper fluttered to the floor.

Esther leaned in to hear Grace's words. "He cleared his phone, there was no listing for me or you, now I can't even be at the grave."

"Sweetheart, you know what he said, it's all for your safety. I've watched too many good people die on these streets. I can't do a thing to take away your pain, Lord knows I would if I could." The women huddled together, weeping hard at the minute obituary. Grace's heartbroken sobs surpassed the sound of the front door unlocking and Kendra returning from school with Antwoine in her front carrier, her backpack over one shoulder. She slumped inside the door.

"What happened?"

Esther looked up; her expression solemn. "Gabriel was killed."

"But was he? We can't know that. He is the second man in my life who's 'dead' without any proof. I think about Daddy. They said it was suicide, but was it? Debris was found without Daddy, and just like that, they declared him dead. Was he? Did they search long enough?"

"Oh, honey, you will drive yourself crazy with questions. Don't you think, if your father made it through alive, he would have contacted you by now?"

Grace spoke with the resignation of a bewildered soul. "I don't know. I don't know about Daddy; I don't know about Gabriel. What do I know? I'm alone."

"You are not alone." Esther's voice was strong and reassuring. "You have me, and you have Kendra. You have your courage and your spirit. You have your mother's fortitude and your daddy's brains, and your own dreams. You have everything you need."

18

The physical scars and pissing blood were evidence of Gabriel crossing Wally's path. His melancholy blue-green eyes were the badge he wore for being restricted from Grace. The new treatment center was, without a doubt, the poshest place he ever parked his duffle bag. Trees hovered over the log cabins, painting a pastoral theme for the jittery clients. Gabriel thought he was the only guy there not shaking like a Chihuahua.

One September afternoon, he checked in as 'Gabriel Bowman'. As he put his few remaining donated belongings in his dresser, a quiet man entered the room, head down, hands in his pockets. He was a youthful late forty-something judging by the silver hair at his temples. Wearing an Izod golf shirt and Madras patch golf shorts, his braided leather belt strained a bit at the belly. Gabriel thought he could have stepped out of a television sitcom as the ultimate father figure.

"Are you Ted? I'm Gabriel, Gabriel Bowman. I guess we're bunk mates? Okay, this is strange. It's the Navy all over again." *Or maybe prison...*

"I'm an Army man myself." The man self-consciously pulled his tremulous hand out of his pocket and extended it to Gabriel. "I'm Ted, Ted Warner. It's my third day here." He clenched his hands together. "They tell me this gets better."

"Yeah, it does, hang in there."

"You don't look like you're too much in withdrawal."

"No, you're right, I went through it a while ago." He shrugged. "On the other hand, you're probably not pissing blood, so…"

The older man drew back. "Jeez! What kind of drug does that?"

"No, that's not from a drug, man. That was courtesy of a couple of street punks." As Gabriel closed the drawer, he smiled. "Nothing good happens on the streets after nine P.M."

Ted's eyes creased with sympathy. "Looks like they worked you over pretty good." He said tentatively. "The cops must have been involved."

Gabriel raised an eyebrow and immediately regretted the sharp pull on his stitches. "I'd like to say, you should see the other guy, but that wouldn't be true. This is a program of honesty, right?" He hung his jacket in the closet. "Cops aren't much interested in street fights."

"Hell, I'd be dragging the cops into it whether they like it or not. I mean, look at you!" Ted shook his head, the salt and pepper hair moved out of its controlled style to fall onto his forehead.

"Wouldn't know who to tell them to arrest. They got me from behind."

"That's too bad. I feel for you, kid. You need any hangers or anything?" Ted gestured at the closet.

"Nope. I travel light." Gabriel grimaced as he shoved the small duffle into the closet. "It's a hangover from the Navy. I'm all stowed away."

"You coming to First Step Class in fifteen minutes, or did they give you some move-in time?"

Gabriel shrugged. "Might as well come, lying in bed just makes me ache."

Ted started to put a fatherly arm around his shoulder, "C'mon I'll introduce to the other newbies." He drew his arm back. "Oh, man, I'm afraid to touch you. What area didn't they break?"

Gabriel laughed with gallows humor. "Oh, they just ran the bases on me. My feet are pretty good."

****

Gabriel didn't know if it was good fortune or bad that he came into treatment already out of withdrawal. It certainly gave him perspective on behavior. Most of the patients, except Ted, with whom he was becoming close, went through wild mood swings. At least they were a better class of junkies. He was moving up. Especially since these were people, who didn't want to be slaves to a habit any longer. He did find, for the most part, they were solely focused on themselves. All the counselors told him it was wrong, but he couldn't stop focusing on Grace. He missed her like a starving man missed nourishment. He'd tried to keep in mind what Kerry said about her safety, and any time he talked about her, he called her Princess and altered all identifying info. He just couldn't see the harm in letting her know he was alive and would come for her as soon as he was able.

He weaned himself off the nicotine gum. His blackened eyes faded, and the stitches eventually dissolved. He could walk two miles now, without leaning on Ted most of the way back. Ted teased him he should be the one propping Ted up; he was old enough to be his father. If Gabriel could have picked a father, Ted would be the man for the job. He'd lived a good and stable life until his wife died of cancer. The disease, a medical rollercoaster, sent him into alcoholism. Gabriel could understand in a perfect world like Ted's, losing the love of his life, could unleash the hounds of addiction. But Ted had forgotten more about living successfully than Gabriel would ever know, at least that's how it seemed, and Gabriel paid attention.

****

Ryan, a self-indulgent trust fund baby, beat a drum solo on the butcher block and barked, "Bow-man, what's the holdup? It's a sandwich not quiche! Which, I might say, I would eat– if you could get it served."

Gabriel held up one finger. "This is a work of art, worthy of a Princess. Do not rush me."

Ryan spun a skillet lid on his finger. "Just put it all out. We'll make our own!"

"It's an assembly line process, Ryan. First the turkey, then the…" Gabriel turned to the list he'd given his counselor. He sighed. "I think they forgot the fontina cheese."

"Just give us the orange stuff," Ryan demanded while the other men shook their heads.

Ted stuck his head in the kitchen. "Give that kid a hunk of cheese to gnaw on and shut him up. I'll take over helping. Go, Ryan! Out!"

Ted and Gabriel took over, heads down over the sandwich assembly line. It was turkey, avocado, bacon, and yellow cheese, not Grace's favorite fontina, on top of crusty baguettes. After he slid the tray in the oven, Gabriel washed his hands and summoned Ted. He didn't look up when he spoke. "If I asked you to mail a letter for me, you could do that, right?"

Ted folded his arms over his chest and dropped his head close to Gabriel. "Why aren't you mailing it?"

"You're not going to let me get away with this, are you?"

"Get away with what?"

"They don't want me contacting anybody. People think I'm dead. People I love could move on if they don't know I'm alive."

"This sounds serious, Gabriel. Who are 'they'? It sounds like the law, to me. If it is, and they don't want you to contact anyone, there must be a reason."

Gabriel made a dismissive gesture. "You know the cops; they're always looking for a worst-case scenario."

Ted's brows knit, and he drew in a deep breath. "Maybe so, but if I loved a girl, I sure as hell wouldn't risk the worst-case scenario happening to her. Plus, you can't even look at me while you ask, so, what's going on, Grease? This is a program of honesty."

Gabriel shuffled his feet. "You're right, Pops. There's a criminal case. I can't say more. I don't want to get anyone hurt." He brooded as he pulled the tray out of the oven and placed the sandwiches on a platter. "Ah hell forget it. It was a bad idea, anyway."

"I'm sorry you're in this mess, Grease-man. I'll help you any way I can, but not by corrupting your program or mine."

"Yeah. Yeah, you're right."

****

That afternoon found the group tubing down The Gunpowder Falls. It was part of the recreation program, helping the patients to see there were enjoyable activities that didn't include alcohol or drugs. Gabriel admitted it was a great time, and something he could enjoy while resting his half-broken body. If he lay still and listened to the other voices in the parties ahead and behind them, he almost felt Grace holding his hand in a tube next to him. *Maybe there's a way... Maybe I can work it out...*

Before he dozed off, the pullout spot was covered with people dragging their inner tubes to the shore. He trudged behind Ted and rode home in silence. After a good, hot shower, Gabriel moved stiffly around his room, toweling his growing hair. *I need a haircut; I'm starting to look like a rock star.*

There was a hard knock on the door. He swung it open to see Detective Kerry standing there, looking grave. "Hey." Gabriel ducked his head. "What's up?" For a moment, he held the soaring thought, *maybe this is over.*

"You look good, Bowman. I have a couple of questions for you."

"Then let's go to the fire circle, away from prying eyes and ears." Gabriel led him out to a circle of cut logs around a fire pit. The tall trees danced in the breeze and shimmered in the bright sun. "You here to tell me it's over?"

"Naw. I need to know if you've heard of a guy, worked at Wally's, name of Juan?"

"Juan, the detailer, yeah. He's a family man. Good guy! Not involved in any of this, at least not seriously." Gabriel folded his arms over his chest. "All he did was call me."

Kerry's lips were a grim line. "You say a family man? Wife, two kids?" Gabriel nodded and closed his eyes. "Bowman, you need to thank your lucky stars you are considered dead."

Gabriel rose from the log and kicked at the pebbles and dried leaves. "No! No, not them!"

Kerry got up and looked around, not wanting to draw a crowd. He stalked up to Gabriel and whispered, "The family was found this morning when they didn't show up at a baptism." Gabriel's eyes teared as his hand wiped at his face. "They were shot in their beds as they slept. This operation is bigger than Wally, the top believes in scorched earth."

Gabriel hefted a tree limb and beat the closest tree viciously. "They were immigrants. Legal all the way. They were good people. Don't tell me they were killed because of me." Dried wood splintered in every direction. Kerry turned his face away from Gabriel. "Goddamn, son of a bitch!" When he was left with a twig in his hand, he turned to Kerry. "I can't live with this on my head."

"It's not you, Gabe. Everyone associated with Wally is going down one way or another. You blowing the whistle just sped it up. I suspect Juan was involved in ways you didn't know."

"He couldn't be…"

"For somebody who spent time on the inside, you are a raging optimist. Every one of Wally's crew was involved. The night you were beaten, they had a shoot-out on the docks. That's why the cops didn't get to you. Juan was eliminated because of his connections in South America. You see why I say you can't contact your girl."

A chill ran up Gabriel's spine, thinking of how close he'd come to making Grace a victim. He wouldn't make that mistake again.

"Listen, we ran your credit report, and a joint listing on a few accounts came up. Your girl's name is Grace Lerner?"

"Yes."

"If I know her name, they know it too. The mob pulled a credit report, we saw an affiliated company ran it. This place where she works, she's working full time, on the record?"

Gabriel mulled it over. "She gets regular paychecks, yeah."

Kerry shook his head ominously. "That means she has a W-2, it's just a matter of time before they crack through enough records if they're still interested in finding her."

"You need to get us into witness protection…"

"It doesn't work like that, Gabriel. You are where you're safest. They think you're dead. As long as she's not spending your money, odds are they think she's in the wind and that's what we want."

"You need to call her, or go see her, tell her not to touch the bank account."

Again, Kerry shook his head. "I can't do that, but we can freeze the account. So even if she wanted to, she wouldn't have access."

Gabriel was resigned. "Whatever it takes to keep her safe." He drifted back to the cottage, absorbed in Kerry's alarming news. Ted bounded out the front door carrying a football and nearly bowled him over.

"Oh, man, sorry, Grease. I didn't mean to knock you down." Ted's hand steadied his friend. "Are you okay? You look pretty bleak."

Gabriel bit his lip and shook his head. "I'm gonna head for the chapel. I'll see you at the meeting, tonight." He wiped his face with the back of his hand and then worried the gold ring on his pinkie as he headed to the rustic chapel past the cottage.

****

Daily, Grace checked the mail slot in the front door for any type of letter. She tucked away the debit cards with Gabriel Lee, and Grace Lerner embossed on them. Aware of the need for security, she made a point of going to the largest branch of the library to use a public computer. *If he's alive, he may be using the money.* She wanted to check the account balance. Although Esther and Kendra tried to tell her he was dead, "You've seen the obituary." Grace's heart could not accept it as fact. She felt the energy of his love guarding and surrounding her. *He can't be dead.*

Gabriel told her to use the money if anything happened to him, she just couldn't do it. Today's inquiry was met with a stern image on the computer screen. "Speak with our online department for inquiries on this account."

Do I want to walk into a trap? No. What happened to the account? Did the authorities seize it or freeze it? Did it go into Probate? *It couldn't, I'm on the account. If they mailed something, it would go to the motor court.* No one has Esther's address. Has Gabriel emptied the account and taken off for parts unknown? *He said he loved me, he couldn't bear to have me hurt, but it would be easier to be on the run alone.* The obituary was published Monday, but the obituary didn't sound real. Grace didn't know what to think, so she clung to the concrete. The account was frozen.

****

She borrowed Esther's car under the guise of grocery and bank errands, but today's goal was discovering more about Gabriel's disappearance. On her way to the Eastern Avenue Police Station, she slid low in the seat and cruised by Wally's Garage. The FBI made no mistake about their intent with the massive warning signs. Every window was boarded, and the garage doors were padlocked with tamper-resistant tags. She saw the sooty remnants of a car fire at the curb. Unnerved, Grace goosed the gas pedal and got the hell out of the neighborhood. As her heart raced, she thought, *I am one big ball of wonky emotions.*

The modern colonial style architecture of the Southeast District Police Department stood out against the neighborhood. The later-built, stylish Johns Hopkins medical campus ate into many blocks of brick rowhomes. The police building was stark and perfunctory, just like their services. It was like a set from a 90's cop show.

Not knowing where else to go, Grace started with the lobby information desk. Her voice was low and hesitant. "Um…I don't know who to ask about this…my boyfriend, Gabriel Lee, was involved with helping the police catch a car theft ring? He…the papers said…he's…dead." She could feel the color drain from her face, and the officer behind the desk ran to guide her to a chair.

"Sit down, Miss, you look like you're gonna faint. Let's put your head between your knees." Grace felt the sweat slide down the sides of her face, even though the day was quite temperate. After a few moments, she felt better and sat up.

"Can you help me?"

The female officer with a kind face sat down next to Grace. She was spit and polished from her shiny black oxfords to the top of her severe bun. Her approachable eyes smiled as she spoke. "Do you know the detectives he was working with?"

"No."

"How long ago was this?"

Grace's thoughts pinballed in her head. *Will anything I say make sense?* "About four weeks ago…we have a joint bank account…he told me he might not make it out alive, so I kept watching the account.

Suddenly, it's frozen, and I can't see it. If he's spending the money, then I know he's alive. I watched for four weeks, and there was nothing…his obituary was just weird, it didn't sound like his life…Wally's Garage is boarded up with FBI signs…can anyone tell me what's going on?"

The desk officer was incredibly patient. "What's your name?"

Grace paused and covered her warm cheeks with her cooler hands. "Grace Lerner."

"Okay, you wait here, Ms. Lerner. I'll call Auto Theft, and I'm sure someone will be out to speak with you. May I get you some water?"

"Oh, thank you." Her eyes filled with hot tears. "I'm not feeling very well."

"You just wait here. I'll be right back."

****

Grace was given a bottle of water and escorted into what looked like the quintessential interrogation room by another female officer. "Would you care for coffee or a soda, Ms. Lerner?"

Grace raised the bottle of water from her lap and said, "No thanks, water is fine."

Detective Barbaran opened the door with more force than necessary. His silhouette filled the doorframe, and he stood there, silent for a beat, looking down at a file in his hands. Grace felt his gaze, and when he walked to stand before her, she raised her head to stare up at him. She sat, ankles crossed, hands folded in front of her on the metal table.

"Ms. Lerner? You're here about confidential informant Gabriel Lee?"

"Yes, sir."

"What's your relationship to Mr. Lee?"

"He and I are engaged." The diamond ring on her left hand felt tight when she tried to spin it as was her nervous habit.

"I see. So, you weren't married. You're not actually family."

"We have a bank account together…"

"Alright. Why don't you tell me what you already know?"

Does he even know what he's doing? Why is he asking me? They know what Gabriel offered.

Grace took a deep breath. "Mr. Lee offered a long history of auto thefts and their locations. He told me he would detail when and where the cars were delivered. Gabriel feared he would be blown off. He demanded I stay with people who didn't know him, for my safety. Now, I'm in the dark. What is going on?"

"The officer on the desk said something about you seeing an obituary on him?"

"Yes."

"I don't know what to say. Obituaries are pretty final."

Grace's throat closed, and she fought to speak. "Are you telling me he's dead?"

With a stony face, the detective smacked the file folder on his open palm. "A lot of people involved in this case are dead."

Grace wanted to scream. "Is Gabriel one of them?"

"You saw the obituary." There was a sharp rap on the two-way mirror. The detective turned and frowned. "I'm sorry, Ms. Lerner, I have an interview waiting for me. I'm afraid I have no other information for you." He walked out the door without a backward glance.

Grace dropped her head into her hands, her world spinning. The female officer who blended into the corner stepped up. "Do you need medical assistance, Ms. Lerner?"

Grace stood unsteadily. "No…I'm just a little dizzy. I'm fine. Let me get to my car."

"If you're unable to drive, we'd like you to sit in the air conditioning until you feel you can drive safely. Have you eaten today?"

"No, my stomach has been upset. I drank a bottle of water with my vitamins."

The woman raised a brow at her. "Have you seen a doctor lately? You must be stressed by the case."

"I'm stressed because I believe Gabriel is alive. I know if he could, he'd be with me. I know something has happened to him. Before I met him, his girlfriend shot him. He's been through so much…"

The female officer took Grace's elbow and led her to the front of the building. "There's a medical center to the right when you leave here. Do yourself a favor and see a doctor." It was great advice; Grace had no intention of taking.

"Thank you."

The officer's searching look was not lost on her. Grace felt the woman's scrutiny on her body and felt the officer suspected she was pregnant. Grace suspected it too. Her next stop would be the drug store for a pregnancy test.

****

Barbaran swaggered into the observation room. "Why'd you pull me out?"

Kerry narrowed his eyes, immune to his bluster. "You were done. You told her just enough, not too much, anymore, and you lose."

Barbaran copped an attitude. "I coulda got some info from her."

"She doesn't know anything, Barbaran. Gabe hid her to keep her out of it. He made a list after he dropped her off in Charles Village. Fishing would make her more suspicious."

Barbaran tossed the folder on the table. "You heard her. She doesn't believe the obit. Kids like that don't take no for an answer."

Kerry shook his head. "Do you know who she is?"

Barbaran assumed his pose. Hands on his hips, fingers splayed to emphasize the shield on his belt. "Who? The Governor's squeeze?"

Kerry picked up the empty folder and slid it under his arm. "That's Linda Lerner Darby's one and only child. The day that gal figures out how to rip us a new one, she'll remember your name, buddy." Kerry's laughter died after the door closed behind him. *If there ever were two kids in love, it was them.*

****

Tonight, Grace had a secret. The tangible evidence of Gabriel's love, their child, would not die from a gunshot wound. It would be her primary duty to deliver a healthy child, whether Gabriel was alive or not. The thought was daunting, raising a child without a father. Esther had done it, Kendra was doing it, she could do it, too.

Each evening Grace recorded a few thoughts in a journal from the dollar store before sleeping in the guestroom's twin bed. Her musings began with wondering if her tiny nugget of their love would be a car-loving tomboy or a tiny toe-dancer. Her left hand rested solemnly over her belly, praying a son would have the example of his loving father to guide him.

After a few lines of wild ideas, Grace listed all her justifications for believing Gabriel was alive, but in her heart, even she was beginning to doubt, and she had new responsibilities now.

On the occasional evenings, the three women were together, they watched DVDs and popped popcorn. Regardless of the show, she developed silent tears as the credits rolled. Work kept her sane. If there was an extra shift, Grace always volunteered. It was easier to fall exhausted into bed at night than to lay awake tormented by the thought of their lost future. Their tiny dividend exhausted her physically, but she'd heard the first trimester was energy sapping.

Eclectic concerts at the nearby university saw the trio out on Friday nights. It was free music and cheap eats at the various food trucks along the sidewalks. She calculated in her head the investment needed to run such a business and the revenue she might expect in return. She saw a snowball truck and missed her nightly walks with Gabriel for the frozen treat. The idea of having a root beer snowball with marshmallow topping made her think of the smile it brought to his blue-green eyes.

"You guys want anything from the snowball truck?" The craving was hitting hard.

Esther and Kendra shook their heads as they slurped on their smoothies.

"Okay, I'll be right back." She took her place in the long line, and the guy in front of her immediately turned around. Seeing her alone, his bright smile grew wider.

"It's not music without a snowball, is it?"

Grace looked around, wondering who he was talking to. He was tall, with a swimmer's build and dressed in Hurley's gear from his sandals to his tee shirt. His thumb was hooked in the back pocket of his jeans. Dark hair was professionally styled, and his black eyelashes framed sky-blue eyes, exquisitely. He was handsome in a mother-approved way.

"Absolutely." Her tone was non-committal a definite challenge to a guy who gave her his panty-dropping smile.

"You go to school here?"

Grace shook her head, no.

"I'm in the bioengineering program." He announced proudly. "Third year."

"Nice." She nodded.

"Are you a native Baltimorean?"

"Sure, hon." She affected Baltimore's Hamden accent.

"I get such a kick out of John Water's films."

She nodded her head and grinned, silently. The line shuffled a bit further. *Is this guy hitting on me or am I overly sensitive?* "Do you know what time it is?"

He glanced at his watch, a Chrome Shinola, that wouldn't have stood up to Ocean City surf. "About seven forty-three."

"Oh, that's good. I'm meeting my fiancé over there." With her left hand, she gestured vaguely across the street to a block of taverns. "I like to have something in my stomach before I start drinking."

Although her ring was small, the college junior received the message. His smile evaporated, and he nodded mutely and turned around. The thought of meeting new guys gave her a stomach ache. Although she found herself several weeks away from Gabriel, she was no further from being devoted entirely to him and their child.

****

Grace woke to jazz music from her alarm clock. It was a Monday, still a special day in her mind, even without Gabriel. She hadn't slept well Sunday night, and dragging herself out of bed was a real chore. In dawn's early darkness, she padded quietly to the bathroom. Her nausea surprised her. *Morning sickness?* Here it comes. She dug for crackers in her purse and sipped on a soda. Dressing for work, in a trim black skirt and smart white shirt, she wondered how soon she'd show and then the secret would be out. She grabbed her backpack and left for the restaurant. This secret pregnancy was a treasure. Gabriel's gift of new life was incredibly precious to her.

The rocking Light Rail upset her stomach further, and she ran for the door two stops before her usual exit. She needed to get to the bathroom and jogged to the back door of the café.

"Looks who's green in the gills today. Too much Guinness last night?" Caleb, the Irish dishwasher, ribbed her as she ducked through the kitchen into the bathroom. She stuck her tongue out at him and slammed the door behind her. She managed to quell the retching with a courtesy flush, washed her hands and returned to the dining area.

19

Ted was an all-around nice guy, the last guy you'd expect to have a drinking problem. That's the way this place seemed, the way a prison never has any guilty inmates. When they weren't working on their sessions and their individual therapies, Gabriel and Ted talked cars.

Gabriel brought two mugs of coffee to the table where Ted was cutting a small tray of brownies. "Pops, why do you call me Grease?"

Ted snickered and put a brownie on a napkin. "Kid, your hands. You aren't a dishwasher; I can see that. Plus, when the golf cart crapped out in front of the cottage, you made it purr in ten minutes. You're either a mechanic or MacGyver."

Gabriel shrugged. "You got me, I'm no MacGyver, I must be a mechanic."

"Like I wouldn't know a grease-monkey if I saw one." He pointed at the brownie. "Have a bite before I steal it. I swear they make these with cocaine."

Gabriel took a bite. "You know mechanics?"

Ted nodded. "Only for about twenty-five years. I'm taking a little break from service management." He tilted his head in the general direction of the car lot.

"Sweet! I'd love to be a mechanic in an honest shop."

"I work for good people. They had my back when Merri got sick, and I started drinking. Once she died, they called me into the office and told me my job would be waiting when I was clean and sober."

"Wow, that's support. You must mean a lot to them." Gabriel was gobsmacked, it probably wouldn't do to say his former employer wanted him dead.

****

The insights Gabriel gained in therapy were a revelation to him. Their group therapist, Jon, was a bear of a man, with mahogany skin, bushy hair and a thick beard. He was someone who cut to the heart of things without pulling punches.

Today was Gabriel's day in the hot seat. This session, he was face to face with Jon in the center of the group. "So, when there wasn't enough money for rent, what did Moms do?"

Gabriel looked around and rubbed his palms on his thighs. "When I was little she'd drop me off at Gran's. It wasn't until I got older I realized what she was doing."

"And what was it?"

"Getting drunk, or high, taking in guys to make some money." He glanced around seeing how the group accepted this. Many obviously couldn't relate. He looked down, and his face flushed with embarrassment.

Jon nodded and looked around at the group. "Oh, I know what you're thinking, man. Nobody here knows what that's like. But watch this. Anybody else in this group have memories of a time when things got rough at home? Say, with your mothers?"

A plump young woman with straight hair and designer jeans timidly raised her head. "When my folks were getting a divorce. My mom would drink or take pills."

A middle-aged businessman who rarely spoke flushed bright pink. "It was like Who's Afraid of Virginia Woolf in my house, only they weren't movie stars, and nobody called 'cut'."

Jon nodded. "Now, all of you folks are from different backgrounds, but you all saw the same thing. The parent or parents who used, all gave you this message: *Child, this is what you do when things get tough. You drink or drug.*"

"Son of a bitch!" Gabriel said. "You're right!"

Jon waited a moment for the group to process his words. "Getting it is one part of the equation. Insight alone will get you nowhere. Now you know, most of you were taught as children, the way we handle problems is to escape in the unhealthiest way possible. Just having insight is crap unless you know what to do with it. So, what are healthier ways of dealing with problems? Gabriel, you're in the hot seat, why don't you start us out?"

Gabriel thought back to the night he confessed to Grace. "Start with honesty. Identify the problem, be frank about it, and brainstorm solutions."

"Good. What else? Who's next?"

****

While their heads were down over the chess pieces, Ted picked up his knight and asked, "You talk about your girlfriend, what's her name? Princess?" He looked up with a twinkle in his eye and Gabriel realized he knew perfectly well she was 'Princess'. "I've never seen her come to family night or family session. You and I are the only two 'baching' it here during family time. What's that about?"

Gabriel lifted his elbows to the table and rubbed his thumbs on his temples as he thought a beat. "She's not around here. But she's definitely the 'one'."

"And yet, she's not supporting your treatment?"

Gabriel rested his hands flat on the table and sat back, shaking his head. "She's giving me the ultimate support. When we met, two very broken worlds collided. We've become each other's guiding stars, but we can't be together." Gabriel looked around. There was no one else in the room. Still, he spoke softly. "You know I have special circumstances. You *cannot* share this with anyone, for everyone's safety."

Ted put the chess piece down and kept his finger on it. "Seriously?"

Gabriel's steely gaze held. "When everything went down, I had to hide her. All we ever needed was each other, but the road to our future has been Death Race: Beyond Anarchy."

"Have I been a target these last few weeks?"

"No. My princess has her own bogeyman after her. Besides, you don't know who I am. We have to leave it at that for now."

"Are they hiding you here?"

Gabriel leaned back and stretched out his long legs, his elbows on the arms of the uncomfortable chair. He steepled his hands in thought for a minute. "I'm a special witness on a working case. If I weren't safe here, they'd carry me out under cover of night, and you'd wake up, and I'd be gone."

Ted shook his head. "I gather the injuries you came in with were no simple mugging."

Gabriel nodded his head. "I can only hope she doesn't believe I'm dead. Ted, the way you talk about Merri… You know, she's my Merri."

"Each man gets one chance for the love of their life." Ted nodded.

"Considering where we are, on a mental health campus, you may think I'm nuts. I don't blame you if you don't believe me. Seriously, I was brought in for my safety and treatment. I've been through a lot of mental and physical changes in the past few months. One day, and I hope it's soon, I'll be able to tell you the whole story. Maybe you can meet her, then." He grinned. "You could write a book."

"I've lived with you long enough to know you're saner than most of the people here, so I guess I have to believe you. I'm guessing the letter you wanted me to mail was to her?"

Gabriel cocked a brow. "Yeah, that was a bad idea. I'm glad you held me to honesty. I found out later that day, some bad things happened to people I cared about. I might have put Princess in danger with that letter."

"I'm sorry this happened to you, Grease. It seems like bad things have driven us all here. So, she's not in on your secret?"

Gabriel shook his head. "They ran an obituary. She probably believes I'm dead."

"Wow, no wonder you want to get in touch with her. You've finally decided against it?" Ted studied Gabriel's face. "I respect that decision."

"It was a bad idea." Gabriel broke off and stared morosely out the window at the wistful movement of the trees. "Who knows if I'll ever get to see her again? I guess I'll have to believe…"

****

Their last week of treatment found the various residents arranging outpatient programs. Ted and Gabriel were advised to seek continued care in a halfway house since they each lived alone.

"Check your mailbox, Grease. I got my letter." Ted waved an open envelope at Gabriel.

"I can't believe it. It's like we just got here." He moved to the bank of cubbies near the cabin front door. The white envelope popped open easily. "Foster House in Towson?"

Ted raised a thumb. "Yup. We got our assignments approved. We move in Friday, and I can report back to work Monday." He turned to Gabriel. "We've got to find you gainful employment, kid. Don't think you can sit on your ass and cook three meals a day for us."

"Gordon Ramsey I'm not! I'm at the end of my recipes. Have I ever shared with you I hate to cook? My girl can make a banquet with tuna and Bisquick. Me, I can't make dinner with a cookbook and a grocery store. We'd be eating Royal Farms chicken every night."

Ted patted his slimmer waistline. "Since you've got me exercising, I think I'll pass. Seriously, on Tuesday morning I want you to come into the dealership and apply for a job."

Gabriel shuffled and grimaced. "I gotta check with my wranglers. My future isn't exactly mine to plan, at this point." He fingered his six-month sobriety chip in his pants pocket.

"I'm sorry, I forgot about that. I understand. You let me know when you're ready."

"That would be sweet, Pops. I'll make a call first thing Monday. I miss working, my hands are getting soft."

Ted prowled around the room, energized. "I miss driving. I'm so glad I didn't get a D.U.I. I love taking trips up to Pennsylvania on weekends. You like chocolate?"

Gabriel spread his hands out. "I heard Hershey sells a ten-pound candy bar up there."

Ted aimed his finger at his friend. "You are so right! We could chew through that!"

****

"Anybody see Grace?" Andy bellowed back to the kitchen staff. "She's got a table out there waiting for silverware." Heads raised and shook, then returned to their kitchen duties. Andy threw open the back door, lazy servers hid back there to smoke, no Grace. He ran down the steps to the basement, he'd rip her a new one now, this made them all look bad. No, she wasn't down there either.

Andy heard the footfalls overhead going to the employee's restroom and then the call for help. Nothing dramatic, just a long, loud, "Somebody!" That brought the kitchen staff to stand in the doorway and stare at their passed-out friend, blood pooled between her thighs.

****

When all the medical attention was rendered, and the emergency passed, Grace was a shell of a girl in a lonely bed. She heard the nurse promise Esther and Kendra they'd be allowed to see her once the doctor finished.

"How pregnant was I?"

"Looks like about eight weeks." The doctor scrolled through the medical notes.

"I was on the pill; I didn't think I'd get pregnant so fast." She whispered.

"When was your last pill?" He countered, tucking the tablet under his arm.

"A couple of months ago. I've been on them since I was sixteen. I've read it takes a few months for you to ovulate."

"Every woman is different. You picked up some misinformation. I want you to follow up with the OB/GYN clinic next week…"

Grace stared at her hospital bracelet, then her engagement ring. The blanket was scratchy cotton. The fuzzy socks were an odd comfort as she half listened as the doctor spoke, "…you came through the procedure just fine. I'm sorry for the loss of your pregnancy…" Grace's hands rested on her tummy. She wanted a shower. A long pulsating shower to beat the sadness out of her. "I saw no anatomical abnormalities…" Grace shook her head silently, oblivious to his words "…that would account for the miscarriage." Grace was mute. "So, this type of loss is typically caused by chromosomal problems…" His empathy was touching. "…random, one-time events… you and your partner should have no problems when the time comes for another child."

Their baby had been her last connection to Gabriel. Now, their sweet child was gone. Was their baby a boy or a girl? She was robbed of even dreaming a future for their child. Grace sat in numb desolation. Where was her partner, her fiancé?

****

Esther was her rock. In a moment where Esther could have served platitudes, she kept her mouth shut except to say she was sorry. They rode home in silence, save for Grace's intermittent sniffles. *Today is the worst day.* She bolstered herself. *Tomorrow will be a better day.* She was sure of it.

****

Grace's period returned within a few weeks, and with it, she expected some physical release from the lonely twinges she felt without Gabriel. She circled several memorable dates for them in the Hallmark Store datebook, and now she regarded the little pocketbook as a chronicle of their short love affair. She viewed the date of the D and C as a loss for them and tucked the little book inside her underwear drawer.

"Cici, you ever going to look up from your lap and live again?" Esther posed the question this unusually quiet Tuesday.

"I think I'm going to go to school." Grace began slowly. "I've been looking online, if I can't get into the culinary college, I'll go to the community college."

"I think that's a fine plan. I'm sure your father made arrangements for your education."

"Money for school is tied up with Mother and Arthur. If I want anything, it's up to me."

"I cannot believe your daddy didn't leave you money for school."

"If I have to complete the FAFSA forms, it's going to connect right back to Mother and Arthur. I can't have him finding me. I have to figure out how to stand on my own two feet."

"You go to your Daddy's lawyer, not your Mother's. Start with a phone call." Esther folded her arms over her chest and stood authoritatively. "It's three in the afternoon, make that call."

****

Each workday, Grace rode the Light Rail back and forth to the bistro. Today, there was a smile in her heart. The conversation with the legal assistant in the law office paid rich dividends. There was a college fund administrated by the attorney. Her mother had no authority there. All Grace needed to do was submit her letter of acceptance, and the bill would be paid. She could breathe for the first time since she left home. Gabriel might be gone, but she had a future Arthur couldn't touch.

****

Calvert College, founded in 1895 was the site of Foster House, Gabriel's half-way home.

It was the original woman's dormitory. Now it housed the college's progressive mental health counseling center. The lower floor served as offices for interns in the psychology and social work programs. During the day and early evening, they saw students for individual sessions. At night, the basement rec room welcomed A.A./N.A. meetings and group therapy sessions. The second floor accommodated a communal kitchen, living room and dining room. The rest of the space was renovated into tiny single bedrooms giving the residents a sense of privacy and independence.

To Gabriel it felt like the Navy, the room barely larger than his ship space, was a comfort. Once again, he was part of something meaningful. Gabriel held his room key in his hand and nodded at Ted, a few feet away at his door.

Ted turned the key in the lock. "You know the next move will be to better digs. I've got a place on almost an acre in Fox Chapel. You could live on one side, I'll live on the other, and we can meet at the pool table in the basement."

"I don't know what I'd do with all that space! I might have to stop shopping at Goodwill. Seriously, man, I don't want to intrude on you. You don't have to take care of me like a stray you picked up."

Ted walked toward Gabriel and leaned against the wall. "It isn't like that. I don't have a family. My Merri fixed our home up like a showplace. I earned an executive paycheck, and she made us a beautiful home, but there was never anyone to share it with."

Gabriel blinked at the offer. "I'd learn to cut grass if you want me to earn my keep."

"If you come back there with me, it would be good for both of us. Who knows where life will take us in the future?"

For now, at the half-way house, Gabriel was in a place where he could sleep with both eyes shut. He could be in good company or take a breather and work out at the college gym. And maybe, he was days closer to being done with the investigation.

****

Being the lone resident without a job was a bummer. In fact, he would ordinarily have been required to have a job or be actively looking for one as a condition of staying at Foster House. His 'special circumstances' prevented that. Gabriel knew himself well enough to know if he stayed jobless, he'd circle the drain. Ted was in a position to get him interviewed, and Gabriel wanted that job. He ushered Detective Kerry and a new guy, better dressed than a detective, with a different air about him, into the kitchen. "You want coffee?" He gestured to the stools at the kitchen island while he headed to the coffee maker.

Kerry planted himself on a perch and nodded toward his companion. "Gabriel, this is Special Agent Hawkins from the FBI. Your case is now Federal."

Gabriel's brows rose as his lips drew a grim line.

Hawkins' gaze never left Gabriel. He felt as if the agent's steely persona scrutinized every detail of his walk, talk, and posture. "If you're brewing coffee, I'll take one. Black." Hawkins extended a smile and a handshake across the island.

Gabriel shrugged as he pulled three mugs from the shelf. "Good to meet you, Agent Hawkins. Black is good because I don't have cream and sugar." The coffee pot chugged, and Gabriel took a stool opposite the two authority figures in his life. "Am I the last man standing?" Gabriel leaned his forearms on the counter. That thought sifted through several layers in his mind and a checklist, and he still decided *I need to say this.*

"That's one way to look at it, Gabriel." Kerry made work of shifting the papers in front of him.

Gabriel felt his face drain, then flush. He stared at the specks in the countertop and shook his head. "I should have just packed my car and taken Grace to Frostburg. We could have lived in a little cabin and been done with this."

"Sure, you could have left, and it might have taken years for them to find you, but would you want to live constantly looking over your shoulder?"

"My girl thinks I'm dead. She's eighteen, how long is she going to wait for a guy like me? I'm an ex-con, got no job. I'm a bust. She'd be better off without me."

Agent Hawkins studied him, and Gabriel braced for the worst. "Bowman, I've looked into your records. There's no doubt in my mind you went to prison on a bum rap. I know how hard it is to find legit work after you've been inside. I don't fault you for fighting to survive, working for Wally. By all accounts, you're a damn good mechanic. You tried to get out on your own and came to the authorities when they wouldn't let you out. Your record in the Navy-- moving up to Petty Officer Third Class in less than four years, that's all proof of character."

Gabriel kept his eyes down, wondering what the catch was. "Thanks." He mumbled as he poured the coffee. "That and fifty cents will buy me a pack of gum." Kerry snorted and shook his head.

Hawkins looked up from his notes. "When you left, you missed the exam for Petty Officer Second Class. What was that about?"

"I was antsy. The opportunities weren't opening up. I thought if I left and got my degree, I could come back as an officer."

Hawkins shook his head. "Nobody told you about the Navy Reserve Officer's Training Corp?"

Gabriel shrugged. "Agent Hawkins, I got no guidance coming out of the Navy. Nobody knew anything. I made hasty choices. If I'd known better, I'd have stayed in the Navy, gone to school and lived a good life." He toyed with the coffee cup. "Kids who raise themselves make lots of mistakes."

"Well, let's see if we can't give you a better foundation. I know you want to be with Grace, and at the same time, it's a risk for her to know you're alive. But Gabriel, she can't save you. If you want to make a life, eventually, you have to make better choices. You don't do that hiding in a cabin, waiting to die."

Gabriel turned away from the men and walked to the sink. The sun shone through the small window, and he sought more gracious words, but they were not there. "I thought taking care of Grace and turning Wally in *was* a better choice, and you should see my medical records. They tap-danced on me until they were tired. What's it got me?"

"I think you're looking at this wrong." Hawkins began, and Gabriel wheeled around.

"You have a straight life. You got educated and got a job, and nothing is going to derail you. I've got zip. And when I get out of here, I'll still have a record and no place to live. My car was torched with all my belongings. I'm wearing charity clothes and have been for weeks. My bank account is frozen. How am I supposed to look at this?"

Kerry tucked his chin, his arms folded over his grey lapels, and he rubbed at his left cheek with this thumb. He was mute.

Gabriel huffed out, "Yeah, thanks for being an honest citizen," and then stood stony-faced.

"See, the problem here is, you're not finished. This whole case has got to close before you're gonna see the results you want. I can't tell you everything, but this mob was involved in a lot more than boosting cars. I'm talking about drugs, guns, human trafficking. If you hadn't made a report on that Saturday, a freighter would have left the dock fully loaded. Your info about the car ring was a piece of the puzzle the cops didn't have. You saved a lot of lives that night, and in my book, we owe you."

Gabriel threw up his hands. "Look, I'm not asking for a pony under a Christmas tree. I want to work at Ted's dealership. I need a clean record to work there."

"We're aware of that Mr. Bowman." Hawkins retrieved an envelope from his briefcase. "That's why we created the Gabriel Bowman identity for you."

Gabriel scowled. "Just because the name changes… ex-cons don't get work."

Hawkins continued with a quelling look. "As I was saying, Gabriel Bowman has no record. Everything else is similar, right up to getting out of the Navy, which, according to these papers was three months ago." He slid the driver's license, birth certificate, and social security card to Gabriel. Here are your honorable discharge papers, as well as a resume for your job interview tomorrow."

Gabriel picked each piece up and gave careful scrutiny to the items detailed. When he put the last page down, he was near tears. Holding the birth certificate and remaining documents, he asked, "Is this who I'll be for the rest of my life?"

Hawkins chuckled. "Gabriel, it's up to you. I suggest you see this man." He slid a doctor's appointment card to Gabriel. "Your appointment is Saturday morning for the consultation on laser treatments to remove that tattoo." He gestured to Gabriel's neck. Gabriel's hand flew up to cover the crude barbed-wire ink. "I suggest you keep your collar buttoned at work until it's gone."

"Wow, man, I don't know what to say. I'm sorry if I was an ass. I'm not used to help." Hawkins nodded. Gabriel's mouth hung open. "What about my parole officer?"

"Gabe Lee is deceased. You're done with a parole officer."

Gabriel began to pace, his breath coming in excited gasps. Kerry slapped him on the back. "Oh, now, come on kid, so it's not a pony, but you look pretty excited."

Hawkins brought him a glass of cold water. "You'll have to buy the pony yourself, but that's after you get this job. Look around you. You're on a college campus. Enroll in school while you can walk to class. Make those dreams of yours come true."

When Gabriel pulled himself together, his eyes were damp, and he was humble. "Thank you. That sounds so lame for what you've done for me, but just…thank you, I won't waste this opportunity. I swear to God, I won't."

"Yeah, I know you won't kid, you've paid with blood." He reached out to shake Gabriel's hand. "Mr. Bowman, go get'em, I'll be in touch with updates on the case as they happen."

20

The Light Rail train rocked a tired Grace nearly to sleep. It jerked to a stop, and a young woman in the black and white checked trousers and a white jacket of the Culinary School jumped on. Grace saw her almost every day.

On her day off, Grace went to the school to speak with a guidance counselor. She came in under the deadline for the fall session. *I'm a real adult now*, she thought as she fingered the class schedule. *School starts in one week!*

****

The peace of an afternoon on the front porch glider was broken by the sound of a cranky Kendra attempting to soothe a crabby infant in her back carrier. The stroller with the wonky wheel, carrying groceries, played an incongruous tune to Antwoine's cries. The cacophony drew closer with every rotation of the squeaky wheel. Grace ran down the steps to the front gate. "What can I help you with?"

Kendra turned around and offered her crying child. "Get him off my back before I sell him to the circus!"

Grace unwrapped the straps and lifted the kicking boy out of the carrier. He gave her a gummy grin and then let loose a juicy, wet fart they both knew was not a fart. "Ewe… I'm so glad he didn't do that in the carrier."

Kendra's brown eyes widened. "He's done it before. Thanks, Grace, for being here." The young mother tipped back the stroller and pushed it up the few steps to the porch. "It's October, the caramel corn is out. Look at the bag from the Sav-a-Lot!" Kendra pushed inside the wide wooden front door and into the living room.

Esther came out from the kitchen at the sound of 'caramel corn'. "I heard you two. Put that away till after dinner. I've got seared rockfish with lemon butter over wild rice. You girls get in here."

****

Grace's nightly habit was to clear and wash the dishes. Esther was the cook, and Kendra was on baby bath duty. Esther scooted around the kitchen.

Thinking of ideas for tomorrow's dinner, or watching me wash her dishes? Grace spoke up. "We could use another car around here, couldn't we?"

"We could use a cruise to the Bahamas too. I hear the young men look positively delicious!"

Grace slanted her a satirical look. "Really, Esther? Are you a cougar?"

"If there were prey worthy of gettin' all this movin' I would be!" She held her arms out and shimmied. "It's hard to stop, once I get started. The most I see around here is those old gigolo men who look for women with their husband's pensions. I have no intentions of cleaning up after them!"

Grace pulled the plug from the sink and dried her hands. *What if I could give back to the people who do so much for me? This is the right thing to do.* "Daddy left me a car in storage. Before Gabriel left, he got it running. I think it will fit on the parking pad out back. You already park out front."

Esther shook her head. "That's because that joker next door thinks he owns the street in front of both our houses. But, you're right, we could use another car."

Grace made a face at the thought of driving the Hearst/Olds 442 with the racing paint job. "It was Daddy's Oldsmobile. It's big. We could drive it on vacation."

"An Oldsmobile? We could live in it! Child, those cars are monsters. Have you ever driven anything that long?" Esther poured herself a cold glass of water and sat down. She motioned to the chair next to her. "If you can swing the insurance, I'll clear out the weeds around the pad. You're going to need every square inch of the backyard."

Grace sat down, about to explode with her news. "Can we call Kendra down? I want to share some news with both of you."

Kendra arrived at the kitchen table with the baby monitor in her hand. The caramel corn and iced tea were set before them. Esther leaned back and smiled. "Kendra, Cici has some news for us."

Grace grinned and looked at both of them, then, drew in a big breath. "You were right, Esther, my daddy's lawyer is the administrator over my college fund. He says I have enough for four years of undergraduate, including room and board and books. If I decide to pursue graduate school, they have that covered too." Both women oohed and awed over Grace's good fortune. "But that's not all of it. I was accepted at Baltimore Culinary College, and I start in three weeks. I also have a car in storage up in Towson. That should free us up on transportation."

Kendra's face fell. "Do you have to move into a dorm? Are you leaving?"

"Oh, no, Kendra. In fact, the good news is, the money for my room and board will go into the family pot and make things easier for you, Esther."

Esther shook her head. "Oh, honey…"

Grace pointed to her. "You are about to become a landlady. The check will come directly to you." She saw tears fill Esther's eyes. "I'll be in school for two and a half years, and then I'll have my Bachelor's in hospitality management. The degree is accelerated, it packs more hours into fewer days. I won't have a lot of social time, but that's okay with me. Ladies, our lives are about to get better."

****

At precisely nine the following morning, Gabriel found himself seated before Aaron Golding, the head of Human Resources and Bob Washington, the Service Manager of Mercedes of Towson. After introductions were made, they got down to asking him about why he settled in Baltimore. Gabriel's heel tapped, causing his knee to bobble. He steadied it with his hand. *Maybe they didn't see it from across this vast mahogany desk.*

"You can see I grew up here, and even though my family is gone now, it still feels like home. Plus, I'm interested in enrolling in Calvert College's business management program."

"You would be agreeable to taking our service classes, I assume? That may require some travel and time out of state."

"Yes, Sir, I like to travel."

The Human Resources Manager spoke up. "You have some excellent references here, Mr. Bowman. Even from one of our Corporate Execs, Ted Warner."

"I've been fortunate to meet and get to know some good people." *Lots of scary, nasty ones, too.*

After thirty minutes of back and forth and mutual smiles, the two men asked him to have a cup of coffee in the service area. He nodded and left the room, hoping his knees wouldn't give out. He played with the button on the borrowed charcoal sports coat and looked at himself in the mirrored wall behind the coffee pot. His borrowed navy-blue turtleneck didn't look too bad, and it covered the barbed wire tattoo nicely. He smelled freshly baked chocolate chip cookies, there for the enjoyment of the service customers. *A cookie would be good right now, but I don't want to look like I'm pillaging the service snacks. If I get the job, I'll grab one on the way out.* He over-sugared his black coffee and burned the roof of his mouth gulping it down.

The Human Resource Manager made a half-step out of the office. "Mr. Bowman?" Gabriel snapped to attention. He followed the man back to the stiff chair in front of the desk. He noticed there were papers, face down, before him. *Good God, what are those?*

"We usually take more time in making an offer, but we talked to Ted, and he said you were currently fielding other offers. We don't want the dealership in Pikesville to snap you up."

Aaron chuckled at Bob's comment as he turned the papers over and slid them to Gabriel. "We appreciate mechanics with a strong work ethic, and we like to hire vets. This is our standard offer for a man with your experience. Of course, you can see the benefits on the next page." Gabriel's gaze followed bulleted points, but he was beyond the ability to read each word. "We start health insurance on day thirty-one, and I can give you a few minutes to read this if you want."

The two men sat back while Gabriel tried to swallow his pounding heart. They offered three times what he'd ever made before, plus, he'd have benefits, vacation, health insurance and discounts on things he thought he'd never be able to buy. Plus, the uniforms were included, with a free pair of steel-toed boots every year. He shifted back in the chair as he tried, without success, to comprehend the scope of the offer.

He slowed his breathing and bit his bottom lip, remembering what Grace said about the first person to speak in a deal, loses. He scratched at his jaw and nodded sagely. *That wasn't considered speaking, was it?*

Bob glanced at Aaron, *is he worried a deal is slipping away from them?* "Do you need forty-eight hours to think about this, Gabriel?"

Gabriel sat up straighter and placed the papers on the desk. The men froze. He drew an ink pen out of his breast pocket. *A gentleman always carries a pen.* Gabriel smiled. "Where do I sign?"

"We have three days of orientation in the office. If it fits with your schedule, you can begin tomorrow, and then on Monday we'll put you on the service deck with a team leader to get you started."

****

The two-hundred-year-old half-way house that was Gabriel's home, for now, was damp and chilly. He sat in the common area watching the retrofitted gas flames flicker. He tried to read the pages of his new employee handbook, but having no experience in the civilian job force, it was painfully tedious. One thing was sure, he'd sit down with Ted and go over it point by point.

I can't blow this. In the Navy the rules were simple. Take orders, do the work, stay out of trouble. I'm not sure what the rules are in a traditional and legal civilian world. He stared into the stunted flames and watched for demons to dance, they spelled one word, 'doubt'.

"Gabriel!" Ted called amiably from the doorway.

"Yeah." Gabriel still focused on the dancing flames.

"You were awfully uptight at meeting tonight." Ted read Gabriel as a father read a son. He stood behind the sofa and patted on Gabriel's shoulders, then walked around and sat in the wing chair opposite him.

"Today, when they offered me a great job, I realized I need to be on top of my game. But Ted, there are so many things I'm not used to. Just the benefits are mind-boggling. I've never been given this much."

"Well, you have. In the Navy, it was an all-inclusive package. Here, they call it benefits, but it's not much different. Treat this job as if you're still in the Navy. If you have questions, just ask."

"I've been in bad situations so long, they look normal. I'll snap out of that with my first paycheck." He paused and looked at Ted sincerely. "What you did for me, that's righteous, man." Gabriel ran his hand over his hair, grown even longer in the past eight weeks. "I need a haircut. They'll think I'm a grunge fan."

"I could use one too. Let's take a walk, there's a barbershop the next street over, near the Ice Creamery."

"Em! Ice cream and a haircut, just like when my Gran bribed me to sit still." Ted laughed. As they signed out, Gabriel dug into his wallet for the doctor's appointment card. "You ever heard of tattoo removal?"

Ted winced. "Yeah."

"Does it hurt? Ever done it?"

"I'm sure it doesn't feel good, but it can't feel any worse than getting one. I've never gotten a tattoo – don't like needles." He shuddered.

"Well, I guess I'll be able to tell you all about it, pretty soon. Until it's gone, turtlenecks will be my fashion statement."

"Lucky cold weather is coming."

"Saturday's my consultation with the tattoo doctor, but it looks like they're sending me to Alabama for a week, so I'll wait till I get back to schedule the treatments."

****

Grace dug into the bottom drawer for a sweatshirt, it was chilly downtown, in the mornings.

"Tsavros needs help with his lunch wagon, Kendra, I can't go to the fall fest this morning."

"Tsavros? Who's Tsavros? Does he have a brother who cooks?"

"That's the problem. Tsavros needs help because his family is tied up doing something. I'll be back just in time to wash the Gyros smell off and get dressed to work the wedding reception."

Kendra's eyebrows wagged at her. "Well, make him buy you lunch."

"Oh, he's paying me for this. Ten dollars an hour, cash. He says he makes a ton right there at the hospital on Calvert."

"When the Giant grocer starts accepting 'tons' in payment, that's cool. Till then, cash is good."

****

Grace stood on the sidewalk and directed Tsavros as he backed the stainless-steel lunch wagon right up to the curb. Once he parked, he jumped out, chocked the tires, and started leveling the wagon. "If you hand out these flyers, we can pump up the business. It looks a little slow."

Grace accepted the stack and took off for the lobbies of the hospital and medical offices. People took the menus and nodded following the seductive aroma of Greek coffee and pastries in the morning.

"Grace!" Tsavros waved her back to the wagon. "Don't stand on the corner. The ambulances jump the curb sometimes. I don't want to lose my first non-family employee." He held up the first Gyro of the day. "Now that we're sold out of pastries let's work on the lunch menu."

Grace accepted the lighter blue flyers. "Seriously? Can't you put both menus on a page?"

Tsavros made a face. "You sound like my mother. Sure, I could. Jeez, Grace…"

Grace focused on the crowded sidewalk across the traffic-choked street. An ambulance up the road changed gurneys while the paramedics gabbed. Traffic slowed when a man let his wife off at the medical building and blocked the lane. Horns serenaded the area and drew Grace's attention.

Her ears caught the music of the street sounds, as people strode up and down the sidewalk, most folks in brightly colored scrubs. Her gaze passed over a multitude of homogenized citizens trudging through their day. Suddenly, Grace was drawn to the tallest guy in the crowd, wearing a gray blazer, his dark glasses sitting on a profile a sculptor would envy. The sunlight blinded her, and when she blinked her eyes open, all she saw was the glint of his milk chocolate brown waves as his head bobbed in the rhythm of his walk. It was the *walk*, it was familiar. It was the same kick-out strut with a little saunter that was totally Gabriel.

C'mon, Grace, every guy you see isn't Gabriel. Before she could chase after the man, he ducked into the medical building and disappeared as swiftly as he'd appeared. She looked at her watch. It was noon. She'd keep an eye on the building as best she could, and hope he'd leave by the same door. By three P.M., when the truck was closed down, Grace still hadn't seen him, or perhaps she'd missed him. She sighed. *Maybe he'll be back next Saturday at noon.* It was a faint hope, but she'd watch this building every chance she could. *If fate is returning him, it's taking its own stinking time.*

21

Gabriel walked into the stylishly furnished and antiseptically scented waiting room. He was on edge. When he'd gotten his Navy art, he'd been pleasantly blasted. When the thugs inked him in prison, he was on high alert. *That's another memory I don't want to tap into.* One corner of the room featured high concept motorcycle art and flashy bike magazines. After he checked in, he headed there to pick up a copy of Street Bikes, thumbing through the pages but not seeing them. *I'm going to feel the removal more than I felt the tattoo.*

"Gabriel Bowman?" The pert medical assistant called his name over a chart. With a nod, he followed her through a door and down a long hall. She gestured into the room and the exam table as she pulled out a blue paper gown and drape. "Please, remove your clothes and wear the gown open in the front."

He made a slow turn to see everything in the room. *Those watercolors are supposed to calm me down?* "He only needs to see my neck." He slid out of his blazer and pushed his sleeves up.

The assistant was on her medical-authority trip, "Doctor prefers his patients in their briefs, gown, and drape."

"I'm keeping these." He held up both fists, and his muscles flexed, moving the Technicolor art on his forearms.

"Oh." She backed out of the room; her gaze self-consciously locked on his blue-green eyes. He chuckled and pulled his shirt over his head. The paper was cold and plastic, like deli wrap. He wished he'd brought the magazine with him. Time passed, and he quit looking at his watch.

A light knock on the door, and it burst open. "Mr. Bowman, I'm Doctor Levy, good to meet you." He held out a steady hand which Gabriel half-heartedly shook.

"I'm… I appreciate your help. Is it going to hurt a lot?"

"You've got a lot of art here, let's take a look." The doctor waved his pen at Gabriel's ink.

"Oh, I'm not here for this." His hand flew to his neck. "This, this is what has to go."

"I get the picture, just from your expression. That wasn't applied with the same love and care these were." The doctor took Gabriel's hand, rotated his arm to see the history and travelogue he wore. When he saw the Angel's face, he took a second look at Gabriel's. "Wow, that's quite a likeness." Then, the doctor lowered his headlight and followed the art up his chest to the crudely drawn barbed wire choker. He drew the skin taut and nodded. "Luckily, they didn't have the right tools to go deep…"

Gabriel barely tolerated the inspection. His heart rate accelerated; the post-traumatic stress of the inking shook him. His head snapped away from the doctor's inspection. "Mr. Bowman, are you okay?"

Gabriel clenched his jaw and shook his head. "Bad memories…"

The doctor sat back and continued with the description of the laser treatment. Gabriel had plenty of questions when he walked into the office, but now…

****

Rancid grease, bright lights glinting off stainless steel. There was a time when Gabriel enjoyed a greasy spoon, but not after the forced inking. A quartet of the brawniest thugs held him down on the prison's kitchen stainless-steel work surface. Pots dangled in the stagnant air over him.

"Hollywood, we were drawing straws over what to do to you, boy. Cletus, here, he likes your pretty mouth."

The man with a shaved head and jowly jaw grinned toothlessly. "I wondered if your hiney is as pretty as your lips." Gabriel's face blanched as his body froze. He schooled his features to remain stoic, he didn't dare show weakness. "But, if word got around, then we'd have to fight to keep you. So, Roy, here. See, he's an artiste. He's cooked up some baby oil, nice and black and he's gonna draw some jewelry on you." Sausage-like fingers wrapped around Gabriel's neck. The stench of a prison diet and bad oral hygiene threatened to gag him.

"Hollywood, when Roy is done with you, everybody is going to know you're our boy." Gabriel's gaze darted from man to man to man, each wearing a barbed wire tattoo around their neck.

The thug holding his right arm came in threateningly close. "Then, I get to screw you."

Gabriel's eyes closed. When he opened them again, they were already inking his neck with a sharpened ice pick. One guy held a coffee cup of sooty oil as Roy made a series of shallow jabs from under his ear, and across his throat. Roy's sour body odor infiltrated Gabriel's lungs as the pick clawed at his flesh well into the night.

By the time they dragged him back to his cell he barely made bed check. His clothes were soddened with his own nervous sweat. When he climbed into his top bunk, he couldn't separate the burning pain of the ice pick from the emotional trauma.

****

"They used an ice pick and burnt baby oil for ink," Gabriel whispered.

"I see they only got the front. What stopped it?"

"They ran out of time. My attackers had to hustle me back before bed check. The next morning, I was put in solitary, like the guards thought I did this to myself. When they figured it out, I was moved off that block."

"This wasn't voluntary."

"You have no idea how bad I want this gone."

****

The Goodwill store in Towson was far tonier than the one in Essex. Gabriel was temporarily fascinated with some antique furniture he saw set up like a bedroom. Wouldn't that be cool in his own bedroom? Was Ted serious that he wanted to share an executive home with him? He couldn't fathom the peace and quiet of living in a congenial house with a pool table in the basement and a swimming pool in the backyard.

He found a large section of men's clothing, and since he needed everything from an overcoat to a second pair of shoes, he figured he'd drop a good chunk of his first paycheck here.

Gabriel felt as if Grace were beside him when he walked through the orderly aisles. Today, in the junior's section, the mannequin wore an outfit he imagined would be perfect on her. She should have been in school, moving toward her proper future. He'd screwed all that up for her. *Well, his rational mind argued, that's not exactly true. That bastard, Arthur, had a big hand in screwing her up, but I certainly didn't help.*

As he wandered through the store, he remembered the first polo shirt she picked out for him. She'd looked triumphant when she coerced him into modeling the outfit for her. He could remember the feel of her in his arms when he scooped her up joyously and spun her around right there in the store. His chest ached as he thought of the luscious weight of her in his arms. *A hundred and twenty pounds of love!* He needed to see her so badly, it was physical pain.

A carbon copy of his original polo shirt hung on the rack, *jeesh, how many of those did they sell?* Gabriel picked it up nostalgically. He wouldn't be able to wear it around work, but he could wear it off-duty, and he'd feel closer to Grace when he did. *What did she say about choosing fashion? Classic cuts and colors that mixed and matched, to expand a wardrobe.*

What colors mix and match? In the Navy, blue and white go together, so that's good. Tan pants are like tree-trunks and leaves are green so I can go with that. That means, jeans, blue slacks, tan slacks, white, green and blue turtlenecks. Yeah, that'll work.

One large rack held nothing but pea coats. Perfect! He knew all about those. Shoes? *Ooh, there's a pair of Hush Puppy loafers in black.* They were comfortable too, good and broken in, *just need a good shine.* Now, a trip to Walmart for socks, skivvies and a shaving kit with travel size toiletries, and he'd be set for his training trip to Vance, Alabama.

Wait! I need something else... A Ralph Lauren navy blazer hung among a rack of new Men's Warehouse sports coats and L.L. Bean blazers as if it were waiting just for him. He found his size, and it fit as if tailored perfectly, even Gabriel could see that. Swallowing hard at the price tag, he decided to buy it. He did his best to coordinate it with a crisp white dress shirt, which reminded him of the Navy, and a blue, turquoise and gold print, silk tie. *What the hell, it kinda matches my eyes. Grace would like this.* He wished Goodwill had salesclerks to ask an opinion but guessed he'd have to rely on his own common sense. He headed for check out, a man with a newly discovered individual style. Gabriel felt a rush of warmth over his bargain hunting. He wished his Princess could see how wisely he shopped.

Just before he hit the register, he spied a rotating display of Baltimore-themed postcards. He stopped to check it out. There was one perfectly capturing the view of the harbor he and Grace used to enjoy together, and a plan formed. If he didn't write or sign anything, he could send her a postcard from Alabama, and no one would know it was from him. *But Grace will know I'm alive…*

22

Sunday morning was grey and chilly. Grace poked at the wood-burning fireplace and sat down with her coffee. Recovering from running last night at the Woodholme-Evers wedding, Grace opened the Sunday paper. The up and coming power couple could have filled a ballroom at the Renaissance but chose an intimate wedding reception on the groom's family yacht. Yes, it was two hundred feet long, and Grace's feet felt like every inch was covered in broken glass. If she went up and down stairs once, she must have made a hundred trips with full silver trays of canapes.

She looked in the Living section for the wedding announcement, and there they were, Avery Woodholme stood in a bespoke gown next to her prince, Hamilton Evers. *So, this is what generations of wealth look like. I'll bet mother is seething since she'll never get to plan an event like this one.*

Grace hadn't worn the ivory lace dress since the day she and Gabriel applied for their marriage license. They'd been so close! Another two days and she'd have been Mrs. Gabriel Lee. Her eyes burned, but there were no tears left. She'd lost everything.

Her fatigue from the night before drew her curiosity back to the wedding couple. When Grace entered the new Prep school her junior year, the establishment was still abuzz over Avery. She was the penultimate over-achiever! Avery played goalie on the State Championship Lacrosse team and won a scholarship to the University of Maryland, which her family pooh-poohed. She was bound for Brown, where she met Hamilton

Evers, another Marylander, plucked from the Oldline State. Grace recalled the monuments to Avery's achievements in the trophy cases. Although her appearance in her prep years was obscured by thick glasses and substantial orthodontia, she emerged a graceful swan. *Now, she's as rich as Croesus.*

Grace let the paper drop to her lap. If she and Gabriel had made it in front of a judge and made their love binding, she would have the legal right to know what happened to him. It wasn't enough to know he loved her. *He does love me. You have to make it legal if you want to be protected. When he brings me that wedding ring he promised, the courthouse is our next stop.*

She sighed, knowing she would never have a wedding like Avery's. It didn't interest her, anyway. Any officiant Gabriel wanted, would be fine with her if she was given a chance. She fought off moist eyes as she heard the keys in the front door. *Stop this right now!* She wiped at the tear threatening to fall.

Esther was the first one in the door. "I knew I should have dragged you out of bed and taken you to church! What are you reading that has your face flushed and your eyes red?" The older woman crossed the room, took off her flowered hat and sat down on the sofa next to Grace.

"You'll never believe the wedding I worked last night. Look!" She held up the newspaper.

"Oh! That little scamp! She was a charmer! That boy doesn't know what he's in for!" Esther took the paper from Grace and tilted her head to see the photo better. "I worked for her family; you know. They were nice enough folks. They down-sized to one of those big condos on the water when Avery left for college. Look how she turned out! Where's that mole on her neck? They must have taken that off."

"Oh, Esther! You're as bad as me!" Grace sighed. "They seemed deliriously happy."

"Well, that's good, honey. I just hope the bride's prepared herself to do more than give parties." Grace made a curious face. "You never know what life is going to hand you. My Robert was a good man. Worked hard every day. Bought this house before Black people lived on this street. He didn't live to see his forty-fifth birthday. I became the head of the house, those kids needed to get through school, and when Kendra's mother died of cancer, I brought that little girl back into my home to raise."

Kendra put her son in the playpen and brought out cups of steaming cocoa. "Those were hard years for you, Momma."

Grace shook her head. "I can't imagine what a frightening time that must have been."

"You've got that right. I'll regret to my dying day not taking the opportunity before I was married, to go to nursing school. If I had done that, we'd still have had some hard times, but it wouldn't have been as bad as it was. Girls, listen to me, there is nothing more important than an education that gives you a career. None of this art history stuff, I'm talking about what you girls are doing right now to give you a job in your field. People enjoy good restaurants, and then they need their dental health."

"Yes, Momma. I know. I grew up knowing."

Esther wagged her finger at the girls. "A year ago, Kendra, did you think you'd be raising your son alone? For Heaven's sake, a bullet intended for that good-for-nothing-dealer across the street took your man. That's the streets in Baltimore. No man should come between you and your future, because you may love him, and lose him tomorrow…"

Kendra nodded, "Drink your cocoa, Momma, before the marshmallows get hard."

Esther was on a roll. "… But you still have to earn a living, and living is more than work. Grace, Kendra, your men are dead and gone. Don't be like me, filling your lives with work. When you can stand on your own two feet, meet men of quality, who are worth your time."

Grace held her steaming cup in front of her smile and thought, *I may have missed church, but I didn't miss the sermon.*

****

After lunch, Kendra stuck her head in the kitchen as she bounced her son on her hip. "Are we gettin' the car today? Do we need to buy a second car seat?"

Grace chewed the marshmallow treat as she nodded. "That was my thought, too. The Highway Patrol can get us connected. I bought a leather portfolio to hold the registration and the insurance cards. It's on the television stand in my bedroom. Is Momma ready to go?"

Kendra nodded effusively before she stuck her head into the basement stairway and bellowed, "Momma, Grace is ready to go."

Esther bellowed back, "Child, you're the one who's ready to go. I'll be up in a minute."

Grace washed her hands. "The lawyer's office sent me the new license sticker, so I'll be legal." She watched Kendra grab a red sports drink from the fridge. "You aren't bringing that in the car, are you?"

Kendra's head shot up over the door. "What?"

"A red drink -- in the car?"

Kendra shrugged. "It's…. naw…" Kendra grabbed a bottle of water and shook it at Grace. "Happy now?"

"Yes."

****

Esther kept her eyes on the road as she spoke to Grace. "Heard you up and down a lot last night."

"Oh, a lot on my mind…school and the car, you know…"

"The parking slab out back is ready and waiting. I put a new lock on the gate. No one is going to mess with Mr. Charlie's car."

Grace smiled absentmindedly, her thoughts a million miles away. The ride was over sooner than she expected, and suddenly, Esther's car was parked before the blue garage door. Grace spent a moment in silence before she unlatched her safety belt. Esther, Kendra and the baby already stood near the door in expectation.

Kendra played with her son's hair and whispered, "What's taking her so long? She lose something in the car?"

Esther gave her a censorious look. "Hush. Grace lost her man. They spent all kinds of time here, getting this car running. This is more than a car."

Kendra stood corrected and busied herself with her son as Grace walked to the padlock. With a few whirls of the nob, the door was up. Esther threw a halting arm in front of Kendra. "You stay right here with me." They stood, silent, watching Grace.

The shop lights came on, bouncing heavenly light off the luminous silver paint job. At Gabriel's last visit, he used a power buffer to rejuvenate the bright silver. Grace inhaled the scent of the storage unit, the automotive solvents, and especially Gabriel's aftershave. His shop coat hung on the hook below his safety glasses as if waiting for him to return and pick up the next task on his clipboard. The bank pen rested on the bench right below the last steps he'd taken. He'd drawn a smiley face by the note saying the tires were on and the speedometer was synchronized.

Grace opened the heavy driver's door and sat in the butter soft black leather seat. Once she realized it was set to Gabriel's long legs, she grabbed the steering wheel and buried her head in her arms, crying great sobs.

It's as if he was just here. He can't be gone, he's everywhere in this storage unit. His energy talks to me. Is that because he's dead? Or is that because he's alive and doing everything he can to get back to me?

Thoughts and emotions flew through her in a jumble. *I miss Gabriel's touch... I want him to hold me... He doesn't even know about the baby...* All the old doubts surfaced. *Surely, he would have told me if there was a brother... The obituary was wrong... How can that be? What if he comes back here and the car is gone? I should leave him a note.*

She achingly pulled herself out of the driver's seat and went to the workbench where his clipboard waited. At the bottom of the page, she wrote, "*Gabriel, you know where to find me. I have the car and some great news. I'm going to school. I'll tell you more when we see each other. I love you. I'm waiting for you, and I've never given up hope of seeing you again. Don't forget, you promised me another ring. (And not on the phone, either.) Love, your Princess.*"

Grace pulled the key ring off the hook on the wall and grabbed a paper towel to wipe the corner of the license tag. She applied the sticker keeping her legal for two more years and then returned to the open driver's door. She kissed her fingertips and then slid the car seat forward and keyed the ignition.

With a throaty roar, the motor growled to life, the exhaust thrummed like a heartbeat, and she carefully pulled the car forward toward her friends. She hopped out and turned off the shop lights, gave a wave to all the equipment inside and locked the door. Kendra and Esther walked around the purring car, examining every chromed accent and graceful line.

"What do you think?"

Kendra's eyes flashed. "It's like something out of a movie! Can I drive it?"

Esther barked. "No, you *cannot*! You get to drive the Subaru. That's where the child seat is."

"Oh, Momma!"

****

It was three hours since the start of orientation, during which the little class of four listened to the human resources trainer describe benefits in excruciating detail. Gabriel didn't know why they had to tell their employees in so many different ways to show up fifteen minutes before clocking in, and excessive absences were grounds for dismissal. *Wasn't that understood?* He filled out forms for everything from health care, to automatic deposit. The most emotional was the life insurance beneficiary form. He printed Grace's full name but didn't know her social security number.

He raised his hand sheepishly. "Can I get back with you on my beneficiary's social?"

The trainer collected everyone's forms and laughed. "Just don't die between now and then."

If you only knew.

Gabriel worked to stifle a yawn. "I'm gonna run over to Service, get myself some coffee. Anyone else?"

The twenty-something receptionist leaped up. "I'm coming with ya!"

She fell into step with him, talking a mile a minute. "Isn't this the most beautiful car dealership, ever? This is the friendliest place I've ever worked. I'm in reception and switchboard. Where will you be?"

Gabriel watched her wobble on platform, ankle-strap shoes as she tried to follow his long strides in her constrictive, black, pencil skirt. He slowed down. "I'm a mechanic. Three to eleven."

"Oh." She pouted. "I won't see you much. This is kind of like being freshman together."

"Yeah. You could say that." *Yeah, she just did.*

"They're teaching us computers this afternoon."

Gabriel's heart sank as he pulled a second paper cup from the coffee bar and filled all of them. *Oh, help me now, a windowless room after a heavy lunch and the most tedious topic in the manual. I hope this is strong enough to keep me awake.*

Ted came around the corner and found Gabriel grinning distractedly at the young receptionist. "By this time of day, the coffee should be nice and strong…"

"I think this is a fresh pot." Ted held up his coffee mug.

"Mr. Warner! Good to see you. This is Miss…" He looked at her paper name badge. "Rose…I'm sorry, I didn't get your last name."

She giggled, "Donnelly." She gave Ted a girly handshake. "Hello."

He smiled indulgently. "Miss Donnelly. Good to have you with us."

Her shoulders danced up and down. "Before I drink this I have to run to the ladies' room. Nice to meet you!" She waggled her fingers at him.

Ted watched her prance down the hall. "I'll bet she didn't need any sugar in her coffee."

****

In the first week of school, Grace found herself buried under more kitchen implements than books. "When all this is done," Kendra waved her hands over the cluttered dining room table, "Are we going to eat whatever it is you're making?" Kendra balanced the baby on her hip while she read over Grace's shoulder about kitchen chemistry.

"This is my homework, so *no*, we are not eating any of it."

She worked eight hours a week at the bistro, and between class time, practicum and homework, she averaged forty hours of school a week. Her days and nights were plenty full. Grace gave up on the bank, the account was blocked. She didn't even have a photograph of Gabriel, but she copied a six-year-old photo of him off the internet. The picture celebrated his induction into the Navy. She carried every other image in her heart.

****

Gabriel never traveled on a regular passenger plane before, he'd always ridden in troop transports. Hearing he was going on a regular airliner to Alabama was a treat. He toyed with the idea of buying a larger duffle bag, but Ted already said he could borrow a real suitcase, *so why waste the money?* Ted swung off the interstate toward the airport. Gabriel grinned at him. "It's gotta feel nice to be driving your own car again."

Ted nodded. "Sure, beats public transportation. Can't wait to park in my own garage. But that's a few weeks away."

"Nice to have you for a chauffeur. Saturday, it was the Doctor's office, tonight to the airport. How come I'm not riding in the back seat, and you're not in uniform, Jeeves?"

"How come I'm not getting a tip? Speaking of appointments, when are you gonna start the laser thing?"

"When I get home, my first appointment is that Wednesday at ten in the morning. Doc says it's superficial, so it may take three or four treatments, but they have to be timed out. Maybe by Christmas, I can give up the turtlenecks."

"When the bay doors open, it gets drafty, you might want to keep them."

"My return flight gets in while you're at work, so, I'll take the Light Rail home. But I appreciate the lift today, thanks." As Ted pulled the car up to departing flights, Gabriel turned serious. "If it gets hairy, I want you to know I already looked up meetings and I'll text before I go all twelve-year-old-girl on you."

Ted nodded. "I'm proud of you. When you get back, you've got to get a Sponsor."

Gabriel unlatched his seat belt and heard the trunk latch pop. He got out and closed the door but leaned back inside the open window. "I hope I get one as experienced as yours, Pops. See you next weekend." He grabbed the small carryon out of the trunk and rapped twice. He watched Ted drive off and felt like a kid left at camp. *This is ridiculous. I've traveled all over the world with the Navy. I'm sure I can handle Vance, Alabama. But can I handle it sober?* His nagging inner voice asked.

****

A text message appeared on his phone shortly after Gabriel's plane touched down at the Birmingham airport. It informed him that five other guys were arriving from the west coast, but not for another three hours. Their group would be picked up together, that meant a hell of a long wait. He couldn't remember any time he'd flown sober. Liquid refreshment wafted its tentacles out the bar door like a Disney villain and whispered it could make the time fly by. Gabriel wasn't buying it. There wasn't a lot to do at the Birmingham airport, and thrifty though he was, he decided to splurge on a New York Times bestselling paperback. He'd let Stephen King scare him to death, it was better than boredom.

As he pulled his wallet out of his pocket to pay, his fingers skated over the postcard he'd bought for Grace. The airport would be the perfect mailing spot. He saw the newsstand sold stamps and got a folder from the machine. After his mind blew through witticisms and quirky things he could say, he sketched a snowball with marshmallow topping. *It does look like marshmallow topping, doesn't it?* He carefully printed Esther's name and address in generic block letters.

He thought about it for a good twenty minutes before he affixed the stamp. If he closed his eyes, he could recall how the sunlight glittered off Grace's golden-rose hair. He loved the way her pale eyelashes glowed in the sun and framed her hazel eyes flecked with jade. She was naturally exquisite, so delicately poised, soft but strong like silk. And smart.

God, I wish I had half her pluck. No eighteen-year-old woman, gorgeous, smart and charming would be alone for long, not unless she beats them off with a club. *Together we were insatiable, will someone else feed her hunger? I have to let her know I'm alive.* It took him another twenty-five minutes to get up the nerve to drop the postcard in the mailbox. No one could possibly trace this back to him or Grace, but she would know.

Once the card hit the mail below it, his mind kicked into a rabid craving. Jon's words came back to him. "This is how you handle stress, drink alcohol." *I'm not falling for the bullshit.* He paced, and then remembered the meditation chapel he'd seen along the corridor and made tracks there.

All the members of his recovery group were encouraged to carry a pamphlet called "How It Works," which he took out and read cover to cover. Another he'd selected specifically for himself, called "It's Better than a Cell" kept him focused on sobriety. By the time he was through, Gabriel had reminded himself of exactly what he wanted in life, and how he wanted Grace to see him. That was *not* as a black-out drunk. Gabriel felt in balance again, and turning his anxiety over to his Higher Power, walked back to the rendezvous point and Stephen King's storytelling.

****

Friday's lesson in the kitchen lab was the four varieties of roux. Grace and Tsavros concentrated on the different colors, the result of how long the flour and butter cooked. Grace's roux approached blonde as the finance clerk stepped into their kitchen area. "Ms. Lerner, you're needed in the Business Office immediately."

Grace looked over her shoulder at the woman's grim face, still stirring the browning ingredients. "I'm in the middle of my roux. I need a few more minutes to get credit for this assignment."

"No, you don't. Remove your apron and bring your locker key."

Tsavros stepped up to the saucepan. "Go ahead, Grace. I've got this." He frowned heavily at the terse clerk who ignored him completely. "Let me know if you need help."

Grace nodded, numb with embarrassment. Everyone in the class was staring at her. The clerk was not confidential in her demand.

As the women headed downstairs, Grace voiced a demand of her own. "What did I do?"

"There's a problem with your check." She led Grace into the private office of the Registrar and stood to wait expectantly as he got to his feet behind his desk.

In his hand was a bank draft. "Miss Lerner." He straightened the bow tie at his neck. "When we gave you the privilege of admission, you agreed to make timely payments. Your last automatic payment was rejected by your bank twice. Your tuition needs to be paid before you enter the classroom tomorrow morning. Because of your default, we can only accept a cashier's check." He handed the form to her as if it were a burning bag of dog poop.

"But I don't understand…"

"Did I stutter? You are in default. Any further discussion needs to proceed between you and your banker. The clerk will escort you to your locker where you will only remove your jacket and purse. She will accept your key and walk you to the door."

"I still don't…I…I…" Grace moved numbly behind the clerk.

****

Tsavros caught up with them as Grace exited the front door. "What's going on?"

"My auto draft bounced. But that's impossible, it's administered by my father's attorney. School expenses are all that comes out of that account."

"Maybe you were hacked?"

"I've got to get to the bank."

A nondescript man in a blue windbreaker stepped up to her. "Grace Margaret Lerner?"

"Yes."

"Sign here, please." He thrust an envelope and an electronic signature tablet at her.

She blinked and robotically signed the apparatus. Looking at Tsavros with trepidation, she unwound the string securing the envelope. "This is from my step-father." Her mouth went grim as she read. "That son of a bitch."

23

Gabriel raised a root beer to Ted as he trudged into the common room. "Ted! There's a cold six-pack in there. Kick back and have one with me."

Ted's eyes brightened. "Cold root beer? I don't know what I missed more, you or having a cold one waiting for me. In your absence, I've been killing time at the gym, and I can barely walk. Please tell this isn't sugar-free."

"Sugar is my last vice. It's fully leaded."

"Oh, good, I need sugar."

"Then take a load off, tell me what I missed. Has the receptionist gotten flowers from admirers yet?"

"Nah, she's shotgunning the cookie angle, trying to catch any single man. She's peeved I haven't eaten them this week." Ted opened the fridge door, snagged a bottle of root beer, and sat in the recliner chair. "There's a flyer in your cubby. Not that I snooped, but I got mine. We're out of here in two weeks. Apparently, the rehab staff thinks we're doing too well to take up space."

Gabriel moaned and dragged his hand through his hair. "I've got to get wheels."

Ted shook his head. "Merri drove a cushy little pickup she used for her garage sale runs. It's as nice as my sedan. You might as well drive it."

"Man, I feel like you're adopting me."

"I couldn't think of a better son. As hard as you're working, you deserve it."

****

Tsavros Pappas, Grace's friend, and lab partner at school shuffled in place until he saw the restaurant door open. No one, except his mother, thought Tsavros handsome as a baby. At his birth, gazes halted when they got to his Roman nose and friend's 'new-baby-smiles' faltered for a fraction of a second. As a young teen, he didn't attract girls. 'Stavi' was skinny and his cheekbones gave him a skeletal look. But, by fourteen he was filling out, he earned muscles from working in the family food business. By twenty, he'd grown into those classic Greek features, his bone structure fine and perfectly symmetrical. He was virile, strong and in command. "Grace!" He raised a wave to beckon Grace and Esther to the back of Apollo's Taverna.

Apollo Pappas' dream of a restaurant in the city was brought to fruition one year after his fatal heart attack. The entire family was there tonight, although it was the sons, Kosmo, Xander and Tsavros who wore their megawatt smiles, shaking hands with the foodies of Baltimore. His mother, Athena, stood protectively next to her sixteen-year-old daughter, Calista, both the image of Greek beauty. Apollo's restaurant was deceptively gourmet, despite the blue and white checked tablecloths and fairly pedestrian Greek prints decorating the walls.

****

As Esther followed Grace through the lobby, they gazed at the imposing portrait of a distinguished man. Esther noted his painting was encircled by portraits of two sons with their families and Tsavros with his younger sister and mother. Blank spots were saved for Tsavros and Calista's portraits when they married.

They arrived well ahead of the guests for the soft opening, and Esther's antenna was up as she observed the young man's attention to Grace. As they came within arm's length of Tsavros and an older man, her school mate's hands grasped each of Grace's and pulled her closer.

"Uncle, didn't I tell you, isn't she is a rare beauty? Did I mention she is also a goddess in the kitchen?"

Esther registered Tsavros' comments with an eye-creasing smile. *He's smitten.*

"Miss Esther, Grace, this is my Uncle, Constantine Pappas, my father's younger brother."

The older man's face brightened as he made Esther's acquaintance with a European hug and kisses on both cheeks. "My nephew did not tell me to expect such a lovely chaperone for his friend." The uncle held Esther's hand until Tsavros' silent nod prompted him to let go.

Esther chuckled. "I don't know who's chaperoning who, Mr. Pappas. It's been a while since I've been out for the evening." They milled around tables set with the specialties from their family cookbooks and when the doors officially opened, the restaurant filled with laughter under the heady aromas of thyme, bay leaves, and rosemary.

Coming out of the kitchen, wearing a brilliant white and blue embroidered peasant blouse, Grace balanced a full tray as she made her way to the buffet table. "The guests are plowing through these dishes, Cici." Esther chuckled as she stacked another skewer of meatballs on her small plate.

"No wonder Tsavros has been exhausted, this place is hopping. I wanted you to be here with me tonight to enjoy this. If you only knew how much I love you, Momma Esther." Grace hugged her. "If anyone in the world deserves a place of honor, it's you."

Athena and Uncle Constantine approached Esther with a plate of antipasto that could have comprised an entire meal. Esther was slightly giggly; the potent Greek wine and effusive company brought a glow to her cheeks.

"Oh! This is so good! What is this?"

Athena grinned. "Taramasalata. Excellent with fresh pita bread and Sancerre wine."

Grace leaned toward her. "It's caviar. Good, isn't it?"

Esther's eyes widened. "Caviar? Really? I never liked the fish eggs before."

Constantine enthusiastically poured her another glass of wine. "You weren't eating the right kind! Perhaps you need to be introduced to more Greek cooking." He led her to a table. On the way, he quipped, "I eat alone too many nights."

Esther giggled. "You're not asking me to wash dishes afterward, are you?" She teased.

Constantine was comically affronted. "You know too little about Greeks, Ms. Esther! You will always be my guest!"

****

Grace knew the legends of Greek hospitality but never experienced it for herself. Now, she understood the concept of Xenia, honor owed by a Greek host to their guests. She supposed no Greek festivity would be complete without the toast of Opa! Which, wisely tonight, did not include fractured pottery. It was late into the evening when the foodies and the critics left, replete with fine Greek cuisine and wine. She and Esther sat together with the family over strong Greek coffee and a custard and whipped cream confection to die for.

Tsavros leaned into Grace and Esther, brimming with the apparent success of the new eatery. "I hope you're prepared to do the work this flourishing restaurant will entail." Esther teased.

"Yes, Ms. Esther, I'm beginning to recognize something will have to give. I want to finish school, and I'll be needed here. I believe our lunch wagon may have to be sacrificed. I'm looking for an ambitious person to take it over." He arched a brow at Grace.

"Are you now?" Grace knew Esther missed nothing. "Who did you have in mind?"

Tsavros leaned into Esther. "The only person I know, with enough talent and determination, is sitting next to you. The family has given me the wagon, and it's my choice who to sell to. I've had lucrative offers, but my uncles and I have discussed it, and we'd like to keep things more in the family if we can.

"What are you asking, Tsavros?" Grace was bewildered.   ·

"If you took over the expenses on the wagon, and the licensing, we'd be willing to float you a loan…"

"Oh, but, you must have family members who want to take over the truck. What about Calista?"

Tsavros laughed and shook his head. "Calista is determined to go to medical school. There is no one else. We've talked about it, and we'd like to offer the deal to you, first. If it's too much…"

"Too much?"

"I know you have some financial problems right now. You can earn some quick cash. I thought it might be a good family business for the three of you, at least until you get your degree. My family has run one per household for the past fifteen years. The corner's been good for us, I think it would be for you, too."

****

Esther tilted her head at him. "I want a word with you, young man." Tsavros stood respectfully, pulling out Esther's chair.

Grace's head, shaking, dropped into her hands. "Oh, no…"

Esther led him to the restaurant lobby, in front of the smiling family portraits. "Young man, your family has been more than cordial to us this evening, and Grace and I appreciate that. And, just looking at these walls, I can see how important family is to you. Might this sudden generous offer be a way to add Grace to your family?"

"Am I that transparent?"

"You are to me."

"From the moment I was paired with Grace in class, I've done everything to get her attention."

"I see. Well, I'm a momma bear when it comes to my girl."

"And, you should be. Beautiful young girls don't just happen. They're taught sensitivity and a work ethic. It gave her an understanding of this life of hospitality." Tsavros gestured to the restaurant. "You filled her with compassion, gentleness, and dedication. Your influence is a part of her beauty."

"She is a glittering jewel, young man."

"You're good people. My Papu, before he died, said the most important thing in finding a partner is integrity. I don't know anyone with more integrity or ambition to create good food than Grace. If you and your granddaughter are willing to help her with the food truck, it will bless everyone."

"Have you asked Grace out?"

"She always says she's busy."

Esther frowned. "Have you discussed any business arrangement?"

"I've tried to approach her about business, subtly. I kinda sprang it on her tonight. I was with her when she was served the legal papers. I don't mean to pry, but, she is wearing a diamond ring. Is that a family ring or does is she bound to someone?"

"You'll have to ask Grace about that." Esther paused. "You realize, your generous business offer will take discussion, there can't be an answer until the weekend."

"I would be hasty to expect an immediate answer. My uncle has the business records for your examination."

Back at the table, Grace broke off her discussion of signature Mediterranean dishes with Xander when Esther and Tsavros returned. She gave Tsavros a wry look. "I see you're still in one piece."

Tsavros quirked a smile, and his eyes sparkled. "Miss Esther knows how to extract information painlessly."

"Do you have a business deal to discuss with *me*?"

With a raised brow, Tsavros waved his hand. "Tonight is not a night for business. Tomorrow, if you'll meet with my uncles and me, we might reach an agreement beneficial to both families."

****

Gabriel dropped his lunch box in the kitchen and wandered back to the common area with a cold bottle of root beer. He unlaced his work boots before he put his feet on the coffee table. Clicking on the repeat of the eleven o'clock news, he sat back.

"Dinner at Eight was at Apollo's Taverna, on Eastern Avenue, for their opening night when we spoke with Athena Pappas." The newscaster bubbled while the camera swept the congenial crowd in the bright white dining room. Gabriel tried to recall where this restaurant might be when he saw the back of a tall woman with rose-gold hair holding a glass up in a toast. He put down the root beer and watched a younger dark-haired girl clink glasses with the strawberry blonde. He leaned forward when the microphone intruded on her space, and she whipped around.

For the first time in months, he was face to face with Grace. Her hair was longer, she was subtly made up for the evening, and wearing a Greek peasant blouse that was the costume of the female servers. She ducked shyly from the cameras when a tall and fiercely handsome young man threw his arms around the shoulders of the younger girl and Grace. The darkly masculine guy whispered or nuzzled in Grace's direction. Her cheeks glowed, and she looked down and then at the glass in her left hand. Then the tape cut to his formal announcement. "The Pappas family welcomes devotees of fine Greek cuisine to our tables. We're here seven days a week to indulge your taste buds!"

The scene was gone as soon as it appeared while the newscaster described the location and menu. Gabriel was gobsmacked. He dared not shadow Grace. Kerry and Hawkins made it clear his attention could trigger a threat. Here was his greatest fear laid out. Grace stood in the arms of another man. True, an innocent embrace, she apparently worked there, but what if it was more? The guy was built, athletic, close to her age, and shared her interest in the restaurant business.

Jealousy washed over him in a malignant wave. It wasn't like he hadn't had offers! That receptionist was baking cookies like a Keebler elf in the hopes of seducing him. He was so damn horny he fantasized about driving her out to the Loch Raven Reservoir with a blanket for a quickie in the woods. Maybe not even a quickie.

Dumb move, you don't fish off the company pier. It isn't cool to bring a date back to a halfway house, but the campus was full of girls who weren't shy about hanging a scarf on their doorknob. Wasn't that cutie with the tight tank top giving me the once-over in a composition class? *I'd like to conjugate some verbs with her! My being under-educated has never gotten me this much positive attention!*

His being horny wasn't Grace's fault, and she wasn't doing anything wrong. Hell, for all Gabriel knew, she believed he was dead. Did the postcard help any? She looked healthy. As always, she looked beautiful. He pulled out his cell phone and went to the network website. Once he found the restaurant review, he took a screenshot and cropped the guy as far out of the image as possible. She looked into the camera. She still wore his ring, it glittered under the video camera light. *Is she looking for me?*

****

Sunday dinner dishes were cleaned, and Antwoine put down for the night before Grace, Esther, and Kendra sat down to plan out the next step in their lives. "I know Tsavros does good business from the lunch wagon, I could see that the first day I worked with him."

"He may do good business, but does it cover his overhead?" Esther raised a brow. "I know he says it does, but what do the books say?"

Kendra looked confused. "Why do we care? We wouldn't be working for other people."

Esther shook her head. "You don't wanna work for somebody who's broke, especially if that somebody is you."

Grace slid a photocopy of the month's receipts and last year's income tax returns into Esther's hands. "They gave me two years of records, and I didn't know what else to ask for."

Esther considered the paperwork page by page. "They've grown year over year, and they have a good tax man, so they aren't giving profits away." She bent over the papers and compared month to month, nodding with her appraisal.

Grace pointed to the expenses. "I think Tsavros's family has been doing business with the suppliers for such a long time, they have quantity discounts. I don't know if that would apply to us, or how much more we might have to pay."

"That's part of the negotiations. I don't know everything we need to know, but I've worked for good people who can advise us. Grace, your daddy's attorney would be a start."

"Yeah, I've already got a call into him because of school. He's out of town until Tuesday."

Kendra leaned back in the chair. "Sounds like we look into this deeper."

Grace nodded enthusiastically. "Did we get any mail this week?"

Kendra pointed. "It's all on the mantle. Mostly junk mail."

Esther went into the kitchen for cookies and tea. Grace wandered to the mantle hunting for rebate checks. She flipped hurriedly through bright advertising flyers and dental ads. A bent and abused postcard fell out of the bunch and dropped to her feet. She picked it up curiously. Nobody sent these anymore. And why would anyone send them a postcard of the Baltimore Harbor? Her gaze wandered over the back. It was addressed to Esther; she was about to put it back in the stack when she saw the note. Well, it wasn't a note. It was a drawing of something. She studied it. It was a drawing of a snowball. *What the hell... A sketch of a snowball with marshmallow topping? What?* Her world went silent. The street noise dulled. The kids on the sidewalk winked out of existence. She stared.

"Grace?" Kendra asked. "What you got there?"

"A postcard," Grace whispered through numb lips.

Kendra jumped up and grabbed her friend, dragging her into the kitchen. On the way, she fanned her with the mail. "Momma! You gotta see this!"

Grace felt the blood drain from her face and then flash back up again in a bright flush. She became conscious of holding her breath and took in a deep gulp.

"What is it now?" Esther glanced at Grace. "Lord, child, what do you have there?"

"It's a postcard from Gabriel..."

"What?" Kendra snatched the card from her hand and passed it to her grandmother with a puzzled look. "There's nothing on it but some scribble."

Esther studied the card carefully and handed it back to Grace. "What makes you think this is from him?"

"That's where we used to eat. That's the snowball we used to have with marshmallow topping. He always wanted to own a condominium right there." She pointed at the picture and gawked. "You know this means Gabriel is alive!"

Esther sat down opposite her and sent Kendra to the stove to answer the whistling teapot. "I hope it does mean that, Cici. I can see why you think it does."

"It does! I know it does! I knew he was alive! He still loves me! This is his code."

Esther took both of Grace's hands and folded her hands over them. "If that's true, the Lord has answered a prayer, for sure." She patted her hands. "Now, Cici, as good as this news is, I want you to think for a minute that this is not an 'all clear'. I do believe he's trying to tell you he's alive. But he's also saying that anonymously. This card is mailed from," she glanced at the postmark, "Birmingham, Alabama, a long way from here. We, none of us, know what that means. We do know he isn't here."

"Why do you always say that? Why can't you just be happy for me?"

"I am happy for you. I'd be the happiest woman on earth if your handsome young man walked through my door right now." She looked at the door as if expecting that to happen. "I suppose I'm trying to protect you. That's why he brought you here, remember?"

Tears came in a torrent. "Yes." Grace choked out. "You've always tried to protect me."

"That's why I have to tell you, it's wonderful news that he's alive. He's also telling you he can't be with you right now. We don't know what that means for the future, but I'm thinking if he were sitting with us right now, your Gabriel would tell you to remember him but go on with your life."

Kendra stepped towards her with a wad of paper towels to wipe away Grace's tears. "You're always telling me 'patience is the ability to count down before you blast off." Kendra folded her arms over her chest, just like her grandmother, and narrowed her gaze. "I can look at you, and I know you're ready to throw every plan out that window and get on the first plane to Birmingham, right?" Grace laughed through tears and nodded. "But that won't do you any good." She shook a finger like Esther. "You don't even know if he's still there. In my mind, you have no choice but to go on with your life, happy he's alive." Grace drew in shuddering breaths, threw herself into Esther's warm arms and cried.

24

Grace joined Tsavros at the food wagon every morning to learn the business. Breakfast was brisk on this sunny day, and Grace looked forward to a good lunch crowd as well.

"I think you've got it. I'm heading to class." Tsavros gathered his backpack and headed to his car. Grace wiped down the stainless-steel front of the pickup window and laid out the lunch garnish tray. She caught sight of a bright Oriole team logo on the newsy cap of a tall, slender man in a pea coat and froze. She spent weeks watching for the Gabriel look-alike, but he never reappeared. Now, he was there, six traffic lanes away.

She abandoned cooking meat and an unlocked till and ran from the wagon to catch the man's attention. "Gabriel!" Her cry was lost in the autumn breeze and muffled by six lanes of busy traffic. She watched his guarded body language. He scanned the rushing cars from under his hat as he texted on his phone. Grace ran to the corner and frantically pressed the crossing button to hail the light. "Gabriel!" She called again, and waved, as she watched a sleek, red Mercedes convertible pull up to the curb in front of him.

A dark-haired beauty, wearing Jackie-O sunglasses, her perfect, full lips curved in a beguiling smile, jumped out of the driver's seat and leaned into the man's personal space. Her head tilted as her hand slid around his waist. He nodded actively and smiled. The look-alike escorted her around to the passenger's side. He returned to the driver's seat, adjusted the mirror and pulled into traffic, the mufflers rumbling over the other car sounds.

He only had eyes on her.

He drove off without ever glancing around.

It can't be a coincidence. This is the second time I've seen this guy. I know it's Gabriel. Is she why he hasn't come for me? Am I just a fool?

For the first time, she doubted Gabriel was ever coming back. Was she a delightful plaything for a moment, but expendable? Maybe he wanted to move forward cleanly. But then, why did he send the postcard? Grace's hopes drowned in confusion.

****

Gabriel exited the medical office's revolving door as a text message arrived. *'Grease, got tied up here. Sent Rose to pick you up in the red SL demonstrator. She couldn't wait to drive that car. See you soon.'* Gabriel sighed. As much as he appreciated the ride, half an hour alone with Rose would be tricky. She was the queen of happy hour, and he'd been the last hold-out, citing his three to eleven work schedules. He didn't drink, and he didn't hang out in places with people who did. He didn't date. He was devoted to Grace. None of these were facts he wished to share. *This will be a long thirty minutes.*

****

That night, Gabriel wiped his hands on the clean shop rag and reviewed the ticket. Although the tech in the next bay couldn't find the source of the squeal, he'd put his finger right on the issue. Now it was 11:05 at night and the rest of the late shift clocked out, but the G-class was purring. He backed the sports utility vehicle out of the shop and lowered the door. Heading toward the cashier with the key, Gabriel stopped when a man in a leather trench coat stepped out of the shadows into the beam of the headlights.

"I've brought this thing in here three times, and it took until 11:00 at night to get it right?"

"I apologize. It was an issue I was familiar with, and I'm night shift. I'm sorry it took so long. She's checking out at one hundred percent, now. Here's the key." Gabriel walked into the headlight's glare and extended the keys.

"Hey! Don't I know you?" The man got in Gabriel's face.

I hope not. "Mr...." Gabriel glanced at the ticket. "Mr. Johnson, right? I don't believe I've worked on this car before, but..."

"No, no, not here. I know you from somewhere." He studied Gabriel's face, and then yanked Gabriel's forearm into the headlights' beam. "I do know you. You're Wally's boy. You worked on my SLK."

Gabriel jerked his arm away and tugged his sleeve down. "I don't know who you think I am, but I don't know you. Your car's ready, you can drive it away." He turned from the man and headed toward Ted's waiting car.

"Don't you walk away from me! You Russian gangstas think you've got it all tied up." He stalked behind Gabriel. "I know how you guys work. You throw in with the city, close up one shop and open another with the seed cars, split the profits. You got my SLK when they boarded Wally's up." Shorter than Gabriel by several inches, the hood still had the nerve, or meth high, to grab Gabriel's collar from behind. He wore the stink of crack.

Gabriel rounded on the thug and spit out his words. "Look, buddy, I don't know who you are or what you think I know. I don't like your tone, or you puttin' your hands on me. So, you need to get in your car," he pointed to the vehicle ten feet away, "and go home."

Ted, wearing an elegant business suit, threw open his door and stepped out of his car. He watched the two men interact. Johnson blustered on meth bravado. "I'm not going anywhere until you pay me for the ride I lost."

Ted powered into the conversation. "I'm a Division Manager for service, Sir. I believe Mr. Bowman has told you he was not involved with your loss. You need to leave, or I'm calling the police."

Johnson escalated the aggression. "You need to know who you got working for you, Slick. G, my man, here, he can chop a car like fruit in a blender. Just sucks when it was my ride that got clipped."

Gabriel ground out his words. "I'm telling you one last time, Sir. My name is Gabriel Bowman. Mr. Warner has asked you to leave. I've asked you to leave. Staying is going to mean a visit from the police you don't want..."

Johnson's left hand grabbed Gabriel's coat lapel and was met with what should have been an easy enough takedown until the thug pulled a

Glock with his right hand. Johnson, down on one knee, leveled the gun barrel in Gabriel's face. Gabriel eluded the hoodlum's aim as Ted moved in. Between the two of them, disarming Johnson seemed like a sure thing, something both of them learned in the military.

The thug, wide-eyed and fearless, sprang from his crouch levying the barrel toward Gabriel, who feinted behind Johnson. With Ted's strong arm across Johnson's neck, the three men danced closely until a shot rang out and Ted slid to the ground.

"You son of a bitch!" Gabriel wrestled the gunman into a choke hold. The screaming and grunting morphed into shrieks, joined by the yells of the security guard, as the parking lot lit under the broad beam of an L.E.D. spotlight. Gabriel fought to subdue his opponent, and the man suddenly went limp in his arms. The two slumped to the ground. Gabriel immediately grabbed for the gun. He turned to check on his friend. "Call 9-1-1!" He looked up at the gaping security guard who suddenly backed away from him.

"Put down the gun, Mr. Bowman."

"Come on, get the gun and guard this guy! He shot Ted!"

Gabriel spun the gun toward the guard, and his breath caught as he crouched over Ted, who was covered in blood. Desperately seeking a pulse and finding none, he listened for breathing. Nothing. He stretched his friend out and started CPR. Nothing. The guard was still frozen in place. "Call 9-1-1! Get an ambulance. He's dying!" The man was finally galvanized into action. Minutes felt like hours as Gabriel continued CPR, knowing, even as he worked on breathing life into his friend, it was too late. Another death laid at his feet?

****

Within minutes it was a three-ring-circus. The first EMT crew arrived at Gabriel's side to relieve him. Gabriel rocked back on his heels to catch his breath and hoped they could help Ted. The patrol officers interviewed the security guard who pointed toward Gabriel, and the second EMT crew checked Johnson. "This guy's dead." The EMT chief called out after a cursory assessment of their attacker. *Fu...*, Gabriel thought. *Now what?*

He looked beseechingly at the paramedic working on Ted, but the man shook his head sadly. Gabriel knew it anyway. *Everyone I touch dies.*

The patrol officer walked up as Gabriel stumbled to his feet. "I need to see some identification, please, Sir." Gabriel handed over his wallet. "Please come with us." They walked him to a waiting squad car.

****

Gabriel sat on the hard bench of the holding tank cataloging the usual Friday night miscreants. The drunks, the crazies, and the usual suspects. He'd been finger-printed and searched and informed the interrogating detectives would be there to speak with him soon. He called Detective Kerry when he finally got his one phone call, to notify him he was in County Holding and it was bad. *Kerry will be here soon with a lawyer.*

The correctional officer escorting him to the cell was snide. "Oooh! Out of the gate, murder? You first-time offenders are over-achievers; you start with double murder."

Gabriel guessed they efficiently purged his record. If they hadn't, the county cops would know he was Gabriel Lee, and he'd been in before.

"We hope you enjoy our accommodations over the weekend. Good thing you showered before you went into work today. You work, right?"

Gabriel ground his jaw. He knew better than to comment. *Just keep your mouth shut and be the water, not the rock.*

****

Detective Kerry became impatient with the two-months-past-the-Bar Assistant D.A. He pitied the kid, actually, knowing a murder suspect with a Baltimore detective and an FBI Agent in his corner was a step above unusual. *Does this kid shave daily?* He wondered. Kerry acknowledged, even as he requested Gabriel's immediate release, the kid didn't have the chops to make it happen.

The newbie's shaky bravado transmitted over the telephone line. "Just because Mr. Bowman has friends in the city and the FBI, doesn't mean I'd let a suspect in two murders go on your say-so. He'll have to wait until my boss gets back on Monday."

"I understand." Kerry infused his voice with false sympathy. "You're gonna find out when CSI and the investigation are finished, that my guy is clean, so, until then, I'll ask you to do what you can to put him with a non-violent offender and keep him safe. This man is a personal friend of mine, Lindsey. If you want to start a good relationship with the Baltimore City Police, you'll take care of your suspect. And none of the perp-walk crap. You'll only wind up embarrassed if you let that happen."

"I can do that for you, Detective," Lindsey affirmed. "If your faith in him is justified, he'll be out Monday morning."

****

Gabriel was shown to a single cell by the same corrections officer showing a clear change of heart. "We're putting you by yourself, Mr. Bowman, and we'll try to keep it that way if we can. But you know, it's Friday night so we may be giving you a roommate."

Gabriel flashed a grim smile. "That'll be fine."

Sleep was impossible. Gabriel relived Ted's shooting every time he closed his eyes. The appearance of a cellmate was almost welcome, anything to take his mind off the anguish of losing his best friend.

Jeremiah Watson was in no way equipped to weather time in a cell. Gabriel suspected the wetness on his cheeks was not the remnants of the de-lousing shower.

The man stood before his lower bunk, blanket in hand, lost entirely. "There's no pillow." He said before he lowered himself on shaking legs to the hard bunk mattress.

Gabriel took pity on the non-descript young fellow with the dejected air. Any former college-polish was swept away with the last wave of the shower hose. Gabriel swung his legs over the side of the bunk. "It's a pretty warm night. You can roll your blanket up to make a pillow." The young man stood there staring at the bunk and swallowed, bleak-eyed. Gabriel hopped to the ground, and the man took a backward step away from him. "I'm Gabriel Bowman. What's your name?"

"It doesn't matter. My life is over."

Gabriel shook his head. "It may feel like that right now, but you're still alive, buddy. Things will be better after you talk with your attorney." He looked closely at the man and held up his hands. "I'm not gonna hurt you. You should lie down and try to get a little sleep."

The jailhouse cacophony and ribald taunts punctuated Gabriel's words. The man before him looked bleaker still. "How can anybody sleep in here?"

Gabriel shrugged. "It's not summer camp. You get tired enough, you'll drop off. C'mon, give me a name, I'm tired of saying 'hey you'."

The man pushed his glasses up his nose. "I'm Jerry."

Gabriel asked the age-old question. "What are you here for?"

"Drugs and soliciting. What about you?"

Gabriel paused. "A misunderstanding." He sure as hell was not going to tell this uninitiated he was in for suspected double-murder.

Jerry lowered himself to the bunk, head in his hands unable to stop the tears. "They might as well keep me. I'll never be able to show my face back home again."

"You can't say that. You have a family, don't you?"

Jerry cried harder. "That's the problem. I have a family in Kansas. My wife will divorce me, and even if she doesn't, she'll make me pay every day of my life." He coughed. "Her father's one of those Holy Roller preachers, a pillar of the community." He leapt up, agitated. "Oh sweet Lord, I am so done."

Gabriel considered the man's vocabulary. What the hell happened to this kid in Baltimore? "So, you're not from Baltimore. How'd you come to town?"

"I came for the Software and Animal Husbandry Convention."

Holy Bill Gates, computers have infiltrated everything!

"I do business with the guys from Chicago all the time. This is the first time we met. When people clock out at night, they're different. I've been dealing with them for two years. I never knew once their minds were off business, *they* were the animals."

Gabriel began to get the picture. "Do you usually take drugs? What happened?"

"I used a little weed in high school, but I've never used coke." The kid wept harder.

"They charged you for coke?"

"We were in the hotel bar… and they were getting ready to go out… they wanted to know if I was going with them. I said I was going upstairs to call my wife and eat some Maryland crab cakes from room service." He looked around as if embarrassed. "They called me pussy-whipped, and told me to stay for one drink, and that's the last thing I remember until… next thing I know, I'm in a bed, and somebody's banging on the door, yelling police. Do you know, I was in bed with a man who looked just like a woman? I thought that was just in the movies… and she's dumping her purse in my lap… with all these little packets of white powder…"

Gabriel groaned. "You were set up, for sure. Did you tell the arresting officers this?"

Jerry shook his head. "They just said, 'tell it to the judge'. They took my phone and flipped through the pictures. There wasn't one photo of my wife and me. There were a bunch of selfies with me and a bunch of different women – if they were even woman – why would they do that to me?"

Gabriel shook his head. "There're assholes everywhere." The kid seemed to blanch at his language. "What's important now is getting you cleared and making your family understand."

"Understand? They're never going to understand. I walked into a bar. The Bible says, 'the wages of sin are death'."

"That seems a little harsh under the circumstances…"

A guard appeared at their cell door. "Bowman?"

Gabriel walked to the bars. "Yeah. Here."

"The Assistant D.A. wants you for questioning." Gabriel nodded. "Present your hands." It was a time-worn procedure, he extended his hands through the bars for cuffing.

****

Gabriel was resigned, he was here for the weekend. Once again, he racked his brain for anyone Ted may have mentioned as even distant family. Someone to stand beside him at a good man's funeral. Well, the guys from the shop will be there. The folks from A.A. Probably even some company brass…

As the guard walked him closer to his cell, he could see Jeremiah virtually in the arms of the criminal in the next cell. They were separated by bars, but as close as two men could be when one-inch vertical iron was between them. Gabriel had seen this kind of thing before; the veteran thug working the newbie into a suicidal lather just to see how fast they could make a guy piss himself. The candymen gave themselves extra points if they could get a cry-baby to off himself. It was inside sport.

Eyes down, Gabriel watched the retreating corrections officer, and when he heard no footsteps, he turned toward the duo in the back corner. He could hear the devil's voice.

"Mr. Sunshine there, don't know your burden. He probably came back just to say goodbye."

Gabriel's eyes narrowed. "Let him go." The thug's arm bore the same ink as Scratchy Jimbo, the pusher who robbed him of Carla and his baby. They were part of the cancer plaguing the drug addicts of Baltimore.

Gabriel's words pushed Jerry closer to the thug. "Let him go. He doesn't need your poison."

Jerry quivered under the other prisoner's control. Gabriel thrust his thumb under the seducer's grip, who howled in pain, as Gabriel peeled the guy's hand off Jerry. *Did he just slip something into this kid's other hand?* "Back up, sleaze bag. What did you just give him?" Jerry skittered into the far corner and curved inward like an armadillo on a country road. "Drop that shit, Jerry. Drop it." Pushing the thug back, as far as his reach allowed through the bars, Gabriel spat. "Back off, you rat bastard."

The corn-rowed prisoner sneered as his homeboys cheered him on from adjacent cells. "Hey, Sunshine, you don't give a lick about that farm boy. B-more don't need another hayseed in town. Let him take his way out."

"Feet first." Another hoarse voice called out above the chanting mob.

Gabriel crouched over Jerry, fighting for the words to reach the miserable young man. "Whatever he gave you, let me have it." Gabriel wrestled with the man.

"You don't understand. I've got nowhere to go. Nothing left…"

Jerry rolled and crabbed his way under the bunk. Gabriel heard sobs and crackling cellophane as he grabbed two handfuls of Jerry's orange jumpsuit and yanked him into the center of the cell. "That pusher doesn't understand, either. Don't sell yourself short. Gimme that stuff." Gabriel rolled on the floor behind Jerry to pin his elbows back. "I swear to God, Jerry, you swallow that stuff and I'll follow you into hell and bring you back, just to beat your ass."

Jerry's slippered feet pummeled Gabriel feebly as he curled to get his hand to his mouth. "Why do you care? You gonna take me home and keep me?"

Gabriel's adrenaline kicked in and he hip-checked Jerry onto his belly and pinned his hands to the floor. "I don't want to dislocate your shoulders, that hurts, I know from experience." He spoke softly into Jerry's ear as he worked his hands toward Jerry's wrists. "Drop the shit, and I'll let you go." The stomping and chanting accelerated in the adjacent cells.

"I'm none of your business. Get off me."

Gabriel watched Jerry's head drop to his chest, and that did it. Gabriel was up with Jerry in a misguided Heimlich maneuver bouncing the two of them off the walls of the cell. Jerry's grip loosened, and a packet hit the concrete. Gabriel kicked it out of the cell. Jerry collapsed, dead weight, crying. "What makes you think I won't do it when I get out of here?"

The muscle in Gabriel's jaw jumped with the tension of the room. "For one thing, Jerry, I'm not convinced whatever drug they gave you is completely out of your system. Plus, think about how you could impress your father in law's congregation by turning yourself around. You were a sinner but saw the error of your ways."

Jerry's tears dried up in an instant. "You think that would work?" He sniffed loudly.

"It can't work if you're dead. Then, the wages of sin *are* death. I don't think that's how the good Lord wants you to end."

Jerry slid on his backside to the wall, his gaze darting at the hungry faces around him, but listening to Gabriel. "You could be right about that."

Gabriel paced a circle in the cell, staring the crowd down to silence. "You're damn right I'm right." He moved the back of his hand over his mouth. "You've got this backward." He ran his hand up his face and his fingers through his thick hair. "Your wife is going to do the Christian thing and forgive you, so you need to repent. Claim that forgiveness and swear off going into a bar ever again."

Jerry rose to pace in the same circle, straightening out his jumpsuit and wiping his face. "Yeah, yeah, I can't be forgiven if I don't repent. They'll probably ask me to give testimony."

"There ya go. You were lost, but now you're found."

"You must be some kind of angel sent here to rescue me."

"No, just a guy trying to get his own life right."

The surrounding inmates had no interest in redemption and withdrew into their cliques.

****

Sunday morning, Grace's phone woke her. "Hello?" She sat up at the sound of her attorney's voice.

"Grace, I apologize for being out of town and missing your call. My office contacted me this morning. I'll be back in town on Tuesday. Meanwhile, my paralegal will look over the suit.

She wiped her eyes and swung her legs onto the floor. "It's a real kick in the gut. My Trust account is frozen. The school's auto-draft bounced, and they won't let me back in until I bring a cashier's check."

"My office will take care of that tomorrow. But, this is quite serious, Grace. It's a frivolous lawsuit, but with Darby's connections, he could drain your father's assets in legal fees."

"What if he faced criminal charges?"

"Criminal charges, what type?"

"Do you have the mailer I sent in early June?"

"I'm not in front of your file."

"I marked it to be opened in case of my death?"

"That's not the type of thing an eighteen-year-old girl mails. Is he threatening you physically?"

"Not now."

"Are you in a safe place?"

"Yes."

"Good. I'll have the banker's box brought to my office early Tuesday. Can you be there at eight?"

****

Earlier than Gabriel anticipated, a corrections officer stood before the bars of his cell and called his name. Ironic, in that Jerry's family hired a high-priced attorney who sprang him yesterday, and Gabriel was alone. Didn't matter to him how it happened, he was just relieved to be heading out of his cell.

"Gabriel Bowman." The Corrections Officer held up a set of handcuffs.

This isn't what I expected. "Yes, sir." He presented his wrists through the slot in the door and experienced the degradation of being cuffed again. "Am I getting out?"

"D.A. wants to see you."

25

*W*ill I ever be a morning person? Grace maneuvered her car into a side street parking space and thought about resting her eyes for five minutes. *No, I need to be there to help Tsavros park the wagon.* Tsavros tapped on her window and startled her.

"I didn't mean to scare you. I didn't know you were a sleepy head." His engaging grin made her return the expression.

Tsavros does all the right things at exactly the right time, but... he's not Gabriel.

"You have no idea. I was going down for a five count. You're early."

"Well, I brought something sweet for you and good, strong, Greek coffee." He held up a steaming mug and a white paper bag.

If I just sit tight and let all this unwind, will I be alright settling for this? Grace's heart dug past the turns she might have taken. If she'd gone to Esther's first, she would never have known her lost 'Angel'.

"Smells fattening. Yum!" Grace opened the car door and slid out. His words about 'something sweet' reminded her of Gabriel asking if she wanted a snowball. They were such different men. Gabriel, for all his seeming confidence and presence, was quite insecure. Tsavros, raised in a loving family with hard but rewarding work was genuinely confident. Both were handsome, both were attentive, both seemed to care about her, but Tsavros was here, and Gabriel was last seen with a brunette in a red Mercedes. *Why isn't he here?*

After they traded grins over the fresh, warm pastry, they got to work. Tsavros pulled the tray of divided meat to the grill. "Portion control holds our profit margin, Grace. The little bit of prep time also cuts your delivery to your customer…" His words broke off following Grace's distracted gaze toward an approaching figure in an unseasonably heavy hooded coat.

Grace's attention was diverted to the young woman. "I hope she orders something hearty because it looks like she's swimming in that coat."

"She doesn't look homeless. Maybe she's sick…"

Grace put on her kindest smile and called to the approaching woman, "We're not open just yet, but give us about ten minutes to finish setting up…"

The woman nodded, and the hood fell back to reveal an unkempt strawberry blonde dye job framing an anorexic face. When she blinked hard, her artificially hazel eyes dominated her face. She looked positively lupine. "Could you help me for a minute?" She asked weakly.

Tsavros leaned out the window. "What is it, miss?"

"It's kind of a girl thing. Will you come out here?" The waif nodded to Grace.

Tsavros turned and shot Grace a warning glance. The two of them moved toward the door. "She looks odd. I'm going out with you." He led them out toward the unfortunate.

When they were five feet away, Grace peeked around her tall friend to see the girl raise her head along with a handgun. Tsavros threw his arms out to the side and yelled, "Grace, run!" Grace froze and felt for her phone, usually in her apron. It wasn't there. "Get out of here, Grace."

Street noise battled with the odd popping of three shots. Tsavros went down with a grunt as he lunged toward the attacker, knocking her back as Grace booked it toward her car around the corner. Grace's heart thumped harder than the footfalls of the shooter.

Where are my keys? She fumbled in her jeans pocket. *How am I going to get this boat of a car out of a parallel parking spot before she shoots me? What does she want? Money is in the trailer.*

The footfalls stopped. "Face me, you ungrateful whore!"

Grace's mind ground to a halt as she ducked behind a mailbox. "What?" She recognized the woman was insane. Armed and insane. The woman stalked her as they danced around the mail and Fed Ex boxes. Sirens raced toward them, but this was a hospital intersection. Sirens raced constantly.

"Arthur was right about you. You collect men like charms on a bracelet."

Grace missed a step in their dance, and a shot whizzed past her, a passerby on the sidewalk went down behind her. She froze in shock and hit the concrete, thrown back by the impact to her chest. Viscous red was everywhere. In a remote part of her mind, Grace guessed the stories were true, people didn't feel a bullet when they were shot. There was another shot, and her thigh stung. When her hand flew to the burgeoning red blossom, she rolled to her side. Thump, thump, the force pushed her face into the concrete, and her ears rang. *Is this the way Gabriel died?*

It was as if she'd awoken from a feverish sleep. Grace ached all over. *Where am I?* Slowly her senses returned, and she saw Tsavros kneeling beside her. He had put himself between a bullet and her. *How is he alive? How am I alive? Are we both dead?* Her field of vision widened, and she saw the on-lookers gathered around her.

"I'm a doctor, let me through." A concerned woman powered her way to Grace, and the look of noticeable relief on her face was puzzling.

Someone threw a sweatshirt down beside her. "Careful, Doc, kneel on this, don't get any on you." Grace thought everyone was amazingly cavalier about her blood.

She heard a scuffle. "Drop the gun. Now." It was a paramedic with her shooter in a restraint hold. There was a hollow sound of plastic as the black gun hit the pavement. She saw him speak into his shoulder. "9-1-1, we've got an assailant with three victims. We're on the southwest corner of thirty-third and North Calvert. We need an officer. Victims are being escorted to the MedStar E.R." He listened for a beat. "No fatalities, this was a paintball gun, thank God."

It took Grace a moment to process the notion of a paintball gun. That explained why she was alive. Her ears still rang.

"What's your name?" The doctor asked as fingers palpated her skull through the thick fluid.

"Grace."

The doctor smiled. "Hi, Grace, I think you're okay, but you might have a concussion, and I'm concerned about your neck. Don't move until the squad comes and we get you into a cervical collar."

****

The tall man was impeccably dressed, with salt and pepper hair and a smile for the six o'clock news. He starred down the guard. "Take those cuffs off." The officer shrugged and removed the restraints. *This is not the beginning of a good Monday.* "Mr. Bowman, I'm D.A. Lang Blackmon." The fortyish man struck a pose that would appear concerned to a camera. "I want to apologize on behalf of Baltimore County for any trauma you endured because of the bungling of this incident. I assure you, had I known your circumstances, you would have been a free man Friday night."

Gabriel blinked. *What does a guy who's never been arrested before say to this? I just want to cut and run, get the hell out of here.* In the end, he settled on the most neutral response he could imagine. "Apology accepted. When can I leave?"

Blackmon put a brotherly hand on Gabriel's shoulder. "Between you and me, Gabe, may I call you Gabe? This sort of thing happens way too often in this state." Gabriel stared at Blackmon's hand on his shoulder, and his mind raced back to a night on the east side when a police cruiser pulled him over with his larcenous friends in the back seat. He waited. "I'm running for Governor, Gabe. I don't know if you knew that?"

"Uh…"

Blackmon powered on, not needing a response. "I mean to change the way law enforcement handles things."

Gabriel nodded at the hand still on his shoulder.

"This was a clear tragedy, and you were a victim…"

Gabriel stepped back from under Blackmon's hand. "I…don't know where you're going with this…Mr. Blackmon."

"It's Lang, Gabe. Have a seat. Let's talk." He gestured to the small table and two chairs.

Gabriel sat down, but Lang drew his chair around the table to sit directly in front of him. Leaning forward, his gaze grew thoughtful. "I've looked into your record, Gabe." A part of Gabe twisted ominously. "You are the face of Baltimore. You've beaten addictions, you're a Veteran, you've gone back to school, you work full time." He had an evangelist's zeal. "And on that job, you were assaulted by a common criminal. This career thug should have been in jail. Instead, you're in jail."

Where the hell is this conversation going? "Yeah...but he's dead now, so..."

"Have you ever heard the saying 'There but for the grace of God go I'? If it happened to you, it could have happened to any of our good citizens." *Sure, if a thug recognizes you from a chop shop...*

Gabriel slid his chair back from Blackmon's reach. "I appreciate the apology, I need to get processed out, so I can get to work..."

Blackmon shook his head reverently. "Even after this hellacious weekend, you have the drive to get back to work!"

The attorney's room door ripped open and bounced off the wall. Special Agent Hawkins stood red-faced in the doorway. "This man is a protected witness of the FBI."

Blackmon sat astonished. "For what?"

Hawkins glared him deeper into his chair. "You should know, D.A. Blackmon, I'm not at liberty to say."

Blackmon stood up and amiably approached Hawkins.

"I'm not trying to hold him, hell, I want to make him part of my campaign."

Gabriel chimed in a beat late with Hawkins's "What?"

"Yes. He's the perfect example of the citizens my governorship could help."

"You need to find another poster boy."

Blackmon stood, mouth agape, his distinguished gray brows furrowed. "This morning, as the D.A., I came to apologize to Gabe. I also came to extend my invitation to a political luncheon at the Marina to talk about his participation in my campaign."

Hawkins motioned Gabriel toward the door. "Find a new face for your cause, Blackmon. Forget you met either of us or the Feds will come to your political luncheon."

****

Gubernatorial candidate Lang Blackmon hunkered down in the two-toned leather of his BMW. "It's a no go on Bowman."

There was the sound of a deep inhalation through the receiver. "When will you forward the camera feed? I want to see his picture."

"He can't do it. Something about being a federal witness."

Arthur Darby leaned back in his office chair and fumed. "Send the camera feed, Lang, I'll see you at lunch."

****

Vincent Spooner swirled the ice in a half-empty glass of Johnny Walker Blue Label while he waited in the enclosed bridge of Darby's ninety-three-foot yacht. It was his first meeting on the Viking Conquest. Previously, he'd only met Darby at football games. He watched Darby shoo a girl down the gangway as he tucked his shirt into the back of his Hugo Boss dress pants.

Spooner stood as the blonde man entered the bridge smoothing back his pompadour. "Stress relief." He gestured toward the departing girl's ass as she gyrated down the dock. "My sainted daddy knows I need it!"

Darby held up the liter of liquor to refresh Vince's drink, and Vince asked, "What can I do for you, Mr. Darby?"

Darby poured three fingers into his glass and motioned Vince to have a seat while he paced in front of him. He flicked on the television's sound as Penelope Frazier recounted the paintball attack. "…Universal Blue Water…" Darby winced at the mention of his company.

"What the hell!" He squinted at the television as if that would expand the news report. "Do you hear this?"

"Uh…yeah…" Vincent pulled out his phone and Googled the report. "Three people were hit with paintballs. Says the attacker was Emily Watkins, one of your employees." He held up the phone to Darby who grabbed it out of his hand.

"Jesus H. Christ! I need this…" The phone in his back pocket chimed, and he flung Vince's back to him. He thumbed to the message and opened a series of photos. Shaking his head and grinding his teeth, he paced the deck mumbling to himself, twisted his heel into the ivory carpet and then drew in a deep calming breath. "I AM vehement in pursuing my goals. I Am vehement in pursuing my goals." He closed his eyes momentarily and then stood directly in front of Vince. "I need you to get rid of Emily Watkins."

"What? Kill her?"

Arthur thought for a beat. "No, not kill her. Put her on the Blue Angel. It's shipping to China day after tomorrow. Reassign her as a ship's clerk."

"You think she'll just go?"

"Of course, she won't just go. Drug her put her in the clerk's cabin, and by the time she wakes up she'll be halfway to China, with no identification." He challenged Vince's disapproving look. "What? I didn't send her to North Korea."

Vince shrugged. "Okay. If you say so."

Darby returned to his tumbler of Scotch and downed it in one swallow. He brought the photos back to his phone screen and pulled out the street fair picture of Grace and Gabe. "The guy here, is he the same guy in both pictures?"

Vince stood to look over Darby's shoulder at the two images. "I dunno. The hair's different. No neck tattoo on the perp."

Darby gaped back at him. "You're an idiot."

"Have I ever messed up?"

"Don't start now."

"Okay, what do ya want me to do?"

"He needs to have an accident." Darby shook his phone at Vince. "He needs to have a fatal accident."

"You *do* mean kill *him*."

"Yes. Make it look like an accident."

"Well, okay, but why? I mean, what's he ever done to you?"

"He's seen my face somewhere I shouldn't have been." Darby poured sparkling water into his glass and slugged half of it. "I thought this bastard was dead already. I guess I have to handle *everything*."

Vince swallowed hard. "Who is he? How soon?"

"You're the detective. The kid's name is Gabe Bowman. I don't want to know how you do it. Just do it." Darby rolled up his dress shirt sleeves. "Don't just sit there. I'm taking the boat out. Go!"

****

Grace sat amid the soft, overstuffed chair facing the television. She was pink from scrubbing red paint from her face and hair. Now she relaxed, wrapped in a luxurious comforter. Esther and Kendra sat on the sofa while they watched the local news. Aside from slowly shrinking welts surrounding ugly bruises, she, Tsavros and the poor guy on the street were no worse for wear.

"In a bizarre incident in the city this morning, two food truck attendants and an unrelated citizen were attacked by a woman wielding a paintball gun. The police say, Emily Watkins, a twenty-four-year-old secretary at Universal Blue Water, appears to have mental health problems. Mr. Norman Craig of Charles Village spoke with our own Penelope Frazier shortly after he was released from the emergency room."

"It was the damnedest thing. I was headed home after a doctor visit, and this goofy girl is chasing another girl, and the next thing I know, I'm on the ground covered in red paint. Who's paying for my dry cleaning?"

"Ms. Watkins's other victims declined to comment. Police state she is detained on a mental examination hold."

Grace turned to Esther, her eyes wide, and mouth agape. "Universal Blue Water is Arthur's company. Did he send that…nut…after me?"

Kendra leaned back into the sofa and shook her head. "That is the most ghetto looking, white girl, I've ever seen."

Grace shrugged. "One look in her eyes and you can see she's off."

"Look at her mug shot, Cici. The dye job, the phony eye color, she's a wanna-be."

"Wanna-be?"

"That girl wants to look like you."

"But why? If her gun had been real, I might be dead. Tsavros took the first shot trying to save me."

Esther lowered her head as in prayer. "There is no greater love than to lay down one's life for one's friends."

Grace shrugged. "How do I repay that?"

Esther's smile was broad. "Both of you lived. What a wonderful beginning."

Kendra shook her head. "What about Gabriel?"

"The truth is, I don't know if Gabriel is dead or alive. If he is the man I've seen at the medical building, he's moved on."

"What do you mean moved on?" Kendra rose abruptly, hands on hips.

Esther's scrutiny passed from Kendra to land on Grace. "Why is this the first time I've heard you say he's moved on?"

"It's not easy to admit, but, I saw that guy again, yesterday. He was picked up by a leggy brunette in a Mercedes convertible. What if it *was* Gabriel? I don't know what's going on with him, but I'm sure of what's happening with Tsavros."

Esther relaxed on the sofa and nodded, her brow rising skyward. "I wondered if you'd give that man the time of day."

Grace sighed. "He has an amazing dedication to his work and his family. He'd make a wonderful husband. You saw how his brother's wives worship Xander and Kosmo, those women have beautiful homes and… security."

Esther's arms folded over her chest as she pursed her lips. "Um hum."

Kendra's face screwed up. "Security? As good looking as Tsavros is, what about passion?"

"Yeah, sure, he's…very appealing…"

Kendra flopped on the sofa. "But you're not catching what he's throwing down. Are you the employee of the month? Because he brings you coffee and goodies. He likes what he sees."

Grace's face fell. "What I know is, I like him. We have a lot in common. I could do worse, and I'm tired of counting on a dream that may never come true. Whether Gabriel is dead or moved on, he's not with me. Tsavros has had my back in many ways, and I like him."

Esther's hands folded softly in her lap as she bowed her head. When it rose, shaking slowly, she spoke. "When you met Gabriel, he had your back from the get-go. He had your back when he brought you here. You don't know *that man* is Gabriel, and if it is Gabriel, you don't know what that woman means to him. I know you like Tsavros, and I think you love Gabriel, but you are hurt. So, don't do something spiteful, that would end in a world of pain for all of you. Wait, a little longer. Have a little faith."

Grace nodded thoughtfully. "Okay, Mama, your advice has always been sound. I'll wait. And anyway, I have to deal with Arthur. What does he really want? He can't need my tuition money."

"He obviously wants your attention, which is the last thing you're going to give him."

"But…"

"Oh, no. What did you tell me when Gabriel brought you here?" Grace frowned. "You told me you would rather be alone than take his abuse. Show him you are not alone. You have us, and you have an attorney."

"As long as there's money, attorneys don't work for free."

"No contact with Arthur."

26

Gabriel functioned on autopilot as he showered and dressed. He hadn't known this type of devastation since the DeRosas died. That was one thing about death, it was final, and there was no arguing. His counselor kindly added program support while driving him to the dealership. The powers that be decided Gabriel was welcome to stay at the half-way house for another twenty-eight days if he needed. He had no idea where he'd live after that.

****

Gabriel pulled into the dealership employee parking lot and entered through the back door heading for Human Resources. When he stepped inside, he was engulfed in a wave of sympathy from his coworkers.

He ran a gauntlet of motherly hugs and brotherly pats on the back, ending with his arrival at Aaron Golding's office. Standing outside the open door, the HR Manager greeted him. "Gabriel, may I see you for a moment?" Regardless of the man's kind expression, Gabriel's stomach plummeted to the basement. *What if Ted was the single reason I'm working here?*

"We're all devastated to hear about Ted. When they took you to jail, you should have called me. I would have had you out in five minutes." Gabriel's head spun. He was half-expecting to be fired. *This is what Ted meant by support.* "The folks here passed the hat for Ted, you know, for a floral arrangement."

"I don't know if he made any plans for a final resting place. I don't know if maybe he bought a plot for him and Merri together, I don't even know what cemetery…I was hoping you could tell me if there were any relatives to contact. I've been driving his little truck…"

Golding gestured Gabriel into a chair and sat behind his desk. "Ted shared with me that the two of you were close. Treatment together, and all, so this morning I took the liberty of looking up his emergency contacts and insurance information. I have that for you here." He handed Gabriel a manila folder. "You're the emergency contact, and he left directions for you to speak with his attorney. The name and all that are in the file." He paused and let the shock sink in. "Are you okay, Gabriel? Is there anything we can do for you?"

"I'd appreciate a few days off…"

"Of course. You'll have three days bereavement, I'm sure I can make more available if you need it."

"I don't know. I've never arranged a funeral before, but I'd like to come back to work as soon as I can. Work keeps my mind occupied."

Golding nodded. "I understand that feeling. If anything changes, you let me know. You're part of our family, here."

****

It was a short drive from suburban congestion to suburban peace. A few twists and turns through what looked to Gabriel like rolling green forest opened to large residential plots with bucolic, pastoral scenes. His navigation system told him his destination was three hundred yards to his right. He pulled into the circular driveway of the white-washed brick ranch home. The double leaded glass doors beckoned him, but in his heart, there was an uneasy feeling he was about to invade Ted's privacy.

He and Ted had intended to move in this past weekend, and Gabriel never dreamed an attorney would be handing him the keys along with the rights to Ted's estate. The winter sun's color painted the flagstone path to the house. Gabriel figured he better open the door and check things out before he lost his nerve.

He opened the door to the smell of lavender Pine Sol and Windex. Ted arranged for a thorough cleaning before they moved back in. The slate floor in the foyer led him through a mid-century formal living room where a realistic Douglas Fir tree sat untrimmed in the corner. Its boughs were heavy with lights ready to twinkle. He moved further, into the recently renovated kitchen and den, flipping lights on as he walked through the rooms. Over the fireplace in the living room were a series of framed portraits beginning with Ted and Merri's wedding photo.

Gabriel stared at the couple's portraits depicting them through the years. He knew they'd shared a limited lifetime together. Unexpected emotion welled from his chest, and Gabriel rubbed at the pain over his heart. He gave into tears he'd been unable to shed since Ted's death. Once again, life turned on a dime. He would miss Ted like a father. Finally, gasping sobs gave way to shuddering sighs, and he sat in Ted's overstuffed chair, exhausted and numb.

I have to be able to handle all this. Ted expected me to use it wisely. This house is now my house, the car is my car. I'd trade it all to have Ted back, but that's not going to happen. He'd expect me to bring my A game.

He remembered the look on the face of Mitchell Arden, of Arden, Preston and Cruz Attorneys at Law. "Ted was one of my oldest clients and a good friend. He and Merri took vacations with Emma and me and the kids. I can't believe they're gone."

"I can't believe it either. I'm looking for Ted's family. The human resources people told me to come here."

"Ted recently changed his Will, and he made you the Beneficiary of his Living Trust."

Gabriel felt the blood drain from his face. Head down, he paced a small circle behind the chairs. Mitchell asked, "Are you still with me, Mr. Bowman?"

Gabriel thought he might be having a heart attack. For a moment, he couldn't breathe, and then his breath came out in gasps. "But there's got to be some family, a friend… hell, *you,* someone who deserves this more than me."

"Well, honestly, I asked him about that. He said I don't need the money, and you do, so that ended that. He did bequeath a portion to Scouts, Ala-non/Ala-teen and the Red Cross, but the majority of everything goes to you. He set up a Living Trust so there wouldn't be a probate. You're the Administrator of the Trust, as well as the Beneficiary. So, once I hand you the house keys, the place is yours."

"Do you know if he made final arrangements for himself? Does he want to be buried with Merri? I…"

"Have you ever known Ted to leave details undone?"

Gabriel looked around the office. "I guess not…"

"Yes, funeral arrangements are all made with Ruck Mortuary. You'll find that as part of the Trust." He handed Gabriel a leather, three-ring-binder detailing the provisions.

"I don't know what to do," Gabriel muttered.

Mitchell took the chair adjoining his. "I know you and Ted were both part of the Program. I was the one who referred him to treatment. I'm Program too. This is a new part of town for you, so if you'd like to come to a meeting with me, I'll be happy to introduce you around. Have you eaten today, Gabriel?"

Gabriel shook his head.

"That's not good. Remember, 'never get too hungry, too tired'…"

"Or too lonely." They recited together.

"I expect you're going to have a problem with the 'lonely' part for a while, you've got to eat, and you've got to sleep, or at least as much as you can. If I were you, under the circumstances, I'd make a meeting every day."

Yeah, Mitchell was great. Gabriel could see why he and Ted were such good friends. He'd need a new sponsor once he left the half-way house. Maybe Mitchell would agree.

Gabriel's palms pressed flat on the long kitchen counter. The granite was frosty white over a black under-mount sink. He saw his expression in the reflection.

Grace, are you already making sandwiches for somebody else? Have you found some other kitchen? I swear, I'm coming for you, as soon as I know we're safe. These delays are eating me up.

He spoke aloud, adopting a relentlessly cheerful tone. "You can make sandwiches or any other wild recipe you can think of in this beautiful kitchen. I can sit right on the other side of this counter and watch you." His smile left his eyes and settled at the corners of his mouth. He turned to take in the view from the kitchen, and his voice broke. "All this house needs is some happy noise. It's too quiet here…"

He jogged from the kitchen, down a long hallway where four bedrooms were spaciously laid out, sharing two bathrooms. *Where's the master bedroom?* He turned at the end of the hall and looked across the family room. Double wooden doors with brass lever handles waited for him. The soft carpet muffled the sound of his leather soles. He drew in a deep breath and threw open the doors on the grandest bedroom he'd ever seen. There were twin wing chairs in a corner in front of a brick fireplace and a king-sized bed with cherry wood nightstands. The luxurious beige carpet ended at another set of doors. Behind the doors were twin dressing rooms and a massive bathroom with his and her vanities.

Which side would Grace want? The one closest to the tub? Did she even like bubble baths? The wall of mirrors reflected and multiplied his astonished expression. *None of this will mean anything without her.*

He turned to the closets and dressing rooms, drawn by subtle perfume. Merri's fashionable clothes hung orderly by color. The lady wore lots of pastels. There wasn't a pair of jeans on the racks.

Poor Ted. No wonder he struggled after she passed. He was unable to let go. What a lonely feeling to see the two wardrobes hanging with no one to wear them. *I'll find a worthy charity.*

He opened Ted's closet and regarded the executive wardrobe Ted preferred. There hung lots of pinstriped dress shirts, tailored, pleated wool trousers, blue blazers, and charcoal three-piece suits. A rack of jewel-toned sweaters, pullovers, and cardigans waited for harsh weather. There was a gap between the blazers and the suits. *The blazer I borrowed came from here.* In a lonely two-foot length of the closet were the more frequently used items Ted wore once his drinking bloated him. These were the subdued colors he was used to seeing Ted wear. He slid the remaining hangers closer together and smiled.

Gabriel looked upward and nodded. "It would be an honor, Ted, to wear some of these fine clothes."

When Gabriel closed Ted's mirrored closet door, he spied a tall, wooden box on Merri's vanity. He lifted the lid wondering why someone would use such a finely carved box for makeup. His jaw dropped. This was Merri's fine jewelry. He'd heard of Tiffany, they were in the mall in Towson, but he'd never had the nerve to walk in there. He picked up the aqua ring box, and a sparkling diamond ring sang in the L.E.D. lighting.

No way! This is real! In the pocket of the large wooden case, there was a small card with faded ink. *Happy twentieth anniversary, Merri, here's a carat for every ten years.* His eyes stung with unshed tears at the sentiment. Ted was now peacefully with his Merri.

He checked the security system directions on the keypad and set a new combination 0-2-2-1 and drove back to the quiet half-way house. His belly rumbled. He hadn't been able to stomach his whole meal when Mitchell insisted they eat lunch. Now, understanding where his future was headed, he could eat an entire pizza and twelve wings.

****

Grace keyed the ignition and entered the address for Holden and Bothwell Attorneys at Law into her phone. The chore of driving downtown in Tuesday morning traffic was something she usually avoided. Today, there was an excellent cause to make the trip to her father's law firm on the harbor. She drove on autopilot, Arthur's hated face more in her mind's eye than the surging traffic. She'd gone to great lengths to protect a mother who probably didn't deserve it. Other than self-preservation, Grace's primary objective was to make a life for herself while avoiding Arthur's snares. Despite all her machinations, she was back in his grip.

Oh, Gabriel, I wish you were beside me. Yes, she thought the tall man on the street was Gabriel, but she didn't want to. For all she knew, he was safely hidden in Alabama. *What the heck is going on? Whatever safety I have at Esther's house will evaporate once I file charges against Arthur. There's bound to be a media frenzy, and it will be a crap shoot who gets to me first, Wally or Arthur. I can't drag Tsavros into this. I have to keep business strictly business.*

****

Grace advanced into the quintessential law office of old money. Her father's attorney came from one of the first families of Maryland, and his reputation was unparalleled. Her feet sank into the thick carpet, and Bothwell rose from his seat as she entered.

"Grace!" His deep voice was somehow comforting, a hold-over from childhood security. "Please have a seat, dear." He motioned her to a chair.

"Hello, Mr. Bothwell. Thank you for seeing me so quickly."

"Of course. Grace, this is Mrs. Sandusky, my right hand." He gestured to the grey-haired woman who sat in a leather wing chair in front of his desk. "She'll be taking notes on everything we say today. First, I want to put your mind at ease about that school payment. I'm going to court as soon as we're done here to request an injunction against freezing your account. It's trivial, we'll simply demand an itemized accounting of all the charges Darby says you owe. It's just a delay tactic but will buy needed time and allow your payment to go through."

"Thank you."

"Now, Grace." His tone and demeanor turned grave. "I want you to explain the meaning of this." He held up the mailer marked *open only in case of my death.* "Why in the world would a teenager from a good home write such a thing?" Bothwell and Mrs. Sandusky stared at her with eyebrows raised.

****

Grace, drained as always by speaking the truth aloud, sagged into the back of the dark blue leather wing chair. She considered the effect her tale had on them. Bothwell was apparently trying to hold his legal persona together and stick to the facts, but it cost him in blood pressure if the redness above his collar was any indication. Mrs. Sandusky, on the other hand, fidgeted and pushed her hair back repeatedly with an agitated hand.

"Do you think the police will do something, Mr. Bothwell?" Grace murmured.

"Do something?" His raised voice betrayed his agitation. "Oh, yes. I think they'll do something!"

"But it's only my word against his. I have no proof…"

"Grace, dear, your recording is more powerful than you know. It showed a premonition of danger when you thwarted Darby. It shows your intent to leave an untenable situation, and it documents some of the abuse you endured. In the next days, you and Mrs. Sandusky will commit to paper every date you can think of when you suffered his advances. We'll correlate those dates with photos, security footage, witnesses, anything that can prove you were together with him at times and places you catalog. With this evidence, I assure you, the police will act. Clear your calendar for Friday. You and I will go to the police on Friday morning, and I have no doubt by Saturday at the latest, Darby will be under arrest."

"But what happens then? Won't there be publicity?"

"Yes, I expect there will be. Unless Darby agrees to a plea bargain, there will be a trial."

"You don't understand. The whole reason I'm with Esther is that Gabriel wanted me hidden from Wally and his gang. I have no idea if they're still interested in me, but if they are, I'll be putting good people in danger by staying with them. I have no place else to go."

After she related the story of Gabriel and Wally, Bothwell and Sandusky were more alarmed. The attorney glanced at his paralegal. "You have the correct spelling on all those names?"

"Yes, Sir."

"Grace, I need to look into your Gabriel a little further with some friends downtown. Before we do anything, I need to be sure of your safety. Stay with Esther. Say nothing until I contact you. I'm headed to court for that injunction. You and Mrs. Sandusky get to work on the documentation. We'll talk again when I know more."

****

When he woke and felt warmth in the bed alongside him, Gabriel remembered how he let Grace 'experiment'. She was shy and awkward at first, so he encouraged her to get her bearings and explore her instincts. He lay there while his lover drove him wild slowly and methodically. She became acquainted with his body's roadmap of pronounced veins and roped muscles. Her sweet lips worked on the hard velvet flesh she found most intriguing. She was especially fascinated with fondling him awake. It amused him that her curiosity could send him wailing a prayer to God before he let it all go. His minx would fall back, satisfied with accomplishing her joyful task, and then let him return the loving favor.

When he woke fully, he realized the warmth was a phantom. In his tossing and turning, he left warm patches all over the twin bed. Gabriel was alone, and Grace was a zephyr in his mind.

He showered and shaved, trying to coerce his hair into a style, and then dressed and stood for inspection. If there ever was a time to remember his Navy days, this was it. He stood tall before the mirror on the closet door. He felt downright 'ship shape' as they used to say. The hated barbed wire tattoo was almost gone, just one more laser session needed.

He picked up the keys to Ted's dark Mercedes, his car now. He'd drive to the funeral home for the memorial, and later, alone, he'd carry the urn to the mausoleum. Sitting, he adjusted the rearview mirror, and his eyes fell to the passenger seat, where he hoped he'd soon be allowed to have Grace. But today, he'd summon the most gracious words at his command to speak about a man who changed his fate. *Without Ted, where would I be?*

****

Grace handed a gyro sandwich to her next customer just as her cell rang. She turned from the food truck window with a hurried. "Excuse me a moment." Esther stepped up to serve the next guest.

"Grace, this is Tom Bothwell. I want to let you know, the cashier's check for your tuition has been received by the school. You may resume classes tomorrow."

"And the other matter?"

"I've spoken with several people. The garage has been seized, and no one will answer any of my questions about Gabriel Lee. As far as any of my contacts know, this is a federal case. Anyone involved is either dead, in jail, or in hiding. If you were in danger, they'd be obligated to tell me. With your permission, I believe we should go together to the police on Friday morning about Darby."

"If there's no danger, I agree." *But no word on Gabriel?* "Arthur has victimized me for the last time."

"That's the Grace I know. Your father would be proud of you."

****

Gabriel slipped on his sunglasses in winter's glare and glanced at the brass urn in the box on the passenger floor. "Well, Ted, I'm *your* chauffeur today. I'll bet you and Merri have been dancing up a storm." The CD marked in a girly script 'Merri's Mix' sat in the console. "Let's see what Merri is playing for your last ride." Gabriel keyed the ignition and slid in the CD. He slowly pulled into heavy traffic and headed toward the Silent Home Cemetery.

Eric Clapton sang about taking his queen and their love ruling in a 'kingdom we have made', while Gabriel began his conversation. "You sure changed my world, Ted." Traffic was bogged down with Christmas shoppers. Gabriel crept along at ten to fifteen miles per hour, longing for the moment when he hit the country and could do thirty-five. He carried on his one-way conversation with his friend. "I've decided to move into the house this weekend. I think I'll ask a designer to help me redo the bedroom." He paused a second. "I know you'll understand it would be a little creepy to sleep in your bed. And I want it to be nice when I bring Grace home."

The farther out he drove, the freer he felt. His foot gave in to the siren's call of empty pavement and winding rural roads. Gabriel beat the drum line on the steering wheel, bobbing his head with Hootie as the speedometer needle passed fifty-five. "Yeah, I know what you're thinking. But I'll bet you can see it all coming together. So, any insight is welcomed."

The road crested in a series of rolling curves, and he grinned at the sedan's responsiveness. *This is why people drive these cars.* Up ahead he saw the ornate gates of the cemetery. He checked his speed. *This road got the best of me.* "Hey, Pops, why didn't you tell me to drive the speed limit?" He was pushing sixty miles an hour when he approached a thick copse of evergreens.

Out of the corner of his right eye, something tan and quick entered his field of vision. "I believe in love…" Elton John sang when the trio of deer bolted to the culvert and considered doing their rendition of the 'cow jumping over the moon'. Except their moon was a black sedan streaking down the gravel-strewn pavement.

Gabriel's reflexes blocked the music, his mind calculated the chance of flipping the auto in the deep ditch to his right if he broke and swerved. Would all three deer leap and clear the narrow country road? Or stand stock still mid-road? With hands at five and seven on the wheel, he prepared to brake. "Stay with me, Ted, I need some divine guidance."

As if he wasn't the driver, he shouted 'brake and steer', reinforcing the focus on his thought process, begging time to avoid hitting Bambi and his friends. He squeezed the brake pedal firmly, without a real response. When he should have felt a skid, he was hurling closer to impact. His foot held hard on the brake with none of the 'machine gun' effects that usually comes back through the pedal. *If the brakes don't work, what good is the parking brake?*

Gabriel downshifted and jerked into a long patch of gravel, prompting the largest deer to pivot and course back into the woods. The back wheel slid onto the shoulder, and he yanked it straight, heading for the shallower ditch ahead. *The rushes might retard my speed.*

The second deer cantered back and forth in confusion, and his hindquarters struck the driver's front bumper. Guts obscured the windshield before it shattered in a bloody spider web. With no brakes and no visibility, Gabriel braced his hands to avoid fracturing his fingers on impact. *This has been one hell of a year.* Although he tried to keep his eyes wide open to see his inevitable journey, all he saw was the blur of impact.

Gabriel sat, in the wreckage of his Mercedes, sandwiched between airbags with the auto's safety operator asking if he was okay. He held a hand to his bloody nose and responded. "Yeah, I think so. I know I need a tow truck." He looked down at the urn which thankfully sat pinioned in its Styrofoam holder. "Ted, you held it together better than me."

****

By six p.m. Gabriel had the car up on the rack and was pointing out the damage to all of the brake lines. "Pinholes. The system didn't leak until I was in the country doing fifty. I'll bet I left a trail of red brake fluid like Hansel and Gretel."

Agent Hawkins shone his own flashlight from wheel to wheel. "In this case, it could have gotten you killed. Kerry, get pictures of this, will you?" He turned to Gabriel. "Bowman, I can't believe you didn't flip this thing."

Detective Kerry followed along snapping photos of the car's undercarriage. "You've got an admirer, Bowman. This is out of nowhere."

Hawkins muttered. "I thought we were coming to the end of this. Could this be Johnson's gang, the thug who recognized you?"

Gabriel shook his head and laughed. "That group is lucky to find the gas cap on their cars. They're not smart enough to do something like this."

Kerry frowned. "Let's back up. The car was working okay this morning?"

"Yeah, it was fine. I drove it to the mortuary for the service."

Hawkins considered. "If it were sabotaged it would have happened at the mortuary. Let's hope there are security cameras in their parking lot."

****

Danny from Service looked at him and shook his head. "You're gonna have black eyes tomorrow."

"Maybe I'll get lucky, and the ice will keep it down." Gabriel winced. "So, do I get an employee discount on this?"

His friend curled his lip. "Insurance, man. You're fully covered. Wait here a sec, and I'll get the ticket for you to sign."

Gabriel leaned against the counter, idly watching the news on the big screen TV as he waited. He touched his nose gingerly. It was a miracle his face didn't look as flat as a pug's at this point. It was a good thing he had strong cartilage.

"D.A. Lang Blackmon, the candidate for governor, addressed the annual Port Authority luncheon today, amid supporters of his campaign." Gabriel noticed the man was wearing the same suit he'd worn to the jail. *That must have been the luncheon he wanted to drag me to.* His eye was caught by a short blonde guy standing next to the candidate. *Where have I seen that guy before?*

Danny came back to the desk. "Well, you don't get an employee discount, but we're waiving the deductible. So that should help you out."

"Hey, that's really nice of the bosses, but I was just joking, I can afford to pay..."

"No, it's a done deal..."

****

Thursday morning Gabriel pulled into the convenience store and nodded to Larry, the clerk, as he headed to the tall coolers for a quart of milk. "What does the other guy look like?"

Gabriel stared at his reflection in the row of cooler doors. He winced at the purple bruises across his eyes and cheeks. "Venison."

Larry didn't chuckle. "I use a shotgun when I'm hunting, it's old-fashioned, but I spend less at body shops..."

Gabriel looked back at Larry. "So, I guess you won't let me keep my face in your coolers today?"

"Same old, same old, buddy. Buy it and skedaddle, it's time for the college girls to come by." They shared a dark laugh as Gabriel opened the cooler door. Chocolate milk on the bottom rack got his attention, and he dropped down to score a pint. One gunshot rang out, piercing the four gallons of milk in the row above him. It spread like white arterial spray.

"Jesus Christ, those deer had friends." Larry grabbed his phone and snapped a photo of the retreating Super Duty truck. "Yeah, operator, this is the Royal Farms on York, I just had a drive-by..." He walked over to Gabriel still crouching in the aisle. "I don't see any blood, did they hit you?"

Gabriel turned warily. "Luckily, no, it's broken glass."

"We get a quick response, sit back behind the counter with me while we wait."

Gabriel pulled out his phone and dialed Hawkins. "This time it was a drive-by shooting. Somebody is still after me."

****

A Baltimore County officer stood outside the convenience store as his partner rolled off skid marks. He took a moment to consult with the

FBI Agent. "Agent Hawkins, the clerk got a clear photo of the truck, but it's stolen. It was nabbed downtown this morning. We'll find it later today dumped somewhere."

"I want first dibs on processing it." He waved and headed inside. Gabriel met him at the door, and they made their way to the cooler aisle as Hawkins calculated the shot line from the parking lot. The low chip and candy displays gave the shooter a clear view when he thought Gabriel was reaching for the top shelf. "Chocolate milk saved your life. My wife keeps telling me whole milk will kill me."

"I'd like to see the humor in this situation, but, after all these months, why now? Who's left out there who wants me dead?"

Hawkins looped his thumb in his belt, near his holster. His face grew grim. "That's why we're going to stow you away tonight and take you directly to the precinct in the morning to look at the books. Does any odd face come back to you? Someone whose car you serviced, maybe unnecessarily, like they were in the shop for empty reasons? Were there any hangers-on?"

Gabriel blew air through his lips. "The only one who's taken particular notice of me is that joker Blackmon like I could do something for him."

"He's your average political gasbag. I don't see us turning down that great political offer as a motive for murder. They'll tow your pickup to safety, and you're coming with me. There's a room at the Hyatt with Uncle Sam's name on it."

"What I really need is a meeting. I've had too many changes this week…"

Hawkins nodded. "I'll sneak in your sponsor, and both of you can have all the room service crab cakes you can eat. I don't think it's safe for you to hoof it across the street to a meeting."

27

Hawkins knocked on the suite door. "Bowman, it's us." Gabriel rose numbly from the chair and let in Hawkins and his sponsor, Mitch Arden.

Glumly, Gabriel stepped aside and directed them to the seating area of the plush room. "Sorry, Mitch, I didn't intend to take you up on the sponsor help so soon."

Mitch extended a hand. "Our paths have crossed for a reason." The three men gathered at the small round table where Gabriel spread out a newspaper.

"I was alone with this paper and um, there's a photo here that struck me familiar. This Blackmon guy is suddenly all over the news, and there's this little guy." Gabriel pointed at the newspaper. "What, does he carry his coffee? He looks familiar, but I can't remember from where."

Hawkins slid the newspaper into the light. "Yeah, Bowman, you've had some head trauma this year. Which one is it, this little guy?"

Mitch Arden squinted at the photo and drew out his phone, summoning 'Blackmon publicity images'.

Hawkins regarded the photo and caption. "…Arthur Darby… So, you don't recall meeting Arthur Darby? Mitch sniffed and read the Google headline. "Arthur Darby, CEO, International Blue Water, past President of the Reagan Republican Club…"

Hawkins returned the paper to the table. "Wait a minute, International Blue Water, he's a mover and shaker on the docks. Not someone you want to cross. Where did you meet him? Was he a frequent visitor to the garage?"

Gabriel's gaze swept the ceiling for the memory, and his palms smacked the chair arms when he realized it. "Wally's garage, that last night, when Wally set me up. That guy was trying to fade into the background. But between that crazy blonde hair and the gold chain with the dangling charm, he was like a beacon in the dark. It was him, alright. I remember wondering at the time if he was the big boss. I'd never seen him before."

Hawkins tapped the photo with his index finger. "Darby's name has never come up before. But it would make sense, his industry is what moves the contraband."

Mitch stood up and gazed over Baltimore's Harborplace. He shook his head. "You told me everyone involved has been killed or sent up the river. If there is a direct line from Blue Water to the crimes, you'd be the only one able to finger him. Until Ted was killed, you were perfectly safe, right?"

Gabriel and Hawkins nodded thoughtfully. "Right."

Hawkins picked up Mitch's line of thought. "So, what happened from the time the cops picked you up Friday till your car was tampered with?"

"I was in jail, the D.A. came to see me, you interrupted that meeting…"

"What did that caption say about Blackmon and Darby? What's Darby to him?"

Mitch joined in. "I can tell you that. Our side's been fighting him for a long time. He's a mover and shaker for the radical conservatives."

Hawkins gave a half laugh and stood, his hand to his forehead. "This is crazy, but what if, as a member of his campaign staff, Blackmon sent Darby your picture? You know, the preyed-upon face of Baltimore? They wanted to put that pretty mug of yours on every campaign poster. Of course, they would vet you first, and Gabriel Bowman ticked all the boxes. Could Darby have seen your photo and realized Gabriel Lee is still alive?"

Gabriel fingered his sore cheek. "It's a long shot. I looked pretty different when he first saw me, and that was in the dark…" Gabriel's demeanor crumbled. "You know, Wally put surveillance on Grace and me. There was a candid photo tacked to the wall. Wally promised it to me when I returned with the stolen cars. I remember the guy in the suit looking at that photo a little too long."

Hawkins expelled a deep breath. "I can check the inventory. We cleaned out that office. I looked at papers, but don't remember a photo."

Mitch shook his head. "Look, guys, I'm a family practice attorney, but I can see a good criminal attorney getting Darby off on circumstantial evidence. You don't have enough to arrest him and make it stick."

Gabriel paced in front of the window. "What worries me, he's seen that photo. He knows about Grace and me. Neither of us is safe."

Hawkins rubbed the back of his neck. "Let's think this through. I agree that Darby looks suspicious, and he may well be a missing link in the Federal case, but we have no good evidence that he's behind the attacks on you." He grinned at Gabriel. "You haven't been sleeping with anyone's wife, have you?"

Gabriel rolled his eyes. "I haven't even slept with my grammar tutor, and she's been after me for weeks."

"For sure, I need to open an investigation on Darby. I haven't seen the security video from the mortuary lot or the convenience store. Though I think it's doubtful, we'll see Darby sliding under a Mercedes. If we can flip the actual perp, we could get him that way. Let's stick to the plan. Gabriel, be ready to leave here at seven thirty tomorrow. I brought your kit and some clean clothes." Hawkins moved toward the desk and tossed them the guest room binder. "You and Mitch, have a good conversation over dinner and I'll see you in the morning."

****

The early December morning bit with wind and humidity. Gabriel hunkered in the hoodie and laughed at the clear blue sky. "Liar." He shook off the cold as he and Hawkins bolted from the car at the curb into the overly warm police precinct. He bobbed down the corridor, surrounded by four armed agents. "I could have used you guys yesterday." Their serious manner never acknowledged his humor.

Kerry met them halfway down the hall. "Bowman, good to see you in one piece. Hawkins, welcome to my house. I'll tell you what, we're going to set you up with Officer Packard, let you look at some photo arrays while Hawkins and I meet with the brass."

Gabriel was led into a small interrogation room. Being offered coffee and having certain courtesies extended to him as a victim, still didn't rest his soul. He blinked at the flashbacks of being cuffed to a table when he saw the bolt before him. And even though they politely told him, the men's room was down the hall to his left, he wondered if, when they exited, the door was locked.

****

Grace reflected on the last time she visited the precinct. People were polite, but not quite so eager to please as when she entered with one of Baltimore's legal heavyweights. Bothwell told her he'd called ahead, and they were expecting her.

He led her across the lobby, and then up the bank of elevators to the third floor marked Sex Crime Division. Bothwell knocked on a closed office door, and it opened to reveal a smallish room with two metal desks crammed into the space, each adjoined by a metal chair. A pleasant looking detective dressed in a navy suit extended her hand. "You must be Mr. Bothwell, I'm Detective Carnegie, and this is my partner, Detective Romero."

Bothwell met her handshake. "This is my client, Ms. Lerner. I believe you'll find more than enough evidence here to act on her complaint."

Carnegie smiled encouragingly at Grace. "Why don't we go into the conference room, where we have more space?" Grace found herself unexpectedly tongue-tied wondering how she would find the words to expose such intimate details.

How many times have they heard these stories? I'll pretend I'm describing what happened to someone else. I didn't keep my cool when I tried that with Gabriel, let's try it again.

"I know this isn't easy, Miss Lerner. Just tell us what happened."

"My stepfather, Arthur Darby, repeatedly molested and raped me in his home, and..."

****

Hawkins and Kerry interrupted the steady stream of photos. When you put a face on crime, it wasn't pretty like in the movies. Gabriel identified Darby in the midst of dozens of other blonde men. He'd identified him in casual, candid shots, posed corporate images, and his driver's license photo. Officer Packard looked up with a smile. "He knows his guy; he's called him out every time."

The three men stood while Gabriel looked up at them. "We've been through the surveillance tapes. We can't get a clear enough picture to run facial recognition."

Gabriel covered his face with both hands and cussed under his breath. He slapped his palms down on the table and asked. "What now?"

The older guy, next to Hawkins spoke up. "We do what we always do in these situations, Mr. Bowman. We investigate."

Gabriel stood. "I don't think you guys are getting my biggest concern. If Darby is after me and he knows about Grace, he might try to hurt her to get to me."

Officer Packard pulled out the formal event photo of Darby and an attractive, taller blonde. "Do you recognize her?"

Gabriel scrutinized the tall blonde. He knew he'd never met her before, but the posture was eerily familiar. "Man, she's with him?" He laughed.

"Yeah, Arthur and Linda Darby. Why would he hurt his own stepdaughter?" The only sound was the wheeze of air moving through the dirty ceiling vent.

Gabriel's eyes widened. "What? Grace is his stepdaughter? That's her mother?" He picked up the picture and sneered. "If Grace is his stepdaughter, he's her rapist." He stared at the lawmen waiting for a reaction. "I met Grace because she was done with living with them. She took off, he closed all her accounts. She was broke, I took her in. That makes me even more concerned that he might do something to her." The men around him glowered, working to process this new development.

"Don't you get it? If it's too hard to get to me, Darby will move on her. I don't want him to get desperate. If you want to sting him, I'll be your bait."

Kerry frowned. "If you're right and Darby is at all interested in her, there's bound to be some police report on it."

Gabriel waved his hand. "The day we met; she was scared shitless he'd have her arrested for assault. She never filed a rape complaint; she was afraid how it would affect her mother."

"Let me check the reports. Let's see if there have been any other incidents involving Grace Lerner."

****

Grace started to relax. The calm and matter of fact demeanors of Carnegie and Romero were somehow comforting in such an emotionally charged situation. Romero handed her a fresh cup of coffee. "So, Grace, on the tape you say Darby might try to kill you. What made you say that?"

"No matter what obstacle I erected to get away from him, he barreled through them all. And he told me, "You'll never get away from me, Grace. I'll kill you first. He has a boat big enough to take to the Bahamas. Once he made that threat; I never stepped on that boat again.""

Carnegie nodded while Romero made notes. "Grace, I know this will be hard, but can you tell us anything about him physically, that would help support your charges? Does he have any distinguishing physical markings on his private areas? Tattoos…"

Grace's eyes grew wide with remembrance. "Oh, my God, yes. He has a small port wine stain on his penis. About half way up the shaft on the right side, his left side." She covered her face and shuddered. Carnegie waited. Grace began to cry jaggedly. "He made fun of it, he told me to watch it get bigger as he got hard." She folded her arms on the table and buried her face, muffling her sobs.

****

The cops moved Gabriel into a conference room, set up for lunch. He looked at all the things in the salad that Grace would have picked out.

She despises cucumbers, tomatoes, peppers, onions. How can she cook so well with those items, when she doesn't eat them?

He smiled sadly. Kerry burst into the room, a sheaf of papers in his hand. "I hope you saved me some. I've got some good stuff here."

Gabriel stood with such force the chair skidded behind him. "What, what is it?"

"Saturday morning, Grace, her coworker and a passerby were attacked by a gal named Watkins who is a secretary at Darby's headquarters."

"Attacked? Is she okay?"

"Yeah, it was a paintball, it was close range, but she was treated and released. Now, the kicker is, the attacker was held seventy-two hours on an involuntary psych hold. She listed no family, but the gal walked out of the hospital and right into a black town car. Her landlord says her studio is empty. She's a ghost..."

"That's it!" Gabriel insisted. "We've got to do something..."

"I'm not finished. This asshole, Darby, is suing Grace Lerner for care and feeding while she was living under his roof."

"While she was his victim?" Gabriel huffed and shook his head. "If he's suing her, he must know where she is. We need to send him my way. I'll take out the trash..."

Hawkins moved into Gabriel's hard gaze. "No, Bowman. That's not how we handle it." He put a hand on Gabriel's tense shoulder. "If we do agree to use you as bait, I say *if*, I want your oath, you'll keep your head and let us do our jobs. No street justice."

Gabriel avoided his gaze and waved him off. "Yeah, whatever..."

****

Grace picked apart most of the Subway sandwich she ate with Bothwell. *If Gabriel were here, he'd eat the stuffing. What a waste.* The detectives came back into the room, and Romero handed her two sheets of paper. "The stenographer has typed your statement, Grace. I need you to read it over carefully. If there are any corrections needed, correct and initial and then sign at the bottom."

Carnegie slid into a chair beside her. "All these addresses you've given are correct?"

"Yes. Arthur will probably leave his office by three. It's Friday, and he'll go to his Harborview condo until Sunday's game." She shuddered.

Carnegie traded gazes with Romero who shook his head. "If we start at the office, they'll tip him off. We'll have the warrant by five o'clock; we'll go straight to the condo. I hope his mouthpiece has left town for the weekend."

Grace grimaced. "Game weekends, they're joined at the hip. That snake wouldn't miss free food and booze."

Bothwell grinned. "Well, maybe Hamm will get drunk and give bad advice."

****

Gabriel force-fed himself, barely chewing while the members of his law enforcement team planned a sting. He touched his nose gingerly. *The last time I did this, I was left for dead.* But he knew in his heart, Grace was worth any danger he might face. The door opened, and a new, cheerful face ducked inside. "Hey, Kerry, weren't you asking about a victim… Lerner? Grace Lerner?"

Kerry's jowls halted; he wiped his mouth. "Yeah?"

"Do you know she's on the third floor in sex crimes? We've got a fresh complaint in the system."

Hawkins swallowed. "Is there a warrant request?"

"Yeah, Judge Allyson Chaney is signing it now."

"Who's it against?" Gabriel held his breath.

"Some guy named Darby. They're going to pick him up now."

Gabriel stood. "Is Grace still here?"

"Far as I know."

He didn't even need words for the communication to pass between him and Hawkins. A nod from both did the job. "Take me to her, now." Looking at the shocked expression on the officer's face, he added. "Please."

****

Grace was alone for the first time in hours. *Have I been to the bathroom today? No. That explains all the caffeine coursing through my body. I feel positively electric.* She sighed heavily, grabbing her purse, and headed to the ladies' room.

****

Gabriel tried hard to be polite. The police probably wouldn't allow a wild man to interact with their witness. He pushed slightly ahead of his guide and threw open the door to an empty room. "She's gone, where is she?"

"There's a coat on the chair. Maybe she's powdering her nose."

Gabriel self-consciously touched his own nose. He hoped she'd recognize him under all the swelling and bruising.

A lilting feminine voice he hadn't heard in months spoke from the hallway. "Excuse me, that's my coat in there."

The cop stepped back. "Yes, ma'am. There's a man here says he knows you."

Grace shrank inward and stepped back from the officer. "Who?"

"He's inside, waiting for you. A young guy."

28

Grace lifted her gaze over the cop's shoulder to the tall dark-haired man whose hands rested on the shoulders of her coat. She knew instantly it was Gabriel because his presence filled the room. Her voice caught in her throat. She stepped around the officer and Gabriel turned. "Princess."

She flew into his arms, and her gentle hands framed his handsome, beaten face. "Why do they keep hurting…"

His lips stunted her question.

The cop receded from the doorway. "Yeah, I guess you do know each other." The door closed.

Time stood still while Grace enjoyed his kiss and the feel of his arms around her. No matter how close they held each other, she needed to be skin to skin with him. His hands traveled down to her backside as he clutched her against his tightening jeans.

The door flew open, and three detectives followed the FBI Agent into the room. Gabriel broke the kiss and chuckled. "You guys have great timing."

Kerry grinned. "We didn't want you to get too far before we interrupted. We have a plan."

****

Gabriel and Grace held hands, sitting as close as two people in separate chairs could sit. Their respective teams traded introductions. "We have a plan to take down Darby." Hawkins slid a timeline in front of the young couple. "For security, we're moving the two of you into The Pendry, got you a Harbor suite for the weekend. One catch."

Grace clutched Gabriel's hand in both of hers. "What's the catch?"

"We have a burner phone." He slid the cell to Gabriel. "We're assuming Blackmon will be with Darby in the M&T Bank Stadium suite. You call Blackmon, tell him, you don't care what the FBI says, you want to work on the campaign. Tell him you want an invite to the suite for the Pittsburgh game on Sunday. Your servers there will be agents, and we'll take over the suites on either side of you."

"So, you're hoping Darby will try and take me out, then?" Gabriel asked. Grace gasped.

Hawkins shook his head. "No, he's too precious to get his hands dirty. But, he has a guy, obviously. If he knows you're going to be there, we figure the most likely trick will be slipping you a mickey and carrying you out like you're drunk. Once you're in the elevator, you're toast."

"Wait a minute!" Grace stood. "What do you mean he's toast?" She turned to Carnegie. "I thought you were picking Arthur up?"

Carnegie and Romero were quiet since entering the room. They stood with their heads down over folded arms. "FBI outweighs the Baltimore PD."

"I don't understand why you're doing this?"

"Princess, we're pretty sure Darby is behind two attempts on my life in the past forty-eight hours." Grace shook visibly as her brows furrowed. Gabriel massaged her shoulder. "I'll explain the ins and outs more completely later. But, you need to know old Arthur probably isn't going to stop until I'm dead. Even if he's arrested on rape charges." A tear ran down Grace's cheek. "I could potentially get him the death penalty. We figure rather than waiting around for him to take the next shot, a controlled sting will take him and his cronies down at the same time."

She pointed at Hawkins. "But he said you'd be toast."

Hawkins walked behind Gabriel and Grace. "That's only if they manage to get him out of the elevator alone, Miss Lerner." His two hands rested on their shoulders as his gaze warmed. "We're not going to let that happen. He's not going to get drugged because he'll only be accepting food and drink from our agents." When he finished speaking, Grace nodded along with Gabriel and Hawkins. "This is our forte. We're not going to let our prize witness get hurt."

"You promise me?" She took in the myriad colors of Gabriel's bruises.

"I promise you. You know, Gabriel is kind of a hero around here."

"That doesn't surprise me." She threaded her fingers through Gabriel's.

Carnegie spoke up. "If the goal is to get Darby off the street, you may never have to file rape charges, Ms. Lerner."

"Because he'll be in jail anyway…?"

Hawkins nodded. "For a good long time depending on his survival skills inside."

Grace sagged with relief and turned to Gabriel. "You're convinced this is the right thing to do?"

"We have to quit running. Yeah."

****

Wearing only a bath towel around his lean hips, Gabriel hung back in the bathroom doorway and relished the sight of his princess. She stood in profile at the floor to ceiling windows overlooking the Baltimore Harbor. Her hair was long and damp down the back of her fluffy white robe. In the reflection of the harbor lights, she stood pensively drawing a wide tooth comb through her hair. "I could look at you for the rest of my life and not get enough of you." She turned her face to him, and he saw the curiosity in her expression.

"We have a lot of catching up to do." Grace slid the comb into her robe pocket. "When did you start driving a red convertible?"

Flummoxed, Gabriel shrugged. "Red convertible? Ah! I've only driven a demo."

"How about the brunette? Was she a demo too? Part of a sports package?"

"Babe, probably fifty guys have test driven that ride. Probably a few women too."

"But I saw *you* come out of a medical building and into her arms."

Gabriel scowled. "What the…oh, the day Rose picked me up. Baby, she's the receptionist at work. She was just picking me up because my friend was busy. He sent her."

"She was certainly chummy with you!"

Gabriel crossed his arms over his chest and leaned back into the door frame. "You a little jealous?"

"Jealous?" Grace sputtered. "What was I supposed to do? Make a Superman leap over six lanes of traffic and bitch slap her?"

"It wasn't what it looked like. Rose is touchy-feely and if you think back to it, did you ever see my hand on her? I was in defense mode from the minute she drove up. I'm the one guy who hasn't chased her skirts, and she is determined."

"Oh." Grace glided over to cuddle against him. "Now that you mention it, I didn't see your hands on her…"

Gabriel slipped away from her and picked up his phone, calling up a photo. "Let's talk about hands." He pulled up a photo of Tsavros nuzzling Grace's neck. "When I cropped this to get you, his paw got cropped out. Who's Mr. tall, dark, and godlike?"

"That's a friend…"

"Yeah."

"Uh, my lab partner and my business partner."

"If this is business, wouldn't being this close be considered harassment?"

"That's Tsavros and his sister. We were celebrating opening night."

"Anything else open that night?"

Grace grabbed the phone out of Gabriel's hand and deleted the photo. "Not a dang thing. He's just a friend."

Gabriel took back his phone and dropped it on the counter. "We've been separated by time and strangers, and this is exactly what I was afraid of. It's so easy for both of us to misinterpret innocent situations, but Princess, there was never anyone but you."

"No one could ever compete with you; you're the man I love."

"Yeah?" He drew her against his awakening body and nuzzled her neck. "I've been going to composition classes, and I've learned that love is a verb and verbs are action words!"

"You want to conjugate verbs with me, Gabriel?" She rubbed closer, slipping her hand around his waist. "If you think I'm too tired after that marathon shower, you've forgotten how much I need you."

"Well, that feeling is mutual." He moved smoothly to pick her up. "I ordered antipasti and some root beer and ice cream. I figured we could pick at the food after we pick at each other…" Gabriel took a couple steps to the bed, and as he released her feet to the floor, he whispered. "I love the smell of your hair."

She moved her cheek back and forth over his chest, trailing tiny nips on his pecs. "I never want to get dressed. Let's just stay in bed till Sunday."

"I do have to answer the door for room service, and I should probably wear a robe. The FBI knows a lot about me, they don't need to know anymore."

"The more I love you, the harder it is to put into words. Just when I thought I could show you every day, we were torn apart." Grace held him fast from lunging for his robe on the bed. "You could be the moon, and I'll be your stars, and the night can go on forever."

Gabriel's lips slowly turned up in a cunning smile. "But if it doesn't, you can be my sun and I'll be your blue sky."

There was an intrusive knock at the door announcing, "Room Service." Grace tightened the belt of her robe and giggled as Gabriel shook the towel from his hips and whisked on his robe, working overtime to tame his hard-on.

"Does it show?" He grinned like a teenager.

"They've never seen anything like that, go… bring back food."

Rolling the cart back, he watched her grow thoughtful.

****

After Gabriel and Grace playfully gnoshed on the table full of finger foods and made suggestive sucking sounds with the root-beer floats, Gabriel extended his hand to her. "This is a big place, c'mon, explore with me." Grace joyously took his hand and followed him back to the bedroom.

This part of the Harbor Suite was softly lit by the busy lights of the Baltimore Harbor businesses and tony high-rises. Behind generously insulated floor to ceiling glass, it was still, almost too tranquil with the plush furniture and luxurious acoustics. The design style spoke of both the business elegance an executive would demand and the artistic feng shui of a museum.

If only we could freeze our time within this opulent marble, wood, and stone. Too bad it's December, what a waste of an airy, expansive patio in this weather. Weather? Haha! Grace mused the only seating she wanted was Gabriel's lap.

After their turbulent months apart, hunger dictated a pell-mell coupling, and their marathon in the shower earlier only sated their sharpest needs. Now, with their bellies half full, they rode on a delicate sort of sensual calm. Not the sensory peace in prose, but the gliding grace of music. Their bodies were symphonies together, teetering on tangible reality. The luxurious sheets, glowing white and whisper soft, were a perfect nest for two lovers to reconnect and pass away hours in one another's arms.

There was something flawless about where they lay. Tucked in, pillows tossed here and there, the gentle caress of a soft cotton coverlet thrown barely over the back of their legs. The warm swoop of the broad-bladed ceiling fan moved temperate air over their naked bodies. Grace rested on her stomach, her hair flooding over her ivory back and shoulders. Gabriel lay beside her, his strong fingers gently tracing some lace-like pattern down her spine and over the gentle curve of her hips. The heady and delicate aroma of sex and intimacy hung like a fragrant whisper in the air.

She could feel the designs becoming more and more intricate as his touch lightened. They became a sweet tease as he lay on his side, his fingertips trailing above the sloping cleft of her buttocks. His other hand slid up to rest against her cheek. Their gazes were locked, as though some spell held them fast. Each move blended them into more profound sublime pleasure.

His lips came closer, resting momentarily against her forehead. His descent to kiss his way down her cheek strummed a particular chord within her. His lips started to make their way over her face, brushing over each of her now-closed eyelids. He leaned into her ear, a gentle purring growl escaping his sensuous lips and flooding memories into her senses. Tenderly, he reached out his long fingers to brush the hair off her shoulders, revealing her ivory flesh.

Softly, more like a dance than anything, he pressed himself against her, effortlessly turning her on her side, keeping their faces mere inches from one another. Resting one large, steady hand on her waist, sliding one of his legs atop hers, he stroked back and forth. He created carnal friction between them as if she needed him to stoke the flames.

Gently easing his hips between her legs, moving his hand over her neck, his fingers splayed into her riot of strawberry blonde hair. Cradling the back of her head, he ran his chin over her lips, teasing her with his stubble. With her lips she savored the divot there, eliciting a shiver from him. His tongue teased, pressing and probing to slip effortlessly between her honeyed lips.

Skin to skin, a soft groan escaped her. With indulgent pressure, Gabriel guided his hips against hers, his masterful hands caressing her soft shoulders. Grace emitted kittenish whimpers, and he continued onward as her hands reciprocated light petting and cuddling. Her hands cupped the musculature of his well-defined glutes, repeating her gentle teasing again and again. *My, oh my, isn't he delicious?* With all that flesh on flesh, a heady rush of well-earned longing released their energies. Now, more energetically, their kissing and caressing accelerated to wrestling tumbles, sheets caught on his or her foot while they moaned, hungers finally released.

Without a word, smoothly and softly, he pressed into her. His steely strength penetrated her welcoming warmth as they initially trembled against one another. Time stopped, her mind rushing and frozen, simultaneously. Her fingers trembled, seeking his muscled shoulders, her head falling back as the sheen of perspiration graced their torsos pressed together. Their erect nipples brushed, causing the music of their moans to increase in volume and strength.

Silently, her soul buzzed with the reality of their reunion. Moving incredibly slowly, pressing deeper and deeper within her, suddenly, he broke their silence with two lone words, almost a groan, almost a moan, almost a cry.

"My Princess."

A spell broke. A flooding rush of emotion, passion, fire, and lust released in chorus. Heavenly moans rose to flood the room. Only two words were spoken. His name on her lips, and her name on his. Nothing else came to mind. *You are all I can see; all I can feel. I know I'm everything to you.*

"I love you."

Who spoke the words was a mystery? Their pleasure rocked them. She clutched him in slippery embraces, drawing him deeper within her. Grace's hips tilted, flipping a switch and breaking a dam holding months of passionate desire and physical craving. Breathless, with the glow of sweat covering them both, they collapsed back against a lavish mountain of pillows.

"I love you, always."

"I love *you, alway*s."

****

Gabriel broke his kiss and held her face in both hands. "Things have turned out for the better. I want to take you home with me."

Grace's love-struck gaze widened. "Home?"

"Yes, home. Will you let me?" Before she could answer, his lips curled upward along with his smiling eyes.

Grace leaned back in Gabriel's arms and let out a dreamy sigh. "Okay…"

His nose brushed hers and they each crinkled theirs playfully. "If you want me, I'm yours. I work an honest job, I'm a mechanic at the Mercedes dealership, and I'm in college part-time. After we get through this weekend, there will be no worries, Grace. No worries at all."

"It's Sunday, I'm worried about, babe."

"Tonight and Saturday don't think of it. I want to tell you about this Christmas."

"You do?"

"Ahum. I have a nine-foot Douglas fir with twinkling bulbs in the living room. There's even something for you under the tree."

She wrapped her arm around his back and nestled to him. "But, I have nothing for you…"

"Haven't we discussed this before?" He held her close, spooning as he whispered in her ear. "I can barely keep the secret, sweet lord, Grace, I can't let you go!"

"Secret? What kind of secret?" She wiggled her hips slowly back against his.

"I told you I'd bring you another ring."

"Oh, you stinker, you're giving the secret away, and now I'm anxious to see it. But, how is all this good news possible? What happened?"

He pulled himself up in the mountain of pillows and cradled her in his lap. He held her hand and looked at where the ring would sit. "It all started with a beat down that Saturday night…"

"When they reported you dead?" Her eyes filled with tears at the memory.

"I was hoping you wouldn't see that. I don't have a brother, and my mother is still alive. They were playing fast and loose with that."

She pumped her fist. "I knew it!" Then she looked at his heavenly blue-green eyes.

****

After finishing his terrible tale of their separation, they ran out of words and Gabriel led her to the sofa in the suite's living room. Comfortably dressed in their lavish robes, he fired up the gas logs and joined her on the sofa. "We've each done a lot in the past six months…"

Grace hesitated to mention their lost pregnancy. "Oh, Gabriel, when I thought you'd died I realized I was pregnant."

Gabriel sat up abruptly in alarm, his gaze fell to her flat stomach. "But…"

Grace folded her arms over her robe. "I lost the baby at eight weeks. The doctor said we shouldn't have any problem when we want to plan another pregnancy."

Gabriel's eye glazed with unshed tears. "Oh, Princess, I'm so sorry you were alone." He caught her back in his embrace and nuzzled her ear. "When do we want to plan another pregnancy?"

Melting into his strong arms, she considered. "When we're married and done with school?"

His cloudy demeanor brightened, and with a chuckle, he nodded. "Sounds about right."

"Right now, I want you all to myself. I plan on being selfish." Grace ran a delicate fingertip to the divot on his chin.

Gabriel sat silent for a beat. "Without Ted's friendship, I would have slipped up and possibly gotten you hurt. He was a force in my being patient."

"He must have grown to love you."

"He was more of a father than a friend. I'm sure that love is why the home feels so right. Their happiness is everywhere. I want us to continue that tradition. Maybe with a couple of kids?"

"Well, you say you have the ring. We might have a day or two left before our marriage license expires."

"Monday it will be, Princess." With that, Gabriel bared the last of his truth. "If you marry me, you're gonna have to get used to a new name."

"Well, of course! I'll be Grace Lee." She reached out and pinched him cutely on the chin.

He caught her hand and nibbled the end of her ring finger. "Not that easy, Princess. The FBI thought it was necessary to kill Gabriel Lee. My new identity, thank heavens, does not include a criminal record. Do you think you could love Gabriel Bowman?"

"I would love you if you were a boy named Sue."

"That's good! Get used to calling me Mr. Bowman then. We can't confuse the neighbors."

She smiled and ran a loving hand down his cheek. "Yes, Mr. Bowman."

He made his move.

****

His lips found the shell of her ear, and his tongue swept over it torturously slow. Grace shuddered, collapsing back against him. "Princess, you've been my waking dream since I left you at Esther's. Everything I've done has been about right now."

She turned in his arms and pressed tightly to him. "Well, no pressure there, huh? Where did we leave off? Was it here?" She cupped him, and his knees went weak. "Or here?" She stroked his length as he quivered in her hand.

"That's a great place to pick back up, yeah, but what about you? Where did I leave off with you?"

She nuzzled the center of his chest. "I thought your short-term memory was better. You remember where everything goes and why, right?"

He reached around and caressed her ass. "Vividly."

She licked up his chest to his neck and into the divot in his chin. His cheek dimple creased at the pleasure she invoked. His hands caught her face, and he returned the deep kiss, releasing her to skim his palms down her arms. With a sly stroke up both her breasts, he shook his head and bit his lip. "It's good to be together again."

"You have the most fantastic ass! You've been working out, haven't you? And that's no flattery." She caught his waist and coaxed him to face her. The reality of the beating he'd survived stared back at her. The inch-long incision from his chest tube was fading, but she found many small suture lines publicizing the abuse he suffered. "Are these sensitive?" She lightly stroked the pencil-line scar from his sideburn to his jaw.

"Nah, I heard chicks dig scars."

"Well, they are rugged." She swooned in his arms. "Take me, I'm overcome with your virility!"

"Well, look who else has been going to school! That's a big word." He chuckled and drew her close, swaying her in his arms.

He shivered when she caught his sex with both hands. "Now class, *this* is virility! Remember when you gave me the mechanic's tour of the male body?"

"I've thought about it every night. Oh, Princess, I've missed you..."

29

Sunday morning arrived too soon. While Gabriel and Grace spooned under the down duvet, past noon, each of them grew more serious. Grace rolled on her tummy and put her chin in her hands. "What time are they coming for us?"

He narrowed his eyes and ran his fingers through her hair. "Us? I don't think you're included in this spy game."

She rapidly covered him with her body. "I'm not moving."

"Ah, Princess, after today, we'll never have to deal with any of this again. Believe me, I'm much safer now with the FBI than I ever was with the BPD."

"I still don't like it. Arthur's a snake."

"Yes, he is. Luckily the FBI's forte is dealing with snakes. This is not their first rattlesnake roundup."

Grace lay her cheek on his warm chest. "I think I missed your scent the most." Then her gentle hand slid down his flat belly and wrestled his sex.

His generous smile curled into a smirk. "I told you how I love the taste of your lips, I just didn't clarify which lips."

"Okay, dirty boy, show me."

The knock on the door was heavy, compelling, not to be ignored.

****

"Damn it," Gabriel muttered as he turned from her, grabbed his robe, and stalked to the door. He looked out the peephole to see Kerry and Carnegie, and he threw open the door. "I haven't ordered room service."

"You kids have made enough noise in here. Time for a shower and some go-juice." Kerry held up the two extra-large donut store coffees, and Gabriel pouted.

"You're a buzz-kill."

Kerry shrugged. "It's my job." He held up a bag of fan gear and headed for the dinner table. "We got you a Flacco jersey, a hat, and we brought your clothes from home." He thrust the overnight bag and fan gear at Gabriel. "The purple jersey matches those bruises on your face. Shower, shave and let's shove off."

Grace exchanged forlorn glances with Gabriel as he headed to the bathroom. "Did I hear coffee, Detective Kerry?" She halted at the sight of both detectives in plain clothes. "Detective Carnegie, I didn't expect to see you again. What's up?" She accepted the coffee and dug in the donut box.

"I'm your company until this day blows over."

"Gabriel said he didn't think I could go with him."

"He was right. I have a transmitter, and we'll see it on the computer." She held up a suitcase. "I brought your clothes and things from home, too."

****

Agent Hawkins was in the van and briefed him on the short drive from the hotel to the stadium. "Got you an earbud." He clicked on the battery and handed Gabriel the minute device. "Press it deeply in your ear, your hair should cover the sight of it. But you can see," he turned his own ear toward Gabriel, "they're small. The suite has been swept, they didn't have anything electronic, but now we've got cameras at every angle. A fly can't fart without us knowing about it. All the servers are agents, if there's trouble, they'll grab you."

"Strange as it sounds, I'm not worried about them trying something on me. I'm worried they won't. So, just in case, is there anything I can get Darby talking about that would help? Do I act like I know Darby?"

Hawkins thought a beat. "Absolutely. Ask him if you ever worked on his car. Make reference to Wally's shop being close to the docks. Drop names, let's rattle his cage."

"Should I mention the hot redhead I'm dating? How about I ask him his preference for women?"

"Make it look inadvertent. Just pluck those strings of his. You're a young, buff guy and you love life. You want to connect with Blackmon and him, let them know you're a red-blooded Baltimorean."

"So, talk trash."

"Oh, yeah."

****

Gabriel was at the open door of the suite on the dot of six PM, the appointed time he'd discussed with Blackmon. He took a deep breath, put on his wildest smirk and held his head high as he strutted into the room. *I'm on my block and word is, I'm a killer, I got this.* He glanced at the quiet buzz of the suite, seeing familiar faces from the evening news downing drinks and making casual bets. He heard his name shouted from across the room and looked in the direction to see Blackmon leaning over the crab cakes with an empty china plate and Arthur Darby at his elbow. *Damn, that guy's short.*

"Gabe, over here." Gabriel advanced toward the waving, smiling man. "Hey, fella. We're all on a first name basis here. This is my buddy, Art." He gestured at Gabriel for the introduction. "This is Gabe... well, I think it's Gabe underneath all that bruising. What happened to you?"

"I argued with my airbag."

"Looks like the airbag won! You hungry? The crab's fresh today, we've got shrimp if you prefer it."

Gabriel smiled at the buffet he would have enjoyed eating. "You sure do have shrimp!" Gabriel stifled a yawn and nodded.

Blackmon prompted, "Late night last night?"

Gabriel licked at his swollen bottom lip and nodded to Art. "You know, the kind of night that goes into the afternoon." He twisted right and left. "I can barely walk..."

Arthur leered. "Oh, to be young again."

Gabriel held up a halting hand as Blackmon attempted to pass him a plate. "Nothing for me, thanks. She fed me before I came." He winked at Arthur.

Arthur elbowed him. "You have to keep up your strength."

"Yeah, those debutantes look delicate. But get one in bed, and she'll ride you like a hurricane." Gabriel shifted from his right to left foot. "I love redheads. What type of gal do you like, Art?"

"I like 'em young and fresh; you know? The kind that fights back."

"I like the way you think," Gabriel paused, "don't I know you from somewhere?"

"You may have seen me on the news. I don't think we travel in the same circles."

Gabriel bit back a retort. *Oh, but the Russian mob thinks we do.* He grinned genially. "I might surprise you. You have a Mercedes?"

"Yeah, I do."

"There you go, I got one too. Well, I should say the deer got it." Gabriel dramatically pointed both index fingers at his bruised face. "When Bambi gets a hard-on for you, you're toast." Gabriel returned to taunting. "Are you the new Eastwood Auto Paint Rep? I'm sure I saw you at Wally's garage. You dress sharp for a paint rep."

Blackmon broke into the conversation. "No, Gabe. Art, here, owns a shipping company."

"No shit, I'd never have guessed."

Arthur looked daggers at him. "Excuse me for a moment, will you?"

Gabriel heard Hawkins chuckle into his earpiece. "You got him now. He just told the guy in the purple plaid sweater to mix you a special cocktail and get you out of here."

Gabriel smiled innocuously at Blackmon. "How's the fundraising this week?"

The sweater-clad guy approached at Gabriel's elbow. "Brought you a drink, compliments of Mr. Darby."

"That's nice of him. But I'm sorry, I don't drink. Enjoy it for me." The guy stared at the drink he was holding, unsure of what to do next. "Or better yet, you should take it back to him. He's got the tab." Gabriel watched from the corner of his eye as the guy sat the drink on a table in front of them and walked away.

Blackmon looked down at the glass. "Well, I hate to see waste, I'll drink it."

Gabriel's satisfaction in deflecting the mickey faded at the idea of the guest of honor passing out in the next ten minutes. "Hey…" He began, but Blackmon cheerfully downed the tainted liquor in three swallows.

"Good night," Gabriel muttered.

"I don't remember Raven's punch tasting like that." Blackmon moved his tongue around his mouth and grabbed for bottled water.

"Why don't we have a seat, you can bring me up to speed on what you need from me."

As Blackmon and Gabriel settled on the sofa, Arthur returned with a glass on a tray. "I didn't realize you were a teetotaler, but we have a tradition. First time in the box, the virgins guzzle Raven's punch. Here's a virgin punch for you."

"You know better than to drink that, right?" Hawkins whispered into Gabriel's ear.

"Yeah." He stood up with a jerk, bumping into the tray. "Oh, look at the mess I caused. Let me get a punch from one of those nice ladies over there, and I'll come back with a bar rag."

Arthur nodded distinctly at one of the servers who smiled and returned the nod. Hawkins spoke again. "He thinks she's about to hand you a doctored drink, so about five minutes from now, start slurring your words."

Gabriel ambled back to Arthur, took a big slug of the drink and gave him a leering grin. "I got it. I know exactly where I saw you. You were in Wally's office, the night we boosted twelve rides. That was my personal record, you know? You gotta be the top dog, cause everyone's dead but you and me." Gabriel downed the next third of the drink. "And I'm not the top dog."

Arthur's smile grew thin. "I don't know anyone named Wally."

Gabriel gestured to Arthur's vest. "You were there, that key of yours was glistening in the dark." He intentionally stumbled forward. "Whoa, do you know, I feel exactly like I had a drink."

"I wouldn't worry about staying sober tonight, Mr. Lee. This might feel better if you're a little drunk."

Gabriel sagged, and Arthur gestured two men forward. "Take him out of here. Vince, you've had two attempts at killing him, make it happen." He glanced over at Blackmon passed out on the sofa.

Gabriel never worked so hard to stay limp. Arthur's men weren't gentle as they yanked his arms over each of their shoulders and dragged him down the dim hall toward the elevator. "Ouch, that had to hurt." Gabriel heard Hawkins. "Stay relaxed. We've got eyes in the elevator." Gabriel muttered a low groan, more for Hawkins than for effect. Hawkins snorted. "You'll be fine. They don't want blood in the elevator. We've got their town car surrounded."

"Thanks for making my life hell, asshole." Vince twisted Gabriel's arm unnecessarily as he backed him into the corner of the elevator, and Gabriel made sure that same arm fell from around Vince's shoulder.

When they dragged him from the elevator into the garage, his swinging arm mysteriously found itself rocking hard into Vince's crotch. *For a big guy, you're not playing with a whole lot down there.* Vince coughed and stumbled onto one knee, Gabriel hesitated as the other guy moved forward and the goon tripped over Vince.

Gabriel allowed himself to sag to the pavement. Vince aimed a kick at his kidney. "I'm going to enjoy killing you, Lee." The two men picked him up and carried him to the open town car trunk.

The admonition Gabriel waited for rang out in Hawkins' best FBI voice. "Halt, FBI." Gabriel peeked open one eye to watch the takedown. He sat up, cross-legged in the trunk and smiled cheerfully at Vince.

"Watching you go away will make up for pissing blood, Vince." He looked at Hawkins and spoke like a game show host. "Okay, Agent Hawkins, what's on deck for two thugs who attempted murder three times?"

"Well, Gabriel, we've got a cornucopia of charges. They range from kidnapping to attempted murder and conspiracy. Yes, Gabe, the use of firearms on the second attempt is going to enhance their sentencing. They'll be spending time in a lovely maximum-security prison, being counted five to six times a day. Who knows, they might have a Somali pirate as a cellmate. Darby could talk about shipping with him."

Gabriel laughed. "Anyway to shorten their sentences, Agent Hawkins?"

"Well, Gabe, confession, and information go a long way with the prosecutors. We'll see how cooperative our contestants choose to be."

Gabriel climbed out of the trunk as the two men were led away. "Thanks for playing our game." He looked around as the elevator opened. "Here comes our main contestant now. Tell us, Mr. Darby, how do you feel about being the big prize tonight?"

Arthur sneered and spit on the ground. "Fuck, you."

Gabriel returned a bright smile. "Arty, is that any way to talk to the street thug that brought you down? Save that thought for your cell-mate." Gabriel had a generation and more than a few inches on him, although he no longer handled his business that way.

Hawkins smiled between the two men. "Gabriel, we'll be processing these gentlemen for the rest of the night. You and your lady should go home and get a good night's sleep. The courthouse opens Monday at eight-thirty, you could be married by nine AM." He turned to Darby, who seemed uninterested. "This fine young man will be your son-in-law before you're arraigned."

"That's bullshit." Darby impudently raised his chin at Gabriel, who walked within a few feet of the handcuffed prisoner.

"What's bullshit is you've preyed upon anyone you could step over. It's ironic that a sweet young girl like Grace put all this in motion. And now, you're destined to be the bitch of the gnarliest man you'll ever meet."

"Agent, I'm being threatened. Are you…"?

Hawkins put a firm hand on Darby's shoulder. "It's not a threat if it's true. Get tough, Darby."

Gabriel raised a parting hand. "Have a nice night. Hope you get the top bunk."

30

"**I**sn't it kind of cool? We're starting all over again on a Monday?" Gabriel grinned as he walked his bride to his rental car and opened the door, the way Frankie always did for his wife. Before Gabriel closed her door, he caught her left hand and planted a sweet kiss over her original tiny diamond ring. He buckled in and keyed the ignition.

Grace watched the ring sparkle in the morning light. "So, tell me about this fir tree, you said it has twinkling lights, have you decorated it yet?"

"There are ornaments, but they aren't ours. I was waiting for you to come home to me."

She braced her hand on the dashboard and leaned over the console. "I'm going to go crazy doing our first tree. But tell me about the kitchen."

"The property inventory said it was a cook's kitchen, have you ever heard of Viking?"

"You have a Viking kitchen?" She turned pink.

"*You* have a Viking kitchen; remember I don't cook." He caught glimpses of her excitement as she interrogated him about every room in the house. She watched the small, middle-class neighborhoods slide by her view as he motored the purring rental up Falls Road.

"Oh, I have to check in with Esther."

"Great, when I get you home, you'll be all mine."

"Wow, you answered on the second ring. My husband, Gabriel, says good morning and he wants to know if he can keep his bride tonight." Gabriel shook his head at her humor. "Are you and Kendra able to handle the wagon for a couple of days?" Grace made a wincing face.

"We've handled it for the last three days, what are three more?" Esther chided.

"We are going to need someone to take over for about a week."

"A week?" Kendra bellowed back.

Gabriel and Grace announced in unison. "We're taking a honeymoon!"

Grace exclaimed. "The engagement has been long enough!"

Gabriel bellowed. "Too long. I'm kidnapping my bride for a week at The Hotel Hershey."

Kendra made a derogative noise. "It's winter, go somewhere warm!"

Gabriel's smooth voice countered. "I'll keep her plenty warm."

Grace butt in. "But, he's taking me to our house first."

Esther stammered. "*Our* house?"

Grace shot Gabriel an indulgent look. "I'll text the address, and maybe you can convince Uncle Constantine to deliver a few dinners for a little wedding celebration tonight?" Gabriel nodded enthusiastically.

Esther paused, and Grace could hear the smile in her voice. "You want me to pack a bag for you? Text me what you want."

Gabriel grinned broadly. "Whatever she's missing, I'll take her shopping."

Kendra sent up a scream. "Oh, that's the kind of man I want. Grace, we love you. We love you, both."

Grace shook her head euphorically. "See you for dinner. Not a moment sooner."

****

Gabriel made a right into the quiet neighborhood. "Do you want the grand entrance through the front door or the family entrance through the garage?" Grace checked herself in the visor mirror, having the absurd feeling she was about to meet her in-laws.

292

"Oh, let's go in the front door." She sat primly with her hands in her lap until he opened the car door and took her hand. He gathered her into his arms and savored her warmth against him. He kissed her slowly, and his tongue found the seam of her lips. "I'm getting ahead of myself."

"Take me… take me inside…"

He led the way, entered the electronic code on the door and slipped his hand up the inside light switch. Even in the day, the Douglas fir's twinkling lights illuminated the living room. "Merry Christmas, Princess! You have a seat right there." He pointed to a pair of leather wing chairs. "I'll be right back." He disappeared into the bedroom, and she sat patiently.

Grace recognized the turquoise box. Tiffany's. Her face flushed with excitement as her shaking fingers reached for it. He went down on one knee and presented his gift proudly. Both shook with expectation. Gabriel nodded toward the case. "Princess, may I make you my queen?"

"'Kay!"

He sprang the lid and the lights danced in her eyes. "Oh! Oh, my God! Gabriel!"

"I told you I'd bring you another ring."

"But this is huge!"

"Do you like it?"

"You know I'll always treasure its little sister." She looked lovingly at the first engagement ring on her hand.

Gabriel acknowledged the sentiment. "When I called them about cleaning and sizing, they told me if you didn't like it, they could trade it in."

"On what? What would I trade this for? A yacht?"

Gabriel's eyes gleamed. "I think two carats only buys a pontoon boat. Is our marriage still a deal, anyway? I mean, if you want a pontoon boat, I could swing that too."

"Please, put it on me! I'll say yes to anything!" Her rushed embrace knocked them to the plush oriental carpet.

"Anything?" Lying on their backs, he held her hand as he turned the first ring to look like a band and slid the new ring on her finger. "I love you, Grace."

She admired the fire in the stone. "I love you, too, Gabriel."

"Let me show you that kitchen. I ordered a little something for lunch. It's not your cooking, but we have a lot of catching up to do. I have some small batch root beer and vanilla bean ice cream." He was up and dragging her to the kitchen.

"Jesus, Mary, and Joseph! This *is* a chef's kitchen!" She spun in a circle taking it all in. "Gabriel, I just…"

"Yeah, me too."

Epilogue

Gabriel Bowman strolled through the garage and into their kitchen. He dropped his keys on the end of the island. Grace fussed over a tray of eggplant parmigiana coming out of the oven. His crafty hand reached for a breadstick in a wicker basket behind her, and she quickly slapped him away playfully.

"I just smacked your son's hand for the same thing."

Gabriel shook his head. "Because you have to be the pack leader."

Grace fell into her husband's arms. "Yeah. Here I am, your mighty pack leader, at least in the kitchen."

He kissed the top of her head and flipped through the mail she'd dropped on the bar earlier. "It's been twenty years, and I still think I'm opening someone else's mail." He waved a letter addressed to Gabriel Bowman.

Grace shook her head as she put the dinner on the bar. "I've enjoyed being Mrs. Gabriel Bowman. It's a nice name." She stepped into the den and waved at Charlotte and Frankie. "Dinner. Dad's got a meeting about cross country tonight, Charlie. We have to speed it up."

The two teenagers locked the video game and took turns washing their hands at the sink.

"That's not until March. Why do we have to meet about it now?" The thirteen-year-old girl whined.

Gabriel levied his 'dad face' at Charlie. "We have to make sure the snack rotation is peanut and gluten free, etcetera, etcetera..." He slid out of his blazer and rolled up his dress shirt cuffs. "Of course, if you're tired of cross country, you could help me with the afterschool self-defense classes at St. Mary's." He rose on his toes and turned femininely. "Or begin ballet lessons? You know about the activity policy in this house."

Charlie exaggerated a groan. "It's all Mom's fault."

"When I was your age, I rowed five times a week, and I sailed and swam -- a lot."

The family sat down to their usual places along the ten-foot length of granite and bowed their heads for the blessing.

Frankie stole two breadsticks and passed the basket to his dad. "Owen is gonna test for his yellow belt at this weekend's promotion. I need to be there for him. Can I use Grandpa's car?

Grace and Gabriel shut Frankie down with a look. "In what Universe?"

"Geesh! I've been driving in the neighborhood since I got my temps."

"Not in that car, you haven't" Gabriel waved a breadstick at his son and then bit the end of it.

"C' mon! It's my best friend!"

"And you will go. Mom will drop you off on the way to the restaurant, and Owen's folks can bring you home. Don't forget you're working at the sandwich shop on Sunday."

"Aren't we having dinner at Aunt Kendra's Sunday? Aren't Grampa Constantine and Gramma Esther gonna be there, too?" Charlie grabbed more salad.

Frankie glared. "Why are you two the responsible parents?"

Grace swallowed her iced tea. "It's our job. When we irritate you, we know we're doing it right."

Charlie vied for attention again. "Mom, I need a check with a permission slip signed for the play at the Hippodrome. It's something about a green witch and a good witch."

Gabriel winked at Grace. "Sounds interesting. Maybe we should get tickets?"

Charlie groaned. "Not with my class! The girls always stare at Dad. It's embarrassing."

He wagged his eyebrows at his daughter. "That's okay, the boys stare at your mother, so it balances out. Frankie will have the same skills soon."

"Soon? I've got game now!" Fifteen-year-old Frankie posed, then vacuumed his dinner plate and scooped seconds.

The wall phone shrilled. "Why do those telemarketers call at dinner, dammit? Everyone, let the call roll to voicemail."

Within seconds, the phone rang again. Gabriel grimaced. "I'd better get that. It might be work."

****

The machines on the third floor of Holy Angels Hospital blipped and blinked ominously. The cold linoleum resonated with the clattering of carts as they walked to the room. Fluorescent lighting paled Grace's cheeks. Gabriel hated to see her go through this.

What had twenty years together taught them? You 'roll with it', through fat and lean.

****

Grace and Gabriel raised their family far apart from Linda, so the late-night call from Holy Angels seemed due. Grace always expected a deathbed declaration. Tonight's dinner dishes were left for the kids after the call came. Gabriel picked up the keys, and they rode in silence through the city to the waterfront hospital.

Tonight, Gabriel's clothing came from a men's store, not Goodwill. He walked the walk of an executive rather than the framed ex-con of his early twenties. Grace was quiet and composed considering the circumstances.

Twenty years separated Mr. and Mrs. Arthur Darby. While Arthur sat in federal prison, Linda returned to hawking condos and living as a resident manager. Though Linda made hesitant overtures toward her daughter, Grace saw the wisdom in Esther's advice to keep her distance. Especially after the children arrived, Grace exercised her maternal rights to protect them.

Tonight, Linda's heart problem wasn't that it was two sizes too small, she was sixty-something and suffered from cardiomyopathy. Arthur sat in a cell, awaiting his third parole hearing. Using the inmate/patient interface system, Linda's parish priest held the tablet connecting Arthur with Linda. When Gabriel and Grace arrived, Father Jerold whispered, "She's lucid, she knows you're coming."

The inmate, Arthur Darby, was initially poised, considering his eyes were blurry from prison stress and grief. His gaze widened at the sight of the girl he'd 'had' a lifetime ago. Seeing Gabriel behind her, Arthur shuddered.

Even though Arthur was behind bars, Grace kept the hospital bed between her and his image on the tablet. He hadn't changed in twenty years; he was still straight-lipped with cold eyes. She pushed the table away from the bed and brushed her mother's platinum hair away from her forehead.

"Mom, it's Grace."

Linda's eyes opened slowly. "Baby." Was all she mustered with labored breath, her eyes pale and scared.

Linda and Grace whispered about the prognosis, and Linda's gaze traveled to Arthur as he spoke up. "Father Jerold spoke with me at length when your mother was admitted. She isn't a candidate for a transplant, too many things going on." Arthur was apparently resigned to her end.

Grace wasn't surprised by the news. She stepped to the end of the bed and crossed to the tablet deliberately. She faced the screen and looked him eye to eye.

"It's a shame she isn't a transplant candidate, Arthur, you could always give her your heart. You've never used it." There it was, all out in the open after all these years. Linda turned from Arthur and cringed, clamping her eyes closed.

Arthur didn't answer, a stony affront chiseled his lined visage. He adjusted his jumpsuit as he turned his face away. Gabriel held out his hand to the priest for the tablet, and Father Jerold obliged. Gabriel excused himself and headed to the empty family waiting room.

****

Did Arthur feel Gabriel's eyes burning all the way from Baltimore? *He should.* Gabriel propped the tablet at eye level and watched in silence as Arthur fidgeted his unease, attempting to strike a regal pose. The old man squirmed under his son in law's silent scrutiny.

From the first night, Grace confessed what Arthur put her through, her husband waited for *this night.* Gabriel sat back, squared shoulders leading to strong arms folded over his robust chest. The athletic cut of the blue blazer outlined his developed biceps and forearms. "I wondered when you'd try for another parole hearing." Gabriel's soft baritone belied his true feelings. He unfolded his arms and scratched at his five o'clock shadow as he leaned forward, one palm on his knee. Gabriel's hand went from his scruff upwards to smooth back his salt and pepper hair, a habit from his days 'inside'. When he brought his hand down, he regarded his wedding ring and thought about Grace before taking a deep breath.

Arthur swallowed hard. "Right, I realize Grace has avoided contact with us." There was silence, and then Arthur pursed his lips and added. "The two of you look healthy, happy…" *A stranger could look at us and see more than that.*

"Did you ever hear how we met?" Gabriel posed the question innocently, and Arthur shook his head. "It must have been… a couple of weeks after the last time you raped her. You came home early from Bali and surprised her." Arthur sniffed, and his jaw tightened. "She was living on the street and needed help with her laundry. She needed a place to stay, and you know, Arthur, even a swinging dick like me could leave her alone." Arthur's eyelid developed a nervous tic. "The night I met you, I spent the day at the police station giving testimony on every boost Wally sent me on. I did not know we were tied up with the Russian mob."

"Gabriel, I was only there, in that office because they demanded I repay them a favor. They demanded I meet Mr. Kozlov. Until I saw the photo of you and Grace, I had no idea who you were."

"You just take out hits on the men who date your step-daughter?"

"No. No, not at all. But you saw who I was. Once it was reported you were dead, I was certain no one could report my complicity. I allied myself with Blackmon, we'd discussed my being Lieutenant Governor. When he chatted about a mechanic who was accused of a double murder, something made me nervous. Once I saw your photo, your fate was sealed."

"No, Arty. Your fate was sealed. Yes, it separated me from Grace for months, and that was rougher than giving evidence on those bad mofos in the Russian mob. I made a lot of friends in law enforcement from the B.P.D. all the way to the FBI" The two men sat in stony silence for a beat. "To this day, all I have to do is call when I need something." Gabriel's voice was barely above a whisper, it might as well have been a bullhorn from Arthur's physical reaction.

As Arthur sat in tense silence, Gabriel continued. "I've spent long hours thinking about everything I know about you. When Grace shared her nightmare with me, I wanted to break into your place, cut off your balls and stuff 'em down your throat. My luck, I'd get caught, and you'd bleed out and not suffer enough." Gabriel watched as Arthur's breathing deepened. "You do like them young, don't you Arthur? I mean, what was Grace, sixteen when you started? That secretary who attacked Grace on the street, was she trying to catch your eye?" Arthur's brows furrowed in confusion. "The one with the dye job and the hazel contact lenses."

"She was a gadfly. She was two years ahead of Grace and idolized the life we led."

"She had you pegged. It took her four years in China to get back to the states, and all because she wanted to catch your eye."

Arthur's fingers moved to loosen the jumpsuit collar that was already open, and he froze for a second, and then dropped his hand in his lap.

Gabriel's keen gaze focused on Arthur's hands. "Arty, do you get hard just thinking about it, at your age?" Gabriel shook his head, "What a bad boy. You are truly a fortunate son. You know the song: 'Fortunate One'?"

Gabriel got up and moved the hassock back. He rolled his shoulders as if he were winding up for a pitch and the jacket outlined the power in his physique. "Great song, I used to sing it when I was all hopped up and feeling like I owned the world… goes something like this. 'Yeah! Some folks are born silver spoon in hand, Lord, don't they help themselves, oh'."

Gabriel included the air guitar performance while Arthur froze, his face a mask of fear.

"So, I want you to know, I'm aware of your sick little appetite, and I also know how to keep you in check. You see, with Linda alive, Grace never wanted to raise hell about your parole. You positively convinced Linda it was Grace's imagination. You're good, diabolically good. When Linda passes out of this world, you better hope she's one helluva a guardian angel because you are going to need one."

Gabriel sat back down and leaned his palms on the arms of the wing chair with his face inches away from the camera. "Within twenty-four hours of Linda's passing, the federal prison system is going to change their mind about your parole hearing. In fact, your case is going back to the bottom of the list."

Arthur's complexion went ashy. "You can't control the prison system."

"No, I can't, but Langford Blackmon, the new Director of the Federal Bureau of Prisons of the United States, doesn't believe someone with your proclivities should be on the streets. He might have been gullible enlisting you on his campaign back in the day. But the man is a great listener. We met at length after you were convicted. He knows you'd hit the streets like a hungry sexual predator." The old man's sneer was papier mache against Gabriel's granite tenacity. "You are going to wake up tomorrow and tell the warden, you're not seeking parole. Your wife has died, you might as well serve your sentence."

Gabriel inhaled deeply as his gaze narrowed and he pulled out his cell phone. "I have Lang's number right here." He held the phone, poised to dial and Arthur's liver-spotted hand waved him to stop.

"I heard you, I heard you, yes, yes… Tomorrow morning. Now leave me in peace, God damn you." Tremors moved through his words. He was finally a broken man after breaking countless young women.

****

Gabriel's head was down over his folded hands, and the monitor was on hold when Grace entered the family room. "Mother wants to speak to you, Gabriel." He kissed her forehead, and they walked back to the room, his arm around her waist, bumping hips, they were so close.

Pale and wan, Linda's slight body melted into the mattress, the fluorescent bulb in the light over the bed did nothing to flatter the formerly stunning woman. Gabriel stood close and touched her fingertips to wake her. "Linda, you wanted to speak with me?"

Her eyes fluttered open. "I was wrong, wrong about so many things, and thank you, thank you for taking her in and loving her." Shallow breaths pushed out Linda's grateful words.

Gabriel wanted to be softer for Grace's sake. He sought to be warm-hearted at the hour of his mother-in-law's remorse. Being human, all he could do was nod and let her know what he thought all along. "She's so easy to love, Linda, it just came naturally."

"Then you were meant to be." Her eyes fluttered a bit, and she weakly lifted the corners of her mouth.

Grace bent from the other side of the bed and kissed her mother's cheek, she smelled rubber tubing and medical tape, antiseptic and hospital laundry detergent. She was accustomed to the fragrance of her mother's Boucheron perfume and natural French hand lotion. *How sad Mother has fallen so far*. Grace pulled out the pocket tube of the same product and warmed some in her hands. Watching her, Gabriel reached for the lotion and followed her lead. The two of them gently stroked the plant infused cream into her formerly radiant skin. Linda's breathing steadied, and she fell into a restful sleep, her eyes less tense, her lips gently parted.

"How long does she have?" Gabriel lip-spoke to Grace silently.

"Hours," Grace's eyes were beginning to puff from fighting tears.

"Let me call Frankie, let the kids know we're okay."

****

Gabriel excused himself and walked back to the empty family room. He didn't give Arthur any thought as he dialed the house and Charlotte answered. Not wanting to upset her he said, "Scrappy, we'll be home in the morning before school, lock up the house and get to sleep, okay?"

"Dad, Frankie says Mom's Mom is dying, is Mom alright?" Charlotte was the tender-hearted one of the family, even for a teenage girl. She hated to see her mother upset.

"Tell Frankie to drop the subject. Yes, your Mom is upset, her mother is critically ill. Get some sleep, Scrappy. We'll talk when we get home."

Gabriel returned to the room to find Grace drawing a wide tooth comb through her mother's hair.

****

Linda Benson Lerner Darby passed from this life at 3:12 A.M. after the turmoil of the family reunion dulled to a low static hum. Gabriel took Grace's hand, and they grabbed hot tea from the family room and left to walk along the harbor.

Wrapped in a light hospital blanket, Grace held her tea with both hands while Gabriel wrapped an arm around her shoulder. Both silent, both serious.

Was it twenty-plus years since they ate their first meals in the shadow of The Inner Harbor? The buildings multiplied; many old ones were torn down to give way to grander, taller edifices of wealth. They found a bench near the marina and watched the boats bobbing up and down with the water's rhythm as they took a seat to drink their tea.

Grace pointed to the tall, sand-colored condos Gabriel coveted in another lifetime, "Are you sorry we never got a place in there?" She watched him blink and with a flutter of those long eyelashes, he looked down into his tea and shook his head no.

"I got what I wanted, I wanted you." He turned his head sideways to make eye contact with her, as he wrapped her tighter to his chest.

She sighed. *That smile of his is still sublime.*

"What about you, did you get everything you wanted?" He asked, his voice a husky mix of temptation and innocence.

"I'd say I have, yes. We're still young, there's so much more for us to do once the kids are grown, and that will be before we know it. Then it'll be just us again." She smiled as she sipped the warm honeyed brew of chamomile and lemon.

"Remember that day?" Gabriel slipped into his happy place, remembering their reunion at the police precinct. He took a deep whiff of her hair, and she swung her legs across his lap and nestled to him. Gabriel sat down his tea and wrapped both arms around her.

"I remember seeing you from behind, your hands on the shoulders of my coat…" She looked up at him and shook her head, the tip of her tongue passing along her bottom lip. "Then when we kissed, you got so hard, I wanted you to take me right there." She blushed.

"I seem to remember you were quite disturbed by the officers filing back into the conference room." Her weight on his lap woke up old reflexes and urges. He took the cup from her hands, and she melted into his arms. They sighed together with soft giggles as they traded kisses as light as dragonfly wings.

"Let's get out of here…" He invited her to no particular destination. They gathered the blanket around her and made their way back to the valet station to retrieve their sedan.

****

"Where are you headed?" Grace was curious about the captivating smile on his face.

"Making a stop," he admitted as he drove to the hotel where they spent two whole days in bathrobes making satisfied noises two decades ago. He rang the front desk while he drove. "You wouldn't happen to have the premier harbor suite on the end available, would you? I'll be arriving within the next fifteen minutes." He nodded as he drove, and Grace smothered a giggle at checking into a luxury suite at four in the morning. "I need one of your antipasti trays, a six-pack of root beer and a quart of vanilla bean ice cream."

"Oh, you aren't ready for a couple of rounds in the back seat?" Grace snickered as he pulled up to the valet.

"We've never had sex in a car. You want to start now?" Gabriel chuckled as he put his arm around her shoulders to enter the hotel.

****

The porter opened the door on the dark suite and preceded them to flip on every light. "No, no lights, the harbor lights are bright enough."

Gabriel slid a crisp bill into the retreating porter's hand, and Grace waited to hear the finite click of the locked door.

She slid her hands under his blue blazer and pressed her cheek on his muscled chest. "I'm sure that tip did nothing to erase his ideas about why we're here."

"And he'd be right." He chuckled.

Looking at him, she flung his coat on the back of the sofa. In the harbor light, her mind skipped back to the Friday twenty years ago when they arrived here. After their dreadful separation, the first stop was the shower and a hasty coupling. Then, dry and warm in their robes they surveyed the opulent surroundings before they embraced silently in the living room. It wasn't long before he escorted her back to the king size bed. Her soft, lightly freckled cleavage awaited his touch and his lips. Their fresh reunion began, and within seconds they were lost in rediscovering each other's bodies.

"I missed you so much. All the places I'd been shoved, none of them smelled like us." Gabriel confessed as he buried his nose behind her ear. His hands kneaded her thighs where they became her cheeks. "Princess, when I'm with you, I'm home."

"Home is wherever you are..." He lifted her over him, and she scurried down his body to grab and lick at his thick hardness in her hands.

"Home smells like you, like your hair and here." He ran light fingers between her breasts. "Home is where I can stroke you long and hard." Gabriel gritted his teeth as she bore down on him with both hands and her pink lips.

****

Tonight, after the drama at the hospital, he respected her heartache and took it slow. His hands were gentle, cupping her generous, pale breasts while he kissed each one reverently. Her sighs were the music he sought as he strummed her like a delicate instrument. Her softly audible moans directed his lips and fingers. Gabriel longed to excite and coerce her appetite to the fore.

He knew how to stir her longing and liberate her from grief's pain. If tonight her world was crashing down, he was going to hold it up with his shoulders and protect her from reality's brutal blows.

His lips soothed her as she arched into him, pressing her hips to his. He strained to touch as much skin to hers as possible, licking and lapping at the crevices of her elbows, her knees, and the hollow of her thighs. He delighted in her taste where her soft skin ducked into her dark pink flesh. He went down on her with such hunger she offered no resistance. She lay back and invited his tongue to kindle deep moans and fervid cries. She clutched at the luxurious bedding and drove her hips toward him.

Grace tasted different tonight as if grief elicited a new layer of succulence. Gabriel caught his breath at the thought of delivering her through tonight's sadness. It inspired him to kiss a little deeper and touch more delicately. She clutched at him, fueling his hunger for her lips to dance across his flesh, yet he wanted to please her *first*.

When she quivered and caught her breath in a possessed wail, Gabriel poised on his knees between her legs and captured the sight of her soft flesh covered in a subtle sheen. The rich aroma of her orgasm drove him rigid. Their eyes met, and she blew a kiss and reached to draw him closer.

Their thirst gave way to their fever. Her succulence drove him to ecstasy. When it all came to his finishing strokes, Gabriel prayed his ministrations delivered Grace from her suffering. They collapsed into a stunningly satisfied place together.

It was never pretending with her, it was always their wild, beautiful truth when they lay together. "Tonight, even with grief as an invisible guest, being here like this, we're all we need."

He lay with her in his arms, their skin slick, and he realized, *for two people in love, pain and strife have no hold. Those torments form you. They refine your heart and mind. Pain is temporary because, from it, you realize it's not who you are, it's who you become.*

The End

WHAT IS CHILD ABUSE?

Child abuse is when a parent or caregiver, whether through action or failure to act, causes injury, death, emotional harm or risk of serious harm to a child. There are many forms of child maltreatment, including neglect, physical abuse, sexual abuse, exploitation, and emotional abuse.

If you know someone under the age of eighteen is experiencing child abuse. Help is available at:

Childhelp USA

Website Address https://www.childhelp.org/

(1-800) 4-A-Child or 1-800-422-4453

The Childhelp USA National Child Abuse Hotline is anonymous, toll-free, and available 24 hours a day, seven days a week. Counselors are paid professionals. Childhelp USA offers crisis intervention, information, literature, and referrals to the 55,000 agencies in their database and has the capacity to handle calls in 140 languages.

Need Help With a Drinking Problem?
What Is A.A.?

Alcoholics Anonymous is an international fellowship of men and women who have had a drinking problem. It is nonprofessional, self-supporting, multiracial, apolitical, and available almost everywhere. There are no age or education requirements. Membership is open to anyone who wants to do something about their drinking problem.

Remember, there is no disgrace in facing up to the fact that you have a problem.

A.A. World Services, Inc.

475 Riverside Drive at West 120th St. - 11th Floor

New York, NY 10115

(212) 870-3400   https://www.aa.org/

Amber Anthony's Newest Releases

Roman's Revenge, Roman's Adventures, Book One

Jax Roman is the image of courage, nobility and strength. A clever mind and agile body propelled Roman to the head of his SEAL class. Handsome and disarming, Jax is in charge of his world, vertical and horizontal. Now, at the pinnacle of his game, he leads his own team until…the Lobos Cartel, the worst Jax has ever fought, sets out to eliminate him.

Lovely and compassionate, Dr. Kameo Alana meets Jax in his most desperate hour. Her family has borne the cartel's punishment. Without Kameo, Jax would not be free to topple the depraved cartel.

Kameo is more than a balm for his pain. Together they sizzle white hot. Jax's mission for a 'happily ever after' with Kameo is an exercise in 'taking no prisoners', SEAL style.